RUINED ROCKSTARS BOOK THREE

HEATHER ASHLEY

Broken Player
Copyright © 2020 by HeatherAshley

ISBN: 9798767925025

All rights reserved. No part of this book may be used or reproduced in any manner whatsoever without written permission except in teh case of brief quotations embodied in critical articles or reviews.

Published by DCT Publishing

Cover Designed by Dee at Black Widow Designs

Contact the author at:
www.heatherashleywrites.com

The characters and events portrayed in this book are fictional. Any similarity to real persons, living or dead, is coincidental and not intended by the author.

We've got that love, the crazy kind.

HALSEY

BOOKS BY HEATHER ASHLEY

RUINED ROCKSTARS:
STEAMY ROCKSTAR ROMANCE

DEVIANT ROCKERS
FALLEN STAR
DIRTY LEGEND
BROKEN PLAYER
VICIOUS ICON
TAINTED IDOL
WICKED GOD

HOLLYWOOD GUARDIANS:
DARK BODYGUARD ROMANCE

CAPTIVE
CHASED
HOSTILE
DECEIT

TWISTED SOUL MAGIC:
MAGICAL REVERSE HAREM ROMANCE

CROSSED SOULS
BOUND SOULS

EMERALD HILLS ELITE:
ACADEMY REVERSE HAREM ROMANCE

TWISTED LITTLE GAMES

HE BROKE ME.
NOW, I'M GOING
TO GET EVEN...

PROLOGUE
RYAN

Sixteen years ago...

"I bet she has a dick, too!" Tyler shouted through his laughter.

Oh, no. Not again.

I tried to curl into myself as my cheeks burned. I'd gotten used to Tyler and Jacob teasing me, but that didn't mean it wasn't embarrassing. Just because I wore pants instead of dresses and liked playing sports with the boys during recess didn't mean I *was* a boy.

"What do you say, Ryan? How 'bout we see for ourselves?" Jacob taunted as they moved toward me. I couldn't let them pull down my pants in front of everyone. My heart pounded, and my eyes darted around, looking for anyone to help me. But all the other kids crowded around the bus stop were ignoring me.

As I continued to back up, step by step, trying to put distance between my bullies and me, my chin wobbled. Even as my eyes stung, I refused to cry. These two boys had been bothering me all year. I didn't wear a ponytail anymore because if I did, they'd pull my hair. I didn't understand why they couldn't just leave me alone. What did it matter that my parents had given me a boy's name? I'd always thought my name was cool and different. I was proud of it.

At least until this year. Now I wished my name was anything else so I could blend in. My sister Charlie told me to ignore them, that they were picking on me because they liked me. I didn't believe her, though. Why would they call me names or hurt me if they thought I was pretty? It didn't make sense. Why would they embarrass me in front of everyone over and over again?

My back hit the signpost that marked the stop, and I tripped, falling onto the dusty dirt-covered ground and scraping my palms and knees. I tried not to show fear, lifting my chin and narrowing my eyes defiantly at the boys who towered over me.

"Leave me alone," I said with a shaky voice.

"Boys aren't allowed to cry, *Ryan*. If you cry, I'll punch you." Jacob moved his lanky body toward me. He was only ten, like me, but he was the tallest kid in my class. When he was standing practically on top of me, his shadow blocked out the sun, and I looked up into his face. He wore a sneer that made him look like he'd smelled something gross.

I was more convinced than ever that Charlie was dead wrong. These boys didn't like me. They *hated* me. Tyler sauntered over and reached down, wrapping his hand around my upper arm and squeezing so hard it hurt. I flinched and tried to pull away, but he was stronger than I was.

My lungs were burning because I was breathing so fast, but I couldn't lose focus. I kicked out my foot and hit Tyler in the shin, and he squeezed harder. "Jake, grab her other arm."

Jacob reached down and dug his stubby nails into my skin, and even though I tried to completely relax my body so I'd be harder to pick up, they still dragged me to my feet.

"Please don't do this," I begged, hating myself for showing weakness. They looked at each other and then cracked up laughing, which made me cringe. I hadn't done myself any favors trying to get them to stop, but I couldn't let them torture me. They'd humiliated me over and over, putting paint on my chair so I ruined my pants and had to walk around with red marks on my butt all day, tripping me when I walked up to turn in my homework.

They'd done too much stuff to even count, every time breaking another little part of me down. This year, I'd gone from happy and carefree to the mess I was right now, shaking and on the verge of tears. Tyler and Jacob made me feel weak, and I hated it. When I got bigger, I'd never let anyone make me feel weak again. But right now, there was nothing I could do.

Even if I was strong enough, two on one wasn't a fair fight.

Tyler let go of my arm, and I swung back to punch him, but Jacob caught my flying fist and trapped both of my hands behind my back while Tyler gripped the waist of my jeans. He'd have to unbutton them to pull them down, and I twisted, trying to keep the clasp away from his grubby fingers.

"Let her go." A low, menacing voice came from over my shoulder, and relief washed over me. Someone noticed. Someone cared enough to take on my two bullies for me. It started to sink in that the group of kids at the bus stop wouldn't be seeing my underwear today, and I could cry from happiness.

Tyler laughed at my mystery guardian. He still stood behind me, and I couldn't turn myself to see who it was. "I don't think I want to. What do you think, Jake?"

Jacob glanced uneasily behind me and back to his friend. "I don't know, Ty. Maybe we should see Ryan during recess instead."

Tyler's hands were pried off my arms, and I shook out my wrists before turning around. I had to tilt my chin up to see him, but the boy who saved me wasn't a stranger. He lived on the ranch next door, and I'd met him a handful of times, but we weren't friends. He missed more school than he went to, so I didn't see him at the bus stop very often.

I guess today was my lucky day since he'd shown up and stepped in. His dark eyes locked on mine, anger and concern swirled in them, and I didn't want to look away. "Are you okay?" he asked.

I nodded. "Thank you." I couldn't think of anything better to say.

He pulled me so I was standing behind him and straightened himself up to his full twelve-year-old height. "If you touch her again, I'll kill you. Both of you." The threat in his voice gave me chills. It didn't feel like he was kidding to me, and I think Tyler and Jacob felt the same way. They backed up, hands raised in the air, and ran back to the rest of the group.

The boy stepped forward and grabbed my backpack, dusting it off before handing it back to me. "Those assholes shouldn't bother you anymore, but if they do, you tell me." His eyes were hard, and he cracked his knuckles.

"I will. Thanks again. By the way, I'm Ryan. I think you live next door, right?" I wasn't in a hurry to move away from my protector. I glanced around him, eyeing

Jacob and Tyler wearily. They were whispering to each other and looking my way. I didn't have high hopes that they'd listen to the boy and leave me alone.

"I'm Maddox." His lips tilted up on one side into a sort of amused half-smile. "Yep, we're neighbors." He followed my gaze to Tyler and Jacob, and his eyes narrowed before he looked back at me. "I mean it, Ryan. From now on, you wait for me in the morning, and we'll come to the bus stop together. After school, I'll walk you home. If they bother you during school, I need you to tell me, okay?"

Tearing my gaze off of my bullies, I looked into his eyes, studying them. Did he mean it? The small golden flecks dotting the beautiful dark brown of his irises was mesmerizing. My cheeks heated again when he cleared his throat, and I looked away. I'd never given a boy a second glance before, but Maddox had saved me. His dark hair fell into his eyes, and I suddenly wanted to reach up and brush it away so I could get another glimpse of the galaxy hidden in his gaze.

"What?" I finally managed.

His laugh was dark and low like he knew he'd caught me staring at him, and I shuffled my feet, kicking up some dust as the bus pulled up. "From now on, we go to and from school together. And you sit by me on the bus."

"Okay," I quickly agreed. I felt safe with Maddox. If it meant freedom from Tyler and Jacob, I'd gladly follow him around all day. A flush crept up my neck again when he reached for my hand, tugging me toward the bus. I'd never be able to thank him enough for what he did for me today.

The boy next door was a mystery, one I suddenly wanted to discover more than anything.

ONE
RYAN

A bead of sweat rolled down the side of my neck, tickling my skin. I reached up and swiped it away, adjusting the wide-brimmed hat on top of my head. It was my only protection against the blistering heat of a mid-day Texas sun.

Storm, the horse I currently rode, was impatient and stomped his hoof, causing dust to kick up around us. I bent down and patted his neck. "What do you say we take a break?" I murmured near his ear, and he tossed his head back, his mane brushing against my sticky skin. I gripped the reins and dug my heels into his sides, gently nudging him toward the pond across the pasture.

My body swayed side to side as Storm trotted slowly across the grass. I squinted my eyes, my gaze searching the horizon for Quinn, my best friend and fellow ranch hand. Instead, in the distance, I could barely make out a weathered farmhouse, and my breath caught as the memories washed over me. I tried years ago to shut them off, shove them down to some deep place inside my brain where they were locked away so I could move on.

But it never worked. It never worked because of that house, sitting on the edge of my family's ranch, at the edge of my consciousness, always lingering just out of reach just like the boy who grew up there. Even after twelve years, Maddox still consumed me.

I had just four short years with him before he left one night when I was fourteen and never looked back. He went from my best friend, protector, and first love to nothing all in the span of one night that I hadn't seen coming.

I'd been crushed. Devastated. The kind of inconsolable pain that I didn't think my teenage heart would ever recover from. And I'd been partially right. Time had dulled the ache where Maddox had carved out his place on my soul, but the scars were still there.

I refused to think of myself as pathetic, though. So many aspects of my life had been shaped by those four years. Yet, here I sat, desperately trying to keep my family's ranch going, on top of this horse in the middle of my daily chores. Was this what I had planned for my life? Hell no. But it was where I'd ended up, and I wouldn't be resentful.

I climbed down off of Storm, my boots scraping along the dry ground as I walked to the shaded spot by the waterline. I pulled my hat off my head and adjusted my ponytail, sweeping the escaped tendrils behind my ears and sitting down on the soft grass, leaning back against a tree trunk.

I heard the pounding hooves before I saw him, and a slow smile spread across my face as I looked to my left and watched as Quinn came into view on the back of his horse, Daisy. He rode right up next to me, pulling back on the reins so Daisy would stop.

He hopped off of her back, his boots making a loud thud on the dirt before he patted her haunches and sent her over to the water. Watching him close the distance between us, his sculpted frame, messy dark hair, and hazel eyes framed by long, dark lashes were every girl's fantasy. Too bad for all of us he wasn't interested. That didn't mean I couldn't enjoy looking at him, though.

Quinn flashed me a cocky smile. "My eyes are up here, sweetheart."

I laughed. "Damn, you caught me. If you didn't want me to stare, maybe you should try putting on some weight, maybe around the middle."

He dropped down beside me, leaning against the tree so our shoulders touched. "Not a chance. I don't exactly have a lot of prospects out here in this podunk town, so I'm not about to let myself go and miss out on the random app hookups in the city. I've got to pull them in somehow, and a picture's all I've got to work with."

Biting my lip to keep from smiling, I eyed him up and down. "You do you, boo. Just don't mind me ogling you from time to time. Checking you out is the most action I've had… ever."

Quinn sighed, wrapped his arm around my shoulder, pulled me into his body, and kissed the top of my head. "When are you going to let go of the boy next door, Mr. Manwhore Rockstar himself, and finally move on?"

Resting my head on his shoulder, I closed my eyes, and dark, haunted eyes with gold flecks flashed in my mind. "I don't know if I can."

Working the ranch was so far from the life I'd dreamed it was almost laughable. If I'd told my ten-year-old self where I was at now, she'd be so disappointed—the little girl I used to be had dreams of no longer needing to be saved. No, I wanted to be the one to do the saving.

As soon as I'd graduated high school, I'd gotten the hell out of here. All I'd ever wanted was to be a cop. To put on the uniform, to be able to protect people the way Maddox had protected me. The way the police went to his house over and over when he was a kid, and I'd watched from my window as the red and blue lights lit up the open fields between our houses, helpless to do anything but observe.

I was still so hung up on Maddox that I enrolled in college in California, naively hoping that in a state with thirty-nine million people, I'd run into him at least once in four years. But, it never happened, and I was too scared of rejection to reach out. Besides, what would I have said?

"Hey, it's Ryan. You know, your childhood best friend and neighbor who you abandoned after giving her a life-altering first kiss?" Yeah, right.

Instead, I kept my head down and studied my ass off. I took every self-defense and fighting class I could find from kickboxing to jiu-jitsu, and when I graduated, I got picked up by the LAPD. Thinking back on those days, a wistful smile pulls at my lips. I was so close to achieving my dream that I could taste it.

However, my life wasn't destined to be so easy, and a few months into the academy, I got the phone call that dragged me back to this tiny town and the ranch I grew up on. My dad, the tall and invincible cowboy I always thought he was, had been in an accident. There wasn't anyone else to step into my father's shoes and take care of things around here. So, I came home, and this was where I'd been ever since.

The past four years felt like at least ten. But, I never complained. My parents needed me. While my sisters were out in the world living their lives, I was here, sitting in the shade by the pond, sweating my ass off in jeans and boots before I'd climb back up on Storm and go fix an endless stretch of fence.

Quinn didn't say much else after that, and his breathing evened out. That boy could fall asleep anywhere, and it made me a little jealous. Once I'd cooled down a little and Storm had drunk his fill, I nudged Quinn with my elbow and he startled. "Wake up, hot stuff. We've got a fence to fix."

I pushed myself up and dusted off my jeans. I grabbed my hat off the grass and pushed it back onto my head before holding out my hand and helping Quinn up off the grass. He looked off into the distance, shielding his eyes with his hand. "Do you think we have enough time to tackle the fence before dinner?"

Sighing, I moved toward my dark gray stallion and ran my hand down his velvety nose. He nudged my cheek, and I chuckled. "If we haul ass, we can get it done."

Quinn saluted me before grabbing Daisey's reins and hauling himself up into her saddle. "Aye, aye captain."

Rolling my eyes, I lifted myself into my own saddle, leading the way to the east pasture. Squinting up at the sun, I figured we'd have a couple of hours left before my mom called us in for dinner. She rang a dinner bell and everything. We needed to finish the fence repair before then because tomorrow we had a whole new never-ending list of shit to do around here, and it felt like Quinn and I would never get it all done. With one last glance back at my best friend, I picked up the pace and tried to push the past as far out of my mind as I could.

Rinsing the suds off my hands, I watched the dirt-tinted water swirl down the drain. The smell of my mom's home cooking hung heavy in the air, and my stomach growled. Quinn took off his boots in the mudroom behind me and hip-checked me out of the way. "Move your cute ass, I'm starving."

We both knew my mom would never allow us at the table without freshly scrubbed hands, something ingrained in me since I was a kid and something

Quinn had learned quickly when he'd come to work for my family when he was twenty-one.

I tossed the towel I'd just used at him, and it hit him in the face. He glared at me as he pulled it off, and I giggled. "Now who's holding us up?"

"You'll be lucky if there's any left for you." He pushed past me and threw me a grin over his shoulder.

"You better not hog all the food, Quinn, or so help me I'll hogtie you and make you sleep in the barn," I threatened. When it came to my mom's chicken fried steak, all bets were off.

He laughed. "Sweetheart, I'd love to see you try."

"Knock it off, you two," my mom scolded lightly. We both mumbled our apologies and sat down next to each other at the table. My sisters both came into town for dinner tonight, so they sat across from us. My dad sat at one end of the table, and my mom would sit at the other when she finished piling dishes onto the table in front of us.

"Yeah, you two. Stop flirting at the dinner table," Justice, my younger sister, piled on.

Rolling my eyes, I reached for the salad bowl, scooping a heaping pile onto my plate. "Quinn and I can't seem to help ourselves, sis. Don't be jealous."

Quinn choked out a laugh around the piece of roll he'd shoved in his mouth and pounded himself on the chest. I reached over and hit his back, too.

"You're going to kill the poor guy, Ryan," my older sister, Charlie, chimed in. She shot Quinn a sympathetic smile before stretching her hand across the table to grab the bowl of salad from me.

"Seriously, Ry. Come into Dallas this weekend and come out with us. Even Quinn is coming," Justice said.

I raised my eyebrow at Quinn, and he shrugged his shoulder. "What? It's been a while, and I need to blow off some steam. Literally."

Chuckling, I glanced over at my dad. I'd known Quinn was gay since high school, but when he'd come out to my family, I didn't expect my dad to be so okay with it. He was an old school Texas cattle rancher. But he loved Quinn like the son he never had.

My dad stopped slicing into his chicken and looked up at Quinn with his eyes sparkling mischievously. "You better be staying safe, son. And watch out for my girls." That was as much approval as any of us were going to get.

Quinn straightened up next to me. "Yes, sir. I always keep at least one eye on them. And I'm always careful."

My dad nodded once and resumed slicing into the breaded meat in front of him.

"Well, I don't feel like going out this weekend, so I think I'll stay back," I decided before stuffing a piece of chicken in my mouth and moaning as it coated my taste buds with deep-fried goodness.

Next to me, my best friend cringed. "Jesus, Ry. Save it for the boy next door, will you?"

I nearly choked on my bite and had to grab my glass of ice water and chug some to get the food down my throat.

Charlie shifted her eyes in my direction. "Speaking of Maddox, are you still not over that ridiculous crush you had on him? It's been *twelve years,* Ryan. He's not coming back."

My cheeks heated up like they always did when my sisters brought Maddox up. For a long time, they'd been understanding and sympathetic. Until months had turned into years, and now that it'd been more than a decade, they'd completely lost their patience with me. Every week they'd come to dinner and pressure me to go out with them and try to meet someone.

I just wasn't ready. I didn't know if I ever would be.

Justice studied me with her green eyes narrowed slightly. "She's not going to budge, Charlie. I don't know why we try anymore. You might as well become a nun, Ryan."

My mom stepped in. "Girls, enough. If your sister doesn't want to come with you this week, drop it. She'll come around in her own time." She turned to look at me with a soft smile on her face. My mom had been the one who comforted me all through high school when I wanted to give up and curl up in a ball and never leave my bed again. She may not understand my pain from a personal experience perspective, but she was my mom, and on some level, I think she knew how deep my hurt ran even now. I thought she probably hurt for both Maddox and me for what we went through back then. She always looked at him like he was her son.

My dad cleared his throat. "We went to see the doctor today."

We all froze, stopping mid-bite and turning to look between my parents. My dad had been thrown from a horse four years ago and never recovered his ability to walk. Being confined to a wheelchair was the worst kind of torture for a man who lived for working his land. He'd tried everything he could up to this point to help, but nothing worked. I didn't even know how much physical therapy he'd done over the years, but still, he spent his days in the house or on the porch in his chair.

"You did? What for?" I rested my chin on my fist and my elbow on the table.

"We heard about a specialist with a new experimental treatment. We set the appointment six months ago but didn't say anything because we didn't want to get our hopes up," my mom explained.

"What kind of treatment?" Justice asked.

"It's called stimulation. Doctors implant a strip of electrodes into my spine, and it would potentially activate the nerves that help me walk. They'd had quite a bit of early success, and it looks promising," my dad elaborated.

Charlie tilted her head and sipped her water, looking thoughtful. "I think I read a study on that a couple of years ago, but it was still early. I'll dig into the research when I get home and see what I can find." Charlie was a neurosurgery resident. She'd finished medical school two years ago and was working her way through her residency. She changed her specialty to neurosurgery after my dad's accident because she wanted to help people like him if she could.

"We don't even know if you can get in. There's a long waitlist, and the treatment is really expensive for something we don't know will work." My mom sounded weary, like she'd gotten her hopes up before and been let down. And she had. We all had. We all knew not to put too much faith into any new treatment option that came up. All had failed so far.

Besides that, I didn't exactly know all the details of my parent's financial situation. Still, I doubted they had the money to take something like this on. It made me angry that helping my dad get better depended on how much money he had, but that was how the medical system worked. I looked at Charlie, and our eyes met. We were thinking the same thing. Maybe her connections at the hospital where she worked could help get him into the treatment and with the money aspect, too.

"I'm pulling for you, Alex," Quinn chimed in.

My dad's smile lit up his whole face. "Thanks, Quinn."

We all dug into our food, the mood lighter, but we were all quiet, lost in our own thoughts. When I finished, I stood and grabbed my plate, and Quinn followed me into the kitchen where we dropped our dishes into the dishwasher. "Movie night?" he asked.

I nodded. "Your turn to pick."

He grinned and rubbed his hands together. "Are your sisters staying?"

Charlie and Justice had followed us into the kitchen. "No, we're about to take off, so feel free to torture her with your movie selection," Justice smirked.

Quinn giggled, and I poked him in the side. "Goddamn, Quinn. You sound like a maniac."

"Don't hate, Ry. We're off to watch *She's All That*. Bye, ladies." Quinn wiggled his fingers in a wave before he grabbed my arm. I barely contained my groan. I hated romantic movies, and Quinn knew it.

"Ugh, couldn't you pick a better Paul Walker movie? *The Fast and the Furious*, maybe?" I pouted.

"Nope. Sure, he's hot in that, but he's hot *and* an asshole in my movie. The best combination." He was practically vibrating, and I begrudgingly smiled. "Seems like maybe we both have a type, right, Ryan?" He shot me a smug smile in return.

I couldn't argue with him there. I didn't know what Maddox was like now from personal experience, but he seemed to be a grade-A asshole in the media. "You know me too well. I think we need to break up," I grumbled.

Quinn chuckled. "If only it were that easy to get rid of me. Sorry, Lancelot. You're stuck with me for life."

I sat on my bed next to Quinn and snuggled into his side, burrowing underneath the covers as he started the movie. "I guess I could do worse," I mumbled.

"Damn right. Now shut up and take in all this nineties hotness with me." Quinn wrapped his arm around my shoulders. I tried to lose myself in the movie, ignoring how my thoughts kept drifting to the house over the hill and wondering what Maddox was doing right now and if he ever thought of me, too.

TWO
MADDOX

B lue lights pulsed around me as I tipped back my glass of whiskey and downed it in one shot, barely feeling the familiar burn. The bass rattled the floor under my feet, and my brain shook around in my skull exactly how I liked it. I couldn't hear myself think when the music was this loud. The thinking was what got me in trouble, and I wanted no part of it tonight. Or any night.

Turning, I watched a hot blonde shove her tits in Connor's face trying to get his attention. He flicked his eyes over to me, his eyebrow raising. When we went out together, he always gave me first choice on the women that were ballsy enough to approach us. Being the bassist for the hottest band in the world had its perks, and I enjoyed every single one.

He also knew I preferred blondes. Light hair and eyes. The complete opposite of *her*.

I nodded once, and Connor turned back to the woman perched on his lap, leaning forward to shout into her ear. She moved away from him, sliding off of his lap and locking eyes with me as a predatory grin spread across her face.

Little did she know, she wasn't the predator. I was. For tonight, and only tonight, she'd be my prey.

I held out my hand and pulled her down into my lap, gripping her hips and running a hand up her stomach until my palm rested below her obviously fake tits. I didn't mind as long as they were perky. Her floral perfume floated around me, mixing with the smell of alcohol and sweat in the club. I brushed her bleached blonde hair off of her shoulder and leaned up until my lips almost touched her ear. "Did you bring any friends with you tonight, sweetheart?"

She nodded her head vigorously before stretching her arm out and pointing to two women grinding against each other on the VIP dance floor. I shot Connor a look, and he followed my gaze. His eyes met mine, and silently a plan was made between us. He stood and moved across the floor slowly in a cocky swagger that had everyone jumping out of his way, clearing a path.

It didn't hurt that he was a big motherfucker.

I moved my palm to rest on blondie's smooth, tan thigh and stroked my thumb in circles. I watched as her breath caught, and her nipples hardened, poking through her tight as fuck dress that hugged every curve.

Turning my attention back to Connor, I watched as he moved between the two women, both of them grinding against him to the beat. From here, through the haze of flashing lights and dark shadows, he could have been fucking them, and no one would have been the wiser. Knowing him, he might have been.

I focused back on the girl sitting on my lap, inching my fingertips higher up her thigh until I hit the hem of her dress and then dipped my fingers underneath. When I lifted my gaze to her face, she watched me with hooded eyes, and her tongue darted out to wet her lips. My cock hardened as I thought about those plump, red lips wrapped around me.

Removing my hand from her leg, I tugged her off of my lap, gently guiding her to her knees. She nervously glanced around the club, but it was so dark and loud that no one paid attention. Her eyes found mine, and she licked her lips while she reached for the button on my jeans, popping it open.

Out of the corner of my eye, I watched Connor throw his arm over the brunette's shoulders and grip the other blonde's hand in his, leading them both off the dance floor. His eyes darkened as he watched the girl between my knees reach her hand into my pants and start stroking my dick like she was trying to start a fire. I tensed and gripped her wrist, shooting her a withering glare. "Be careful," I hissed, though I didn't know if she could hear me over the music. I could already tell she was wild and eager to please.

That only meant fun things for me when I got her back to my place. For now, she had to earn the right. I ran my hand down into her hair, fisting the coarse strands and gripping tight while I held her right where I wanted her. She ran her tongue up and down my shaft as I locked eyes with her friend now sitting beside Connor across the booth from me, her pupils dilating as she watched.

A smirk tugged at the corner of my mouth as blondie took my cock into her mouth, suctioning me to the back of her throat, and I threw my head back and clenched my jaw. Closing my eyes, freckles and doe eyes flashed in my mind, and I snapped them open. I pulled the blonde off my dick, stuffed myself back into my pants, and motioned to the waitress. I wasn't nearly fucked up enough for what I had in mind tonight. I needed to forget. I always needed to forget.

Several shots of whiskey later, Connor and I stumbled into my house with the three girls. I ignored the squeals from the brunette Connor claimed as his company for tonight, and I tried to focus my blurring vision on the two blondes hanging all over me. We careened our way to one of my guest rooms. I could never bring myself to take the hookups into my bedroom. That was my private space, and I didn't want it tainted with meaningless sex.

Pushing into the room, we were a tangle of lips, teeth, and hands until we tumbled onto the bed. I leaned back on my elbow, content to watch the show for now.

"What do you like, baby?" blondie number one purred.

"I want to watch… for now," I smirked.

They lunged at each other, pawing and kissing and stripping until they stood naked before me, putting on a show that only had me at half-mast. Maybe it was all the whiskey I'd drunk, or maybe it was the fact that these girls were all wrong. When I watched, I found myself wishing for dark hair and expressive eyes, skin covered in freckles, and a laugh that made my whole heart feel light.

Fuck. I needed to shut that shit down, locking those thoughts away in the deepest vault of my mind. I hated that they'd slipped through. I made my bed years ago and spent the last twelve years lying in it. All dredging those feelings up did was make me hate myself even more. Instead, I refocused my attention back on the girls in front of me.

Might as well make the most of the night.

Groaning, I woke up assaulted by too many feelings: A pounding head, a body wrapped around my left side, and my dick being stroked by a warm hand. I wasn't sure what to focus on first, and I pried my eyes open, watching as blondie number one flashed me a devilish grin and sucked the head of my cock into her mouth. I reached down and pulled her off with a *pop*, a scowl crossing my face.

"Sorry, sweetheart. I don't do seconds," I scolded. She pouted before shaking her friend awake. "Time for you two to go."

I jumped out of bed and pulled on my boxers before striding out of the room, not bothering to look back. I needed coffee more than anything, and even on my best days, I wasn't a morning person. The closer I got to the kitchen, the stronger the smell of coffee became. Connor must have been up already and made a pot.

Sure enough, rounding the corner, I found him sipping a steaming mug, perched on one of the stools at the marble-topped island. I tilted my chin in greeting before grabbing a mug and pouring myself a cup.

"Why the fuck do you live in a house made up of so much glass? It's bright as fuck in here in the morning," Connor bitched.

"You could always stay at your own place if you don't like it." Truth be told, I loved my house, but he had a point. My eyes wandered around the room, taking in the glass walls, light marble floors, and white furniture. This place was the complete opposite of who I was, and I liked it because it reminded me that things didn't always have to be so dark. Or at least I could pretend for a little while.

But when I had a hangover? This place was like a fucking drill right to the skull.

Connor rolled his eyes and took another sip of his coffee. "Fuck off." Clearly, getting his dick wet last night hadn't improved his mood this morning.

I practically gulped my coffee, needing the caffeine to clear my head. "Where the fuck is my phone?" I muttered, glancing around the kitchen. It was clearly not here, so I stalked out to the living room. I sure as fuck didn't want to go back into the guest room until I was sure the girls were gone. I hated myself for this morning routine, but I'd gotten in the habit of checking *her* social media feeds.

Convincing myself this small allowance was okay because I wasn't actually making any contact with her was how I justified my behavior. But Ryan deserved a whole hell of a lot better than me, so I removed myself from her life years ago and tried my damndest not to look back.

At least not much.

Finally, I stalked down the hallway, stopping outside the door and listening, but the room was silent. I peered around the door frame, and the room was empty, so I walked inside and dropped to my knees, searching under the bed. Near the nightstand, I spotted my phone and reached out, pulling it into my hand and swiping the screen on.

I'd been lucky neither of the girls from last night had taken my phone. It wouldn't have been the first time. Or even the tenth. I'd had to replace this phone a dozen times already just this year. I pushed myself up off the floor and made my way back to the kitchen, popping into my room to grab sunglasses and slipping them on my face to block out some of the intense sunlight.

Connor lifted his eyes from his phone when I strode into the room, chuckling as he took in my sunglasses. "I knew you weren't immune."

Lifting my middle finger, I flashed my hand at him, and he chuckled again. I slid onto the barstool a couple down from him. I pulled open my social media accounts, quickly navigating to Ryan's and checking for new updates like a starved man desperate for a scrap of food. I held my breath as the page loaded like I did every day. I'd never seen her post a picture with another man as long as I'd watched, which was longer than I cared to admit. I didn't know what I'd do if I ever saw that, but I had no right to my feelings of possession over her.

That didn't mean I didn't still have them.

I gave up my right to any kind of a relationship with Ryan a long time ago. When her page finally loaded, my insides felt like they'd been shredded. Her latest update was her beautiful smiling face looking carefree and happy, which I wanted most for her. But next to her was a man who looked equally happy, his arms wrapped around her, their faces pressed close together. I recognized her family farm in the background, the familiar barn visible in the frame.

My fingers were wrapped so tightly around my phone that it creaked ominously, and I dropped it onto the counter, raking my fingers through my hair and down my face. I wanted to smash everything near me, to let the storm raging inside of me out. Instead, I swallowed it down like everything else. I tightened every muscle in my body, keeping myself rigidly perched on the stool.

I needed to get the fuck out of here. Suddenly my ten-thousand square foot house felt claustrophobic. I stalked to my bedroom, grabbed a black t-shirt and jeans, dressed quickly before brushing my teeth, and walked back to the kitchen to find Connor staring at me.

I barely contained my rage as I slammed the garage door open before looking back over my shoulder. "You coming?" I asked Connor, grabbing one of the sets of keys hanging on the rack by the door.

Lifting the car door up, I lowered myself into the matte black McLaren Spider that was my favorite whenever I wanted to go fast. There was something about pressing the gas pedal into the floor and watching my surroundings blur as I flew past them that kept me in the moment, pulling me out of my thoughts.

The passenger side door slamming caught my attention as I looked over to find Connor in the seat next to me, his mirrored aviators in place. He didn't say anything, just looked at me expectantly. I pressed the button and waited for the garage door to lift, tapping my fingers restlessly on the wheel. My thoughts were swirling, and my fury was still barely contained. I needed to destroy something.

Pressing on the gas pedal, I tore out of the garage and down the street, the tires squealing. We drove in silence until I tossed Connor my phone. "Put on something loud," I barked. I didn't mean to be such an asshole, but Connor didn't take it personally. It was why I liked hanging out with him. Right now, it was all I could do not to crash us into a pole to try and shut off my brain. My throat was dry, and I struggled to swallow around the huge lump that had settled there.

I'd known this day would come someday, but that didn't mean I'd been prepared for it. "Are you packing?" I asked, shooting a sideways glance at Connor.

"Always."

"Good." I didn't say anything else until I whipped my car into a deserted parking lot. There was a low unmarked building directly in front of us.

Connor chuckled darkly beside me. "Should I even ask what's got you so riled up this morning?"

I glared at him before lifting up the door and stepping out of the car, stretching out my body. I moved to the trunk and tried to ignore the blood pounding in my ears and adrenaline coursing through my veins. I reached in and pulled out my handgun, slamming the trunk shut.

Connor opened the glass door, and I strode in like I owned the place, nodding once at the guy behind the counter and moving through the lobby until we stood outside in the open-air range. Connor reached into his waistband, pulled his gun out, checked it over, and took his place beside me. We'd been here so many times before, we didn't need to talk. Even though I didn't show it, his presence calmed me.

Placing ear protection over my head, I unloaded clip after clip into anything I could find, the kickback of the gun causing my muscles to tighten. My focus was singular, blocking out every other thought and feeling until my breathing regulated, and my heart slowed down.

For the first time since I saw that goddamn picture, oxygen inflated my lungs. Shooting the fuck out everything in sight at the range had calmed me enough that I could once again shove my feelings down and block them out, throwing up a mask of indifference.

That was until my phone vibrated in my pocket. I pulled it out, noting the unknown number with a Texas area code. My heart kicked up, pounding in my chest while I debated whether or not to answer. For a brief moment, I let myself hope that it's her. But I shut that shit down. She doesn't have my number, and even if she did, I made sure she wanted nothing to do with me when I took off without a word.

So whatever this was wouldn't be good. I knew it in my bones.

Resigned, I sighed before answering. "Hello?"

A deep gravelly voice spoke loudly in my ear, and I pulled the phone back a little, wincing. "Maddox?"

"That's me. Who's this?"

"I don't know if you remember me, but my name's Joel. Joel Stewart? I'm a cowboy on your dad's ranch."

Fuck, this was *not* my day. "Hey, Joel. It's been a long time. What's up?"

The line stayed quiet so long I looked down at the screen to see if the call was still connected. "Joel?"

A long, low sigh sounded across the line, and the hair on the back of my neck stood up. "Yeah, I'm here. Look, kid. I'm going behind your old man's back to make this call, but he hasn't given me much choice."

I stayed quiet, waiting for him to finish.

"It's been weeks since I've been able to buy feed, and when I try talking to Russell about it, he gets belligerent and tells me to fuck off. The animals are suffering, and I haven't been paid in months. If it were just about me, I'd walk away. But I can't let the animals suffer if there's something I can do."

Connor stepped up beside me, tucking his gun back into his waistband and pulling off his noise silencing headphones. He shot me a questioning glance. "What do you need from me, Joel?" I asked, pinching the bridge of my nose, sure I didn't want to hear the answer.

"I'd ask you to just send money, but I don't have access to the accounts. If you send money, Russell will drink or gamble it away, and we'll be back to square one."

"I don't think I can do what you're asking."

"Sorry, kid. But the only way to fix this is to come out here. I know it's not what you want."

I clenched my fist, preparing to throw it into the wooden beam in front of me. "If I come out there, a whole lotta shit's going to change, Joel. I can't be around my dad."

"I know. But the animals need you. Hell, *I* need you. Just get your ass out here, spend a day, and go back home. I'll do what I can to run interference."

Suddenly the anger left my body. All I felt was a paralyzing numbness, like I was empty, devoid of feeling. "Fine. I'll fly down tomorrow. You've got me for one day and one day only."

"I'll take it. See you then," Joel agreed, and the line went dead.

My stomach knotted. I couldn't believe I'd agreed to go home and deal with my dad's fucked up life.

"What's going on?" Connor asked, concern lacing his features. Being an ex-Marine and current badass bodyguard meant he picked up on every little thing.

"I have to go home tomorrow." My voice sounded monotone.

"Do you want me to come with you?" he offered.

I shook my head. "It's only for a day, and I don't want to expose you to my shit. I'll be fine. But thanks."

He nodded once and turned around, walking toward the exit. I followed, wondering what the fuck I'd just gotten myself mixed up in.

THREE
RYAN

Dust billowed up off the dirt road as an unfamiliar truck made its way down our long driveway. I shifted my gaze to Quinn, whose narrowed eyes were focused on the unexpected guest. He met my eyes, and we both nudged our horses forward at the same time, moving toward the house.

"Expecting someone?" Quinn asked.

I shook my head as a prickle of unease worked its way down my spine. I looked to my right, gripping the reins in one hand and shielding my eyes with the other, scanning the horizon for the little house next door. When I found it, everything looked quiet. I breathed out slowly, a mixture of relief and disappointment washing over me.

Quinn shot me a sympathetic look. Years ago, I'd confided in him one drunken night about my past with Maddox. At least he'd stopped pressuring me to go out and meet someone for the most part. The parts of Quinn that were damaged from growing up gay in a tiny town in the bible belt understood how flawed I was deep down inside, so he didn't push me.

"I don't think it'd be him, Ryan," he said quietly, voicing and crushing the hope I'd had all in one sentence.

I squared my shoulders and straightened my spine, hardening my heart again. I kicked myself for feeling hopeful in the first place. How many times would I get my hopes up only to be crushed again and again? Maddox was *never* coming back. I doubted he even remembered me. I couldn't blame him. It wasn't like this was a happy place for him filled with sunshine and rainbows. I'd like to think I was a bright spot in an otherwise shitty childhood, but the way he left had me thinking otherwise.

"I know he's never coming back. Maybe one of these days, my head will tell my heart to knock its shit off, huh?" I smiled sadly.

"He never deserved you, and someday, when you're ready, you'll find someone worthy of all your amazingness," Quinn promised. "Until then, you're mine."

I giggled at the way he waggled his eyebrows at me, my spirits lifted in a way that only my best friend could. "Race you!" I yelled, kicking my heels into Storm's side as he took off, his hooves thundering along the dirt. Daisy's gallops rumbled behind me, but Storm was faster. With my head start, Quinn would never win.

My heart was light, and I laughed as I rounded to the front of the house, pulling the reins to slow Storm to a stop, Quinn and Daisy hot on my heels. I laughed breathlessly and hopped down off of my stallion's back. "I win!" I cheered, pumping my fists into the air.

Quinn flashed me a dirty look. "You cheated."

"You're a sore loser," I countered.

The car we'd been watching pulled into the driveway behind my dad's old Chevy truck, coming to a stop. Shielding my eyes from the windshield's glare, I tried to see who was inside, but it was useless. Quinn stepped up beside me and threw his arm over my shoulder. "Who do you think it is?" he asked.

"No idea. Guess we'll know soon enough."

A youngish man in a charcoal suit exited the car and moved toward Quinn and me, a grim expression on his face. "Are you mister and missus Knight?" he asked us.

I shook my head. "I'm their daughter."

"That'll work," he declared, lifting a thick manilla envelope I hadn't noticed he was carrying and holding it out for me to take.

"What's this?" I eyed the envelope warily.

"Just read through it. Everything to answer your questions is in there. Consider yourselves served. Good day," he said airily before turning on his heel and walking back to his car.

My stomach twisted uncomfortably. I didn't like any of this, and that creepy unease I'd been feeling earlier returned in full force.

"What the actual fuck?" Quinn asked, looking down at the envelope held in my shaky hands.

"We better go inside and see what this is all about." I spun on my heels and stomped up the stairs onto the porch, slamming the screen door open. I was scared, and it was manifesting itself as anger. I knew I should rein it in, but this was going to be bad news. I felt it in my bones. I just didn't know how bad.

Quinn pulled out one of the dining chairs, and I sunk down into it. He plopped down next to me, and I slid my finger underneath the sealed flap of the envelope, my heart beating wildly in my chest.

"Do you think we should wait for your parents to get home?" Quinn wondered.

Shaking my head, I slid out the stack of papers inside. "What if they're hiding something? My dad's been a little cagey lately when I've brought up some of the changes I want to make for the ranch."

Quinn leaned forward, his elbows on his knees. "Fuck, this could be bad."

"I know." I turned over the papers, scanning the print quickly. The more I read, the more my stomach dropped, and I started to feel lightheaded. Quinn could read me like a book and tensed next to me.

"What is it?" he asked.

Wordlessly, I handed him the papers so he could look them over. I watched as his eyes ran down the length of the page. "Fuck," he whispered, his hazel eyes lifting to meet mine.

"Fuck's right. Do you think they were going to tell us?" My thoughts were scrambling around in my head, and I couldn't make sense of what I'd just read.

"I don't know, Ry. But we need to talk to them as soon as they get home. This is really, really serious."

"Let's talk to them over dinner. We've got chores to finish and not a lot of daylight left to do them." I stood up, stuffed the papers back in the envelope, moved to my bedroom, and left it on my dresser.

When I got outside, Quinn was already on Daisy's back, ready to finish our tasks for the day, but he didn't look happy. I didn't *feel* happy about it, so I couldn't blame him.

"We better get this done," Quinn said quietly.

I nodded and pulled myself onto Storm's back. Despite the hundred and five degree weather, chills rolled down my spine. Pushing Storm into a trot, I was tempted to gallop across the pastures and into the sunset. That sounded like a better prospect than sitting over dinner and confronting my parents about how we were about to lose our farm.

My heart slammed against my ribcage, and I couldn't catch my breath. I caught Quinn's eye as he lowered himself into the chair next to me at the table. His eyes were wide, and a light sheen of sweat had broken out across his forehead. He looked about as freaked out as I felt about confronting my parents.

Looking at my mom and dad, you'd never guess anything was amiss. My mom cheerfully hummed as she brought the food to the table, and my dad was telling Quinn a joke he'd heard today. Once my mom finally sat down, I waited until everyone dished up their food before clearing my throat.

Quinn reached under the table for my hand, lacing our fingers together and squeezing. I took a deep breath, his support giving me the strength I needed to have this conversation. Both of my parents turned toward me, and their curious stares bored into me. I just wasn't sure what to say to start the most awkward conversation I'd probably ever have in my entire life.

"When you guys were out today, Quinn and I had an interesting visitor," I started.

My mom's eyes darted to my dad before shifting back to me. "Oh?" she asked.

Nodding, I continued. "Yep. A man came by to drop off some papers." I pulled the envelope out from under my chair, setting it down on the table and sliding it towards my dad. "About the ranch."

My mom paled and reached for her lemonade glass, her shaking hand making the liquid slosh around as she brought it to her mouth.

My dad's shoulders slumped, and he let out a long sigh. "We thought we could fix it before it would ever get this far, kiddo. We never wanted you to have to worry about it. You've already done so much for us."

I rubbed my temples. I could already feel the beginning of a stress headache forming. I'd held onto one last shred of hope that they'd tell me this had all been some terrible mistake or they'd fixed it before I'd ever found out. But that clearly wasn't the case.

"What are our options at this point?" I questioned, looking at my dad.

He avoided meeting my eyes, playing with his napkin instead. "We've tried getting another mortgage, getting a loan, and requesting a payment arrangement to pay off the debt, but we've been denied every step of the way. The ranch isn't as profitable as it once was, and we don't have the money to invest in new technology."

Tapping my fingers on the table, I clenched my jaw and took a few deep breaths to calm down. An entire tornado of frustration was blowing its way through my body right now, so I held as still as I could to let it pass. Quinn grabbed my hand again, rubbing soothing circles on my wrist with his thumb. I didn't know what I'd do if he wasn't here right now.

Finally, I opened my eyes. "I've been trying to tell you for months changes we could make to streamline things and save money while not having to invest much, and you refused to listen, dad. You refused to even consider any of my ideas. If things were so bad, why the hell wouldn't you have tried what we could to fix this? Now we're going to lose the ranch!" I yelled, my voice rising more with every word. My chest was heaving. I'd never yelled at my parents before, but I was so angry and frustrated and scared.

My dad sat up straighter, folding his arms across his chest. "I thought I could handle it myself." Ah, now it made sense. My dad was a proud man, and since his accident, he'd felt useless, like his best years were behind him and like he couldn't contribute to the ranch anymore. This ranch had been in his family for generations, his grandfather and father both lived their lives here, worked the land, and raised their families. Now it was his turn, and he'd been too stubborn to ask for help before it was too late.

Waving my hand around at nothing in particular, I said, "Clearly not. We've got a month to try to fix this."

My mom spoke up. "Honey, it's too late. There's nothing we can do."

Pushing my shoulders back, I stood up, pulling Quinn with me by our joined hands. "I am *not* letting go of this ranch. Maybe you two are okay just giving up, but while I still have breath in my body, I will fight with everything I have to save this place. This is our home. No one is taking it from us."

Spinning on my heel, I marched off toward my room. "Where are we going?" Quinn asked, letting me drag him behind me.

"I need to call Charlie and Justice, and then we need to figure out what the hell we're going to do to fix this mess," I fumed. I bet if he looked hard enough, Quinn would actually be able to see steam pouring out of my ears, that's how mad I was.

He followed me into my room, and I slammed the door behind us. I grabbed my phone and dialed Justice, putting it on speaker. Pacing the room, I waited for her to pick up. "Hello?" she answered.

"Hey, sis. Do you have a minute to talk? It's important."

She shuffled around a bit on her end before answering. "Sure, what's up?"

"Hold on, let me get Charlie in on this, too," I said, before dialing my older sister and adding her to our call.

"Okay, Justice?" I asked.

"Mmhmm."

"Charlie?"

"I'm here," Charlie acknowledged.

"Quinn's here, too," I added, shooting him a grateful look. He winked at me from where he was sprawled out on my bed. I moved toward him and sank down into my soft mattress.

"Hey, Quinn," both my sisters greeted him at the same time.

"Hi, beautiful ladies," Quinn sang.

I cut in. "I called you both because Quinn and I got some disturbing news today. We confronted the parentals about it at dinner, and they admitted everything, and now we need to make a plan."

Charlie groaned. "What did they do?"

"The bank is about to foreclose on the ranch. They served us with Notice of Sale papers today. In a month, they're going to auction the ranch off to the highest bidder."

"What?" Justice shrieked into the phone. "They can't do that!"

I scoffed. "Yeah, Jus. They can, and they are. Unless we figure out a way to stop them."

"I want to help. I do. But with my rotations, I barely have time to sleep. I shouldn't even be on this call right now. I'm sorry, Ry, but the most I can offer is moral support," Charlie apologized. "If it makes you feel better, I feel like absolute shit about it, though."

Tears pricked behind my eyelids, and I blinked them back. I had to be strong right now if I had any hope of saving this place. I couldn't crumble or break down. There'd be time for that when the ranch was safe. "I get it, Charlie. You've worked way too hard for your career to slip now. It's okay."

She breathed out a relieved sigh. "I really am sorry."

"We get it, Charlie," Justice added. "And Ry, I can help with research and stuff if you need it, but I'm in the same boat as Charlie. Once I committed to the academy, they owned my ass. There's not much I can do without quitting. I can't miss any time."

I might've been pissed if I didn't love my sisters so much. But as usual, I'd be on my own for this. It had been the same when my dad had his accident. I'd been the one to step up and answer the call. To do what needed to be done. That's why it hurt so much that my parents hadn't told me about the ranch being in trouble. Charlie was chasing her dream of being a neurosurgeon, and Justice was halfway through firefighter training. But I'd given up on my life to be here, to tow the family line and be the good little daughter who carried on traditions.

I breathed out a heavy sigh. "Okay, I'm glad I got to at least get this off my chest."

"I still can't believe they didn't tell us. I'm just as mad at them as you are, Ry," Justice huffed.

"Same," Charlie said through clenched teeth.

"What are you going to do?" Justice asked.

I took a deep breath, but Quinn answered. "We don't know yet. Reading through every line of those papers is a good place to start."

"Yeah, then making dad show me the books on the ranch. I need to see and understand what's coming in and what's going out. I should've forced him to show me years ago," I added.

"That's a good place to start, babe. Let us know what you find out, and we can try to figure out a way to help however we can," Charlie said.

We ended the call with an agreement we'd talk tomorrow after Quinn and I went over everything. Suddenly weakness and exhaustion clawed their way through my body. I stood up, pulling my jeans off and throwing my PJs on. Quinn didn't bat an eye, whipping his jeans and t-shirt off until we were both ready for bed. We climbed in my bed together, and he wrapped his arms around me, pressing a kiss to the top of my head. "We'll find a way, Ry. We always do."

His reassurance made me feel marginally better as I closed my eyes, breathing in his comforting smell. Not for the first time, I found myself wishing my best friend wasn't gay because life would be so much easier if I could just move on and set my heart free. For now, I had bigger things to worry about than Maddox Everleigh's imprint on my soul.

FOUR
MADDOX

Stepping off the jet, I felt like I was walking to my execution. The tiny flicker of excitement I'd let myself feel at the prospect of seeing Ryan again had long since been extinguished by reality. Even if she *was* happy to see me and I did happen to run into her, based on her last Instagram post, she'd long since moved on from her teenage crush on me.

I walked across the hot concrete, cracked and warped under the unrelenting Texas sun, and slid into the waiting Tahoe with blacked-out windows. The truck probably drew more attention than I wanted, but I'd need whiskey to get me through this day, and I wasn't in the habit of driving drunk.

As soon as the door closed me inside, the driver started the hour-long trek to Everleigh Ranch, the last place on Earth I ever thought I'd step foot back on. I pulled out my flask, lifted it to my lips, and took a big swig, the burn making its way down into my stomach. I closed my eyes, leaning my head back against the cool leather seat.

I needed to brace myself for what I was walking into. I hadn't seen or spoken to my old man in twelve years, but I could only imagine he'd gotten worse in time, not better. Beating on me because I hadn't earned any money that he could take to fuel his drinking or gambling habits when I was only ten years old had been my breaking point. I'd finally snapped and decided I would do anything to get out of here as soon as possible.

When I left, I vowed I'd never look back. And I'd tried damn hard not to. But as the dirt kicked up around the truck and we flew down the familiar road that never quite felt like home, I rolled my shoulders. I tried to clamp down on all the memories wanting to break free of the cage in my mind where they lived. No matter what happened today, I wouldn't let this place, my dad, or the girl next door, drag me back.

I'd worked too damn hard for too damn long to end up right back where I started, in the dark hole I'd worked to claw my way out of. If I had any luck at all on my side, I wouldn't have to face my dad at all. I was only here a day, and when I was a kid, he'd disappear for days at a time on drunken benders or gambling binges. I internally crossed my fingers that he'd stay away today, and I could clean up his mess and go home before anyone knew I was here.

If he was there, I had no idea what I'd do. I wouldn't be surprised if I laid hands on him, to return the abuse he heaped on me for years. Every punch, slap, belt lashing, broken bone, bruise, and mark on my body that he'd caused, I itched to return tenfold.

It would take every ounce of self-control I had to keep my temper in check. As we pulled up, I glanced around and didn't see his truck. The small house was in worse condition than when I'd left, the paint chipped and the roof with missing shingles. There were no warm and fuzzy feelings of nostalgia looking at this place. No, my stomach was filled with lead.

My phone vibrating pulled me out of my thoughts, and I glanced down at the screen, a small smile breaking out across my face. It was yet another picture of my niece, True's daughter, Phoenix. That kid was so damn cute, and she had all of us wrapped around her finger, even if it was annoying to get twenty-five text messages every day about her.

Movement out of the corner of my eye caught my attention. Every muscle in my body tensed, not even remotely prepared to deal with my dad. But I breathed out a deep sigh when I saw it was just Joel who'd come onto the sagging front porch to greet me.

Throwing open the door, I slid out of the car, the Texas heat assaulting my body immediately. I forgot how fucking hot Texas was in the summer. I lived in LA, I was used to warm weather, but this shit was unbearable, like the goddamn seventh circle of hell. Sweat instantly beaded on my forehead, and I regretted my decision to dress in my usual all black. At least it was only one day.

Joel dipped his head, tipping his hat at me. He'd worked for my dad for years, but I'd only ever talked to him on the phone. When I was a kid, I'd been the one to do the hard labor around the ranch. My old man never had the money to pay for help, so it all fell to me. At least until I ran away and he didn't have a goddamn choice in the matter.

"Hey, Joel, right? I'm Maddox." I stretched out my hand to him, his rough, tan palm gripped mine firmly before letting go. He wore a sympathetic expression on his face, and a chill ran over my body despite the scorching heat.

"Good to meet you, son. Sorry it wasn't under better circumstances."

I looked past him at the front door, then shifted my eyes back. "Is he home?" I wondered, dreading the answer.

Joel shook his head. "Nah, hasn't been here for a few days, best I can tell."

I swore a fifty-pound weight lifted off of my shoulders as I exhaled. Maybe Russell wouldn't be back today. Maybe I wouldn't have to see anyone and could get the fuck out of here relatively unscathed.

I moved around the porch, bending down and reaching under the withered potted plant sitting next to the door to find the spare key. Gripping the warm metal in my palm, I opened the door, and as it swung open, a wall of stale air and old beer hit me in the face. Joel wordlessly followed me inside, wincing at the smell and the heat.

The old air conditioner sat in the window unused, if it even worked anymore. I found the light switch and flipped it up, but nothing happened. "Guess the power's out," I muttered.

Joel shrugged. "I doubt Russell's paid the bill."

"Let's talk on the porch," I suggested, moving back outside. I couldn't be in that house until I got the power back on.

When we'd crossed over the threshold, I sucked in a big breath of fresh air. Now that I could breathe again, I needed to figure out how to fix shit as fast as I could so I could leave in the morning. Joel leaned against the wooden post holding up the roof, his arms folded across his chest, waiting for me to speak. He seemed like he was a man of few words, and I appreciated that.

"I'll get the electricity on, but I need to know what's been happening around here so I can straighten shit out. This place looks worse than it did when I was a kid," I observed, looking around at the unkempt fields of grass beside the house.

Joel uncrossed his arms and lifted his hat, swiping a hand through his matted hair. "It's been bad for a long time. Russell has no business running a ranch. He can't take care of himself, and he sure as hell can't be trusted to take care of his animals," Joel seethed. I could see this shit really got to him. It warmed my cold, unfeeling heart just a little that he cared about the animals enough to go over my dad's head and call me in. I might have to make some bigger changes around here than I was initially planning.

The gears in my mind started whirring, frantically trying to rearrange the original plans I'd made. A small smile tugged at my lips as I considered taking this entire day in a new direction. The only downside was I'd have to stay longer than the one day I'd first committed to. But, if things worked out like I thought they might, it'd be worth it.

I'd finally show my old man what a fucking useless waste of space he was and get him out of my life for good.

𝄞

Rubbing my temples, I tried to stave off the throbbing in my skull. I was not made for staring at endless pages of spreadsheets. Fuck. I'd been lucky that Joel had maintained at least some semblance of financial records for this place since my old man hadn't done shit.

He'd done worse than shit. He ran this place so far into the red he'd never be able to dig himself out of it. But that's what I'd been counting on. The sun had sunk low in the sky, and so far, I'd been lucky. Russell hadn't shown his face. But just as the thought slipped into my mind, footsteps echoed on the front porch. My whole body tensed up, a habit left over from my childhood that I hadn't outgrown even a dozen years later.

The chair scraped across the scratched up wooden floorboards as I stood, my fists clenched, and I prepared myself for a fight. But as I caught a flash of wavy brown hair blowing on the breeze, I realized it'd be a different kind of struggle I'd be facing right now. One that involved my heart and that I was even less prepared to deal with.

I watched as she lifted her hand and knocked on the screen door, balancing a plate on her other hand and tucking her wind-mussed hair behind her ear. I took a step forward, the floor creaking under my boot.

Our eyes locked through the screen door, and the air crackled between us. I hadn't expected Ryan to come over at all, let alone the same afternoon I showed up. It made me wonder if she'd been waiting and watching for signs of my return. I didn't dare let myself hope. I couldn't. Nothing had changed, I still didn't deserve her.

I threw up my mask of indifference and shut off my emotions. Over the years, I'd gotten good at hiding how I felt, and I'd need those skills now more than ever. No matter what, I would protect her from me. I allowed my eyes to scan over her dark wavy hair, striking brown eyes, and cheeks dotted with constellations of freckles. I'd come across thousands of beautiful women in my life and not one of them compared to Ryan.

A memory tried to push its way to the surface, one filled with clumsy kisses, unsure lips brushing against each other, and soft, freckled skin smooth under my palm. I shut that shit down, though. It was as if being closer to her made the memory of our first and only kiss bubble up out of the depths of my mind. I couldn't deal with that shit.

I turned the handle, opening the screen door, and she moved aside so I could step out onto the porch. No fucking way was I inviting her into the house. There were so many reasons that was a bad idea, I couldn't even list them all.

"You're really back," she marveled, her voice breathless and wispy as if she thought she was in a dream, and if she spoke too loud, she might wake herself up. Fuck, the way she looked up at me with wonder and longing in her eyes instead of hate and resentment like I deserved meant trouble. I couldn't afford to let my walls down when it came to Ryan. It was torture to rip myself away from her all those years ago, misery to keep myself away, and I'd done it all for her.

I could endure anything if it meant she'd be happy.

"So glad you noticed," I drawled as if I was bored, letting my eyes wander up and down her body with a cold smirk plastered on my face. I built myself quite a reputation, one that was well-deserved. I hoped she didn't see through my act here. I needed her to assume the worst of me like everyone else did. Ryan was anything but another conquest, but I needed her to think that's all I saw.

She shifted awkwardly before seeming to remember she held a plate full of food in her hand, which she thrust in my direction. "Here, I made your favorite," she tried again, her tone light but tinged with more uncertainty than a few minutes ago.

My heart swelled as I looked down at the plate of chocolate chip oatmeal cookies. She used to make these for me when we were kids, and I'd had a particularly shitty day of my dad beating the everloving fuck out of me. She, and the cookies, were the only bright spots in my otherwise fucked up childhood.

I took the plate, swallowing hard. My mouth watered, but I kept the cocky grin locked on my face and my eyes as devoid of emotion as I could. "I can't eat this shit. How do you think I maintain this body?" I asked, rubbing my hand down my chest and abs and watching as her eyes sparked with heat and followed my fingers' path before snapping back up. "See something you like, baby?" I taunted, hating myself for the way I was acting, but I had to do it.

She huffed. "Don't flatter yourself."

I handed her back the plate. "Thanks for stopping by, but I've got a lot of work to do." I left no room for argument, and her mouth fell slightly open as she absently took the plate back. I turned and opened the screen door, not waiting for her to leave the porch before letting it slam behind me. Everything in me wanted to turn around, but I knew I wouldn't be able to handle seeing the hurt look in her eye at what a colossal asshole I just was to her.

I long since thought my heart was cold and dead, incapable of feeling anything other than indifference and anger. But I'd been wrong because Ryan just climbed her way back inside and cracked it wide open again.

FIVE
RYAN

*W*ho the hell did he think he was?

I didn't think I'd ever been so angry. My teeth ground together as I stomped off the creaky wooden porch and climbed into my car. I tossed the plate of cookies onto the passenger seat and slammed my hand against the steering wheel a few times, wishing it was Maddox's face. Had he always been such a complete tool, or was that something he'd developed now that he was some big shot rock star?

For a second, I thought I'd seen a flicker of something warm and inviting in his eyes, but it was gone so quick I must've imagined it. The engine turned over, and I put the car into gear, spinning the tires as I pressed down on the gas a little harder than necessary.

A couple of minutes later, I pulled into my driveway and got out of the car, slamming my door shut. I still fumed from my interaction with the boy next door. Had he really changed that much from the boy I once knew and loved? The boy who saved me, protected me, and became my best friend?

Quinn jumped down off of Daisy, his eyes searching my face and then narrowing in the Everleigh Ranch direction. "What'd that asshat do?"

I blew out a frustrated breath, my sweaty hair barely lifting off my forehead as the warm air wooshed past. I clenched my fists until my nails bit into my palms. "Oh, you know, nothing except refuse the cookies I baked him and slam the door in my face after looking at me like I was a piece of meat," I recounted.

I kept to myself how much it actually hurt that Maddox looked me over but deemed me not even worthy of a second glance.

I knew he had access to the most beautiful women in the world and took advantage of that fact often. I wasn't blind or immune. I may not be as obsessive about following his career as I once was, but I wasn't naive. I've read the headlines. I just never thought he'd look at me as not *enough*. I never had self-esteem issues when it came to my looks. I knew I was pretty, and even Maddox's lack of interest in me wouldn't change my mind.

But damn if it didn't sting.

Rather than let the stinging in my eyes turn into tears, I reached into the passenger side of my car and snatched up the plate of cookies. I handed one to Quinn before dumping them on the ground and stomping them into the dust, growling my frustration with every strike of my heel.

"Damn, Ry. I could've eaten at least another two or three of those," Quinn lamented, staring longingly at the pile of crumbled cookies now spread across the ground at my feet.

"Sorry, not sorry, Quinn. But you know what?" I asked, looking up into the hazel eyes of my best friend.

"What?"

"Screw Maddox Everleigh. I deserve better," I declared, dusting off my hands.

Quinn wrapped his strong arms around me, pulling me into his chest. "Yes, you do. And I won't let you forget it. Now c'mon, that hay's not going to move itself."

I chuckled before casting one last glare at the small house on the hill and turning my back on it. Maybe it was time I finally let go of my childhood love once and for all.

𝄞

Groaning, I rolled over in bed and slapped at my phone until it fell off the nightstand, the blaring alarm grating against my last nerve. Leaning far over the bed, I brushed my fingertips along the rough carpet before hitting my phone under the bed. "Ugh!" I growled, sliding off the mattress and falling onto the floor in a heap. Finally retrieving it, I shut off the beeping with a sigh.

Today was already starting off on the wrong foot, and I'd barely stepped out of bed yet. Fallen was more like it. Hauling myself up off the floor, I stepped into the bathroom and started prepping for the long day ahead.

An hour later, I met Quinn in the kitchen, filling a mug with black, steamy goodness. I wrapped my hands around the cup and inhaled the bitter scent.

"Look at you all dressed up. Where're you off to today?" Quinn asked, looking me up and down appreciatively.

Sighing, I took another sip of my coffee before squaring my shoulders. "I'm driving into Dallas. I have an appointment at the bank this morning."

Quinn's eyebrows shot up. "What are you going to do?"

"Beg for a loan."

He eyed me warily. "Do you think that's going to help?"

"Probably not, but I have to try. I don't have any other ideas, but I do have this presentation I stayed up putting together last night." I patted the laptop bag I'd set on the counter next to me.

Quinn perked up. "Are you going to tell them about your ideas for streamlining the feed?"

Nodding, I finished my coffee and turned to rinse the mug. "Yep. I outlined it all in a quick PowerPoint. Hopefully, I'll get them to listen," I explained.

"Hopefully," he agreed. "Do you want me to come with you?"

I appreciated how Quinn was always there for me, but I had to do this on my own. Shaking my head, I reached up and patted him on his broad shoulder before giving it a squeeze. "Thank you, but no. I've got to do this on my own. Besides, who's going to start clearing out the pasture so we can put this plan in place if you come with me?"

He scoffed. "You know that can wait until tomorrow, Ry."

"Not if we're going to save this place, it can't. We need to get it done."

He leaned down and pressed a soft kiss to my cheek. "Good luck. Text me as soon as you know anything."

"I will," I promised. I'd need all the luck I could get if I had a chance in hell at saving my family's legacy.

※

"Ryan Knight?" A middle-aged woman stood before me, a pleasant smile on her face. I imagined she was the secretary of the man I'd come here to meet with today, but I didn't want to assume.

"That's me," I confirmed before I stood from the faux leather chair I'd been in for the last forty-five minutes, unsticking my legs from the material and smoothing down my skirt. I tried not to let the irritation at their lack of respect for my time show on my face. Lifting my laptop bag, I slung it over my shoulder and followed her toward a set of imposing heavy wooden doors.

"I'm sorry for the delay. Mr. Rutherford's prior appointment ran late," she explained, but it did nothing to calm my nerves or squash my irritation.

"I'm sure he's swamped," I replied, maybe a little bit more condescending than I should have, but this guy obviously thought his time was more important than mine. The secretary shot me a disapproving look before motioning for me to enter the office as she held open the heavy door. I mumbled a *thank you* under my breath before turning my attention to the man sitting behind the giant desk.

I blinked rapidly as I took in the man I'd be meeting with today, the man who held my family's future in his overly soft hand. He was a *lot* younger than I'd been expecting, and a whole lot sexier, too.

His dirty blonde hair was longer on top, swept off his face, and a little to the side. He wore a button-down shirt that hugged his defined chest, and the sleeves were rolled up to show off his toned forearms. His tie matched his blue eyes and made them stand out, so the effect was striking. Based on the cocky smirk he wore, he knew it, too.

"Mrs. Knight?" he asked in a rich deep voice that dripped with a mix of professionalism and sexuality. It made me feel a little melty inside, which hadn't happened since I'd heard a certain bassist sing to me as he played the guitar when we'd sneak off to the pond as kids.

I smiled brightly and stretched out my hand. "It's miss Knight."

He brightened before sliding his soft palm into mine. I'd been right. His hand was so different than any man's I'd ever touched before. I was used to leathery skin or calluses, but his hand was smoother than mine. I tried not to judge him too harshly for that.

"I'm Yates Rutherford. Please, have a seat," he invited, gesturing to the chairs in front of his desk. As I settled into the hard seat and reached down to retrieve my laptop bag, he moved behind his desk and sat down.

"So, Rutherford? Like…" I lifted my hand and gestured vaguely around my surroundings. This was the biggest bank in Texas, possibly beyond that, and it was called Rutherford Financial.

He laughed. "Yeah, guilty as charged. Someday my father expects me to take over, but for now, I'm here learning the ropes." I was surprised by how casual and down to earth he seemed. He looked pretentious, but he didn't act like it.

"I don't normally meet with loan applicants personally, but your application intrigued me," he admitted.

I raised an eyebrow. "Oh?" I wondered what made my application special enough that he felt he needed to personally meet with me.

Nodding, he absently typed into the laptop on his desk. I assumed he was bringing up my application or folder or whatever it was the bank kept on me and my parents. "We don't deal with a lot of ranches anymore. Most are selling out to big corporations. From what I reviewed, it looks like your family is on the brink of having to sell. We don't currently hold your mortgage, but from the looks of this, you need help now. Am I right?"

Straightening my back, I inhaled deeply, preparing to explain to him my entire sob story. I was trying to decide what was important to share and what I should leave out. "Yes, you're correct. My dad had an accident a few years ago and wasn't able to work the ranch anymore. I came home after I graduated from college, and I run the ranch now. My parents never let me know how much the medical bills were sucking out of the ranch, but here we are. I'm going to level with you, Mr. Rutherford."

He held up his hand and flashed me his charming smile again. "Please, call me Yates."

"Yates, things are bad right now. But I know I can turn it around. I only just found out because my dad is stubborn and thought he could handle it." I reached over and patted my laptop. "I've got a quick presentation to show you my plan for digging us out of our hole. We just need help to get there," I admitted, hating having to ask for help.

He leaned back in his chair, his finger rubbing his square jaw. "What kind of help were you thinking?"

My palms were clammy, and I tried to discreetly wipe them on my skirt before I answered. "I wasn't sure what, if any, options I had. Either a second mortgage or maybe we could refinance our current loan with your bank."

He sighed deeply as a little line appeared between his eyebrows. "Listen, miss Knight-"

"Please, call me Ryan," I offered with a small smile, which he returned.

"Ryan. I would love to be able to help you, but I've gone over all the financials you provided, and none of the options I have available would buy you the kind of time you'd need."

My shoulders sagged, and my eyes stung, but I would not let Yates see me cry. I reached for my laptop, sliding it back into its bag before standing up. I straightened my skirt and held out my hand to him. "I'm sorry for wasting your time, Mr. Rutherford. Have a great day," I said before turning and starting toward the door. My mind was racing because this had been my last best hope. I wasn't sure where to go from here.

"Wait!" Yates called out, and I turned back around to see him striding across the room until he stopped in front of me. "I know this probably seems like horrible timing, but would you have dinner with me tonight? I have a proposal that I think might work for both of us, but I can't discuss it here."

I had to admit I was curious. I never really dated. And was this even a date? The way he'd phrased it, it sounded like maybe it was a business dinner. But what if it was a date?

My mind flashed to Maddox. His sexy smirk, chiseled jaw, and day-old stubble got him any woman he wanted. Based on the pictures I'd seen of him over the years, I knew he'd filled out, but seeing him here in person, he was so much broader and more defined than the sixteen-year-old boy that'd claimed my heart and refused to let go.

But he'd made it clear he had no interest in me. I couldn't sit around and wait forever, so I'd accept this date, or not-date, with an open mind. Yates may not be my usual type. He wore custom suits that probably cost more than my car, and his face was clean-shaven. He was Maddox's opposite in every way except one: They both looked like they spent a lot of time in the gym.

Yates filled out his suit in a way that most guys around here didn't. I was so accustomed to seeing beer bellies that Yates and his clearly muscled body and likely six- to eight-pack of abs took me pleasantly by surprise. It wouldn't be a hardship going out to dinner with him. Sure, I didn't feel that spark the way I had with Maddox, but that had to be because I hadn't fully moved on yet.

At least that's what I was trying to convince myself.

Yates was hot, and he seemed nice, despite the fact he hadn't approved my loan request. I couldn't really fault him for it, though. He was just following bank policy, and he seemed really apologetic.

I looked up into his eyes, trying to read any sort of trickery or deception, but they sparkled back at me, hopeful and with a little heat in them.

"Okay," I whispered.

The side of his mouth lifted in a smile. "Really?"

I nodded. "Sure, but I'm only here for tonight."

"That's perfect. Can I have your number?" he asked, and I laughed.

"Isn't it on the application?"

He reddened slightly. "Yes, but I thought it'd be a lot more polite and less unprofessional if I asked your permission."

Yates had a point. I fished my cell phone out of my bag and handed it to him. "Here, put your number in and text yourself."

He tapped at my screen before I heard a buzz over on his desk. He slid my phone back into my hand, his fingers lingering against mine for a moment longer than was necessary, but I didn't mind.

"I'll text you in a little while once I make a reservation. Does seven work for you?"

I bit my lip, my mind was already wondering what the hell I was going to wear to this dinner since I'd only packed this one cute outfit for the meeting. And now I'd need to get a hotel for the night since there was no way I was driving all the way back home after a date.

"Ryan?" Yates repeated. Shit, I hadn't answered his question.

"Uh, sorry. Yes, seven works." I hesitated. "Yates?"

"Yeah?"

"Is this a date?" I squirmed a little under the heat pooling in his gaze.

He took a step closer, and I could feel the warmth radiating off of his body through my clothes. "I'd like it to be, yes." He lifted his hand and brushed a stray lock of hair off of my forehead with his fingertips. "Is that okay?"

"Mmhmm," I mumbled, unable to form coherent words. What kind of sorcery was this? He'd managed to turn me into a jumble of nerves and lust. Only one other person had ever done that to me, but I refused to let him into my thoughts. It was time I moved on.

Yates stepped back and flashed me his bright white smile one more time. "Great, I'll text you in a little while and pick you up at seven then. Wear something nice," he added, turning back to his desk. I guess that meant I was dismissed. I bristled at the end of our interaction, but the rest had been great, so I let it go. I was sure he needed to get back to work.

"See you then," I said and made my way out of the bank.

As the spell broke and the adrenaline of the meeting wore off, I wondered what the hell I'd been thinking. I was not even close to ready to date. And what was this proposal Yates and hinted at? A little bit of hope bloomed inside me at the idea that maybe he'd be willing to help me save the ranch outside of the bank's rigid rules and policies.

Whatever happened, I had a feeling everything was about to change. I could only hope it'd be for the better.

SIX
RYAN

I hadn't packed a single thing to deal with the wild mess my hair was after a day out in the humid Texas heat, so I sat in a comfortable chair, sipping sparkling water and texting Quinn. At the same time, a hairdresser tamed the mess on my head.

Quinn: Wait, did you say date?

Ryan: Yup.

Quinn: So, he denied your loan then asked you out?

Ryan: It sounds terrible when you put it that way.

Quinn: …

Ryan: I'm glad you're keeping your opinion to yourself. Now help me with outfits. He said to dress nicely. What do I wear?

Quinn: What does 'nice' mean?

Ryan: Hell if I know. Dress?

Quinn: Definitely a dress. Send me dressing room selfies.

I could always count on Quinn to steer me in the right direction when it came to outfit selection. Having a gay best friend definitely had its perks. When my hair was finished, I jumped in my car and headed to a department store. A fancy boutique shopper, I was not. I didn't have a lot of money to throw around on new outfits, but I wanted to impress Yates.

Maybe it was more that I wanted to impress myself. I couldn't remember the last time I had a reason to dress up, so I wanted to make the most out of tonight.

I loaded down my arms with dresses until they shook under the weight, and I had to stretch my neck to see over the top of the pile. Stepping into the dressing room, I tossed the pile onto the waiting chair in the corner and grabbed the first dress off the top.

Pulling it down over my head, I realized my fatal error. I went to the salon before trying on dresses, which meant every dress was going to go over my head. Sorting through the pile, I tossed out anything that didn't have a zipper, hoping I could find something leftover that would look decent on my athletic body. I had curves, sure, but I also had muscles, so looking feminine could be challenging.

I hoped this wouldn't be one of them.

After trying on at least a dozen dresses and hating them all, I started to sweat, and Quinn's messages were getting snarkier and snarkier.

Quinn: I thought men were supposed to do the peacocking.

I glanced down at the dress I had on, wincing at the amount of sequins and feathery things hanging off of it. This was hopeless.

Ryan: Screw this. I'm grabbing pants.

Quinn sent back a string of clapping and *hallelujah* emojis, and I rolled my eyes. I liked dressing up fine, but I was more at home in pants. They were more *me*. And I didn't have time for this bullshit right now. I only had about an hour before Yates would be picking me up at my hotel, and I wanted to grab a quick shower.

I gathered up the huge pile of rejected dresses and dumped them on the dressing room attendant with an apology and made my way back to the sales floor. I quickly scanned the racks, pulling out a pair of pink wide-leg, high waisted pants, and a white halter neck bodysuit. *Perfect.* I didn't even bother trying them on, I didn't have time.

When I got back to my hotel, I jumped in the fastest shower of my life, did my makeup, and then threw on the outfit. Thankfully it fit perfectly. I snapped a quick mirror selfie and sent it to Quinn for final approval. The butterflies sprung to life in my stomach. I waited for him to reply, noticing that I only had a couple of minutes before Yates would be knocking on the door.

Quinn: Damn, girl. You're lucky I'm gay

Quinn: I expect a text from you as soon as you get back

I grinned, sliding my phone into my clutch. I didn't know what I'd do without Quinn in my life. He always knew the perfect thing to say to make me feel better or put my mind at ease. Plus, it was nice to have someone always looking out for me.

Just as I finished applying a final coat of lipgloss, there was a knock at the door. My heart kicked into overdrive and pounded uncomfortably in my chest. I smoothed my hand over my pants, before striding across the room and swinging the door open.

Yates's eyes widened before scanning up and down my body. "Damn, Ryan. You clean up well." He leaned forward and brushed his lips against my cheek. He smelled clean, like soap and light cologne. He wore blue again, and I was beginning to suspect he knew how the color made his eyes stand out and wore it all the time on purpose. This time he wore a blue blazer with a plaid button-up underneath and designer jeans.

He looked charming, not my usual type, but maybe that'd be okay. "Thanks, you do, too," I finally managed. I couldn't remember the last time I'd been on a date, and I was incredibly nervous. I felt awkward. I knew next to nothing about Yates other than he worked at the bank his family-owned, and right off the bat, it seemed like we wouldn't have much in common. Still, he was hot and seemed sweet. I wanted to go into tonight with an open mind.

"Hungry?" he asked.

"Starving. I skipped lunch." Right on cue, my stomach growled, and he laughed. His laugh was rich and warm, and I decided that I liked it and wanted to hear it again.

"Well, let's go eat. Our reservation's in fifteen minutes," he said, glancing down at his watch.

I closed the door behind me with a soft click, sliding my room key into my clutch. I exhaled deeply before following Yates down the hall to the lobby. We didn't talk, and I wasn't sure what to say. The silence was a little uncomfortable, and I found myself wanting to fill it but unsure how. Instead, I bit my lip and tried to focus on taking deep breaths to calm my nerves.

We walked up to a sleek sports car, and Yates opened the door for me. I slid into the soft leather and tried to make myself comfortable. I needed to break the awkward silence. I couldn't take getting through an entire dinner like this.

When Yates lowered himself into the driver's seat and started the car, I decided I'd go with an easy ice breaker. "So, Yates," I began. "You're being groomed to take over the family business, right?"

He chuckled. "Yeah, you could say that. Why?"

I picked at a stray string on my pants. "Did you go to college?"

He nodded. "Yale, just like my dad and his dad before him. It's a family tradition. I didn't really have a choice. It was expected of me before I was even born."

"Wow, didn't that bother you? What if you wanted to do something else?"

"It worked out. I love business. I guess it's in my blood. So I was happy with Yale," he answered. "What about you?"

I looked out the side window, watching as we passed storefronts and people out walking their dogs or jogging in the cooling evening air. "I went to college in California. UC Irvine. It's always been my dream to be a cop."

He turned to look at me, his eyebrows rising up his forehead. "A cop? How'd you end up working the ranch?"

"My dad had an accident. My older sister was doing her neurosurgery residency, so she wasn't going to give that up to come back. My younger sister was in the middle of college, working toward her degree in fire science. She always wanted to be a firefighter. I was the one who was done with my degree but not very far into my actual career training, so it made the most sense for me to come back." I sighed. I hadn't meant to tell him all of that, but it just sort of poured out of me.

I also left out the part about how I chose UC Irvine because of its proximity to Maddox Everleigh.

He shifted slightly in his seat and adjusted his grip on the wheel before he continued asking questions. "I know you want to save the ranch, and please don't be offended, but wouldn't it be better for you if you let the ranch go?"

I slumped against the seat as my body suddenly felt very heavy as if the world's weight was pressing down on my shoulders. "I'm not going to pretend it wouldn't personally be easier for me, but I could never let that happen. This ranch has been in my family for generations. It's my legacy, just like the bank is your legacy. Would it be so easy for you to just let it go?"

A dark shadow crossed Yates's face before he blinked it away and flashed a grin in my direction. "You're right. No, I wouldn't be able to let it go. It was a dumb question."

I gave him a small smile, grateful he hadn't pushed me further. "It wasn't dumb. That's a legitimate thing to ask me. My dad has never known another home, and neither have I, outside of my years in college. I may not want to raise my own family there, but that doesn't mean I don't want the option someday."

"You really are amazing, aren't you?" Yates asked though I didn't know what to say back to that, so I kept quiet the rest of the way to the restaurant.

We pulled up to a valet, and Yates got out and came around, opening the door for me before tossing the valet his keys. He placed his hand on the small of my back before leading me inside the fanciest restaurant I'd ever been in. I was glad I'd bought a new outfit, but I still felt a little underdressed. It made me feel better that Yates was wearing jeans, even if they were designer.

We were greeted right away by a hostess who seemed to know Yates by name. She led us back to our table and tried to offer me a wine list. I was a beer girl through and through, so I had no idea what to do with it. Instead, I deferred to Yates, and he ordered a bottle of something I'd never heard of for us to share.

I glanced at the menu on the table in front of me, not recognizing a lot of the food and wishing he'd taken us to a burger joint or something instead. I could really go for a burger and fries right about now. Maybe even a milkshake, too.

But, I tried to push those thoughts aside and enjoy tonight for what it was. Even if this wasn't really my thing, it'd be nice to try something new just to say I'd done it once.

"What do you recommend?" I asked him.

"The pork cheek mezzaluna is incredible. You've got to try it," he enthused.

"Okay, done."

Yates chuckled. "That was easy."

I lifted the glass of wine the waiter had just poured me and sniffed it expectantly. It smelled like alcohol. I really didn't get the fuss. "I think as you get to know me, you'll find I'm really not that difficult to impress."

His eyes glinted in the candlelight as he reached across the table and took my other hand in his. "I'm looking forward to getting to know you better, Ryan. I like you."

My cheeks heated up as I took a small sip of the wine and nearly spit it back into the glass, but I managed to choke it down. I set my glass down and slid it slightly further away. I'd had enough of that for a lifetime. I wasn't sure what to say back to him. He was nice enough, but I couldn't say I liked him yet. I didn't know enough.

"How about we start easy, then?" I proposed, smiling up at him. He wore an easy smile himself, and my hand was still clasped in his.

"Shoot."

"Favorite color?"

"Blue," he laughed.

I rolled my eyes, but I was still smiling. "Obviously. I've known you all of one day, and that's all I've seen you in. Even your car is blue."

"How about you?" he asked.

"Purple. The exact shade of the sunset after the sun has gone down, but before the stars come out. There's something about it that reminds me of magic."

He studied me for a minute, not saying anything. The waiter interrupted the intense eye contact when he dropped off our entrees. Yates let go of my hand, and we dug into our food.

As I bit into the little pocket of pasta, a flavor explosion happened on my tongue as the salty pork cheek popped out of its noodle cage. My eyes widened as I chewed. "Oh, wow," I breathed.

A smug smile crossed Yates's face. "Told you."

"Mmm," I agreed while taking another bite.

As we finished our dishes, I pushed my plate back and wiped my mouth on my napkin. I had to admit that it had been more delicious than I thought it'd be when we first walked in.

Yates cleared his throat. "Now that you've eaten, I have something I want to talk to you about," he began.

"Okay." I sat back, curious about where he was going with this.

"I'm not sure how to start this, so I'm just going to say it."

My stomach fluttered, and my heart rate kicked up, but I sat still and kept my eyes on Yates, waiting for him to start talking.

"Okay, so you know how my family owns the bank, right?"

I nodded.

"Well, the bank has been in my family for generations. Like your ranch, the bank is my legacy. My dad runs it now, but he wants me to take over. Also, like you, I don't know what I want to do for sure yet. There's a big part of me that wants to build something of my own. I do love business, but I don't love the banking business. Does that make sense?"

I nodded again, still confused about where this was going.

"I have a trust fund, but I can't access it until I'm thirty. I'd love to be able to get early access to invest in my own projects. I could show my family that I'm capable of running something I'm passionate about instead of what they want me to."

I furrowed my brows. "I understand that, but what does that have to do with me?"

He flashed me a small smile. "I'm getting to that. The amount of money in my trust fund is pretty significant. And that early access I was talking about? There's only one way to do that."

The meal I'd just eaten and enjoyed suddenly felt heavy in my stomach. "And how's that?"

"To get married," Yates disclosed, observing my expression. A chill settled in my chest, and I started to feel a little dizzy.

"M-married?" I stammered.

He nodded. "Look, I know I just met you today, but I think this could be the solution to both of our problems."

"How do you figure? It sounds like it'd help you definitely, but what would I get out of it?" I folded my arms across my chest. My mind was spinning a million miles a second, and I wasn't sure what to focus on first. Was I even considering this?

"If you agreed to marry me, I would buy your family's ranch and sign it over to you. You'd own it outright. No mortgage anymore, it'd all belong to you."

I inhaled sharply, sitting forward, my head falling into my hands while I closed my eyes and tried to process. I lifted my head up to look at him, to study his face. The truth shone back at me in his eyes: He needed me, and I needed him.

"There might still be another way for me to save the ranch," I argued.

He shook his head sadly. "No, Ryan. There's not. I looked over everything. No bank in their right mind would touch you guys. I'm sorry to say it, but I'm your last best hope."

Breathing out slowly, I considered his offer, but he continued talking as he grabbed my hand in his again. "Look, Ryan. I know it's unconventional doing this backward like this, but I really think we could have a legitimate future together. I like you, you're feisty and gorgeous and hard working. You fight for what you believe in. We don't know each other that well yet, but what if we're soulmates? What if we end up still married fifty years from now?"

The room was starting to spin. "F-fifty years?" I couldn't wrap my mind around that. It was absolutely overwhelming.

Yates started to backpedal. "I'm just saying it could happen, not that it has to. It's one possibility. If it makes you feel better, we can write an end date into the contract as an optional clause we can take after a year. Okay?"

I felt myself nodding along, but I wasn't quite sure what I was agreeing to at this point. Yates wanted to marry me? To get his trust fund? That made sense, even if it was a crazy idea. But still, I could see why he'd come up with this solution. And if it meant owning my family's ranch outright? Never having to answer to another bank again, would that be worth a year of my life married to this guy?

I looked him up and down, really taking him in. He looked genuine, and I could respect he was willing to do whatever it took to accomplish his goals. I was the same exact way. "How long do I have to think it over?" I asked, knowing I didn't have much time before we lost the ranch but really needing to wrap my head around everything.

"Unfortunately, I need your answer tonight. I have an event tomorrow where, if you agree, I plan to announce our engagement. Things need to move quickly for both of us, Ryan. I know it's a lot, and it's sudden, but I can't miss out on my chance, and you don't have months to decide. You have weeks at best until you lose everything."

I laid my head down on the table and closed my eyes, trying to drag air into my lungs. He needed an answer now? Could I do this?

I needed to think clearly and to do that, I needed more information. Lifting my head, I straightened my spine. "Okay, I have questions."

He smirked. "I expected you would. Go ahead."

"If we do this, when would the wedding be?"

"In a month. I don't think we can wait longer than that to save the ranch," he said, and he was right. I'd be lucky if we even got that much time.

Nodding, I moved to my next question. "My family knows I don't date. How would I explain suddenly turning up engaged and getting married in a month?"

He sat back and rubbed his chin thoughtfully. "I've thought about that. I figured we'd say we met online or on a dating app because we're both busy. We've been seeing each other when we can for months, but we got tired of that and can't stand to be away from each other anymore, so we decided to get married. What do you think?"

I looked at him dubiously. "I don't know if anyone who knows me is going to buy that."

"Well, you'll have to get them to. Because if you agree and we sign the contract, we'll also both be signing a non-disclosure agreement so you can't tell anyone."

I thought about Quinn, who knew I was going on this date and that I hadn't dated anyone in ever. "My best friend already knows I was going out on this date with you. He'll put two and two together and figure it out."

Yates sighed. "Fine, he can know, but if he tells anyone I'm holding you in violation of the NDA. It would ruin my image if this got out. I'm serious, Ryan. Not a word."

"Fine." The weight on my shoulders eased slightly, knowing I could talk to Quinn about all of this. He was going to freak out. That was if I agreed to do it, which I was still thinking about.

"Where would we live?" I continued my questioning.

"When we buy the ranch, you won't have to make mortgage payments anymore, so use that money to hire help. Then you'd move here to Dallas to live with me. Over the next year, or longer if you fall in love with me," he grinned.

"You'll be expected to go to functions and events with me as my wife. I have appearances to keep up and an image to maintain, so you'd be expected to help me with that."

I could do this, couldn't it? If it meant saving the ranch, seeing my parents happily live out their days in the place they loved best in this world, I could manage to be Yates's wife for a year.

"Last question, but I reserve the right to ask more later if I think of any," I warned, and Yates laughed.

"Fair enough."

"What about…" I leaned across the table toward him. "Sex?" I whispered.

He chuckled. "What about it? I think if it happens naturally great, but there won't be anything in the contract specifically one way or another. If you fall in love with me, great. If you don't, that's okay, too. But while we're married, we're only with each other. Even if that means we're not sleeping together. When you're my wife, you're mine. When I'm your husband, I'm yours. Okay?"

I blew out a breath. "Okay, I like that."

He smiled. "Good. So, what do you think?"

I bit my lip, trying to process everything, but there was no way I could wrap my mind around it all in such a short amount of time. My mind quickly flashed back to Maddox again, but I shoved the thought of him away. He made his feelings toward me clear. Now it was my turn to move on and do what I could to save the ranch. I could do this.

"I think you've got a deal." I just hoped I wasn't signing a deal with the devil.

"Really?" he exclaimed, jumping up and pulling me out of the chair, wrapping his arms around me and hugging me against his chest. I had to admit he smelled good. He didn't excite me like Maddox, and truthfully his hug felt more like when Quinn wrapped me up in his arms, but it wasn't bad, and maybe I could learn to fall in love with him. I guessed time would tell since now I had at least a year.

He let me go and reached into his pocket, pulling out a massive diamond ring and dropping to one knee. I gasped and covered my mouth with my hand, not sure what to make of this.

He flashed a lopsided grin up to me and took one of my hands in his. "I know this is unconventional, but don't the best love stories start out that way? This may be the only proposal you ever get if things work out like I hope, so I want to make it count. Ryan Knight, I just met you, and already I can tell you're an incredible woman, one I want to share my life with. Will you be my wife?"

My heart was pounding so hard I was surprised he couldn't hear it. My hands were tingling, and there was a ringing in my ears, but I felt myself nodding, agreeing to marry this stranger. He stood up, crushed me against his chest, and slid the giant sparkling rock onto my finger. He leaned down and brushed his lips against mine. He looked light and carefree, happy even. I wondered why he wasn't freaking out as badly as I was about this, but that was the least of my concerns.

"Now, what do we do?" I whispered, feeling like my whole world had turned upside down in one evening.

"We tell the world we're getting married, and we start planning."

"I'm going home tomorrow morning, and I'll tell my family then."

He nodded. "I'll tell my parents tomorrow as well. They'll want to meet you as I'm sure yours will want to meet mine. We can do that this weekend if that works for you. Yours on Saturday, mine on Sunday?"

"Yeah, that should work," I mumbled, my head still spinning.

"My mother will want to start planning right away, so you won't have to worry about a thing unless it's important to you. Like your dress or the cake flavor."

I perked up. "Ooh, I forgot about that. At least there will be cake."

Yates laughed his rich, warm laugh that made me smile. At least I knew enough to know I liked his laugh. He lifted the hand he still held and kissed the back of it lightly, obviously getting more comfortable being affectionate towards me. I had zero experience in this department, but I knew I'd have to learn quickly if we were going to convince anyone this was real. "Are you ready to get out of here? We've both got big days tomorrow. I've got the contracts in the car for you to sign."

He paid the bill, and we walked outside, waiting for the valet to bring his car around. "I think this is going to be really good, Ryan. I have a good feeling."

I wished I shared his sentiment, but I still had a lot of doubts. I wished I had longer to see if any other alternatives could save the ranch. Marriage meant a lot to me, and if this didn't work out with Yates, I'd have a divorce attached to me for life. My stomach turned, and I had to push the thought out of my head before it sent me into a panic.

I smiled weakly at him as he continued talking. I didn't think he noticed my unease. "Will you text me tomorrow and let me know how it goes telling your parents? I'll do the same."

Nodding woodenly, I reached for his hand, needing to grip onto something to ground me to reality. He grinned down at me, lacing our fingers together and tugging me a little closer to his side, so our arms were touching.

It's all for my family, I reminded myself.

For their future, it would all be worth it.

SEVEN
RYAN

What the hell had I done? I stared down at the enormous glittering gem on my fourth finger, twisting it around and around. I imagined if I were ever going to get married, it would be to a man that understood a ring like this would never be something I could wear. I hoped he would know me better than that.

But this monstrosity was yet another reminder that I was in an impossible situation, and I had no choice but to keep moving forward. Once I signed my name on that dotted line, I saved the ranch. It'd lifted a weight off of my shoulders and replaced it with a boulder in my stomach.

I always imagined my wedding as a small affair with the man I loved. I didn't care if it was fancy or at the courthouse. The most important thing in my mind had always been the groom, the man I was giving my heart to for life.

But here I was engaged to Yates, a man I didn't even know. I didn't even know simple things about him like his favorite food or what kind of music he liked. My sweaty palms were making it so easy to twist this ring around that I was worried it would fly off my finger. I planned on giving it back to Yates after our year was up. After I got a divorce.

Shivering, I looked down at my phone, which beeped for the thousandth time tonight. Quinn had been texting me relentlessly worried about how my date went, but I hadn't messaged him back yet. I had no idea what to say. How did I even begin to explain what I agreed to do?

Looking around the small hotel room, it felt so impersonal. I missed home. Suddenly, the walls felt like they were closing in. The air was hot and stuffy despite the air conditioner blowing a constant stream of chilly air into the room. I jumped off the bed and started collecting my stuff, shoving it into the tote bag I brought along with me this morning when I made the drive to the bank.

Had that just been this morning? It felt like a lifetime ago. So much happened today. I was having a hard time processing it. I needed my best friend and home.

Pulling my phone out of my back pocket, I checked the time. Eleven. I didn't feel tired. In fact, I was wired, jittery, and wide awake. I doubted I'd be getting any sleep at all tonight, long drive or not. Besides, home wasn't *that* far, only maybe an hour's drive. It would be worth making the drive to sleep in my own bed.

Ignoring all the texts from Quinn threatening to drive here tonight and hunt down Yates if I didn't respond, I shot him a quick message letting him know I was on my way home. I would explain everything when I got there. I doubted that would make him feel much better, but at least he'd know I was alive.

Taking one last look around to make sure I hadn't left anything behind, I left the room, pulling the door shut behind me with a satisfying click. I knew I was making the right choice to get the hell out of here and go home. Besides, maybe I'd run into a certain hot as sin rock star staying next door. My lips tilted up at that thought, as unlikely as it was, and I made my way out to my car suddenly in more of a hurry to get home than I'd been a few minutes ago.

𝄞

Pulling down the long driveway that led to our one-story ranch house, I slowed and rolled down my window, sticking my head out and turning off my headlights. While I didn't plan on living on the ranch much longer, I could appreciate how incredible the night sky was out here. I always took it for granted until I went away to college in southern California. The stars were almost impossible to see through the city lights out there. But here, there wasn't a street lamp for miles. There was nothing to impede on the inky sky full of sparkling stars and faint galaxies. Anytime I found myself outside at night, I couldn't help but tilt my head up to the sky and remind myself of how small my problems really were.

It was a reminder I sorely needed tonight. My phone buzzed in the cupholder and pulled me out of my fantasy. Instead of flying up to a faraway planet and leaving all my problems behind, I squinted my eyes at the bright screen. It hurt my eyes in the dark, and I stared at it, rolling my eyes at Quinn's text threatening to come out here and drag me inside if I didn't walk in the door in the next two minutes. He'd obviously been watching out the window for me to get home.

Flipping my headlights back on, I finished the drive. Finally, I stopped, stepped out of the car, and stretched my arms overhead. I glanced at the house next door, and all the lights were on. I wondered what Maddox might be up to tonight, but I wasn't sure I wanted to know. Instead, I grabbed my bag out of the backseat and walked inside before Quinn made good on his threat.

Closing the screen door softly behind me, I turned, and Quinn stood against the wall in the hallway with his arms folded across his chest and a scowl on his face. He motioned to follow him into the quiet house back to his room, and I did, dropping my bag inside the door before closing it behind me.

Running my hand through my hair nervously, a few strands got caught in the ring I almost forgot I was wearing, and I yanked, crying out from the pain. Quinn's eyes narrowed in on the ring. "What the fuck is that?" he growled. "And do I need to kill someone? I've been going out of my goddamn mind, Ryan, worrying about what was happening to you tonight because you couldn't be bothered to send a simple fucking text."

Quinn started pacing the room and sort of reminded me of a bull before a rodeo. I could practically see the smoke pouring out of his ears as I fell back onto his bed and relaxed into the familiar comfort of his mattress. I was surrounded by comfy blankets and the sandalwood and soap Quinn smell that always comforted me. I'd spent more nights than I could count sleeping in here.

"First of all, you don't need to kill anyone. I don't think," I started.

Quinn bunched his fists. "You don't think?"

"No, I know. You don't have to kill anyone. But can you please come lay down with me? I need my calm and comforting best friend right now if I'm going to tell you everything, not this angry version of him," I requested, patting the mattress next to me.

He sighed and deflated a little before sinking into the bed next to me and grabbing my hand, lacing our fingers together. "Sorry, Ry. But I was a fucking wreck all night worried about you when you didn't text back. You never date, so I was shocked you even wanted to, especially when the rock star showed back up," he gritted out, and I could see he was trying to rein in his temper.

Squeezing his hand, I rolled onto my side so I was facing him and looking into his dark hazel eyes. "I'm sorry, too, Quinny. I didn't mean to worry you, and when you hear what happened to me tonight, hopefully you'll understand why I didn't want to tell you in text and why I wanted to drive home so we could talk face to face."

His eyes softened, and he reached out and brushed the hair out of my face, waiting for me to talk. "You know this morning how I went to the bank, and Yates denied my request for a loan?"

Quinn raised an eyebrow. "Wait, his name is *Yates*?"

Giggling, I nodded my head. "I know. How very *Ivy League* of his parents, right? But it really fits him. You'll see."

"What do you mean, I'll see? Why would I ever meet this douche?"

"I'm getting to that part."

Quinn motioned for me to continue. "So, he picked me up for dinner, and the ride to the restaurant was so awkward. Have I ever even been on a date before?" I wondered aloud.

"Uh, not that I remember. But I wasn't with you in college," Quinn answered, furrowing his eyebrows until a little crease appeared between them.

"Yeah, well, now I know why. We don't know anything about each other, and I had no idea what to talk about, and it seemed like he didn't mind the silence. We got to the restaurant, and it was fine, the place was the nicest restaurant I'd ever been to. I even had wine."

Laughing, Quinn poked me in the stomach. "Look who went to the big city and got all fancy," he drawled with an exaggerated version of his slight twang.

Smacking his chest, I glared at him. "I've always been fancy. Anyway, the food was surprisingly good considering I didn't know what it was, but that wasn't the interesting part. That came after we were done eating."

"I have a feeling I'm not going to like this part," Quinn sounded wary.

"Yeah, I don't like this part, so I don't think you will either. But try to hold off on all your questions until the end, okay?"

He nodded once, and I continued. "It turns out that Yates had quite the proposal for me. He knew all about our problems with the ranch, and he came to dinner prepared. His family owns the bank, and he's in line to take over the family business. But he wants to make his own way, so he needs access to his trust fund."

"I don't like where you're going with this," Quinn said, his voice low.

I kept going as if he hadn't spoken because if I thought about it too much, I'd chicken out. "He made me an offer. He said if I did something for him, he'd buy the ranch and then sign the deed over to me. So, there would be no more mortgage, and we'd own the ranch outright. Then we could hire help, and we could be free Quinny."

He pressed his lips into a tight, flat line but didn't say anything for a long time. Finally, he spoke up. "Based on this," he pulled my hand into his and jiggled the diamond on my finger. "I'm going to assume that it wasn't something easy like being his fake date or something."

"No, it wasn't that simple," I confirmed. "He said we had to get married, and he wanted to do things backward. He said he likes me and wants to get married first and then sort of date and see if we want to stay married. He came to the date with a contract ready and everything. I even had to sign an NDA, but I told him to exclude you because I refused to do it if I couldn't tell you."

Quinn sighed. "What the hell were you thinking, Ryan?"

I pulled my hand out of his and sat up. "What other choice did I have, Quinny? Please, if you have any other ideas, I'm all ears. His bank was my last hope."

Raking his hand through his hair, he closed his eyes. "He took advantage of you. You know that, right? He saw you were desperate and knew he could get you to do whatever he wanted."

My shoulders sagged, and suddenly I felt every minute of this day weighing down on me. I wanted to sink into the mattress and pass out. "I know. But I still didn't feel like I had another option."

"So, you're going to marry a stranger and stay married to him forever?"

Shaking my head, I tucked my legs under my body. "I made him change the contract and write in that either one of us can get out of it after one year. He said that was the minimum, and I agreed. I don't feel any kind of spark with Yates. I don't see any world where we stay married after a year."

"What about Maddox? He just came back. What if he wants to start coming around more?" Quinn asked, almost sounding a little sad.

I scoffed. "Remember how he treated me yesterday? Fat chance he wants anything to do with me. Even if he did, I can't tell him that my engagement with Yates isn't real, and neither can you. We could lose everything, and then all of this would have been for nothing."

Quinn opened his eyes and looked at me before shaking his head. "You know I'll always support you, Ry. And Yates better make a room up in what I'm assuming is his big-ass house because the second you leave this ranch, I'll be right on your heels. You're never getting rid of me, fake husband or not. He'll just have to deal with it."

I laid back down, burrowing into Quinn's chest as he wrapped his arm around me. "I wouldn't want it any other way, Quinny. Love you."

"Love you, too, Lancelot." I smiled at the familiar nickname. Quinn hadn't called me Lancelot in years. He once told me that Lancelot was the bravest and strongest knight he could think of, so the name just fit me. After I'd gotten in a fight with a guy at a bar harassing Quinn for being gay, he'd given me the nickname, but he hadn't used it in months.

I closed my eyes and slowly started to fall into sleep when Quinn's quiet voice jolted me awake. "What are you going to tell your parents?"

Closing my eyes again, I tried to ignore the sudden racing of my heart. "That I'm getting married."

"Shit, they're going to freak out. Want to tell them over breakfast? I'll bake," he offered.

"You're the best. Will you hold my hand, too?"

He chuckled. "Whatever you need."

With his promise, I floated off into a dreamless sleep, dreading the morning and the half-truths I'd be forced to tell in the name of saving the ranch.

The smell of cinnamon sugar and butter danced through the air, and I smiled before I inhaled deeply and filled my lungs with the delicious aroma. Quinn must have been up for quite a while working on breakfast already, and I was glad he'd let me sleep in.

My body still felt heavy and tired from everything that happened yesterday, but I needed to drag myself out of bed and face my parents. The sooner I told them what was going on, the better. I hadn't told Quinn last night that Yates wanted to get married in just a month. Quinn probably would've freaked out, and I couldn't have handled that. He'd get that fun surprise this morning with my parents.

Sitting up, I rubbed my eyes and swung my legs over the edge of the bed before crossing the room to my bag and walking across the hall to my room. I quickly got dressed, brushed my teeth, and washed yesterday's makeup off. No longer looking like a raccoon was an excellent first step on facing the day. Tossing on a sundress, I padded out to the kitchen.

"Breakfast smells amazing, Quinny," I said, walking around to where he stood with an apron wrapped around his body. He held out a coffee cup filled with the perfect coffee-to-cream ratio, and I gratefully took it.

He grinned. "I wish I had more time to cook. Unfortunately, ranch work doesn't leave a lot of kitchen time."

"Maybe when all this is over, you'll have a chance to go work in a restaurant," I suggested. I wanted nothing more than for Quinn to chase his dreams as much as I wanted to go after mine.

"Maybe," he mused before looking over my shoulder at my parents, who were shuffling into the room. They'd given up keeping rancher hours a couple of years ago, so Quinn and I were almost always up before them.

"Morning, Ry. Smells incredible, Quinny," my mom said, grabbing a couple of mugs and pouring herself and my dad some coffee.

"Thanks, Shannon," Quinn smiled, sliding his hand into an oven mitt before looking down at me. "Hey, Lancelot, think you can carry the bacon and eggs?"

Chuckling, I grabbed the platter on the counter piled high with breakfast meat and scrambled eggs. "Lead the way."

I followed Quinn to the kitchen table where my parents sat, suddenly feeling incredibly nervous. My hands shook as I leaned over the table and placed the platter down with a thud. Quinn glanced at me out of the corner of his eye but schooled his expression into his typical calm facade. He slid out the chair next to him, and I plopped down into it, balancing right on the edge and keeping my back stiff and straight. I shook my leg with nervous energy.

My mom studied me carefully. "What's going on with you this morning, sweetheart?"

I exhaled a shaky breath and nervously tucked my hair behind my ear. My mom's eyes followed the movement, widening almost comically. "What is that?" she squeaked, pointing to my hand. Quinn grabbed it and pulled it under the table, squeezing my fingers.

"I'm engaged-"

My mom's squeal made me wince. "Oh, my god! I knew it! Alex, didn't I tell you? I knew they'd figure it out." She jumped out of her seat and rushed around to me, wrapping her arms around Quinn and me.

"I'm so happy for you two. I knew it was only a matter of time. I've been telling your dad for years this would happen."

I glanced helplessly at Quinn, who looked decidedly uncomfortable. My dad cleared his throat. "Shannon, let the kids breathe for Christ's sake."

My mom sniffled and finally loosened the death grip she had on us, and I took a deep breath. I had *not* seen that reaction coming, and by the look in Quinn's face, I bet he felt the same way. Being gay wasn't something you just grew out of, and I thought my parents understood that. There'd been a few times I caught Quinn looking at me with interest, his eyes dark. There were times where he got possessive whenever other guys showed interest when we'd go out together. But he was just a good friend. There'd never been anything there with Quinn, not when I wasn't exactly his type.

Plus, as long as I'd been interested in boys, only one had ever held my heart.

Maddox.

"You guys, Quinn and I aren't engaged. Sorry to disappoint," I started.

"What do you mean? Who else could you possibly be engaged to?" my mom asked incredulously.

"I'm getting to that," I said, glancing at Quinn to see the muscle in his jaw tense up and I rubbed my thumb across the back of his hand and watched him relax slightly.

"I've been seeing someone for a few months. His name is Yates, and we met on a dating app." I thought I'd go with the most straightforward explanation I'd been able to think up. My parents were hopeless when it came to smartphones and apps.

"Where does he live?" my dad asked.

"He lives in Dallas. Yesterday, we had a date, and he proposed at dinner," I explained.

"Why have we never met him, Ryan? I've got to say I'm shocked by this. I figured any guy you ended up with we'd know well by the time you got married," my mom said, her eyes a little misty still.

"He works in finance for his family's business, and he doesn't get a lot of time off. That's why we met online, he didn't have time to date traditionally. He proposed because we're tired of being apart." I cringed at that last part. I wasn't sure if my parents were buying it.

My dad sighed. "I'm not sure how to feel right now, kiddo. But I do know that if you decided he's the one for you, your mom and I wouldn't stand in your way."

"Thanks, dad." I sniffed as my eyes stung with unshed tears. Now it was Quinn's turn to comfort me as he squeezed my hand again. I tried to tell them as much of the truth as I possibly could. Still, I hadn't come up with a good reason to explain Yates buying the ranch without it sounding like a business transaction, so I decided that'd be a problem for a different day.

"So," my mom said, a small smile on her face. "When's the big day?"

My stomach dropped as I glanced at Quinn out of the corner of my eye. "Um, in a month," I mumbled.

"What was that sweetheart?" my mom asked.

"In a month," I repeated, and Quinn inhaled sharply. I knew we weren't done talking about this by a long shot, but I'd never felt so shitty about anything in my entire life. I had to keep reminding myself I was doing all this for a good cause. But if that were true, why did it feel so bad?

EIGHT
MADDOX

"Where the fuck is the coffee?" I grumbled out loud, slamming the cupboards closed. I'd been lucky yesterday. My old man hadn't come home, and I spent the afternoon going over all the financials I could get my hands on. The more I read, the more my new plan solidified in my mind.

But today was a new day, and I woke up hungry and in desperate need of a caffeine fix. Being in this place set every last nerve ending on edge. I fucking hated it here. I wanted to burn this whole fucking place to the ground like it deserved.

Instead, I decided to play the long game. Setting this ranch on fire would be satisfying, and I could move on more quickly, but Russell deserved worse. He deserved to know exactly how little he meant to me.

With my tentative plans swirling in my mind, I jumped in the shower and threw on my uniform black jeans, black t-shirt, and black boots. Not practical in the Texas heat, but signature style usually wasn't a practical thing. This was small-town Texas, but that didn't mean fans or paparazzi weren't lurking around the corner with a phone pointed in my direction. No matter what was going on in my life, I had an image to maintain. One I'd worked too goddamn hard to shape to have it threatened by anything.

I sighed heavily before tossing a black baseball hat on my head and shoving a pair of aviators on my face. I couldn't remember the last time I went to a grocery store on my own. I had people who did that mundane shit for me now. And in this small of a town, people gossiped and stopped you as you walked around because no one could mind their own goddamn business. I figured it'd be too much to hope I could get in and out without talking to anyone.

Calling my driver, I scrolled through social media while I waited for him to pick me up. Ryan hadn't posted anything new since I saw her yesterday. I looked at the picture of her and her boyfriend at least a dozen times, trying to figure out what she saw in him. Even though I pushed her away, deep down, I still felt like she was mine.

I knew I didn't deserve her, that I'd never had her, but that didn't stop the possessive part of my brain from feeling enraged that someone else had taken her from me. I had no one to blame but myself, but thinking in this way wasn't doing anything to help my already fucked up mood. I'd need to avoid Ryan as long as I was here. When I got home, I'd have to do what I'd done for the past twelve years: bury myself in pussy, alcohol, and music until I forgot anything else existed.

I looked up from my phone just as the black SUV pulled into the short driveway. Hopping inside, I looked out the window as we drove the ten miles into town. Town was a generous word for this place. There was a grocery store, a diner, a motel, a post office, and a bar. There wasn't even one stoplight. I hated everything about it.

Pulling into the grocery store, I took in the mostly full parking lot with disgust. If this tiny shithole of a town had any decent restaurant fare or meal delivery service, I'd never step foot in this market, throwing myself at the mercy of the local rumor mill. But a man had to eat, so I'd endure it even if it sort of made me want to throat punch everyone who looked my way.

And of course, because I was in a blacked-out SUV with a driver, every goddamn head turned in my direction the minute we pulled in the parking lot. So much for keeping my trip low key. Grinding my teeth, I threw open the door and slid out of the backseat. I checked my pockets quickly to make sure I had everything then slammed the door shut, probably harder than I needed to. I didn't bring a list with me, but I knew I needed food and I needed coffee so I'd try to get in and get out as fast as I could. I'd keep my head down and try to ignore the stares burning into my back from every direction, too.

Grabbing a basket, I glanced around quickly to get my bearings. It didn't look like anything had changed about this store since I was a kid, which meant I still knew where everything was. Right after my mom left, Russell made it clear buying food was my responsibility, so once a week, he'd drop me off at the store while he went to the bar down the road and drank for a couple of hours before he'd pick me back up. I spent so much time here, all the cashiers knew me by name, and I had every aisle memorized.

Striding toward aisle five for the coffee, I almost bumped into someone. I tried to step around her, but she moved to stand in my way. "Maddox?" she asked.

I glanced up, pulling off my sunglasses when I took in her familiar dark brown hair, now streaked with more silver than I remembered. "Mrs. Knight, it's good to see you," I said, smiling at Ryan's mom. It *was* good to see her, and she was one of only a couple of friendly faces I wouldn't mind bumping into while I was here.

"Wow, haven't you grown into a handsome man?" she teased. "The pictures don't do you justice."

I chuckled. "How's life, Mrs. K?"

"Please, Maddox. I've told you a thousand times to call me Shannon."

"Sorry, Shannon. It's been a long time. How have you been?"

"Well, all my girls are healthy, so I really can't complain too much. I've gotta say I'm surprised to see you back here. Is everything alright?" she asked, concern lacing her features.

I shifted my weight from one foot to the other, uncomfortable with her scrutiny, even if I knew she didn't mean anything by it. I wasn't used to opening up about personal shit to anyone. Ever.

"Joel called me about a few issues with the ranch, so I thought I'd come down and help for a couple of weeks." I tried to be vague because no one could know my plans yet, but I told as much of the truth as possible. I respected Shannon, but more than that, I liked her. She'd always been good to me growing up.

"Oh, well, I bet Ryan will be happy to see you," she teased, a smile crossing her face.

"Uh, yeah. Maybe. How has she been?" I hadn't dared ask Ryan herself, but I thought it'd be safer to ask her mom. I was starving for any scrap of information about the woman I'd been obsessed with since I was twelve years old.

Her forehead wrinkled a little before a small smile popped back onto her lips. "Funny you should ask. She sat us down this morning and let us know she's getting married and in just a month. Will you still be here? I'm sure she'd love it if you came."

My heart stuttered and then slammed against my chest as pain ripped through my entire body. I couldn't have heard her right. Ryan was getting married? I listened to the words, but my brain was having a hard time processing what they meant.

"Maybe," I managed to mutter, surprised I still had the ability to speak a goddamn word out loud with how it felt like my body was collapsing in on itself. I glanced down at the dark screen of my phone, pretending I got an important message. I looked up at Shannon with what I hoped would pass for an apologetic expression, even though it probably looked more like I was losing my shit.

"I've got to go. It was nice to see you, Shannon."

She narrowed her eyes. "Are you okay, Maddox? You don't look very well."

"I'm fine. Maybe I'll see you again before I leave." My head started to spin, and a cold sweat had broken all over my body. I didn't stay and wait for her response, I had to get out. I spun on my heel, dropped the basket to the ground with a loud bang, and practically sprinted for the exit.

My mind was a mess, I couldn't catch my breath, and my heart felt like it was being torn out of my chest. The pain was so intense, I stumbled, trying to get out of the store, and my chest heaved with the effort to pull fresh air into my lungs. But nothing helped.

I couldn't breathe.

How could I have let this happen? I thought letting her go was the right thing to do, but I never considered what I'd do if she actually moved on.

And now she was marrying someone else? No one else would love her like I did. No one else could give her the kind of life I could. She was my best friend. But I threw it all away. I'd never hated myself more. I did this. *Me.* I had no one to blame for this misery but myself.

My eyes stung. Fuck. I *would not* cry. Especially not in public. I learned when I was a kid to never let anyone know they affected me. I endured bone-cracking beatings that left me battered and bruised and never shed a tear. I watched my mom walk away and leave me behind, and my dad tell me he wished she aborted me and not broken down.

But this? This would wreck me. My heart would never recover. And her mom expected me to actually watch her walk down the aisle to another man? I'd fucking murder him. I couldn't do it. There was no goddamn way I could endure it.

Why was the air so thick? My hands were tingling because I couldn't get enough oxygen. Was I hyperventilating? I had no idea. All I knew was I felt like I was going to pass out. I needed to get the fuck out of here, and I needed a drink.

But most of all? I needed her.

I couldn't have her, though. I burned that bridge a long time ago and reinforced it yesterday. Even if I tried to make it right, to explain to her how I did this all for her, she'd never want me after the way I treated her. Right now, I needed the guys. I *never* asked for help. I was the one everyone came to when they wanted shit handled, but I had no idea what to do.

With a shaking hand, I pulled my phone out of my pocket and texted True.

Maddox: I need you guys.

True: When & where?

Maddox: Texas. Now.

True: Give us a couple of hours.

Maddox: Bring all the alcohol.

True: …you got it.

I exhaled a shaky breath and slid my phone back into my pocket as I climbed into the back seat of the waiting SUV without the groceries I came for. I'd deal with it later. "Drop me at home," I demanded. I'd have to deal with myself for a couple of hours until the guys showed up. I couldn't risk getting fucked up at the bar. Odds were either someone Russell knew would be there and recognize me, or I'd end up with a shitty picture on some tabloid by tomorrow morning.

Nope, I'd have to wait until True, Zen, and probably Connor got here. The two of them were into all that romance shit, and Connor would knock some sense into me. Maybe I could still salvage this.

Looking back on all my decisions when it came to Ryan, I realized how colossally I fucked up. She'd always been there, waiting for me to pull my head out of my ass and claim her as mine. But I pushed her away one too many times, and she finally gave up on me. Now it was my turn to show her I wouldn't give up on her.

NINE
MADDOX

"I don't understand," True said, his words slurring together. "If Jericho were here, he'd know how to explain it."

Zen brought his glass to his lips, sloshing a little bit out of his cup in the process before slurping another sip of his drink. "My wife demanded he stays. Sorry." He didn't sound sorry at all as a crooked smile broke out on his face.

Sighing, I pinched the bridge of my nose. We'd already gone over this again and again for the past hour. Now that the alcohol was buzzing through my veins and my thoughts weren't nearly as clear, it was getting harder to answer their questions and focus on the details.

And on top of that, the numbness I was used to from the whiskey hadn't happened this time. No, this time, the pain had gotten worse because that was just my fucking lot in life. My stomach turned, and the sharp stabbing in my chest got worse as I focused on it. Instead, I tried to push it aside and explain why I cut Ryan out of my life.

"Man, you didn't see the way she looked at me back then. We were just kids, and we kissed, and when I realized what happened, I looked down at her, and she was looking at me like I was her goddamn hero. Like I was the only person in the entire fucking world, and I couldn't handle it. I knew if I didn't get the fuck out of here, I'd drag her down with me. The same blood flows in my veins as my old man, and I watched him destroy my mom. He tore her apart piece by piece until she couldn't stand to look at either one of us. The day she left, I knew she blamed me for keeping her tied to him. I refused to do that to Ryan. So I made the choice for her, and I left."

Eyes burned into the side of my face, and I turned to find Connor studying me. He hadn't said much this entire evening, but he sipped his drink and observed like he always did. I wasn't sure if he came along for my benefit or for Zen's since Kennedy was six months pregnant, and they couldn't stand to be away from each other. I was surprised he came at all.

"Dude, that's pretty fucked up. You didn't give her any say in the decision?" Zen asked.

"No, I couldn't. She was fourteen at the time, and I had the only chance I'd probably ever get to get out of here. I couldn't take her with me, but I could have told her I was going or asked her to wait for me. But don't you see how fucking unfair that would've been? I had no idea things would turn out like they did." I raked my hand through my hair, absently noting how my fingertips tingled.

"Well, now she's getting married. You have to tell her how you feel," True announced, standing up from his seat and swaying before throwing his arms out to the side to balance himself.

"True's right, Mad. This might be your only chance to make things right. Now everything makes fucking sense. You've been a goddamn nightmare for ten years, and it's all been over a girl. I never would have guessed," Zen mused, sipping his drink.

"What if she hates me? I've seen her once in twelve years, and I was a complete dick to her," I whispered, my words slurring together even to my own ears. I set my drink down on the table, standing up. The room tilted and swayed but thankfully hadn't started to spin.

"She doesn't hate you. She brought you your favorite cookies as soon as she saw you were back. That girl loves you, asshole. Christ knows why," Connor responded, rolling his eyes.

True stepped around the coffee table and gripped my arm, yanking me toward the door. "Where are we going?" I asked, stumbling after him.

"Do you want to be with this girl?" Zen asked, trailing behind us.

I nodded reluctantly, blowing out a breath that burned on the way out. I bet if I blew against a match right now, it'd light my breath on fire, the alcohol was so strong. "More than anything. I've never been able to let her go."

"Holy fuck. Is she why you've never been with the same girl more than once?" True asked, his eyes going wide.

I nodded again, avoiding all three pairs of eyes focused on me right now by looking at the swaying floor. "I never wanted to risk getting involved with someone else. I think deep down I always hoped I could find a way to show her I'd be good enough for her." Ugh, I fucking hated admitting feelings shit out loud. It made me twitchy.

"You're going to tell her right now how you feel and why you've shut her out for so long. This is your chance, bro. Do not fuck it up." True opened the screen door so hard it banged against the siding, and I winced at the loud noise cutting through the quiet country night. I forgot how quiet life could be out on the ranch with only the crickets making noise.

My heart rate picked up until it was slamming against my chest, and my hands were clammy. "Right now? There's no way she'd hear me out after the way I've acted for the past twelve goddamn years. I'm sure she's aware of my well-earned reputation. And I'm too fucked up to drive, and it's too far to walk in the dark," I protested.

Zen and Connor followed us outside, and True stopped short as Zen almost plowed into my back. "What the fuck, True?" Zen asked, and I wasn't sure either one of them had listened to a word of my drunken rambling.

True twisted his nose ring for a second before he clapped his hands. "Horses!"

He grabbed my arm again and yanked me forward as he took off toward the barn. "What the fuck do horses have to do with anything?" I asked, but True ignored me. Zen was practically giggling behind me. I smirked as I glanced over my shoulder, stumbling against the hard-packed dirt ground. Zen had always been a fun drunk. It was why, until I met Connor, he was my favorite wingman.

The smell of musty old hay and just straight up farm animal hit my nostrils as we crossed the threshold into the barn. True dragged me up to the stable where one of Russell's horses was and flung the door open. The horse startled and made a noise that had all of us backing up and away from him. I may have been drunk, but I was in no mood to have my face kicked in by a horse.

True's unfocused gaze landed on me. "Do you remember how to ride one of these things?" he asked, pointing at the horse in front of us.

"It's gotta be like riding a bike, right?" Zen giggled.

I rolled my eyes again and stepped closer to the horse, reaching my hand out in front of me and waiting for him to come to me. He eyed us warily before snorting and slowly stepping toward me, touching his fuzzy nose against my hand. I rubbed his nose a few times before walking into the stall and grabbing the gear to get him ready to ride.

Once I had the horse saddled up, I led him out into the barn. "What am I supposed to say to her?"

"You stop being a fucking coward and tell her the goddamn truth," Connor growled.

I bristled at his harsh words, then quickly deflated. He was right. "Fine, help me up," I said, my words still slurring together. I briefly wondered if tomorrow this would seem like such a good idea, but now I was determined. I felt like if I didn't tell Ryan how I felt, I'd never get another chance. I lost her officially, she agreed to be another man's wife, and it would destroy me to let her go, but maybe there was still a sliver of hope that she'd hear what I had to say.

Maybe she'd been feeling like she was missing her other half all these years like I'd been feeling half of me was missing, too. I was too afraid to hope that she'd actually want to be with me, but maybe I could convince her to stop and consider giving me a chance. I knew I'd have to earn the right to call her mine, especially after how I'd acted. But I was ready to try.

I couldn't believe I'd gotten to this point where I actually *wanted* to be with someone more than I wanted my next breath, but here I was. It took the threat of losing her to another man to snap me out of my idiocy.

I grabbed the saddle and tried to lift myself into the seat, falling on my ass on the hard ground instead. The room swayed again, but Connor reached down and pulled me up. Zen was bent over, laughing his ass off, and I glared in his direction. Or at least I think I glared. I couldn't feel a lot of my face, so I wasn't sure. It didn't really matter either way because he wasn't paying attention.

I stuck my foot in the stirrup and grabbed the saddle again, but this time True and Connor both helped me balance and braced me as I hauled myself up with a grunt. I swung my leg over, and when the stallion shifted impatiently, I leaned forward. I grabbed onto his neck to avoid falling, slipping my hands into his coarse hair and grabbing on with both fists.

"I'm going to fall and break my fucking neck," I grumbled into the horse's fur.

"You'll be fine," True assured me, slapping the horse on his haunches and sending us out into the night at a trot. I had my eyes closed, but I knew I had to steer the horse, so I gingerly sat up and grabbed the reins, leading us toward the house that I could only see in the dark night because of its porch light.

The ride felt like it took forever, and I wasn't feeling great by the end of it. I'd be lucky if all the swaying didn't make me throw up as I tried to profess my feelings to the only girl I ever loved, but still, I kept going because goddamnit I had to try. I already waited too long, and True was right. I wasn't waiting any longer.

I pulled back on the reins in Ryan's front yard, hopping down and steadying myself against Hex's side until the ground held mostly still. I took a few deep breaths of the still warm and humid as fuck air. Even at one a.m., the Texas heat was stifling.

I remembered her bedroom from when she was a kid, and I hadn't stopped to consider that she might have moved or that her *fiance* might be in there with her. My fists clenched as I thought about another man sharing her bed, worshipping her body. My blood started to boil, and I had to take a few more deep breaths. Fuck, I messed up.

Her window was dark, and I stood off to the side so I wouldn't freak her out when she woke up and saw me standing right outside. When we were kids, I'd always stand off to the side because I never wanted to scare her. I tapped gently on the glass with my knuckle and waited to see if she'd wake up. A few seconds passed, and nothing happened, so I knocked again louder.

I could barely make out movement in the darkness of her room, but then there she was, in a tiny tank top and shorts, her hair messy from sleep staring down at me with wide, tired eyes. She lifted the window and leaned outside, and I couldn't help myself. I dropped my eyes to her tits, which were practically spilling out of her top. My cock and I were in agreement: Ryan had grown into a fucking stunning woman with curves in all the right places. I ached to be inside her, but I pushed my hunger aside. Ryan would never be a quick fuck.

Her orange-vanilla scent slammed into me, a familiar warmth wrapped around me as I was transported back to hot summer days spent with cold popsicles and the girl of my dreams. Her scent hadn't changed in the past twelve years, and the nerves I'd been feeling about talking to her instantly calmed down when I breathed her in.

"Maddox?" Her voice was so breathless and husky it immediately made me hard. She sounded sleepy and maybe like she'd been crying. "What are you doing here?"

"I'm so fucking sorry, Ryan," I started.

She sighed. "Are you drunk?"

"Maybe a little but I have so much I need to say to you, I couldn't wait until tomorrow," I said, leaning against the house's side to keep myself upright.

"Come in," she whispered, moving back to let me climb in. I grabbed the window frame and pulled myself up, but I wasn't coordinated enough to get inside on my own. She grabbed my forearms and helped drag me into her room. I collapsed onto the floor with a thud, and she glanced at her door nervously. I hoped her dad didn't come barging in with his shotgun. He liked me when we were kids, but things were different now.

I hurt his little girl, and I had a reputation no dad would want for his daughter.

She shut the window and moved to sit on the edge of her bed, staring down at me with her big, beautiful brown eyes. She was giving me a chance to talk, waiting for me like she always had. I was such an idiot to push her away. Ryan was way too fucking good for me.

The words started pouring out of me like they'd been on the tip of my tongue, waiting to escape and confess all my sins. "I never should have left without saying goodbye. I couldn't stay, but you didn't deserve that."

"Why *did* you leave like that?" she wondered, her fingers playing with the hem of her tank top.

Exhaling deeply, my shoulders slumped. I moved to sit up and lean against the wall before I let myself admit out loud how much I really fucked up. "Do you remember the night before I left?"

She scoffed and folded her arms across her chest as hurt flashed in her eyes. "Of course I remember. You gave me my first kiss and then took off as if you'd been shot. Then I never saw you again. Well, until yesterday."

I lowered my head, unable to take the hurt in her eyes. I could never tell her it hurt me just as badly as it did her for me to walk away, but I was trying to protect her from me. She'd deserved better back then. Honestly, she still deserved better.

"You'll never know how fucking sorry I am for that, but I hope you can believe me when I say I thought I was doing it to protect you."

She stood up and crossed the room, lowering herself to her knees so she was sitting right in front of me. She reached out and cupped my cheek with her soft hand, lifting my head so that she could look into my eyes. "I believe that. You were always my best protector, Maddox."

I leaned into her touch, never looking away from her intense stare. "I just want to know why you never called or wrote or texted. Why you completely shut me out," she softly demanded.

Reaching up, I wrapped my fingers around her wrist, stroking her soft skin with my thumb as her palm rested on my cheek. Now that she'd touched me, I never wanted her to stop. "I knew I'd never be good enough for you, Ryan. You deserve so much better than me. What if I-"

My voice had gone gruff, and I struggled to get the words out without the emotion overtaking me, my throat clogging, and my eyes starting to sting.

"Shh," she soothed. "I know you better than you think, Maddox Everleigh. There was never a chance you would turn out like him. You're good and kind in here," she said, moving her other hand to rest her palm on my chest over my heart.

The kindness and certainty in her eyes made my chest warm under her palm. A tear slipped down my cheek before I lowered my head into my hands and started sobbing uncontrollably. Fuck, when was the last time I cried? I came here to apologize and beg Ryan to give me a second chance, and here I was, breaking down on her bedroom floor instead.

Instead of being horrified by me like she should've been, she wrapped her arms around me. She held me close to her warm body while I cried, whispering comforting words into my hair, running her fingers through it like she used to do when we were kids, and I ran to her house after my dad beat the shit out of me. She'd always been my safe place, my refuge.

"I'm so sorry," I whispered, and she leaned back, standing up. She grabbed my hand and pulled me up with her. She silently crossed the room and slid into her bed, pulling back the covers and patting the spot next to her. I couldn't believe she wanted me to stay after everything I did to hurt her.

I wasn't going to miss out on any opportunity to spend more time with her. Lowering myself unsteadily to the bed, I untied my boots and pulled them off before moving under the blanket and laying flat on my back. I wanted to pull her into my arms and hold her close to me the whole night, but she didn't belong to me yet, and I wouldn't disrespect her that way.

Instead, I reached out and wrapped my pinky around hers before closing my eyes. Now that I'd unlocked the vault of my feelings, there was no going back. No shoving shit back inside. If she married another man at this point, I was pretty sure it'd destroy me.

TEN
RYAN

The next morning, I woke up to cold sheets in the bed next to me. I had to wonder if I imagined the whole Maddox-drunkenly-crawling-through-my-window-at-one a.m. situation. Was I so desperate for him to reciprocate my feelings that I made the whole thing up? I stood from my bed, stretching my arms overhead as I considered everything that happened last night.

Glancing back, I noticed a small scrap of paper on the side of the bed he slept on. All it said was one word: *Thanks. -M.* I blew out a breath as my heart rate picked up, and a slow smile spread across my face. It had been real.

Maddox did care about me, enough that he put us both through hell to try and make sure I lived a happy life. But what had he done to himself in the process? My smile quickly evaporated as I thought about his stint a few years ago in rehab I saw in the headlines, the constant string of girls hanging off of him in the news. He seemed so broken last night, and my heart ached for him, for what could have been.

But what should I do with his late-night confession? The information burned a hole in my brain, begging me to do *something* with it, but I had no idea what. I always hoped the day would come where Maddox would come back to me and tell me he wanted me like I wanted him. That he'd been waiting just as long and he made a terrible mistake when he left.

My stomach sank when I remembered why I fell asleep with hot tears streaming down my cheeks last night. Yates. I agreed to marry him, signed a contract, and now the ranch would be safe. No one would ever be able to take it away again, and I couldn't walk away from that no matter what.

My good mood instantly evaporated. I had a strong feeling that Maddox wouldn't wait around a whole year while I was married to another man I didn't even know and could never love. My heart had always belonged to someone else.

Why couldn't Maddox have come to me two days earlier? The ranch may still have been in danger of foreclosure, but I wouldn't be engaged to Yates with a wedding on the horizon. The soft click of my bedroom door opening startled me out of my thoughts, and Quinn poked his head into my room.

He smiled at me, but it quickly fell off of his face as he took in my expression. Stepping into my room, he closed the door softly behind him, and then as he stepped closer to me, he faltered, stopping and sniffing the air. Confusion swam in his eyes as he looked me up and down. "Why do I smell cologne in here?"

I winced a little before patting the mattress next to me. "Come sit."

Quinn sank down next to me but leaned back so he could watch my face. "Spill," he demanded.

"Promise not to freak out?" I asked.

"More than when you came home and told me you were engaged to some rando you'd just met?" he countered, his eyes narrowed.

"Yeah, more than that." I was twisting my fingers together, and Quinn reached out and grabbed my hand, lacing our fingers together.

"I probably shouldn't, but I promise. I reserve the right to punch someone if I need to, though." Quinn scooted back on the bed until he leaned against my headboard, dragging me back with him where I sat across from him cross-legged.

"Last night, Maddox came by," I began.

Quinn inhaled sharply. "What could that asshole possibly have to say to you?"

"He was drunk, and he wanted to apologize." I gnawed on my lower lip because I knew Quinn wouldn't react well to the next part.

"For which part? The part where he broke your heart at fourteen? Or the part where he acted like you never existed for the past twelve years? Or maybe the part where he was a complete tool to you the other day?" he seethed.

I shrugged. "For all of it."

That seemed to shut Quinn up, and I watched as he visibly deflated. "Did he at least give you an explanation?"

I nodded. "He said he did it to protect me, but that he shouldn't have. He was afraid he'd turn out like his dad, and he didn't want that for me. He said I was too good for him, that he didn't deserve me."

"He's right about that. He doesn't deserve you." Quinn's hazel eyes locked with mine, filled with a mixture of anger and concern. "Are you okay?"

Blowing out a breath, I bit my lip again while I considered his question. "At first, I was so angry about everything. But then, after he explained, he broke down on the floor and my heart hurt for him. His whole life has been tragic, and I doubt he's ever felt really, truly loved in his entire life." My eyes burned as tears threatened to spill down my cheeks. "When he confessed and apologized, and then I looked into his eyes, I could see every broken and damaged part of his soul. It calls to me. It always has."

Quinn's brows furrowed. "If you're so connected to Maddox, what the fuck are you doing marrying this Yates douche?"

"Quinn!" I scolded, smacking him on the arm. "You don't even know Yates. He seems like a good guy."

He rolled his eyes. "What kind of a good guy has to trap some desperate woman into marrying him to access his money? This whole thing is not right, Ry."

I let go of his hand, sliding back a few inches from him to put distance between us. He didn't understand what an impossible situation I felt like I was in. "I don't know what to tell you, Quinn. He seemed to genuinely need help and wanted to help me in return."

He moved closer to me and pulled my hand into his again. "You know I've always got your back. I'll always support you in whatever you do, and you'll never get rid of me. But I think you're making a colossal mistake marrying this guy. You don't even want to live on the ranch. Why are you trying so hard to save it?"

Squeezing my eyes closed, I rolled my head on my neck a few times, trying to stretch out the tense muscles in my upper back. How could I make Quinn understand why I needed to do this? "This is my family home. This is where

I grew up, where my sisters grew up, where my parents met and got married. Maybe this place isn't my future, but to me, the past is just as important. My roots are here. My dad has never known another home, and I refuse to let him lose this one when there's something I can do to fix it."

Quinn's eyes softened, and he rubbed his thumb soothingly on the back of my hand. "That's a high price to pay to fix something that isn't even your problem."

"I know, okay? But it wasn't my dad's fault that the horse threw him off. He didn't ask to spend the rest of his life in a wheelchair. I have to do this for them. My parents have given me so much, it's my turn to give back to them."

"And giving up on your goals to move home four years ago and take on running this place wasn't enough giving back?" he countered.

Sighing, I laid flat on my back, staring up at the ceiling. "They gave me life, Quinn. Is there such a thing as enough when it comes to giving back to my parents?"

"Your sisters seem to think so. Your dad didn't have to let shit get this bad, you know. He could've asked for help sooner. Hell, he could have listened to the ideas you've been trying to talk to him about for *years*, Ryan. Marrying someone isn't just no big deal. It's a goddamn life-altering choice you're making. You don't have to be a martyr or play hero here, sweetheart. This isn't your mess to clean up."

I knew Quinn would always support me no matter what I chose. Still, I doubted he'd ever understand why I felt like I needed to do this no matter how many times I tried to explain it to him. "Agree to disagree, Quinny."

𝄞

The rest of the week passed slowly. Whenever I was outside the house, I found my gaze drawn to the little house over the hill. I was distracted in my work, watching the guys next door come and go. I only knew Maddox and could always pick him out when he was outside, which wasn't much, but I assumed the others were his friends or maybe the guys in the band. I wasn't a part of his life anymore, so I wasn't that familiar with anyone he spent time with.

But I hadn't seen him up close again since the night he came to my room. I didn't know if I'd get the chance to talk to him again or if he'd leave without saying a word to me like he had last time. Maybe he regretted our conversation. The more time that passed without talking to him again, the more I convinced myself it'd all been one big mistake.

I reached up and wiped a drop of sweat from my forehead before it could roll down my face. It was Saturday morning, and Quinn and I were out finishing up our morning chores before I had to go inside and get showered and dressed. I was a ball of nerves. My stomach churned, and my heart beat faster than normal all morning. I barely slept last night either, despite Quinn climbing into my bed and trying to comfort me.

Today was the day Yates would meet my family. Today was also the day I would go to Dallas with him, meet up with my sisters, and start the wedding planning.

Today was the day shit got real with this wedding.

I wanted to throw up. Yates was supposed to be here after breakfast, but there wasn't a chance in hell I'd be able to eat anything with my stomach in knots like it was.

Quinn rode up on Daisy, pulling her reins to stop next to me. He flashed me a crooked grin. "You ready to do this, bridezilla?"

I shot him a withering glare. "Bridezilla? Really?"

He shrugged and laughed. "If the name fits."

"Stop being ridiculous," I snapped. "I'm not in the mood."

"Further proving my point about the name," Quinn pointed out.

"I'm going in to shower," I grumbled. "Are you coming?"

He tilted his hat at me and flashed me his bright grin. "I wouldn't miss meeting my future sort of brother-in-law for anything. I'll be in after I take care of Daisy here," he said, patting his mare on the neck.

Sliding down off of my stallion, I handed him the reins. "Can you take care of Storm, too?"

Rolling his eyes, he kicked his heels into Daisy's sides. "Fine, but you owe me."

I turned on my heel, and with one last glance at the quiet house next door, made my way inside. It felt more like I was walking to my doom than to a shower and a meet and greet with my future husband and my parents.

Checking the clock on the stove, I realized I had less time than I thought before Yates was supposed to be here, so I took the fastest shower of all time. I threw on a cute sundress and my cutest cowboy boots, letting my hair hang in damp waves around my freckled face. I opted for light makeup, which was how I usually kept it. A swipe of mascara, a tiny bit of blush, and some lip gloss were my usual staples.

Just as I was taking one last look in the mirror, I heard a car pulling into the gravel driveway. A swarm of butterflies took off in my stomach, and my heart slammed against my chest. This was it. Once my parents met Yates, we'd be officially starting on our path to being married.

I looked down at the ridiculously huge diamond ring sitting on my dresser. I sighed heavily before sliding it onto my finger. There was no way I could do ranch work with this thing on my hand for the next year. Except I wouldn't have to do ranch work now, would I? I'd be expected to be some fancy banker's wife which was about the furthest thing from who I really was. What was I thinking jumping into this marriage? Could I hide who I really was for an entire year?

Pushing my unsettling thoughts to the side, I rushed out of my room to greet Yates at the door. He looked just as handsome as the last time I saw him, only this time he was marginally more casual.

He wore tapered khaki pants rolled up at the ankle, a blue plaid button-down with the top button undone, and a blue blazer over the top. His hair was messy in a sexy way, and I had to admit he was pretty hot. Unfortunately for both of us, after Maddox's late-night apology, I wasn't so sure my heart was into giving Yates the chance he deserved. I was glad he agreed to the time limit clause in our contract because, at this point, I was totally sure I'd be taking it.

Mostly.

Except the doubts crept in. If Maddox didn't actually want to be with me, or couldn't wait for this whole thing to be over, what would I do then? I couldn't tell him it wasn't real because I signed the non-disclosure agreement, which meant I had to act like I was in love with Yates when I barely knew him.

"Hey, babe," he greeted me with a kiss to my cheek, and then he slung his arm around my waist and pulled me against his body. I tried not to stiffen up, but it took everything in me to relax my muscles one by one so that we wouldn't look awkward.

"Hey yourself," I smiled up at him and hoped it looked genuine. I was *not* a good actress.

Pulling the door shut behind him, I grabbed his hand and led him into the living room where my dad was reading the paper in his chair. My mom had gone into the kitchen to grab some lemonade and probably something baked, and just as we walked into the room, she popped in from the other side.

"Mom, Dad," I began, moving back against Yates, who wrapped his arm back around my waist. "This is Yates, my fiance. Yates, this is my mom, Shannon, and my dad, Alexander."

Yates moved into the room, greeting my dad with a handshake. "Nice to meet you, sir." He walked over to my mom and held out his hand for her, but she grinned and wrapped him up in a hug, which he awkwardly returned.

"None of that handshake nonsense," she said. "And call me Shannon."

"Hey, now, I appreciate that handshake nonsense, as you like to call it," my dad teased my mom. "It shows the boy is respectful." He nodded at Yates and motioned for us to sit down on the couch. Sinking against the soft cushions, I exhaled. At least the first part of this fiasco was done with now, and it had gone better than I expected so far.

Quinn picked that moment to walk into the room, his hair still damp from the shower. He narrowed his eyes at Yates's arm around me before plopping himself down on my other side. I glanced up at Yates. "This is my best friend, Quinn," I introduced him. "And Quinn, this is Yates, my fiance."

I could tell Quinn wanted to say something sarcastic, but I shot him a pleading look, and he clenched his jaw, no doubt trying to keep his snark inside. "Nice to meet you, man."

Yates pulled me closer against him, and I frowned. What the hell was this? He couldn't possibly be possessive of me at this point, could he? That would be ridiculous. "Good to meet you, too." His tone was a little frosty, and it was the first time in my limited exposure to him I saw him be anything but charming and kind.

Quinn stiffened beside me, and I reached between us and grabbed his hand, squeezing it firmly. I needed him to hold in all the shit he wanted to say to Yates because it wouldn't do me any favors. Quinn was incredibly protective of me, and I could tell by his body language that he already didn't like Yates. If he opened his mouth, this would become a thousand times more difficult.

"Would you like some lemonade?" my mom offered Yates.

He pulled his eyes away from Quinn, and the frostiness disappeared and was replaced by an overly friendly smile that I was beginning to suspect was completely fake. "I'd love some, thank you, Shannon."

My dad cleared his throat. "So, Yates. I've gotta say I was pretty surprised when my girl here came home last weekend and announced she was getting married. We never heard anything about you. Why the rush to get married?"

Yates pulled his arm from around me and started playing with his expensive watch nervously. "We don't feel like we're rushing. We've gotten to know each other, and the time feels right. I'm training to take over my family business, and before I do that, we thought it best to get settled in our new life."

I had to admit, that sounded reasonable even to me, and I knew the truth of our situation. He'd obviously given this a lot of thought. "Yates is right, dad. We're not rushing anything. We didn't want to wait any longer. You and mom got married when you'd only known each other for six months. It's been almost thirty years. It seemed to work out okay for you two."

My dad sat back in his chair and folded his arms across his chest. He was studying me, and I could tell he was considering my words. It wasn't entirely important to me to get my parents' blessing on this marriage. It wasn't going to last, and I was going through with it no matter what they said, but it'd make the whole thing more comfortable if I didn't have to deal with attitude and anger the whole time.

My mom walked over and sat on the arm of the chair my dad sat in, resting her hand on his shoulder. "Don't give the kids a hard time, Alex. We have to let them live their lives," she said softly, and then she smiled at me, and I knew she'd get him on board. My mom had always been loving and supportive, guiding my sisters and me to make our own decisions and helping us through when those decisions went wrong.

My dad grumbled a bit but took a sip of his lemonade and seemed like he let his line of questioning go. After several minutes of awkward silence mixed with small talk and Quinn's stare burning into the side of my head, I decided I'd had enough.

"We should go," I said, standing from the couch with Yates and Quinn both taking their places on either side of me. I could feel the tension radiating between the two of them, and I worried about what might happen if we didn't leave. "I'll be home tomorrow."

I looked up at Quinn. He wore a scowl, and I could tell he was biting his cheek. I knew he wanted to come with me more than anything. He was looking at Yates like he wanted to punch him in the face, but he held his tongue, and I'd never been so grateful for anything in my life. He tore his glare off of my fiancé and bent down, wrapping me in a tight hug. He whispered in my ear, "If you need anything at all, you call me and I'm there. I mean it, Lancelot. Call. Me."

I nodded before tearing myself out of his embrace and forcing a smile onto my face. I shook off Quinn's overprotectiveness and stepped around him toward the door. Yates followed me out, saying goodbye to my parents, and I grabbed my bag off the floor by the front door before walking outside into the Texas heat.

"Well, that wasn't too bad," Yates said, flashing me a crooked smile before moving in front of me to open the passenger door of his vintage blue convertible.

I chuckled, rolling my eyes. "Compared to what?"

Darkness crossed his face for a second that had my stomach in knots all over again. "Meeting my parents." Once I was in the car, he shut the door, and I felt like my fate had been sealed.

ELEVEN
RYAN

"Let's play twenty-one questions," Yates suggested after turning down the music. We were halfway to Dallas, and the ride had been quiet and awkward, much like our first car ride together to the restaurant. I'd been lost in my thoughts the whole time.

Perking up, I glanced over at him, watching his dirty blonde hair blow around in the wind. He really was handsome, but something was holding me back from feeling that spark with him. I wasn't sure exactly what it was, but I suspected Maddox had something to do with it.

"Yeah, that sounds fun," I agreed. "You go first."

He shifted his grip on the steering wheel, so he had just one hand wrapped around it, and he propped his elbow up on the door, resting his chin on his fist. Suddenly, he sat up straighter and grinned at me before putting his eyes back on the road. "What's something most people think is true about you but actually isn't?"

I thought for a second. "That I'm a tomboy. People assume because I have a boy's name, and I work on a ranch all day that I don't like pretty dresses or smelling good or feeling feminine. They would be wrong." I chuckled.

"Well, I for one think I'm going to like you in dresses if this is any indication," Yates flirted, his bright smile making me laugh as his eyes roamed the exposed skin of my legs.

"Okay, my turn," I said, changing the subject. I tapped my chin, thinking. "How useful would you be in a zombie apocalypse?"

Yates burst out laughing. "Not as useful as you, I'd imagine." I smiled at him and motioned for him to continue. "Let's see. I'm in decent shape, and I can throw a solid punch, so if I had a weapon, I could probably do some damage. I'm not going to be good at the things you are like growing food or fixing things. But I'd like to think I'd be a good leader and also a good planner. I think if it came down to it, we both have skill sets that would compliment each other pretty well."

I had to hand it to him, he convinced me that I'd want him on my team even if he looked like he'd never done any hard work in his entire life. As we kept asking each other questions, I felt myself relaxing in his presence. I had no doubt this game would help us get to know each other better, which would help us pull off convincing everyone that we were in love.

I turned to Yates. "I feel like I need to warn you."

He turned to look at me, his eyes narrowing slightly. "About what?"

"My sisters. My parents are the easy ones. My sisters, well… They're going to give you a hard time. Just prepare yourself," I warned.

Yates just chuckled and took my hand in his, resting it on my thigh. "I think I can handle your sisters. It's my mom you've got to be worried about." I could already feel the lump forming in my throat about tomorrow, but I shoved it down. That was tomorrow's problem. I already had enough to worry about today.

I spotted my sisters as soon as we walked into the restaurant. Justice waved her hand frantically in my direction. She was always so energetic, but usually, it was contagious. Charlie was the more serious sister and the one I was most worried about today. However, the glint in Justice's eye as Yates and I walked up to the table didn't make me feel good about her plans for this lunch.

"Hi guys," I said, sliding into the chair Yates had pulled out. "This is Yates." He nodded at Charlie and then Justice before grabbing my hand and pressing a kiss to the back. "These are my sisters, Charlie and Justice."

Yates chuckled before resting his arm across the back of my chair and scooting closer to me. He was taking this whole fiance thing really seriously already, and I was totally uncomfortable. I needed to get over it soon because I was sure my sisters would see right through it. Keeping that in mind, I took a deep breath and leaned closer to Yates, so we were almost pressed together. He smiled down at me and ran his thumb down my cheek, pressing a kiss to my forehead. He smelled good, but I felt indifferent. There was no spark. I didn't want to get closer or bury my nose into his chest like I did with Maddox.

My pillow still smelled like him, and at this point, I'd probably never wash it. Charlie was watching me with her eyes narrowed, and I shook off thoughts of the sexy rock star next door. I couldn't afford to give Yates and me away at this lunch. I needed him to help me too much.

After we all ordered our food and the waitress dropped off drinks, I braced myself. I knew we were about to face the inquisition that was my sisters. Charlie cleared her throat and folded her hands on the tabletop. "So, Yates. Why have we never heard a single thing about you until about two days ago?"

Straight for the jugular. Classic Charlie. There was a reason she'd been top of her class in medical school. Charlie was a straight-up badass who didn't miss a single damn thing. She was sharp and witty, and I bet she saw straight through this ruse. But if I was lucky she'd keep it to herself. I shot her a pleading look, begging with my eyes to keep her conclusions to herself. We needed Yates even if she didn't know it right now, and I couldn't tell her. I hoped she trusted me enough to know I was doing what I thought was best.

Yates smiled and leaned closer to me. "Ryan and I hadn't had time to meet the families yet. It's been an intense year training under my dad to take over, and I haven't really had any spare time outside of the time I've spent with Ryan." He pressed a kiss to my temple again before he continued, smooth and confident in his answer. I almost believed him myself.

"But I was tired of staying away from her, so now we're meeting everyone and making things official."

Charlie nodded her head and shot me a glance that told me she didn't believe him, but she wouldn't say anything. I nodded slightly, and I knew she'd let this go for now, but it'd come up later. I just hoped when I asked her not to press me and to let me handle it, she'd do as I asked.

Justice flipped her long, wavy hair that was exactly like mine over her shoulder. "So, Ryan, Yates must be pretty good in the sack, right? Since he's the only one you've ever been with, right?" She leaned back in her chair and smiled evilly like she was proud of herself for embarrassing me.

My cheeks burned, and I had no idea what to say. "I'm confident Ryan doesn't have any complaints," he said smoothly, winking at her. I wasn't sure I'd ever actually seen anyone wink in real life, but I had to admit he pulled it off. Yates was smooth as butter and alarm bells were going off. I'd need to be careful with him. I didn't know him at all, and he was a little *too* good at messing with the truth.

"Now that you two have thoroughly embarrassed me, are you satisfied?" I questioned, glaring at both of my sisters who wore matching innocent expressions on their faces.

Justice patted her stomach. "I know I am. I'm ready to walk off lunch and do some shopping. Charlie?"

My older sister nodded her head, her eyes locked on me the entire time. "Great," I sighed, reaching for my purse to pay for lunch, but Yates stopped me, handing his card to the waitress as she walked by our table.

"I've gotta run, babe," he said before turning back to my sisters. "Ladies, it was great to meet you. I hope we can spend more time getting to know each other before the wedding." His eyes lingered on Justice, and her eyebrows shot up. I glanced at Charlie, who noticed it, too, narrowing her eyes at him again.

As he slid his chair back and stood up, he leaned down and pressed a kiss to the top of my head. "Hold onto my card and use it while you're out shopping for wedding stuff today, okay?" Yates offered, and I nodded woodenly. "I'll pick you up in the morning." Shit, I was really doing this—the lunch I'd picked at churned in my stomach.

With one last wave, he turned and walked out of the restaurant, and we all watched him leave. As soon as the doors closed, my sisters shot me matching *what the fuck is going on* looks.

I lowered my head, resting my forehead on the cool surface of the table. "Can we not right now?" I begged.

"Fine, but you're telling us what the hell is going on as soon as we get to the dress shop," Charlie demanded.

"Fine. You two know your way around here. Where do we even go for wedding dresses?" I asked.

Justice smiled, plucking Yates's black credit card up off the table where the waitress had just dropped it. "I know just the place."

We pulled up next to a gorgeous white brick building with modern black signage and deep green ivy climbing the walls. It was classy and elegant, and I knew if it weren't for Yates, I'd never be able to step foot in a place like this. If this was my only chance, I'd make sure to enjoy it even if I was a little sad that I'd have to waste this opportunity on a groom I had no interest in.

The sign read *Love + Lace* and the huge front window displays showed off stunning dresses in a variety of sizes. I couldn't wait to try some dresses on and wondered if I could convince my sisters to try something too, just for fun.

As Justice held the door open for Charlie and me, I stopped just outside the door, and Charlie turned around. "Aren't you coming? You can't get married without a dress, even if the wedding is a total sham."

Leave it to my sister to not pull any punches. "Who said it was a sham?"

Justice raised her hand unhelpfully. "Me. I said it's a sham."

"Me, too. I don't know who you think you're fooling, but we know you better than that."

I followed my sisters inside, not really sure what to say. We were immediately greeted by a saleswoman that I was incredibly thankful for because she took the heat off of me.

"Welcome to *Love and Lace*. I'm Katie, and this is my shop, so you let me know if there's anything I can help you with." She looked at the three of us. "So, who's getting married?" she asked with a cheerful smile on her face and sparkling eyes. It was obvious she really loved this wedding stuff.

I slowly raised my hand, trying to look happier about the whole *betrothed* thing than I felt. "That'd be me."

She clapped her hands a couple of times, bouncing on the balls of her feet.

"I've already got about five dresses in mind for you. Follow me." Katie spun on her heel and strode to the back of the shop. My sisters and I looked at each other before hurrying off to follow her.

Katie was moving quickly around the store, pulling dresses off of racks and piling them over her arms. "What's your name, bride-to-be?" she shouted at me from across the shop. I was glad we were the only ones in here shopping.

"I'm Ryan."

"Well, Ryan, why don't you go get undressed in one of the fitting rooms and I'll bring you in the first dress to try." She turned to Justice and Charlie. "You two take a seat on the sofa over there," she pointed to a gray velvet tufted couch facing a circular platform just outside the fitting rooms. I moved toward the rooms, pulling the door closed behind me and stripping down to my underwear. I was glad I thought to wear a strapless bra for this.

Katie knocked on the door with her knuckle. "Ready for dress number one?" she asked.

"Hand it over," I said, reaching my hand out of a crack in the door and pulling the layers of tulle and satin inside. This dress took up almost the entire room, and I had no idea how the hell I was going to get it on by myself.

"Katie?" I asked, a little bit breathless just from wrestling this thing into the room.

"How can I help, Ryan?"

"Can you come in and help me, please," I asked, turning a little bit red at the idea of a stranger seeing me in my underwear. But I didn't want my sisters to see me until I had the dress on. Like I said before, I wanted to have fun with the experience.

"Sure, honey." Katie pushed her way into the room and started sorting through the fabric layers like an old pro. In about two seconds flat, she had created a tunnel for me to burrow into and hope that I'd somehow pop my head out of the top. I was glad I'd asked for her help because before I knew it, she was expertly zipping up the back of the dress. I already knew I wasn't going to choose this one, but I still wondered how the hell I'd ever pee in it if I had picked it.

"Ready?" Katie asked.

I nodded, and she opened the door wide, giving me enough room to squeeze through. My sisters both watched without saying anything as I walked past them and stepped up onto the platform. There were mirrors on one side of it, and I looked at myself from multiple angles. The dress itself was beautiful, but it was just not me. It was too poofy, and I was no princess.

Justice shook her head, and Charlie pursed her lips. "This is definitely not the one. You look ridiculous," Charlie said.

"She's right. Thank you, next," Justice agreed.

I laughed and stepped down, walking over to where Katie held open the door. She quickly helped me out of the dress, and I stood studying myself in the mirror while I waited for her to bring in the next dress. She knocked again before she stepped inside, holding a much smaller lace dress. I liked it immediately and hoped it would look as good as it did on the hanger.

"This wasn't part of the original five I pulled for you, but after seeing you in the last dress, I think this could be *the one*." Katie said the last words reverently, almost like the dress was more important than the groom. I guess in her world, maybe it was.

I couldn't argue with her on the choice of dress, though. As she helped me step into the soft white lace, I pulled the dress up my body, and it skimmed all of my delicate curves. I had more muscle than most women, and my curves were more subtle, but this dress highlighted every single one. I didn't think I'd ever felt more feminine.

When I stepped out of the dressing room, I heard audible gasps from both of my sisters, and I knew this was the dress. When I looked into the mirrors behind the platform, I traced the lines of my body, studying the fitted silhouette of the dress, the sweetheart neckline and thin straps, the way the lace fell into a mermaid skirt with a short train. It was perfect.

"This is the one, Ry," Justice breathed, her hand on her heart.

Charlie nodded her head in agreement. "Sham wedding or not, this dress was made for you."

"Shh! We'll talk about that later, Charlie. Knock it off," I whispered back harshly, my eyes darting over to where Katie was hanging up the dresses she'd pulled off the rack. I hoped she hadn't heard. I didn't know how well-known Yates was, and I couldn't let the reality of our engagement get out.

"I'm going to go change, and we can get out of here," I said, hurriedly stepping down and moving into the fitting room. I took out my phone and snapped a quick picture, sending it to Quinn since he couldn't be here with us, and he sent me back about a hundred *heart eye* emojis.

I slipped the dress off and hung it up gently, afraid that my rough, calloused hands might snag the lace. Carrying the dress up front, I handed over Yates's credit card, and just like that, I had a dress.

"Who's ready for margaritas?" Justice asked.

Charlie and I both raised our hands and laughed. I followed my sisters to Charlie's car, and we made our way to her condo. We were all staying here tonight since I didn't get to see my sisters very often, and both Charlie and Justice managed to get tonight off of work.

We all changed into swimsuits and blended margaritas, which we carried down to the community pool. After we settled into side-by-side lounge chairs, they started in on me. I was grateful I'd been able to hold them off as long as I had.

"Okay, Ryan. What the actual hell is going on?" Charlie asked. I could hear Justice slurping her margarita on my other side. They sandwiched me between them so there was no escape.

"Can you guys trust me when I say I can't tell you? I've got it handled, and I promise everything will make sense in about a year. Until then, I need you to just let it be," I begged.

"Fiiine," Justice whined. "But, you owe us one hell of a story next year."

"Deal," I said quickly.

Charlie sighed sadly. "I honestly thought if you ever got married, it'd be to the boy next door, Maddox?"

Justice nodded vigorously. "Yeah, the bassist for Shadow Phoenix. He's so damn sexy. I can't believe we grew up next door to him."

I sipped my margarita to avoid talking about the guy I'd been hopelessly in love with for more than half of my life. Right now, I was thankful for tequila and sunglasses.

"Do you remember Ryan had the biggest crush on him? You guys were inseparable," Charlie reminisced.

"I remember," Justice said, lowering her sunglasses to waggle her eyebrows at me.

"Yeah, yeah. Make fun all you want, but he was pretty awesome as far as best friends go," I said.

"Don't let Quinn hear you say that," Justice teased.

"Anyway," Charlie continued. "I remember the day I was convinced you guys were going to grow up and get married. It was the day he dared you to climb the huge oak tree by the barn. Do you remember?"

I nodded. "I was terrified, but a dare's a dare. I had to do it."

Charlie laughed. "Yeah, that sounds like you. You climbed up the tree, and you were fine until halfway up, a squirrel popped out of nowhere and scared you so bad you let go of the branch."

Shuddering, I took another sip of my frozen drink. "I hit the ground, and my arm shattered in three places. I still have the scars from where the bone popped out of my skin," I said, tracing the tiny discolored spots on my forearm.

"That's not the part that had me convinced, though, because honestly, you never turned down a dare as a kid," Charlie pointed out. "The part that had me convinced was how Maddox acted when it happened. He forced mom and dad to take him to the hospital, and he slept on your bedroom floor for almost a week. I think he felt bad and he was so worried about you he wouldn't leave your side. I was convinced he loved you even then, at twelve years old."

A tear slid down my cheek at the memory. I hadn't thought about that in years, but she was right. He stayed with me, and every time I cried out in pain because I moved in my sleep or couldn't get comfortable, Maddox was there stroking my hair and telling me it'd be okay, that he'd always be there for me. I guess that was why it hurt so much when he broke his promise to me and left.

"I guess it just wasn't meant to be," I whispered, and thankfully, my sisters dropped it.

TWELVE
RYAN

The next morning, after a leisurely breakfast with my sisters, I slid my sunglasses off of my face and jogged downstairs to meet Yates. Spending the night reconnecting with my sisters was what I needed. I felt refreshed and ready to face whatever shit show with his family I was about to walk into.

I climbed into the passenger seat of Yates's blue convertible and shut the door. He flashed me a smile before taking off toward wherever we were going. "You look nice today," he commented, his gaze sliding down my body. I squirmed under the intense scrutiny, but there wasn't much I could do about it.

"Thanks," I said with a small smile. I didn't want today to be uncomfortable. Even though I was sure I'd never have romantic feelings for Yates, that didn't mean we couldn't get along and be friends.

"It's a short drive to my parents' estate, but I should warn you they can be a lot to handle. My mother will be the hardest to convince, which means we'll have to be more affectionate than we have been so far," he warned.

"What does that mean?" I asked, feeling dread creep into my body.

"We haven't kissed yet, we barely touch when we're around other people. We're going to have to do those things at this brunch, Ryan. You're going to have to get used to me touching you, us being close. We need to be a married couple in every sense of the word," he finished.

I didn't like what I was pretty sure he was implying. Hadn't he said that we didn't need to sleep together when I agreed to this whole thing? "In every sense of the word in public, right? Because I'm not ready to go there with you in private, and I don't know if I ever will be," I emphasized.

I watched his jaw clench, and then he regained his composure. "Of course. Just in public." Somehow I didn't believe he meant the words this time around.

He glanced over at me before returning his eyes to the road. "You're going to give us a fair shot, though, right? Because I like everything I've gotten to know about you so far, and I think we could be perfect together, babe."

We'd been fake engaged about a week, and it already felt like the lines were blurring where he was concerned. On my side of things, the lines were crystal clear. "I think we can be great friends, Yates, but I don't see anything romantic happening between us. I just don't feel that way about you," I said, keeping my voice soft and as gentle as possible.

I watched as he gripped the steering wheel tightly until his knuckles turned white. "I think you're wrong, Ryan. I'll show you how good we can be together. You just need to give me a chance."

I sighed and studied his profile. What was wrong with me that I wasn't attracted to him? That I felt nothing when I looked at him? "I'll think about it, okay?" We were about to go into his parent's lair, and I didn't want him to be upset with me when we did. I'd have to talk to him about this again later.

He relaxed and shot me a crooked smile. "Okay."

A few minutes later, we pulled up to a massive iron gate, and Yates entered a code on a keypad outside. As the gate swung open, we drove inside, and I marveled at how huge the property was. I hadn't even looked at the house yet. I lived on a ranch, and even I was impressed by what seemed like miles of lush green grass and manicured gardens.

The house itself was red brick and gigantic. It could fit at least ten of my house into their one. It made me wonder why Yates had chosen me as his bride to be. His family was loaded, and he was good looking. I was sure I needed him more than he needed me. Maybe that was why he picked me. He knew I wouldn't back out.

He parked in the circular drive and hopped out of the car, jogging around and opening the door for me. He held his hand out, and I gripped it, stepping out of the car as he pulled me against his chest. I guess we were starting with the affection now. He lowered his mouth to mine and kissed me sweetly, but I might as well have been kissing my brother. I pulled away before he could deepen the kiss, but he didn't seem to mind.

He kept my hand in his, weaving our fingers together as we made our way up the front steps. Before we reached the door, it swung open, and a man in a uniform bowed slightly in greeting. Yates didn't acknowledge him as we passed, but I shot him an apologetic smile. I wasn't sure what the protocol was here, but I was sure ignoring someone who did something polite for you was rude as hell.

A middle-aged woman with her hair pulled back into a low bun and dressed in what I was sure was a designer skirt suit stepped into the entryway. Behind her was a man who had salt and pepper hair and stood slightly shorter than Yates. "Mother, father. Meet my fiance, Ryan. Ryan, these are my parents, Jacqueline and Richard Rutherford."

I held out my hand toward his mother, and she looked down her nose at it, distaste coloring features. "Charmed," she said before looking back at Yates. His father hadn't done more than glance down at me. He hadn't even said hello. I knew from Yates's warnings that his family would be difficult, but I didn't expect them to be complete dicks lacking ordinary human decency.

How the hell would I possibly survive an entire year in this situation, having to be around these people regularly?

Jacqueline's cold eyes flicked back to me. "I thought we could discuss wedding plans. We don't have much time to do things properly, so whatever we can throw together will have to do." She said it as if this was all my fault. Maybe she thought I got pregnant and trapped her son. I had no idea what Yates had told her going into this. For the first time, I thought maybe Yates and I should've discussed our story before we did the whole meet the parents thing.

Too late now.

I also noted that she hadn't invited us in to sit down yet. Yates must have read my mind because he finally spoke up. "Mother, can we go sit down before we get into all that?"

She sighed irritably. "By all means, you know where the parlor is, Yates."

He pulled me along behind him deeper into his parent's mansion. Everything in me wanted to turn and run the other way, but I couldn't. Instead, I inhaled deeply to calm myself down. After what felt like miles, we stepped into a tastefully decorated room with bland furniture. The second I laid eyes on Yates's family, I expected nothing other than the place in front of me. Beige sofas, pastels, and nothing with any personality at all. But I was sure it was all expensive.

The two sofas in the center of the room faced each other. I absently wondered if I should have taken off my cowboy boots before I stepped onto the plush white carpet, but it was too late now. I couldn't guarantee there wasn't dust on my sundress either, so I dusted myself off the best I could before lowering myself onto the pristine couch beside Yates.

He still held my hand in his while we watched his parents silently take the couch across from us. Jacqueline crossed her legs at the ankle, folding them off to the side, and she looked every bit the high-class, well-bred woman I took her to be. I played with the hem of my dress which had ridden up my thighs, exposing my knees and a few inches more thigh than I'd like, and her eyes ran over me, filled with disdain.

I got the feeling Yates enjoyed pissing his parents off. When I looked up at him, he was watching his mother carefully. After a few minutes, he took our entwined hands and rested them on my exposed thigh, his thumb stroking the skin just above my knee.

Jacqueline followed the movement as her lips pressed into a thin line. We'd only been seated about thirty seconds before a woman in a classic maid's uniform suddenly stood beside the sofa with a tray in her arms. She wordlessly set it on the table before turning and disappearing to wherever she came from. "Tea or coffee?" Jacqueline offered.

"Coffee, please, mother, and Ryan will have tea," Yates spoke for himself and me, and I bristled. Who the hell did he think he was ordering for me like that? I clenched my teeth together. This wasn't the time or place to bite his head off, but we'd be having a discussion later. I was not a woman who'd shrink beside her husband. If that was what he wanted, this would never work.

I accepted my tea with a mumbled thanks, taking a small sip and relishing the burn. Anything to distract me from the awkwardness of this moment was welcome.

"So, Ryan, my son tells me you've planned to get married in just a month. While I can't imagine what the hurry could possibly be to marry my only son, he's made it clear you've made up your mind," Jacqueline passive-aggressively began.

And what the actual hell was Yates's game here? He blamed this entire thing on me? I wanted to punch him in his damn pretty boy face, but instead, I shot him a quick death glare out of the side of my eyes before smiling widely with the fakest grin I could manage. "Yes, that's right. The plan is to get married next month. I know it seems sudden, but we just love each other so much we can't wait to start our lives together," I said, my voice sickly sweet. I dug my nails into Yates's hand clasped in mine, the only retaliation I had right now for what he just forced me to endure. He stiffened next to me as I broke the skin, and I squeezed a little harder, enjoying his discomfort.

Asshole.

She clicked her tongue while she sipped her coffee, and I looked over at Richard. He was stoically watching everything with a disinterested expression on his face. He looked like he wished he were anywhere else but here, and I couldn't blame him. "We'll have to make do. Of course, you'll have the ceremony and reception here." *Of course.* Who the hell did this woman think she was?

I plastered that fake-ass smile on my face again. "I live on a ranch. I thought we could do-"

"No, that will never do. You'll get married here. What would people think if my son got married on some disgusting farm? Could you imagine?" She laughed as if I was being ridiculous.

"We appreciate you offering the estate, mother," Yates agreed before turning to me with a condescending look in his eye. "While Knight Ranch would be quaint, there are certain expectations when a Rutherford gets married, Ryan. Mother's right. This will be the best place for the ceremony on such short notice."

What people thought of him must be more important to Yates than I thought. He must be really desperate for his trust fund if he was willing to marry me since he couldn't just hide me away. What the hell was his game here? I was just a *lowly* rancher's daughter. How had he ever thought this would work? We came from two different worlds. If we loved each other, that would be one thing, but this seemed like an awful lot of trouble to go through just for some money.

"Fine," I bit out, sure the smile on my face looked a little deranged at this point but not caring in the slightest.

After another twenty minutes of uncomfortable small talk where I learned Yates was his mother's bitch, I'd lost almost all the respect for him I had, and I was beyond ready to leave.

"Excuse me," I interrupted. "Where's the restroom?"

Yates pointed toward a hallway off to the right. "Third door down that hall."

I stood and quickly left the room, reaching into my purse and pulling out my phone the second I was where the Rutherfords couldn't see me.

Ryan: In five minutes, call me with a fake emergency.

Quinn: You got it

I could always count on Quinn when I needed him, and I'd reached my limit of all things stuck up asshole for my lifetime. This was going to be one long year.

I quickly splashed cold water on my face, making sure to turn the ringer up on my phone before sliding it back into my purse and making my way back out to the couch. Sitting back down, Yates slung his arm over my shoulder and pulled me into his body. I didn't want to be touching him in any way right now, I was so disgusted and angry, but his mother's observant gaze lingered on us, and there was nothing I could do. She reminded me of the Eye of Sauron from *Lord of the Rings.*

Right on time, my phone rang out loudly in the room. I shot an apologetic look to Yates and then his mother as I dug my cell out of my purse and swiped to answer. "Hello?"

Quinn's panicked voice filled my ear. "Ryan? You need to come home right now. The main tractor broke down, and we have to hand-feed the entire herd before it gets dark, or they'll starve." I suppressed my giggle at how ridiculous that was. Hand-feeding five hundred cattle in three hours was impossible, but these people had no idea. Quinn was messing with me, and I loved him for it. I needed the laugh, even if I had to keep it inside, and I immediately felt lighter.

"Oh my *god,* are you serious?" I shouted for added effect.

Jacqueline pressed her hand to her chest as she jumped at the loudness of my voice.

"Dead serious, Lancelot. Time to come home," Quinn said, and I could hear the smirk in his voice.

"Okay, I'll come right home," I finished, ending the call, turning to Yates. "Emergency at the ranch. I need to get back."

He narrowed his eyes before turning to his parents. "Mother, father. I'm sorry to cut the visit short, but we'll have plenty of time to get to know each other better. We're going to be family after all."

I didn't wait for them and stood. "It was nice to meet you, Mrs. Rutherford."

"Yates, you'll leave me Ryan's contact information so we can discuss wedding details," she commanded without returning my pleasantries, fake as they were.

"Of course, mother," he agreed. I could never be with someone as spineless as Yates appeared to be. We said goodbye to his father, who I wasn't sure had even said one word the entire time we'd been there and finally, blessedly, made our way outside. I didn't wait for Yates to open the car door for me before diving into the passenger seat and shutting the door behind me. I was desperate to put as much space between me and his family as I possibly could.

Yates slid into the seat next to me and started the engine. "Well, that went better than I thought it would," he mused.

"You can't be serious. That was horrible," I retorted, folding my arms across my chest.

"For my mother? That was downright civil," he laughed. I didn't think any of what had just happened was funny.

"Can you please take me home?" I asked, sinking down into the seat and staring out the window. I wasn't in the mood to talk to him after what I'd just seen. I needed to do some serious thinking about whether I could tie myself to this stranger sitting next to me for the next year of my life. As Yates turned on the radio, I got lost in my thoughts, thankful for the space he was giving me.

THIRTEEN
RYAN

I watched as Yates's taillights disappeared in a cloud of dust as he drove down my driveway back toward the road.

"The asshole couldn't even be bothered to come in and say hi?" Quinn questioned from where he must've walked up behind me. I spun around and flung myself into my best friend's arms, relishing the comfort he always provided me.

His chuckle rumbled in his chest under my cheek, and I smiled my first real smile all day. For the past four years, Quinn had been my home, my person. I was so thankful for his friendship. "I know what you need, Lancelot. Go get changed. We're going out," he stated, leaving no room for argument.

I let him go, stepping back and smiling mischievously. "What, you mean we don't have to go hand-feed five hundred plus cattle?"

Quinn's laughter had me laughing, too. "Hey, it worked, didn't it?"

"It did," I agreed. "Thank god. It was absolutely miserable."

"None of that. We're forgetting about the future in-laws and drinking and dancing the night away. So get your cute butt in something hot, and let's hit the bar before it gets crowded."

Twirling on my heel, I went inside the house to change into my slinkiest dress, already feeling the day fall off of my shoulders. I was determined to have a good time tonight with Quinn.

An hour later, freshly showered, hair perfectly wavy, I pulled on a skin-tight black dress that highlighted what curves I did have. Swiping smokey eye makeup across my lids, I took one last look in the mirror before I stepped out of my room and knocked on Quinn's door. He swung the door open and looked me over. "Good thing you've got me to run interference between you and every guy who's going to hit on you tonight," he commented with a crooked grin.

I rolled my eyes. "And I'll be there to fend off all the ladies that will inevitably be trying to get in your pants tonight, too, like always," I promised.

"Glad we understand each other," he laughed before closing his door. I followed him out to his truck and climbed inside. His truck was ridiculously tall. I wasn't short, but I almost needed a ladder to climb into the damn thing.

The drive to the bar was short, but Quinn and I managed to sing along to almost a full song on the radio before we pulled up into the gravel parking lot. Fancy, this place was not. But it was the only place in town with a dance floor, loud music, and alcohol where we could all go to let loose. Since it was Sunday night, I hoped it wouldn't be too busy, but there didn't ever seem to be an off night at *On Tap*.

Quinn held open the door for me, and I stepped inside, noticing the faint smell of old cigarettes from back when smoking inside was allowed. Glancing around, I noticed there were already several booths filled with people. The faded black and white tile dance floor was empty, but it was still early. Quinn set his hand on my back and guided us forward to the dark wood-paneled bar, and we both hopped up onto the high back tufted green vinyl barstools. This place was quirky and dark and everything you'd want out of a dive bar, and I loved it.

They served cheap liquor and only local Texas beers on tap. "Hey, you two," Garett, the bartender greeted us. As long as I'd been of legal drinking age, Garett had been serving beers up at *On Tap*. "Your usual?"

Quinn glanced over at me, and I knew that look, and I nodded once. He grinned and turned back to Garett. "Me and my girl here are going to try something new. How about two Electric Jellyfish?"

Garett reached to the cooler behind him and pulled out two beers, popping off the tops and sliding them across the bar toward Quinn and I. "Thanks, G," Quinn said.

I raised my eyebrow at my best friend. "Electric Jellyfish?"

He shrugged with a laugh. "I heard they were delicious, and I've wanted to try for a while. Last time I was here, I asked Garett if he could get them." Quinn had always been into trying every local craft beer he could get his hands on, no matter how weird. I drew the line at anything sour. Beer should *not* be sour.

I held out the neck of my amber bottle toward Quinn, and he clinked his against it. We both sipped, and I rolled the bitter liquid around on my tongue before swallowing. "Citrusy," I observed.

Quinn took another small sip, considering. "And I think mango?"

I shrugged and laughed, taking a huge sip and not bothering to really taste it. At least it was refreshing. "So, how was your night, Quinny? Do anything fun?"

"If by fun, you mean binge Netflix and chill with myself, then yep." He lifted his beer to his mouth and gulped it down.

"Sounds like we both deserve a night out, then," I said, jumping off the stool and leaving my empty bottle on the bar. Crossing the bar to the jukebox, I made my pick and then grabbed Quinn and dragged him out onto the floor with me. I wasn't shy, and I didn't care that we were the only ones out here. Usually, it took just one person to get started, and everyone else would pile out onto the floor. I didn't mind being the first person if it meant I got to shake my hips to the beat.

I wanted to start with something more chill, so I picked *Paradise* by Bazzi to start us off, and Quinn's hands rested on my waist as we swayed together. I closed my eyes and let the music flow through my body, losing myself in the beat. Halfway through the song, the hair on the back of my neck stood up, and a shiver ran down my spine. I only had that reaction to one person in the entire world.

Maddox.

My eyes snapped open and locked with his dark gaze across the bar. His eyes were narrowed on Quinn and me, and he suddenly broke our staredown and strode across the room and stopped at the jukebox. He turned his back to me, and the next song that came on made my heart beat faster. *Mine* by Bazzi started playing as I danced with Quinn but listened to every lyric.

"I think someone's trying to send both of us a message," Quinn chuckled.

I shook my head. "He doesn't feel like that, Quinny. It's probably because he thought we liked Bazzi."

"Uh, yeah, no. That's not it. Have you seen the way he's looking at you? He looks like he wants to murder me right here with all these witnesses for daring to touch what's his."

I chanced another glance at Maddox, and it was then I noticed he wasn't alone. He'd come in with three other guys, one of which was talking to him, but his eyes were locked on me. I tore my eyes off of him and looked up at Quinn. "Maybe we should go say hi?"

He looked over my head back at the guys before smirking. "Lead the way. I wouldn't mind getting to know the guy with all the tattoos on a more *personal* level if you know what I mean."

Rolling my eyes, I giggled. "I *always* know what you mean, Quinny."

We wove through the much more crowded dance floor and stepped up to the bar. I stood so close to Maddox, I could feel the heat of his body even through all of our clothes. He turned to face me, brushing a stray strand of hair out of my face before a cocky grin crossed his face. "Ryan," he said my name in a low growl that I was surprised I could hear over the music. I felt it all the way down to my toes, the way his voice alone could set off every nerve ending in my entire body.

"Maddox," I countered, hoping I didn't sound breathless.

We stared at each other, completely lost to the heat building between us until Quinn cleared his throat behind me and broke the spell. Maddox shot a glare at Quinn before a tall guy with huge muscles and a short, military-style haircut behind Maddox turned around and smiled at me. There was something about his grey eyes that were both sad and captivating, and I wondered how he and Maddox knew each other.

"Mad, aren't you going to introduce us?" the guy asked as the other two guys stepped closer to Quinn and me.

Maddox sighed. "Ryan, this is Connor, Zen, and True. You probably know of Zen and True from the band, and Connor is Zen's bodyguard since he's too much of a pussy to bother with learning how to protect himself."

"Fuck off, dude," Zen said, and I felt Quinn perk up behind me.

"Nice to meet you guys," I said and turned to Quinn behind me. "This is Quinn, my best friend, and partner in crime." I noticed Maddox's eyebrows furrow a little before he erased the expression from his face. He did the same thing when I went to see him at his house, and I wondered how often he actually let people see what he was feeling.

"It's about time we meet the famous Ryan we've heard so much about," True beamed, and I liked him right away. His smile was genuine and kind.

"Oh? Have you heard a lot about me?" I asked True, but my eyes found Maddox's, and he looked away.

"Not really, this fucker doesn't tell us shit," Zen answered for True, and they all laughed as if it were some inside joke.

"Oh, well, I don't know about you guys, but I'm ready to get back on the dance floor," I said, signaling to Garett for another beer. He slid it across the bar, and I sipped the refreshing liquid, letting it slide down my throat and cool me off.

"Want to dance?" The hulking guy who must have been Connor held out his hand, and I grinned, sliding my palm against his much larger one and following him back onto the worn dance floor. A more upbeat song came on, and we moved to the music. After a couple of songs, Connor leaned down and whispered in my ear, "Have you seen Maddox's face? I've never seen him more pissed off." He sounded delighted as he let out a deep chuckle.

"Do you like to piss him off?" I asked, chancing a look at the murderous expression on Maddox's face.

"It's not that hard to do, but this is next-level. I wanted to see how he'd react if I asked you to dance, but don't worry. You're safe with me. I'd never touch someone he was interested in," Connor assured me, and I was more confused than ever. Why did everyone think he was interested in me? I kissed him once when I was a kid and he ran away and never looked back. That wasn't how you acted when you liked someone.

I just nodded because I didn't know what to say to that, and I didn't really like talking to Connor about Maddox even if they were friends. I stepped out of his arms. "I'm going to get some air," I explained before crossing the room and stepping outside. The sun had set, and the stars were out. The air outside was more humid, but somehow it was easier to breathe.

It had been a long day, and after a few beers, my thoughts were swirling. I was confused about Maddox, confused about what to do about Yates, and tired. I walked around the bar's side, away from the people coming and going in the parking lot. I rounded the corner of the building, leaning against the wood paneling that had long since faded in the harsh sun.

I closed my eyes, taking a deep breath, and trying to calm my racing thoughts. I felt him before I even opened my eyes, his hard body pressing up against mine. My eyes snapped open, and Maddox was standing in front of me, his hard chest pressed against mine, his eyes dark and filled with lust. He rested his hand on my waist and pulled me closer into his body. His scent wrapped around me, woodsy and masculine and clean, and I breathed him in.

His face was inches from mine. "Other men don't get to touch you," he growled, and I laughed.

"You don't get to say that. You left, remember?" I countered, pushing against his hard chest to try and put some distance between us, but he didn't budge.

"Biggest mistake of my fucking life. I'd take it back if I could, but I can't. But fuck, Ryan. I can't stand watching anyone else's hands on you. When other men look at you, I want to rip their fucking eyes out of their heads and crush them under my boot. Why didn't you tell me you were getting married?" he asked, hurt and anger swirling in his dark eyes.

I dropped my gaze down to the ground as blood pounded in my ears. Being this close to him made it hard to think clearly. With one of his fingers, he lifted my chin until I was looking into his eyes. "Why, Ryan?"

"Because it wasn't the right time," I answered, not knowing what else to say. I wanted to jump into his arms and confess everything. I wanted to tell him he was the only man I'd ever loved, that I saved myself and waited for him for years. That there would never be anyone else for me but him. But I couldn't. My parents' future depended on it, and I wouldn't let them down, even if it killed me.

"You can't marry someone else, Ryan. You know it's always been you and me," he whispered, his lips almost touching mine. We were so close we were breathing each other in, and I closed my eyes. I lifted up onto my toes at the same time he lowered his head, and then we were kissing with an explosion of years of hurt and want, regret and need. Our mouths moved together in the kind of kiss that's life-changing, world-tilting, and hot as hell. He kissed me like he knew he owned my soul, and like he wanted to know every inch of my body. He pressed me into the rough wall behind us, one hand on my hip and the other tangled in my hair.

This was the kiss I'd waited more than half my life for, and my toes curled as I melted against his muscular body.

Our tongues danced together, his taste familiar and comforting. Having him close snapped into place something I'd been missing since the first time we kissed, and warmth exploded in every corner of my body as I felt *complete*. My fingers sunk into his hair, and I pulled him even closer. He pressed his hips against my stomach, showing me just how much he wanted me. Moaning, I pushed myself against him, needing more. I'd been waiting my entire life for this kiss, and I never wanted it to end. But instead of getting closer, Maddox growled and tore himself off of me. Both of us were breathing heavily, and his hair was disheveled from my fingers running through it.

He blew out a breath and ran his hand down his face. "I shouldn't have done that, I'm sorry," he said, and my heart sank. "You're engaged, and I won't be the other man." He turned, and I watched him walk away even more confused than I was before.

FOURTEEN
MADDOX

"Are you ready to talk about it?" Connor asked me and I bristled. Last night, I stormed back into the bar and demanded we leave. I knew I was being a dick, but I didn't even wait to make sure Ryan got back inside safely. I couldn't face her after what I did. I told myself I'd be better, that I would show her that I deserved her and respected her, and I blew that all away with one kiss.

One perfect, life changing, hot as fuck kiss that I was still replaying in my mind over and over.

"Leave it alone, Connor," I warned.

He folded his massive arms across his chest and narrowed his eyes, not at all intimidated by me and less than impressed at my slamming cupboards open and closed looking for some goddamn food.

"You need to calm the fuck down," he stated as if that were the simplest thing in the world to do. Gritting my teeth, I inhaled deeply trying to exhale all of my self-loathing and demons in one giant breath. It didn't work. Just as I was about to tell Connor to fuck off for at least the tenth time this morning, there was a knock at the door.

Shoulder checking Connor as I walked by him towards the front door wasn't as satisfying as I thought it'd be considering I barely even moved him, but at least I got out a little bit of my irritation. I pulled open the front door to a smiling Shannon holding a basket. "Hey, Maddox. I figured you and your friends were starving in that house. Your dad has never been one for taking care of himself or you, so here," she said, the words pouring out of her as she thrust the basket into my arms.

I looked down, peeling back the cloth covering the still-warm muffins piled inside. Smiling my first real smile of the day, I stepped forward and hugged her gratefully as my stomach growled. "Thank you so much for this, Shannon. You were right, we've been wasting away."

She laughed. "So I hear. Well, I won't keep you but don't be a stranger. Our house is always open to you, you know that."

I did know that, but it wasn't that simple. Especially after last night. Still, I always appreciated what a goddamn saint Ryan's mom was. "You still make your famous pot roast on Sunday nights?" I asked.

"I do. I think Alex and the kids would riot if I ever stopped," she joked.

"I might just have to stop by then," I said, hoping by next Sunday I'd have figured my shit out with Ryan. She was getting married in less than a month and I needed to convince her to give me a chance. And I needed to figure out who the fuck she was marrying. I assumed it was that Quinn guy because he was the one on her social media, but it was clearly not him. The way he eyed Zen last night told me all I needed to know.

So who the fuck had stolen my girl?

Shaking myself out of those thoughts for now, I said another thanks to Shannon before carrying the basket of muffins into the kitchen, swiping a blueberry off the top and shoving it into my mouth. "Thank fuck," Connor said, snatching his own muffin out of the basket and practically inhaling it. As he reached for another one, I yanked the basket out of his reach. "We're going out back," I declared, and spun on my heel, taking the muffins with me.

It was still early and while it was always hot as fuck, it wasn't stifling just yet. Grabbing the bag and pistol I left on the back patio before I went in search of breakfast, I stuck it in my waistband and lifted the bag, marching toward the open pasture. Connor followed close behind me but was smart and didn't say anything. I wasn't in a talking mood right now and he never wanted to talk about heavy shit. That made this morning's jabbing from him even more fucked up. I must be a disaster if he actually wanted me to talk.

Eventually I'd have to figure out what the hell I was going to do, but first I needed to blow off some steam in the best way I knew how: shoot some shit. I strode right up to the fence, dropping the bag and basket of muffins into the soft green grass. I leaned down and pulled out a couple of cans I found lying around Russell's house and lined them up, walking along the fence and placing them on every post. Finally, I picked the basket back up and walked back to where Connor stood, several yards back from the fence.

He glanced over at me before reaching out for another muffin and I rolled my eyes as he devoured it. The dude could eat like no one I'd ever met. Once he dusted the crumbs off of his hands, he reached around and pulled out his own pistol, checking the clip and safety. We did this so many times together, we didn't need to talk. He stepped back and I took aim, squeezing the trigger and feeling the kickback as the can fell off the post in the distance.

For just a few minutes, I forgot all the hard shit and just breathed, focusing on the shot. It was pure fucking relief. I emptied my clip, hitting almost every target I set out before I exhaled and then went to reset for Connor.

Once he finished, we both sunk down onto the grass. "This place is actually okay," Connor said finally and I chuckled. "High praise."

"You know what I mean," he growled. "Why are we here? Why didn't you come home after the first day?"

Plucking a long piece of grass out of the ground, I stuck it between my teeth and sucked on the sweet tip while I gathered my thoughts. "We're here because I'm finally ready to show Russell that he can't fuck with me anymore. I'm going to take this place from him," I disclosed.

Connor sat up straighter. "What do you mean?"

"I mean the one safe place he's always had, this ranch," I elaborated, sweeping my arms out wide. "It's going to be mine because I know what his weakness is and I'm ready to exploit it."

"Why now?" he asked.

"I was never ready to face this particular demon of mine before. But when Joel called, I didn't have a choice. Now that I'm here, I want to sever the last hold Russell could ever possibly have on me. I want him to fucking suffer knowing he's lost every goddamn thing he ever had in his life to his addictions.

He's made his choices, and now I'm making mine."

Connor looked thoughtful. "What does that look like? You're not exactly farmer material."

"No shit," I sneered. "Once this place is mine, I'll figure it out from there. The first step is confronting Russell and giving him no choice but to sell it to me."

"When's that happening?" Connor asked, looking out at the fields surrounding us instead of at me.

Shrugging, I watched as the breeze blew the blades of grass until they were swaying all around us. "Fuck if I know. Whenever he decides to show his pathetic face."

"I hope I'm here when he does," he said menacingly, making a show of cracking his knuckles. I might have laughed if I didn't know he'd killed men with his bare hands before.

Wanting a change of subject, I turned my attention to him. "What about you? How long are you staying here?"

"Until Z says it's time to go, unless you need me to stay."

"Let's play it by ear," I suggested.

"The new guys I've added to my team are holding their own right now, so I'm okay spending some time here if you need me. Say the word."

"Thanks, man," I said and I meant it. Connor had been the one by my side for almost the entire last year. He slowly replaced True and Zen as my best friends as they found their wives and peeled away from our group. I still considered them brothers and nothing would ever change that. Jericho, too. But things were different now. Connor and I were in the same place: Fucked up in the head and too stubborn to deal with it.

So we shot shit, got drunk, and fucked as much as we could. It worked for us, but now that I opened the lock box of feelings I carried around for Ryan, and now that I'd tasted her again after all these years, I wasn't so sure I could go back to the way things had been before yesterday.

I wasn't sure I wanted to.

"I should actually get going. I'm supposed to be watching Z's back and not out here fucking around with you," Connor said with a hint of amusement in his tone.

"Not my fault he keeps your ass on a tight leash," I insulted him.

Lifting his huge body off the ground, he ambled back toward the house and disappeared inside. I got up and collected the cans and the basket of muffins before I started making my way back. Before I got to the back porch, I glanced next door, wondering what Ryan was doing right now and if she was thinking about last night as much as I was.

After a shower, a restless nap, and scrolling aimlessly through Netflix but not actually watching anything for what felt like hours, the sun was starting to set and I wondered if I should call the guys and see if they wanted to hit up the diner in town. Instead, I turned my head toward the lights that had just flashed across the living room wall through the huge bay window.

I stood up, raking a hand through my hair before bracing myself, my muscles tensing and my senses on high alert. I peeled two of the blinds apart and watched my father stumble out of the driver's side of his old beat up Chevy. Fucking *finally*. I could confront the asshole that gave me life and hopefully be done with him once and for all.

By the looks of him as he stumbled his way up the front porch, barely staying upright, he was not even close to sober. I flinched, remembering the kind of damage a drunken Russell inflicted on me as a kid. Suddenly it was like I was twelve years old all over again, small and cowering from my strong and angry as a tornado father who took out every injustice he felt the world had handed to him on me.

My palms went clammy and my heart rate skyrocketed as I waited for him to swing the door open, slamming it against the wood paneling of the wall behind it as he did so many times before. I couldn't stop my body from reacting to the inevitable slam of the front door as I practically jumped out of my skin. Fuck. I hated the fact he still got to me.

I watched as my father stepped into the room, his gait uneven as he steadied himself on the wall, watched as his eyes locked with mine. "Who the fuck are you and what are you doing in my house?" he bellowed, his words slurred. Anger simmered in my veins. How could he not recognize his own son?

"It's your son, you fucking alcoholic," I answered.

"Can't be. The one good thing my fucking cunt of an ex-wife did was get rid it. Sacrificed him to the devil like I done told her to do. So, I'll ask you again. Who the fuck are you?" Russell glared at me from across the room.

This was pointless. He was clearly out of his mind high on something and the fact that even fucked up like he was he looked glad to have been rid of me was a fucking gut punch, even if I knew my whole life he felt that way. It didn't feel good to hear it again.

"You're too fucked up to talk right now, so I'll see you in the morning," I fumed before trying to push past him to get outside. There was no fucking way I could stay here tonight with him like this.

"The fuck you will," he thundered, pulling a knife out of a holder on his belt loop and holding it out toward me, a few inches from my face. Blinding rage tore through me. "I need to send you back to hell. They've been looking for you, whispering all the things they'll give me if I spill your blood. And look, here you are. Didn't even hafta look."

Goddamn, what the fuck was he on?

"Last warning, Russell. Back the fuck off." My fists clenched at my sides and my eyes narrowed into slits, tracking his every jerky movement. He looked hyper now, his eyes darting around the room, his breathing fast.

"Or what, demon? Hell's got a spot waiting for you and I'm about to send you home." A maniacal smile broke out across his face and I wanted to vomit. This shit right here was why I pushed Ryan away. What if I was looking at my future?

While I was figuring out how to get out of this house without my dad going completely psychotic, he decided he'd had enough waiting and lunged at me, knife slashing through the air. I caught his wrist and bent it back until I heard a pop but he didn't drop the knife. With my other hand, I punched him in the face and he laughed as blood poured out of his nose in a river that turned his skin red and dripped onto his shirt.

Instead of falling back or recoiling, he punched me in the ribs harder than I thought possible considering he looked frail as fuck, like he hadn't eaten a decent meal in years. Between the alcohol and whatever the hell he was on right now, I doubted he had. I kicked out, trying to sweep his legs from underneath him so I could pin him to the floor but he was fast and moved out of the way.

While I still held his obviously broken and dangling wrist, the one that held the knife, he took advantage of the fact I wasn't watching his other fist and it connected with my cheek just below my eye. Fuck, the old man could pack a punch, just like when I was a kid. My skin split and hot blood dripped down my cheek. I needed to end this shit now.

The fact he was freakishly strong was throwing me for a loop. It had to be whatever drug he was on. I'd have to do something fucked up but I didn't have a choice. I jerked my knee up and connected it straight with his groin, dropping him instantly. As he moaned and writhed on the floor, I jogged into the kitchen and grabbed a zip tie out of the junk drawer before running back and trapping his hands behind his back.

I sat back on my heel as he glared at me with so much hate, it burned through me, consuming any thoughts I might've had that someday my dad might actually outgrow his demons and realize what a fucking mistake he made all these years. That maybe someday he'd actually be proud of me. With one glare, every small fraction of hope I held on to throughout my life went up in smoke and I didn't have the energy to feel anything.

Panting, I stood up, unsure what to do with myself. My legs moved on their own and before I could process where I was going, I stood outside Ryan's bedroom window. My hand moved as if on its own accord and I found myself tapping on the warm glass. Less than ten seconds later, Ryan was there, lifting the window and leaning out of it like a breath of fresh air.

"Maddox? Are you okay?" her voice was concerned as she looked over my battered face, her forehead wrinkled with worry.

"I don't even fucking know," I answered honestly.

"Come in," she demanded, leaving no room for me to argue with her. I climbed into the window and she slid it shut behind me. I looked around her room, the floral quilt covering her bed and the thousand throw pillows of all different colors made the room bright and cheery. It was the same room I'd been in a hundred times as a kid, only more grown up. This was a woman's room now.

"Sit," she ordered, pointing at her bed. I lowered myself onto the pillowy mattress and looked up at her. My mind had gone completely blank and all I could focus on in this moment was Ryan. Her soulful brown eyes locked onto mine, her sweet, plump lips turned down slightly in a frown as she inspected my cheek.

"I'm going to get the first aid kit. Stay here." She turned and left the room, shutting the door with a soft click. I blew out a breath, not even sure where to start with processing everything that happened in the last hour with Russell. This was why I left and never looked back. Russell was toxic, poison of the always fatal variety. Subjecting myself to him was asking for drama and a lot of fucking pain.

I dealt with a lot of shit in my life, made a lot of problems disappear. I'd done things I wasn't necessarily proud of, but I was a protector at heart. I always had been. And when someone fucked with my family, I was the one who stepped up and fixed shit. But when the problems were mine, it was different. Ever since I opened my heart to Ryan, I'd been obsessing about how to make her mine. How to make her see that she'd always been mine.

But the reasons I left still held true. Just look at what happened tonight with Russell. No matter how bad I wanted her, I would never put her through what I just experienced at the hands of my father. No fucking way. I needed to rid myself of the weight on my life that was Russell Everleigh for good before I could fully be the man Ryan needed me to be.

The door swung open and she walked in carrying a white box. Shutting the door, she crossed the room until she stood in front of me, kneeling down until she was at my eye level. Her creamsicle scent wrapped around me and as her fingertips brushed across my cheek, I closed my eyes.

"I don't think you'll need stitches, but this is going to hurt," she stated, pressing an alcohol wipe against the cut. I hissed, but as quickly as the sting started it was gone. I watched her as she took care of me, a deep longing settling in my chest. I'd never had anyone to take care of me except Ryan when we were kids. Flashes of memories ran through my mind as I watched her. We spent so many nights like this as kids, Russell taking every bad thing life threw his way out on my body and me fleeing to the safety of Ryan's house.

She bandaged up my face and wordlessly cleaned up the supplies. "Do you want to talk about it?" she asked, looking up at me from her spot on the floor.

I shook my head. "There's nothing to talk about. Shit never changes."

She bit her lip and I watched intently, wanting to take that plump lip between my teeth like I had last night. Every whimper, moan, and taste we shared during that kiss had branded me for life, the heat of the moment leaving a raised scar with her name across my soul.

I watched as thoughts crossed her mind. Her face had always been so easy to read for me. She brightened up suddenly, her eyes twinkling. "Blanket fort?" she suggested.

I chuckled, the first cracks of sunlight breaking through the blackness of this night and she'd been the one to punch through. "We haven't done that since we were kids."

Ryan sat up even straighter, tucking a piece of hair behind her ear. "I know, it'll be awesome. C'mon, Maddox. Pleeeaaase?" she begged, her hands clasped together under her chin while she batted her eyelashes up at me.

Truthfully, the idea of spending time in a blanket fort with Ryan was both a dream and a nightmare and I wasn't sure I'd be able to keep my hands to myself. I wanted a repeat of last night more than I wanted anything, but it wouldn't be fair to her on so many levels. But was I strong enough to resist?

I sighed heavily. I was way too emotionally drained to go back to Russell's right now or deny myself more time with Ryan. "Depends. What movie are we watching?"

She smiled wide because she knew she had me. "What else would we watch? *Jackass*, duh."

I grinned despite the pain in my face and the darkness still lingering inside me. *Jackass* had been our favorite movie as kids. Her parents told us we weren't allowed to watch it, but we got our hands on a copy and never let it go. We watched it so many times we both knew all the words.

I stood up off the bed, grabbing the quilt and tossing a few of the pillows onto the floor. "I'll make the fort, you grab the popcorn," I suggested.

"You know if I go make popcorn, Quinn's going to smell it and be in here right in the middle of us, right?"

Quinn seemed like a good enough guy when I met him last night. He'd been looking out for my girl when I wouldn't let myself. But I didn't know if I liked him enough to spend the night cuddled up next to him in a tiny fort.

"Better try to avoid him then," I said with a smirk.

She laughed, shaking her head. "You obviously don't know Quinn at all."

"Obviously not," I agreed, tossing more pillows on the floor. Why did one person need so many goddamn pillows?

I watched as she darted out the door and it took me all of five minutes to set up the structure. I did this so many times when I was a kid it was like riding a bicycle. Everything came right back like I never left at all. When it was done, I crawled inside, kicking off my boots and arranging the pillows and blankets on the floor into a makeshift bed.

The door closed softly and the buttery smell of popcorn wafted into the fort. Ryan's freckled arm shot out, holding the bowl out for me to grab so she could crawl inside. She settled next to me, pulling a blanket up over both of us as we laid back against the pillows. My left side was touching her right side, the heat of her skin searing me through my clothes. I wanted to pull her into my arms, hold her close to my body and forget about everything outside this fort. But I couldn't.

I was quickly realizing this night was about to be torturous as fuck.

"Ready to watch?" Ryan asked, looking up at me with bright eyes and a smile. I loved that she knew exactly what I needed right now. She didn't make me talk about it, she didn't ask questions. She knew I needed to forget, to distract myself with something good. I grabbed a handful of popcorn and tossed a couple kernels into my mouth, nodding at her.

She leaned back pressing play on the laptop she'd pulled in with us. As we settled in for the movie, she moved closer to me, resting her head on my chest and lacing her fingers with mine. My breath caught as every cell of my body was hyper aware of Ryan and how close she was to me right now. She looked up at me with such compassion in her eyes, I fell into them, lost in a sea of warmth and caring that no one else had ever shown me. Her gaze darkened and I knew she wanted me to kiss her, to lean down the couple of inches separating her lips from mine and show her exactly what she did to me.

But Ryan was my future. I didn't want to just sleep with her, I wanted to wake up next to her. One night with her would never be enough and that was why

I wouldn't let myself kiss her now. Not when she was tying herself to someone else. Not until she admitted that she'd always been mine and that she would always be mine.

Instead, I wrapped my arm around her and pulled her closer, closing my eyes and enjoying a few minutes of peace before the world inevitably shit on me again. She wrapped her arm across my stomach and when I cracked open one eye a few minutes later, her eyes were closed and her breathing was steady. She'd been going through a lot lately, too, and I wondered if she was getting much sleep. I studied her face, every freckle, every dark eyelash fanned out on her soft cheek wanting desperately to trace every line with the tip of my finger. Instead, I closed my eyes and let myself succumb to exhaustion.

Waking up the next morning, heat enveloped my body. I looked down and Ryan had completely wrapped herself around me, our legs tangled together and she gripped my shirt tightly in her fist as if she were afraid I'd leave her while she slept. Her breathing was still slow and even, and despite the fact I spent the night on the floor, I felt surprisingly rested. I needed to get home, though, and deal with the fallout of last night.

I let myself have one more minute watching Ryan sleep, enjoying her closeness. She had always been the most beautiful girl I'd ever seen and I doubted that would ever change. If I could wake up every day like this, there would never be anything else in my life that could compare. But for now, I had shit to handle.

So I gently peeled Ryan's clenched fingers off of my shirt and untangled my body from hers. I immediately missed her warmth as I watched her curl up under the blanket. I pulled it up over her and leaned down, ghosting a kiss over her forehead. It was all I'd let myself have for now. Crawling out of the tiny fort, I slid into my boots and lifted the window up as quietly as I could. I climbed out and started the walk back to my childhood home.

The last place I ever wanted to be.

The place I had to go if I was ever going to be free.

I trudged up the front porch, dread creeping into my body, a cold sweat breaking out across my forehead. This was it. All the planning I'd been doing for the past week would hopefully payoff today. The old screen door creaked as I swung it open, not bothering to be gentle or quiet. If Russell had a hangover and the loud noise pierced his skull that would be just fucking perfect.

Right on cue, he yelled out, "What the fuck, boy?" Ah, so he *did* remember who I was afterall. My teeth grinded together as I clenched my jaw to keep from lashing out at him. I needed to stay focused. That was the only way I was going to rid my life of the man who reluctantly gave me life once and for all. Instead of answering, I marched through the house to the room I'd been staying in. Predictably, it was ransacked, no doubt as Russell searched for money to fuel his habits. At least I kept my wallet on me last night.

I grabbed the envelope that contained the key to my freedom and walked back to the kitchen. My heart was racing a million miles an hour. I'd never been good at standing up to or confronting my dad. He held some weird, sick power over me that I fucking hated him for. I tossed the thick envelope down in front of where he sat at the kitchen table.

He lifted his bloodshot eyes to me over the rim of his coffee mug. Whatever he had in there wasn't coffee since there wasn't any in the house. "I saw what you did to my room. You had no right to go through my stuff," I gritted out. I didn't know why I even bothered, but I was starting to boil over with anger and I needed to say my piece.

"No right?" he scoffed. "I have every right when you barge into my house and make yourself at home. I didn't ask you to come here."

"No, you didn't. Joel did since you can't manage to take care of the animals that you're responsible for. So I stepped in. *Again.* And how the fuck did you get out of the zip ties?" My fists were clenched at my sides so tight that they were starting to go numb.

"Broke a beer bottle." I looked at his wrist, spotting the dried blood where he'd missed and cut his skin instead.

His eyes turned calculating and then he smiled up at me as if he flipped a switch from the monster to an actual human being. I knew better than to be fooled. "Well, thanks for taking care of the feed. I appreciate it. You know, if you could just lend your old man a little bit more, I could really turn this place around," he tried.

I threw my head back and laughed. Was he fucking serious? I had to hand it to him, he had balls. At the sound of my laughter, the monster was back and he was glaring at me, his livid expression almost funny.

"You must be out of your goddamn mind if you think I'll give you one more cent to blow on alcohol and whatever drug you were high on last night," I scoffed before shifting my tone into something more neutral. "You know, if you want money and to be free of this place, I may be willing to help."

I watched as he perked up, the predictable fucker. "Help? How?"

I nodded toward the envelope that sat untouched in front of him. "Open it."

He reached his shaky hand out, but I knew the shake wasn't from nerves. The tremors would only get worse the longer he went without feeding the beast that lived inside him. He pulled out the papers and scanned over them before his nostrils flared and he slammed his fist down on the table, shaking his mug so the liquid inside sloshed out. "No fucking way," he shouted.

Shrugging, I studied the worn and faded room around me, not wanting to give him any sort of indication how badly I wanted this. "Fine, have it your way."

I reached to pick up the papers and he snatched them out of my grip, his eyes narrowing. "How much?"

I grinned like the goddamn Cheshire Cat because I knew I had him. "Fair market value, minus the repairs needed and the amount I already paid for the feed and upkeep this week." I wasn't offering him a dime over what I thought was fair. And I knew he'd accept because he was completely consumed by his demons. Nothing was more powerful in his life.

Not one goddamn thing.

He sat in the chair stewing and I could practically see the steam rising off the top of his head, but finally he sagged in his chair. "Never wanted to be a rancher anyway. Fine, you've got a deal," he reluctantly agreed and internally I pumped my fist in the goddamn air. I was about to be free of my nightmare.

"Sign here," I pointed to the sticky arrows my attorney had placed in every spot a signature was needed and handed Russell the pen I'd stuck inside the envelope. I didn't want even one second to allow him to hesitate. I watched as he scrawled shaky signature after shaky signature and after the last one, I blew out the breath I'd been holding.

I pulled a check out of my pocket and slid it across the table to him, his greedy eyes lighting up at the amount even if it was almost nothing to me. "You've got twenty four hours to get the fuck out of my house," I said, reaching down and stacking the papers neatly in a pile before sliding them back into the envelope.

I didn't wait to hear a response from him before walking back to my room to shower, change, and go into town. There wasn't a chance in hell I'd be spending any more of these last hours in this house with Russell. Our ties were officially severed.

I was officially free.

FIFTEEN
MADDOX

I might as well have been floating for how goddamn light I felt now that I owned the ranch, and Russell was gone for good. I hadn't realized when I came out here how much I needed this. How much I needed to take control of my past, face it head-on, and let that shit go. I was ready to move forward, to embrace the man I knew I could be. Seeing the mess Russell had made of his life all these years later, I realized something. Ryan was right. I was *never* going to become like my old man.

Not a fucking chance.

I watched him become a monster when I was a kid, or maybe he'd always been that way. Either way, I'd never been more determined to prove that that would never be me. Sure, I had a little too much fun when Shadow Phoenix had first made it, but I'd gone to rehab and a shit ton of therapy to learn my lessons and get as healthy as possible.

Had I still held onto the anger and resentment? The abandonment issues? Yep. But, I ripped the chains off of myself by buying the ranch. The feeling of kicking Russell out of my life permanently was indescribable. Looking around the house that was now mine, I realized I needed to get a cleaning crew in here to throw out everything. Better yet, calling a contractor might be the best move. I wanted to strip this place down to the studs and start fresh.

Short of leveling the building to the ground and rebuilding something entirely new, this was the best plan. I made a mental note to talk to Joel about it. Despite the sexy as fuck girl next door who I was pretty sure I was still in love with all these years later, I had no plans to live here permanently. I doubted I'd spend much time here at all. Still, I had plans for this place, and I wanted it to be somewhere I felt comfortable visiting if I ever felt the need.

Now that I'd thought of Ryan, she was like a beacon to my brain. I wanted to see her, spend time with her, get to know who she was now. I wanted to make her mine. Glancing at the calendar hanging on the wood-paneled wall, my heart sank a little as I realized there were only two and a half weeks until she married another man. I was running out of time.

Skipping breakfast and downing a scalding mug of black coffee, I set the empty cup into the sink. Now that shit was squared away here, it was time I focus my efforts on Ryan. I was determined to make her see we belonged together.

Locking the door, I slid my keys into my pocket and pulled the black baseball hat I wore down over my eyes. The sun was fucking intense out here, and the walk wasn't exactly short to the Knight's house. But I didn't mind, it gave me time to think about how I wanted to approach things with Ryan. I knew she didn't fully trust me, considering what I put her through. I never thought my walking away would affect her like it had, that it would hurt her like it did me.

I figured she was just a teenage girl with a crush, that once she saw what I became, she'd be glad I spared her a life with me. Fuck, I'd been so stupid. So incredibly stupid.

The wooden porch steps creaked under my weight as I climbed them, rapping my knuckles on the front door. I didn't have to wait long before the door swung open, and Quinn looked back at me through the screen door, a slow grin breaking out across his face.

"Let me guess. You're not here to see me?" he asked with a chuckle.

"Not today, buddy. Sorry," I smiled back. I figured being friendly with Ryan's best friend was probably my best bet to getting on her good side. Maybe he'd even put in a good word for me. Plus, he seemed like a good dude. "Is Ryan around?"

Quinn pushed the door open, standing back so I could come in. "Yeah, she's just finishing breakfast. You know where the dining room is?"

I nodded. "You aren't staying?"

"Nope, I was just on my way out. I've got an appointment in Dallas," he explained before leaning in a little closer and lowering his voice. "If you want to get on her good side, stick around today and help with the chores. Since I won't be here, she'll have to do it all on her own."

I reached over and patted him on the back, thankful for his advice. I had a feeling I had an ally in Quinn when it came to Ryan, but I wanted to be sure. "Why are you helping me?" I questioned.

He glanced over my shoulder before his eyes darted back to me. "I want Ryan to be happy, and I have a feeling you might be just the guy to give her that, even if you obviously don't have a clue how to treat a woman."

Narrowing my eyes at him, I hated to admit he was right. I'd been a complete asshole to every woman I'd ever spent time with, no matter how short. Ryan had always been different, but I still ended up hurting her. Finally, I sighed deeply. "I want to make her happy, Quinn. But she's fucking engaged to another man, and I don't want to cross lines and make her into a cheater."

He raised an eyebrow. "Didn't you already make out with her behind the bar?"

"Yeah, and I've been guilty as fuck about it ever since," I admitted.

"Don't be. Trust me when I say to keep doing what you're doing. I think she'll come around. But you better get your ass in gear if you want to have a chance. There's not a lot of time left."

"Yeah, I hear the goddamn clock ticking, man. Trust me, I'm aware."

Quinn moved back to the door, pulling out his keys before looking back at me. "Good luck," he said before closing the door softly behind him. Taking a deep breath, I turned and walked toward the dining room I'd spent so much time in as a kid. The only reason I knew what a family dinner was like was because of Ryan's family.

Stepping into the room, she didn't notice me right away, so I took the opportunity to watch her. She leaned over a book she had open on the tabletop next to her plate. Her hair fell over her shoulders in waves, brushing her upper arm. She lifted her coffee to her lips, taking a small sip as her eyes never left the page. As I studied her, my chest constricted, the beauty of her almost painful for me to look at.

Ryan must've sensed my staring as she finally looked up at me. Her doe eyes widened as she lifted them to meet mine before smiling like she was actually happy to see me.

"You gonna stand there staring all morning?" she teased.

I couldn't help my smile back, moving to take the chair beside her. "Would it be so bad if I did?"

She laughed, brushing her hair behind her shoulder and watching me over the rim of her mug as she took another sip. "I don't know how to answer that," she said honestly.

"Okay, well, a little bird told me you might need some help around here today." I reached out and took her mug, taking a gulp of the hot liquid before passing it back. I watched as her eyes darkened before she snapped herself out of it. My cocky smirk told her I knew the effect I had on her. I did it on purpose. I might not be able to kiss her or do other less innocent things to her right now, but I was going to pull out every other flirtation and seduction technique I'd ever learned.

Hopefully, by the end of this day, she'd be wound up and needy for me. At least that was the plan. I hoped I had enough self-control to hold myself back from taking things too far if it came to that. The making Ryan want me part of my plan wasn't in question. I had no doubt I could do it and quickly, too. The part that I was going to struggle with was when she looked at me with hooded eyes, practically begging me to claim her body as mine.

That was going to be a fucking struggle.

She blew out a breath, bringing my thoughts back to my offer. "So? Mind if I stick around and help today?" I offered.

Nodding, she pushed her chair back and stood up. "That would be great, thanks." I watched as she collected her breakfast dishes, the smooth skin of her arms on display under the clingy tank top she wore, her curves just the right proportion. When she bent over to grab the final plate, I had a view down the front of her top to the swell of her breasts spilling over the top of her lacy bra. I bit back a groan as I tried to discreetly adjust my hardening cock under the table.

She stood up, taking away my unobstructed view of the most perfect set of tits I'd ever seen. I couldn't wait to get my hands and mouth on them, and I knew it was only a matter of time before it happened. Ryan and I had always been like fire and gasoline. Put us together, and the chemistry was explosive. We'd never explored it, but I felt it in every brush of her skin against mine, every longing look we exchanged.

Ripping myself away when we kissed the other night had been the hardest thing I ever had to do, and that included confronting my dad after everything he did to me. When she finally became mine, I knew I'd never want to leave her body. The magic we would make together would be like nothing I'd ever experienced before. I could already tell.

She walked back into the room, her hips swaying slightly with each step, and my eyes were locked in. I couldn't help it. The best part about Ryan was she didn't know how fucking sexy she was. She didn't try to put more sway in her hips or wear layers of makeup or spend hours getting ready. She was just naturally beautiful, enticing, and fucking perfect. She didn't need all that shit, and it was refreshing, especially compared to the girls I normally came across in LA. They felt like cheap imitations now in comparison.

Following her out to the barn, we walked side by side, our arms brushing every now and then. "I wanted to apologize," I began.

"For what?" she asked.

"The other night. I shouldn't have brought my fucking mess to your doorstep. When I left, it was to keep that side of my life from you." I stopped and looked down into her eyes, brushing the hair the wind tossed around her face behind her ear.

Her eyes were so open and concerned, emotion swelled up inside me. No one had ever cared about me like Ryan did. "Don't you ever apologize for that, Maddox. I'll always be here for you, no matter what happens. Always have been, always will be," she promised.

I lowered my head to rest my forehead against hers. "I don't know what I ever did to deserve someone like you in my life," I murmured, forgetting I was supposed to be keeping some fucking distance between us. But I could already feel my emotions getting tangled up. If she didn't end up picking me when this was all over, I wasn't sure I'd survive it. But I couldn't think like that now.

She raised her hand and cupped my cheek, closing her eyes for just a second before letting me go, stepping back but still holding eye contact. "You deserve everything," she breathed, and I didn't know what to say.

Instead, I turned and closed the last bit of distance between us and the barn, looking at the horses in their stables. "Which one do I get today?" I asked, grateful for the change in subject.

Ryan followed me inside, walking up to the grey stallion and petting his nose. "You'll be on Quinn's mare, Daisy," she said, pointing to the white mare in the stall a couple down. Once we had the horses saddled up, we both climbed up, and I followed her lead out of the barn and into the pasture.

"So, besides being engaged to some mystery guy, what have you been up to the past twelve years?" I gripped the reins a little tighter as we trotted further into the field.

She laughed, the throaty sound making me smile. Ryan always had the most infectious laugh, the kind that when you heard it, you smiled and wanted to laugh, too, even if you didn't know why. "Do you remember what I wanted to be when we were kids?" she answered my question with one of her own.

"Sure, a cop, right?"

She nodded. "Do you know why?"

"No, I guess I never knew. I always figured you were power-hungry and wanted to lord your authority over the peasants in this town," I teased.

She laughed again. "Not quite. I wanted to be a cop because of the times I watched them come to your house and how they were the only ones who could make your dad stop. They made things better, even if it was only for a little while. I wanted to protect you for once," she admitted, and warmth crashed over me as I fought to keep myself composed at her confession.

Clearing my throat, I hoped my voice sounded steady because I was feeling anything but. Ryan had always knocked me off balance. "So, what happened? Why didn't you do it?"

She sighed and glanced out at the wide-open pasture in front of us. "Short answer? My dad's accident."

My eyebrows furrowed. "What accident?" Why hadn't I heard about her dad up until now?

"You didn't know? His horse threw him about four years ago. He had a spinal injury, and he's been in a wheelchair ever since. It's why I'm here."

"Fuck. I'm sorry, Ry." I wasn't sure what else to say.

She shrugged. "Nothing we can do about it. That's why I came back after college. Did you know I chased you to LA? I didn't know exactly where you were, but I knew from the tabloids that's where you went after you left, so I ended up applying to only California schools when I decided where to go to college."

Her confession floored me. She went to California after high school? For me? That meant she'd still been thinking about me four years after I left. "Where did you end up going?"

"UC Irvine. I got my degree in law enforcement and planned to stay out there. There's nothing quite like palm trees and sand between your toes, you know?" She sighed wistfully, and I chuckled.

"You're goddamn right. That's why I live right on the beach," I agreed.

She laughed. "Lucky bastard. Maybe someday I'll get to see where the other half lives, huh?" Her eyes lit up when she talked about my home, and I had to admit I liked it a whole fucking lot. Maybe all hope wasn't lost after all.

"I'll take you home whenever you're ready," I promised, aware that there was more than one way she could interpret my words, and I meant every one of them.

"I'll keep that in mind, cowboy." Her eyes twinkled mischievously. Her face sobered before she continued. "After college, I actually got hired with the LAPD and had just started the academy when the accident happened."

"What about your sisters? Why aren't they here?" I wondered where Charlie and Justice were, but I hadn't felt right asking until now.

"Charlie was in medical school, and Justice was in the middle of college. I'd just started, and so it was easiest for me to walk away and come back," she said simply as if it weren't a huge fucking deal for her to give up on her dream to come back here.

We rode up to the fence, and both hopped down. I tied Daisy's reins around the post before turning to Ryan. "You're fucking incredible. I hope you know that. There aren't many people who'd put their dreams on hold the way you have." I stepped closer to her, wanting to pull her into my arms and feel her against my body, to wrap myself around her and never let go.

She brushed me off, waving her hand in the air as if she weren't the most selfless and extraordinary woman I'd ever met. If I hadn't been convinced before, I was now that there was no one equal to her, no one who deserved her. But she made me want to try to be worthy.

"All the boys who want to get in my pants say that," she flirted, trying to lighten the mood. I could tell my praise made her uncomfortable, but she deserved it all and more. She was the one who deserved everything.

Raising my eyebrow, I stepped closer to her until there were only a couple inches between our bodies. "And how often does it work?" I didn't want to come off like an asshole, but I was possessive when it came to Ryan. The thought of another man inside of her made me crazy. I wanted to kill anyone who dared to touch her. I was her first kiss, and now I was struck with a burning inside my chest as I clenched my jaw, fighting not to let the jealousy out.

"What? Boys getting in my pants?" She looked like she wanted to laugh at me, but I scowled right back, nodding once. "Uh, never? I was waiting for you, remember? But then you never came back, and I got tired of waiting. So, I met Yates, and here we are, getting married in a couple of weeks."

My heart soared and then crashed. She saved herself for me? Fuck, I hadn't been expecting that. And now what had always been made for me was going to be some other man's. A quiet rage started to build inside of me. Wait. "Yates? That's his name?" I questioned.

I swear Ryan winced before nodding. "That's his name. Yates Rutherford." Damn, I could just picture the kind of guy he must be with a name like that. I committed his name to memory for later.

I clenched my teeth. "Let's change the subject. What are we doing out here?" I asked, hoping for a distraction and a way to let my anger out without letting Ryan know how bad it was.

She pointed at the grass and brush that had died and taken over a lot of the pasture. "Clearing all this brush out of here so the cattle can start grazing here again. We'll start over there," she pointed to the far end of the field, "And work our way back here. Tomorrow Quinn and I will gather it up and burn it."

I turned back to Daisy and dug into the bag I'd attached to her saddle, pulling out the tools I'd need. "Lead the way, boss," I said, turning back to Ryan and following her across the pasture.

We started working next to each other, side by side, hacking at the overgrowth. Sweat poured down my back, and I lifted my hat, swiping at my forehead. Ryan's breathing was heavy as she took a break, too, grabbing a bottle of water and tossing one to me. "Now that you know what I've been up to, how about you? I've seen a lot in the headlines, but I know a lot of that can't be true."

Unfortunately, more of what they wrote about me was true than not, which wasn't the case with the other guys. But I didn't mind the fame. I embraced the paparazzi and liked making headlines. Or at least I had early on. Now not so much.

"What do you want to know?" I asked hesitantly, not sure how much I should share about the past decade for me. I lived the rockstar lifestyle to the fullest, enjoying every single perk that came along with being a celebrity. The girls, the booze, the drugs, the money. I loved it all and embraced it wholeheartedly.

She shrugged. "Whatever you want to tell me."

"When I left here after that night," I started, not wanting to remind her of that night. "I ran straight to True's house. We met online on a message board for musicians and chatted for months. His parents offered to take me in, and I finished high school with him. Not long after I showed up, we started messing around musically. He played guitar, and I played bass so we'd jam together. Junior year we met Zen. Jericho went to school with us, but we weren't friends with him until I decided to take band as an elective."

She giggled. "Oh my god, you were a band geek."

I chuckled. "Yeah, yeah. Laugh it up. You haven't met Jericho yet, but when I saw what he could do with a set of drums, I convinced True we needed him. It wasn't even a conscious thing that we were making a band. We just had fun playing together. Once we had Jericho, we needed a singer, and that's where Zen came in. He and True had a couple of classes together and instantly became friends when he moved to our school."

"Yeah, I could see that. True seems pretty friendly and outgoing, at least from what I saw the other night," she agreed.

"He is. But once we realized what we had, we got more serious. We'd practice every free minute we had. Zen wrote our music, and Jericho arranged it. True and I helped, too, but mostly it was them. Once we graduated, we decided to really pursue music as a career, and things happened pretty fast after that. By the time I was twenty, we'd headlined a world tour, had a multi-platinum record and won our first Grammy."

"Damn," she said, pulling her cowboy hat off her head and brushing the sweat-soaked strands off her forehead before tightening her ponytail.

"Yeah. The next couple of years were a blur that I don't really want to get into. I wasn't exactly someone I was proud of those years. There were a lot of drugs and a lot of women, both of which I regret. But the guys dragged me into rehab about four years ago, and I've never looked back."

She looked a little lost in thought, and I held my breath and waited for her reaction to all the worst parts of my new life. Finally, she looked up at me with nothing but kindness and understanding in her eyes, neither of which I deserved after how I'd treated her. "How about the last four years?" she asked.

I chuckled. "Things have gotten a lot more… domestic, I guess. Not for me, but Zen and True both got married in the last couple of years and either have kids on the way or have kids already. I have a feeling our next tour is going to be wild for a whole new reason."

She laughed. "Better invest in earplugs. Crying babies are no joke."

"I don't mind. I'm the fun uncle, so I'll get them all hopped up on sugar and then hand them back over," I explained.

"Smart man, I'd do the same thing," she smiled before she sobered. "Have you heard from your mom?"

I shook my head. "I hired a PI a few years ago because I was curious about what happened, and I found out some shit, but I haven't done anything with it."

She tilted her head to the side, her eyes locked on me. "What'd you find? I always wondered what happened to your mom after she left."

I stared off into the distance over the top of her head, thinking. "She got remarried a couple of years after she left. She's still married to the dude. She…" I paused, taking a deep breath. This part shouldn't hurt as much as it did but fuck it stung. "She had another son. One she stayed around to raise this time."

Ryan's eyebrows shot up her forehead. "You have a brother?"

I nodded. "A half brother, yeah. He's twenty-two."

"And you haven't met him?" she questioned.

Shaking my head, I ran a hand down my sweaty face. "I don't think he knows I exist."

"Are you going to?" she stepped closer, taking my hand and squeezing.

"I don't know. Maybe someday. Depends, I guess."

"Depends on what?" She wasn't going to let this go.

"Forget I said that." I wasn't about to tell her that wanting to meet my brother was something I'd only feel brave enough to do with her by my side. That if she went through with the wedding, I'd be too wrecked to do much other than drink myself into oblivion for the rest of forever.

She studied me before shaking her head and letting go of my hand, but I wasn't ready for the closeness to end.

Instead, I stepped a little closer, unable to keep my distance being this close. We were sweaty from a couple of hours of hard physical work, and she had little pieces of dry brush caught in her hair. I reached out, plucking a small stick out of the strands. She looked up at me with big eyes that I found myself lost in. They were deep and captivating, inviting me to sink into the depths of her mind.

Fuck, I wanted to kiss her, and I didn't think I could stop myself. Talking to her was too easy. Even sweaty, she smelled delicious, and I wanted to lick every inch of her skin until she was writhing beneath me. Instead, I ran my hand along her neck, feeling her pulse under my palm until I finally gave in and pulled her toward me.

Our lips connected, and I was lost, falling into an abyss I never wanted to crawl out of. My body sparked, and every nerve ending was on fire. I needed her touch, needed to be closer to her, needed to feel her in every inch of my existence. As I deepened the kiss, she opened to me, twining her arm around my back, and her other hand found my neck, stroking my stubbled jaw with her thumb as her tongue explored my mouth.

I knew this was a mistake, but I couldn't get myself to stop. I ran my hand down her back until I grabbed her ass, pulling her tighter against my hard as fuck erection. I couldn't seem to get her close enough, and the whimpers she was making told me she felt the same way. She jumped, and I caught her, gripping her thighs as she wrapped her legs around my waist. She ground herself against me as a growl tore from my throat. "Fuck, we have to stop," I groaned, pulling her closer instead of putting her down like I should have.

Her lips found mine again, and I forgot every reason we shouldn't be doing this. The sound of approaching hooves pulled me out of my lust-filled haze as I placed one last soft kiss to her swollen lips. "Someone's coming, Freckles," I said, gently sliding her down my body and groaning at the feel of her body against mine.

She glared over my shoulder. "Fucking Quinn," she hissed, and I chuckled, watching him ride up to us. Based on the looks he was shooting my way, I knew he'd seen plenty. I smirked, daring him to say shit to me.

I looked back at Ryan, where she still held onto me to steady herself. I brushed my finger down the side of her cheek before dropping my hand. "Hey, Quinn," I greeted.

"You two look like you've been busy," he teased, still shooting knowing glances Ryan's way. I stepped in front of her, interrupting his silent interrogation. She didn't need to deal with that bullshit, even if he was her best friend.

"Yep. Ready to help?" I asked, making it clear that it was time to get back to work, and there would be no questions about what he just witnessed. The last thing I needed was Ryan analyzing everything and regretting what happened. I was finally starting to making progress, and no one would fuck it up for me.

He stayed quiet as he grabbed the tools from his horse and made his way over to where we were working. We all resumed working in silence, clearing the brush going a lot faster with three of us now. As the sun started to set, we had a massive pile of dead sticks to burn tomorrow and were all in need of a shower and dinner.

Quinn spoke up first. "I don't know about you two, but I think we earned a night out."

"I'm in," I said, tucking my tools back into the bag on the saddle.

I swear Quinn blushed. "So, Maddox. Any of your hot as fuck friends gonna be at the bar with us tonight?"

I laughed. "Subtle. No, Zen and True flew home a couple days ago and Connor's in Dallas visiting an old Marine buddy."

Quinn deflated. "Damn. Well, it should still be fun. Meet at the bar in an hour?"

We all agreed, and I made my way home to shower and call a car. I probably needed to get a rental if I was going to stay here much longer.

An hour later, I strolled into the local dive bar, finding Quinn and Ryan in a quiet corner booth. "First round's on me," I announced.

"I'll take whatever micro brew they've got," Quinn said, and Ryan agreed.

"Be right back." The place was pretty busy, so I had to weave in between quite a few people to get to the bar. I placed our order and stood to wait for the bartender to bring it over. While I waited, I pulled out my phone and scrolled through social media absently. Someone brushed against me, but I didn't pay much attention because of how crowded the bar was. When it happened again, and I felt a hand move against my stomach, I looked up.

A girl with fake eyelashes and bleached blonde hair in a tight red dress that left nothing to the imagination looked up at me with a wicked grin. I stepped back, pulling her hand off of me. "What the fuck are you doing?" I hissed.

"Don't you remember me?" she pouted.

I wracked my brain, but it was just a blur of blonde hair and long legs, none sticking out more than any of the others. Shaking my head, I turned back toward the bar. "Sorry."

"Maybe you'll let me jog your memory," she purred, skating her arm back around me until her tits pressed into my side. I was getting seriously pissed off. Why the fuck was this girl touching me?

"Hard pass," I snapped.

"I bet I can snap you out of that cranky mood," she offered, sliding her hand lower. Why the fuck wouldn't she get the goddamn hint? I glanced across the bar toward Ryan. If she saw this girl all over me, I knew she wouldn't take it well, and suddenly the thought of anyone else touching me was repulsive.

"You need to back the fuck up off of me now." Ryan's eyes locked with mine as she made her way up to the bar, and I knew she'd seen the whole thing. Fuck.

The blonde finally got the hint and stepped away as Ryan moved to my side. Blondie shot Ryan a glare before finally backing off and slinking back to whatever hole she'd crawled out of. I doubted this would be the last time that shit happened. I'd been with a *lot* of women, and I left most of them wanting more since I was never with the same girl twice.

"Friend of yours?" she asked with a voice more casual than I could tell she looked. The hurt in her eyes killed me. I vowed never to hurt her again, yet here I was doing just that. Would there ever be a day when I wouldn't cause her pain?

"Not even a little bit."

"Right. I'm going to the bathroom." She spun on her heel and stalked away from me.

"What the hell are you doing, man?" Quinn stepped into the spot Ryan left open, grabbing two of the bottles the bartender slid in front of me.

"Grabbing beer?" I grabbed the last one, and we made our way back to the booth. I slid in across from him, taking a sip of my beer.

Quinn rolled his eyes. "You're not that fucking dense. With Ryan."

Picking at the corner of the label, I sighed. "I can't let her marry another guy. It will wreck me. I made a mistake leaving all those years ago without reaching out and at least being her friend."

He nodded, sipping his beer. "Yeah, you really fucked her up. I stepped in to try to fill your shoes freshman year of high school, and we've been best friends ever since. But she's waited for you for twelve years, Maddox. Do you understand what I'm saying?"

"That she's missed me?" I really didn't know exactly what he meant, and I wanted him to spell it out.

He narrowed his eyes at me. "She didn't just miss you, bro. She saved herself—every part. Up until Yates, she hadn't kissed anyone else. She's never had a boyfriend until him. I'm the closest thing she's got, and it's only because I'm safe. You don't know the power you've got over her. It'd be so easy for you to break her. But if you break her, I'll fucking kill you myself." That last part he growled at me threateningly, and my respect for him went up even more.

And she'd never even had a boyfriend until this Yates guy? We'd lived such different lives. While I'd been hung up on her, I shoved her to the back of my mind, pretending she didn't exist so I could try and move on. Except I never had. Subconsciously I had all these rules to keep me from really finding someone else.

And I felt guilty as fuck every single time. It was why I always had to be drunk when I hooked up with girls. I couldn't handle the guilt.

I stared across the table at Quinn. "Do you think I really have a chance to stop this wedding and get her to see that she belongs with me?"

He leaned back in the booth and ran his hand through his messy hair before nodding. "I do. But it's going to take a fuckton of work. Lucky for you, I'm on your side."

"Why?" I asked, unsure why he'd want Ryan with a fuck up like me.

"I've known our girl for a long time, but I've never seen her light up the way she does when she talks about you. Even before you came back, when she told stories about the past, she always talked about you so reverently. I love Ryan, probably more than I should." A dark shadow crossed his face, and I sat up straighter. He was gay, right? "And that means the only thing I want for her is to be happy. I don't know you very well, but what I've seen so far, you seem like a good guy. I saw how you tried to get that skank off of you. I don't think Ryan was thinking clearly enough to see that part," he noted.

"So, how do I fix it?" I took another big sip of my beer, letting the cold liquid slide down my throat.

"Treat her like the motherfucking queen she is. Show her you want her more than anyone or anything else. And most of all, never, ever give up on her and run away again. No matter what." He finished, his eyes boring into mine. The threat was implied. If I did this, if I went down this road with her, I better be sure because if I tried to back away, he'd be there inflicting every bit of pain on me that I do on her.

Except I knew I'd never back away. I'd never wanted anything like I wanted Ryan, and now that I'd unlocked the feelings from the depths of my soul, there was no putting them back. There was no containing them, and there was no stopping what I was about to do.

No matter what it took, Ryan Knight would be mine.

SIXTEEN
MADDOX

After my talk with Quinn yesterday, and the decidedly frosty way Ryan had treated me for the rest of the night, I woke up this morning with a new determination to show her how I felt. I had a little over two weeks left until she walked down that aisle, and I planned to use every second I could get with her to my advantage.

I needed to be around her. It was a physical pull to be closer, to be in her presence even if it was just being nearby. Like an addiction, I'd take any bit of her I could get. I'd replayed yesterday's kiss over and over until I had to take a cold shower last night and relieve the pressure that'd built up. Jerking off under the cold water was as miserable as it sounded and left me sexually frustrated.

I'd wait as long as I had to for Ryan, but I hoped it wasn't long. Tossing on my clothes, I slid into my boots and left the house before the sun was fully up. I couldn't remember the last time I'd been up this early without having stayed up the entire night. I quickly closed the distance between my house and Ryan's, eager to not miss a second with her.

Before I even climbed the last step on the porch, the door swung open, and Quinn held out a steamy mug of coffee for me. I took it gratefully. "Thanks, bro."

Quinn gave me a small smile before closing the door behind me. "She's probably not even up yet. For a rancher, she's not even close to a morning person," he grumbled.

"I'll get her up," I promised, and Quinn chuckled.

"Get her up, Maddox. Not keep her in bed all day," he chastised, rubbing his eyes.

I chuckled darkly. "No promises."

He groaned but didn't say anything, and I stepped past him, making my way down the hall as quietly as I could. I knew the layout of this house like the back of my hand, and I turned the handle of her door, pushing it open and closing it behind me with a soft click.

Ryan was curled up under her quilt, her dark curls wild and messy around her face as she breathed evenly. The relaxed look on her face drew me closer. I didn't want to wake her, but she needed to get up. I stretched out next to her, moving closer and tracing my finger down the soft skin of her forehead and cheek. The corner of her mouth lifted in a slow smile as she slowly came out of sleep.

She whimpered softly before reaching up and covering my hand with her own. I wanted to kiss her so goddamn bad, and at this point, I'd already crossed that line twice. Would it be so bad to do it a third time?

Still, we were on her bed, and if I kissed her now, I wasn't so sure I'd be able to stop. Quinn was waiting on her, and she still hadn't chosen me over her fiance. Things were actually pretty fucked up, but at least I still had hope. I had to believe that if we spent enough time together and I showed her that I wasn't running, she'd dump him and give me a chance.

"Freckles," I spoke softly. "Time to wake up." I tried to coax her the rest of the way awake gently, freeing my hand and running it down her arm, brushing my fingers up and down the smooth skin.

Her eyes fluttered open before closing against the bright morning sunlight pouring in through the window. I chuckled at her struggle. Both times I managed to stay over with Ryan since I'd been back, I left before she'd woken up. I was getting my first glimpse into what she was like in the morning, and I had to admit she was pretty goddamn adorable.

"C'mon, gorgeous. Quinn's waiting for you, and if you want me to stick around today and help out, you've gotta get up now." I thought bribery might help even though I knew I'd be sticking around either way.

She rolled onto her back and threw the blankets off, sitting up and glaring at me through the chaos of curls, and I bit my lip to keep from laughing. "Fine, I'm up, but if you try to leave before we're done with chores, so help me…"

"And miss out on even a second in your presence? Never."

She flashed me a small smile before kicking me out of the room to shower. It took everything in me not to follow her into the bathroom and use my powerful persuasion skills to convince her to let me join her. Just knowing she was totally naked under a cascade of water made me hard, and I knew I'd need a distraction to keep from at least going and taking a peek.

Luckily, Quinn was in the dining room when I walked in, and I knew he'd be just the guy for the job. "What's on the agenda for today?" I asked, sitting down across from him at the table and taking a still-warm croissant out of the basket.

He lifted his eyebrow over his steamy mug of coffee. "Is that really what you want to talk about?"

I wanted to know everything about the competition, and he knew it. "You know it's not. Tell me about the fiance."

He snorted. "You mean *Yates?* The yuppy, old money douchebag?"

"That's what I guessed based on his name, but I figured I was a little bit biased when it came to the guy Ryan's marrying."

Quinn shook his head, buttering his own croissant. "I've only met him once but-"

"Once? That seems a little weird considering you're Ryan's best friend. How long has she been with this guy?"

Quinn shifted in his chair, his eyes darting away from me. I could tell he was hiding something, but his loyalty wasn't to me, so I didn't press. I waited for him to answer.

"Uh, I'm not exactly sure. She says for about six months. She didn't want us to meet him until she knew it was serious," he answered, still not looking at me. I'd let it go for now.

"So, why does she like him? What does he have that I don't?"

Quinn shrugged. "Stability, I guess. The fact he's here. Plus, I don't think he has the ability to really hurt her."

My stomach twisted, and I dropped the croissant I was about to bite, suddenly not hungry. Fuck, I really hurt her. I didn't know if I'd ever be able to make up for the choices I'd made. "Is he really here, though? You hadn't met him for six months, and I haven't seen the guy once since I've been back."

Quinn shrugged, not knowing what to say, I guess. "Level with me, Quinn. Is there any chance at all that she'll ditch the douche? Am I just making shit more complicated for her by being around?"

"No, there's more than a chance, Maddox. Don't give up. Yates doesn't deserve Ryan. The jury's still out on if you deserve her, but I know her deep down better than anyone. She never really moved on from the dream of you. I don't think it'll take much pushing on your part to convince her if you just keep showing her you're around and not going anywhere. You have to build back that trust, but lucky for you, Ryan's the most forgiving person I know," he said, and hope filled me.

If there was even a tiny remote possibility she'd call off the wedding and be with me, I'd never quit trying. Not for anything. I'd give up everything and move to Texas and become a rancher if that's what she needed me to do.

Fuck, I hoped that wasn't what she needed from me.

Still, right now, it didn't matter. What did matter was Ryan and showing her I knew I fucked up and that I was willing to do whatever it took to make up for it. Showing her that no matter what either one of us had been through, she was always it for me. There'd never been another woman who made me feel like she did, like I was willing to rip out my heart and hand it over on a silver platter for her to do with it whatever she wanted.

We both straightened up as Ryan walked into the room, bringing with her a lightness of energy and her orange-vanilla scent that woke my appetite back up in more ways than one. "You slackers ready to hit the hay? Literally?" she asked, laughing at her own lame-ass joke.

Quinn groaned, and I rolled my eyes as she snatched a croissant for herself, shoving it in her mouth and holding it between her teeth as her eyes sparkled. She took a huge bite and grabbed the bottle of water Quinn handed her before spinning on her heels and walking back out.

I glanced back across the table at him, and he was already standing up, dusting off his hands. I slid my chair back and stood, picking up my plate. "Leave it," Quinn insisted, waving his hand. "I cook breakfast, Shannon does the dishes. She likes to feel useful."

"You made those?" I asked, pointing at the buttery croissant, and I swear he blushed a little.

"Yeah, I love to cook."

"You've got to meet my buddy, Grayson. He owns this fucking incredible restaurant that has a waitlist for forever. If you ever come to LA, we'll go," I promised.

"I'd like that," Quinn agreed, and we walked to the barn, just shooting the shit.

Ryan had already pulled out her and Quinn's horses, but there wasn't a third. "I see the horses for Quinn and me, but what are you going to ride?" I asked her, flashing her my cockiest grin while I swaggered up next to her.

After my little chat with Quinn over breakfast, I decided today I was going all-in with the charm. I didn't have time to waste taking things slow, but I also needed to tread carefully. I still had to be myself. She wasn't some groupie I didn't care enough about to even learn her name.

She looked up at me through her thick, long lashes, heat flashing in her eyes. "Why, you offering?" she practically purred, and I was instantly hard as a goddamn rock. Fuck, I hadn't expected her to play along, but it excited me like never before. My heart was pounding, and I leaned forward, brushing my lips against her ear as I whispered, "Always, baby."

"If you two aren't going to make room for one more, there's shit to get done," Quinn grumbled, climbing onto Daisy's back and effectively ruining the moment. I stepped back from Ryan before shooting a glare in his direction.

"Yeah, that's what you get for being so hot," he shrugged, and I laughed. I couldn't argue with his logic; even if I was still irritated he ruined the moment. I would have bet every cent I had that Ryan would have let me kiss her again in about ten more seconds if he hadn't interrupted. Maybe it would be better to let the tension build up throughout the day, though.

I looked back down at Ryan, wrapping one of her curls around my finger. "We can share," I declared, letting go of her hair and climbing up on the saddle before she could argue. I reached my hand down, and she took it, letting me help her up. She threw her leg over Storm's saddle, and she settled her back against my chest. I wrapped my arms around her waist, pulling her even closer.

Burying my nose into the crook of her neck, I breathed her in. She was so fucking enticing, I wanted to take my time and run my tongue along the curve of her neck and up her jaw, but I didn't. Instead, I leaned back slightly and let her take the reins, enjoying the feel of her body swaying with mine as we rode to one of the outer pastures.

Her hair brushed against my cheek as it blew in the breeze and tickled as it caught in my stubble. I laughed as I untangled it from my face, and she twisted to look at me. "What's so funny?" she asked.

"Your hair keeps getting caught on my face," I said, still chuckling. "Don't get me wrong, I like it. It just tickles. But I can think of other things of yours I'd like on my face more." I stopped fighting to keep her hair off me. Instead, I lowered my hands to her hips. I pulled her back against my body even closer, close enough that I'd bet she could feel the semi-hard dick I was currently sporting from having her pressed against me.

Her body was like the best drug I'd ever tried, but I had a feeling it'd be more addictive if I ever got a real first taste. I'd be lost to an addiction so bad that nothing would ever compare. I wanted to fling myself headlong into it without any fucking hesitation.

"Hmm," she hummed, and I had a feeling she didn't know exactly what to say, but that was okay with me. I liked how innocent Ryan was. Her inexperience was a fucking turn on like no other.

All too soon, she pulled on the reins, bringing us to a stop. We climbed down and got to work in the hot as fuck sun, but I didn't mind these chores now that I was out here with Ryan and even Quinn. The dude was honestly pretty badass, and I found myself liking his company, which was saying a lot, considering I hated almost everyone.

After a couple of hours, my muscles were straining, I was thirsty as hell, and my stomach was trying to eat itself because I was so goddamn hungry. I hadn't done this much manual labor since I was a kid, and I remembered why I fucking hated growing up on a cattle ranch. Could I do this kind of work day in and day out? Sure. Did I want to? Fuck, no.

"Break for lunch?" Quinn panted, sweat pouring down his face. I was sure I didn't look any better as I pulled off my baseball hat and wiped my face with my shirt. I didn't miss the way both of their eyes lingered on my abs, and I chuckled. "I can take it off if you want," I offered, reaching for the hem of my shirt and pulling it over my head.

I knew I looked good, and if my girl wanted to check me out, I had absolutely no problem with it. As an added bonus, I'd get to ride back to the house with her body pressed against my shirtless chest. I was getting hard just thinking about it and took a deep breath to calm down.

It didn't work.

We loaded the tools and climbed up on the horses, and I gripped Ryan's hip in one hand and moved her hair away from where it stuck to her neck with the other. I couldn't help myself and pressed a soft kiss to her damp skin, opening my mouth just enough to brush my tongue against her skin. She tasted salty and sweet, and I wanted more.

A breathy moan came out of her mouth, so I kissed her again, and she melted into me, resting her head back on my shoulder. I let the hand on her hip drift down to her thigh and back up to her stomach, pushing up the fabric of her tank top and letting my fingers tease the soft skin underneath. I was so captivated by her that I didn't notice where we were until I felt her stiffen against me before she sat up. I pulled my hands back and looked around her to see what she'd reacted to.

"Douchebag at three o'clock," Quinn muttered as he rode past us up to the front porch.

A tall blonde guy that looked like he'd stepped straight out of an Abercrombie and Fitch catalog stood on the porch with his arms crossed and an annoyed look on his face. I had to assume this was the fiance, Yates.

Every picture his name had conjured up for me had just been proven right. But he couldn't be all bad if he managed to get Ryan to agree to marry him, right?

Still, my gut told me there was something not right with this guy. I didn't know what yet, but my intuition rarely steered me wrong. I wasn't exactly making a great first impression, but I really couldn't give any less of a fuck. This guy had stolen my girl, so I immediately hated him on principle.

Ryan pulled herself even further away and climbed down off of Storm. I glared at Yates, not at all happy that he was the one to make her pull away from me. I felt like I'd made some real progress with her today, and he came along and wiped all that out. My fist clenched around the saddle's horn as I climbed down behind Ryan and tied the reins off on the porch rail.

I grabbed my shirt and pulled it on, watching as Ryan climbed up the porch to greet her fiance. Quinn moved beside me, having already tied up Daisy. He leaned close but kept his eyes locked on Ryan. "Pretty sure the dickhead's here for lunch. We should fuck with him," he whispered, shifting his eyes to look over at me where they were practically sparkling with mischief. I almost laughed, except I noticed Yates's stare burning through my skull.

I wanted to lift my hand and flip the fucker off, but instead, I glanced over at Quinn, who still stood shoulder to shoulder with me. "I'm in."

Ryan and Yates walked ahead of us, and their conversation drifted back to Quinn and me.

"Where's your ring?" Yates asked.

"Oh-" Ryan started, but Quinn cut her off. "She can't wear that monstrosity working on a ranch, dude."

It looked like Yates was biting his lip to keep from telling Quinn to fuck off, so I chuckled but kept my mouth shut.

"Sorry, but Quinn's right. I'd break it or lose it or get it caught on something and hurt myself. But it's safe on my dresser. Promise," Ryan confirmed.

After that, the silence was awkward as fuck, but Quinn and I shot each other looks. He was about to make this lunch a lot more fucking bearable.

We followed Ryan and Yates into the house, washing our hands and making our way into the dining room. Shannon was placing a couple more dishes on the table, and even though Yates and Ryan walked in the room ahead of Quinn and me, Shannon lit up when she saw us. "My boys! I'm so happy to have everyone here for lunch," she fawned over us, wrapping her arms first around Quinn and then me. "The only thing that would make this better would be if Charlie and Justice were home."

Out of the corner of my eye, I watched as Yates frowned, his jaw muscles tense, and my chest swelled a little. I'd always fit in with the Knight family. They took me in and accepted me as one of their own when I was a kid. This family was the only bright spot in my entire childhood, and I missed them more than I'd thought.

Coming back here and being with them felt like coming home. As an added bonus, it made Yates uncomfortable that Ryan's family had included me more than him. I went over and patted Alex on the shoulder. This was the first time I'd seen him since I'd been back, and the first time I'd seen him since his accident.

I was glad Ryan told me about what happened before I saw her dad because it was shocking seeing the powerful and indestructible Alexander Knight so broken. Even still, he wore the warm smile I remembered from when I was a kid. If I ever had kids, and that was a big *if*, I'd want to be the kind of dad Alex was, or even True's dad, Chris.

"Good to see you, son," Alex declared, clapping his hand over mine. His eyes were warm and welcoming, and a little part of me that had been knotted up inside for a very long time loosened at their forgiveness and compassion. I convinced myself a long time ago that the Knights all hated me because of how I left. It wasn't just about Ryan. Yeah, that was fucked up, but they all had been like family, and I disappeared without a word.

"You, too, Alex. Hope you don't mind I've been helping our girl out the past couple of days," I added, knowing it would probably piss Yates off. Quinn coughed behind me to hide what sounded like a laugh, and I moved to the chair next to Quinn. Ryan sat across from me, and Yates was next to her.

Ryan's dad chuckled, probably well aware of what I was up to, but that was fine. I doubted he liked this idiot any more than Quinn or I did. "Not at all. Imagine if your fans could see you now," he mused.

Shannon passed me a tray of ribs that smelled both spicy and sweet, and I pulled a couple onto my plate before giving the dish to Quinn. Yates was studying me across the table, probably trying to figure out who I was. "Fans?" he finally asked.

A cocky smirk spread across my face, the one I knew pissed people off when I used it. "Mhmm, fans," I drawled, not really caring to answer his question. He had Google. He could figure it out if it mattered that much to him. My eyes drifted to Ryan, who looked like she wanted to crawl under the table and hide. I wouldn't mind if she did, maybe I'd join her.

"So, Yates," Quinn began, pausing his forkful of baked beans halfway to his mouth. "What is it that you do again?"

The blonde dickhead sat up straighter, obviously on more comfortable ground talking about this. "I'm in finance," he stated proudly, even puffing out his chest a little. I didn't even try to hide my eye roll, and I watched as his face turned red. But then he smirked, tossing his arm across the back of Ryan's chair and stroking the skin of her shoulder with his thumb. I clenched my teeth but wouldn't take the bait.

"How *interesting*," Quinn mocked. "Doesn't your dad own the company or something?"

Yates scoffed and opened his mouth to speak, but instead, Quinn turned to me, effectively cutting him off. "When we're done with the hay, we should take our girl for a swim. You in?"

"The old pond in the east pasture?" I asked, wanting to make it clear I was more familiar with this place than Yates would ever be.

Quinn nodded before turning to Ryan. "What do you say, Lancelot?"

"I think that sounds lovely," Shannon spoke up, her eyes dancing as she looked at me and winked. Yeah, she knew exactly what we were doing and was on board. I loved these people.

"Uh, yeah. It's hot out there today, so a swim sounds good," Ryan agreed, shifting in her seat a little further away from Yates's wandering fingers. Interesting.

"Bathing suits optional," I tacked on with a wink in her direction, and I watched as her eyes flashed.

"You're just going to—" Yates slammed his mouth shut mid-sentence, probably thinking better of whatever he was about to say. "Sounds like fun," he said instead.

"Sure does." I flashed him my cocky grin again, keeping my eyes locked on his. This prick would never beat me at this game.

Alex's voice cut through the tension. "So, Mad, I hear your dad moved out."

I nodded. "I bought the place, but it needs a lot of work. Speaking of, I'm having a new AC installed, and it's going to take a few days." I turned to Ryan.

"Do you mind if I sleepover for a night or two while they do the work? I could get a hotel, but it'd be easier to stay here so I can keep helping out."

She stiffened next to her fiance. "Sure."

Quinn clapped his hands together once. "Perfect. We can all cuddle up in the fort and watch movies like the other night. Maybe even trade massages. Hauling hay is hard work."

I took a sip of my lemonade to keep from laughing. Yates's eyes were cold as he stared at Quinn and me from across the table, and I could read every way he wished he could fuck me up in his hard glare. I couldn't have imagined a better way to get under his skin and let him know I was stepping back into Ryan's life and had no intention of leaving again. Ever.

"I'm great at giving massages," I agreed. I'm sure my face gave away all the ways I was thinking about my hands running over every inch of Ryan's soft and smooth body.

Ryan's parents stayed silent. I was sure they didn't know what to say, and we sat in awkward silence. Yates was shaking with barely controlled fury, and I wondered if I was the only one who noticed, but one glance at the smirk on Quinn's face told me he saw it, too. I wanted to high five the fuck out of my new partner in crime, but I held it in, at least until we cleared the dishes and took them into the kitchen.

I held up my palm, and Quinn slapped it heartily, leaving a sting behind. I didn't mind one bit. "Fuck, yes. Did you see the look on that dildo's face?" he laughed.

"I thought he'd stroke out when you talked about cuddling and massages," I cracked up.

"We need to actually do this whole sleepover thing tonight and post a picture to her Insta," Quinn added.

I nodded. "Imagine what'll happen when we tag me in it."

"Oh, fuck, yes. We are one hundred percent doing this."

Right as I finished rinsing our dishes, there was a knock on the door, and I heard a familiar voice a few seconds later. Drying my hands, I walked back into the dining room to find Connor's hulking form taking up the entire doorway. "Hey, man. What's up?"

He nodded at me once. "Sorry to interrupt. Zen called to let me know you have files to review since he couldn't get ahold of you."

"Yeah, I left my phone inside this morning so it wouldn't get broken. Here, come in," I offered, pulling out a spare chair next to Quinn. "This is Alex and Shannon, Ryan's parents," I started introductions, and Connor shook their hands. "You know Ryan and Quinn, and this is Ryan's fiance, Yates," I said last as Connor's eyebrow raised, and he took Yates's hand, squeezing no doubt harder than necessary. He knew what Ryan meant to me and supported me completely in trying to win her over. He supported me so much that he was still in the middle of fucking nowhere Texas with me even though Zen had gone home.

I hadn't missed that he assigned Julian to guard Zen and Kennedy while he stayed here with me. "Everyone, this is Connor. He's my friend and," he met my eyes with a subtle shake of his head. "Someone I work with on occasion." I finished, hoping that was good enough. He obviously didn't want Yates to know he was part of the band's security for some reason.

Yates turned to Ryan. "Babe, do you normally have this much… company?" He smiled, but it looked forced, as if it was the last thing he wanted to do, which made it look more like a sneer.

Ryan shook her head. "Not normally."

"Hasn't been for a while, but it's about to become your new normal since I'm not going anywhere. Right, Freckles?" I challenged.

She looked at me with pleading eyes, and I figured that was my signal I'd pushed hard enough, and I needed to back off just a little. At least for now.

"Right," she said in a small voice.

"Well, I should be getting back to the city," Yates cut in, sliding his chair back and standing up. Quinn and I stood up with him, and Connor followed our lead. We all wanted to make sure he got the fuck out of here and didn't make Ryan pay for us fucking with him.

"Good to see you again, Yates," Shannon insisted with a bland smile, and Alex murmured a simple goodbye.

"You, too, Mrs. Knight, Mr. Knight. Thank you for lunch, it was delicious." The dude was smooth, I had to admit. The problem was he was *too* smooth, and that shit rubbed me the wrong way. It was like he wasn't actually showing any of who he actually was or hiding his true self or something. I didn't like it.

We all followed him out to the front porch, and I held out my hand. He took it, squeezing so hard his muscles strained and shook, but my ice-cold stare never faltered. Neither did my grip. This motherfucker thought he could scare me with a hard handshake? Pathetic.

"Keep your fucking hands off my fiancee," he demanded in a low voice so Ryan wouldn't hear him over the conversation she was having with Quinn. Connor's eyes narrowed, though, as he watched our exchange.

"Yeah, not gonna happen. I don't like you, and if you think I'm going to stand by and watch you marry *my* girl, you're out of your goddamn mind."

He stepped closer, trying to pull me forward by the grip he still had on my hand, but he was both smaller and weaker than I was. "Listen, jackass-"

"No, *you* listen," I growled over him. "I will *never* stop fighting for her. And if she chooses you, I'll still be there, making sure you don't hurt one single hair on her perfect head. And if you do? I'll fucking kill you. Just so you know," I promised before shoving away from him. He stumbled once in the dirt, the dust dirtying up his perfectly polished dress shoes.

He was shaking with the effort to contain his anger. I considered that mission accomplished.

He moved over to where Ryan stood by Quinn, and I watched with a smirk as Quinn threw his arm over her shoulder and pulled her into his side so Yates couldn't get his grubby hands on her. Yates clenched his jaw as he leaned forward and pressed a kiss to her cheek before shooting Quinn one last glare and stomping off to his car.

"I don't like him," Connor said, stepping up beside me as we watched the bastard climb into his imported car and take off down the driveway without a backward glance.

"What's to like?"

"I mean, he's up to something," he clarified, running his hand through his close-cropped hair and watching Yates's retreat through narrowed eyes. I'd never met anyone with better instincts than Connor, so when he said something wasn't right, I trusted him.

Quinn came up beside us while Ryan went back to the house. "We hate that guy, right? Like it's not even a question?"

"Fuck, yes. I've never wanted to punch anyone more than him."

Connor nodded. "He has a punchable face, but I think there's more to it than that. I'm gonna do some digging."

Quinn perked up. "If you need help taking him down, I'm definitely down for that."

The screen door slammed behind us as Ryan passed by our little group and made her way to the barn without glancing at us once. I winced. "How mad is she?"

Quinn shrugged. "I think she's more embarrassed and doesn't know what to do with it. She'll get over it in a little while." He turned to me. "You coming back out with us this afternoon?"

The corner of my lip twitched as I almost smiled. "Were you serious about swimming and massages?"

He laughed, and Connor's eyebrows shot up. "Massages?"

I waved him off. "We spent the entire lunch fucking with Yates."

"And yes, I was serious. Skinny dipping in the pond this afternoon and massages tonight while we cuddle and watch movies. We can make a Ryan sandwich, as long as you don't mind sharing *your* girl with me," Quinn flirted.

"You have the samples Zen sent. He's waiting on you to listen and give him feedback this afternoon," Connor reminded me.

"I'll give her some time to cool down while I work. What time do you want to meet at the pond?"

Quinn glanced up at the sun, shielding his eyes. "Four?"

I nodded. "I'll see you out there then."

Turning, I headed toward the big, black truck Connor had rented and waited for him to unlock it to drive us back to my house. Zen was already gearing up for our next album, and I couldn't wait to hear what he'd come up with sound-wise.

But what I was even more excited about? Getting naked and wet with Ryan later this afternoon. Time couldn't pass fast enough.

SEVENTEEN
RYAN

What a complete disaster. Having Maddox around was throwing me so far off balance, I wasn't sure I even know how to walk straight anymore. Everything was confusing. I didn't know what he wanted or expected from me. He kissed me, he told me that it had always been the two of us. And he and Quinn had both made it abundantly clear at lunch today how they felt about Yates.

But I didn't know what to do with all these feelings or information because the truth was it didn't change anything. I still had to save this ranch. I closed my eyes for a second, feeling the gentle sway of Storm's walk and taking a deep breath, letting the humid air center me. I opened my eyes again and steered Storm toward the pasture we'd been working in earlier today, the hay half gathered.

I didn't know if Maddox would be coming back with Quinn, and if he was, I didn't know what I'd say to him. I got my answer a couple of minutes later when Quinn rode up on Daisy by himself. He tilted the brim of his cowboy hat at me with a sly smile as he rode up beside me. "You okay?" he asked, sliding off of Daisy and tying her rein to the wooden fence post in front of us.

Following his lead, I did the same with Storm before sighing heavily. "I honestly don't know, Quinny. What was that in there?"

He shrugged. "Yates is a tool and doesn't deserve you. Maddox and I wanted to make sure that message got across."

Quinn met my questioning gaze with a crooked smile, and I felt my own smile tug at the corner of my mouth. "I can't deny that it was a little bit fun to watch you two make him squirm."

Quinn laughed and patted me on the shoulder. "I had a feeling you'd enjoy that."

I groaned. "How am I going to stay married to him for an entire *year*? The more time I spend around him, the more I realize we have nothing in common and come from two different worlds."

"One look at him and I could have told you that," he pointed out. "Besides, what about Maddox?"

"What about him?" I asked, knowing I sounded defensive but not caring one bit.

"He likes you. Maybe even loves you."

I scoffed, turning to walk toward where we were working earlier, and Quinn followed, falling into step beside me. "He left Quinny. He's back now, and maybe it's the nostalgia, but he hasn't exactly asked me not to marry Yates. I'm just his fun new toy," I argued.

Beside me, Quinn stopped walking, gripping my elbow and spinning me, so I faced him. He cocked his head at me while he stared as if he were trying to figure me out. "What's wrong with you?"

"Nothing." I tried to yank my arm out of his grip, but he held on tight, refusing to let me walk away before facing whatever he thought I needed to. This was one of the things I both loved and hated most about my best friend.

"Nuh-uh. That's not gonna work on me, sweetie," Quinn said, using a finger to tilt my chin up, so I had to look him in the eye. "Tell me what's going on with you."

It was a demand, and we both knew it. Sighing heavily, my shoulders sagged. "I don't know. He confuses me because I thought I had everything figured out. I was going to do this whole thing with Yates, and our problems were going to be over. It wasn't exactly clean, but it seemed simple enough. Then Maddox fucking Everleigh comes strolling back into my life, and he actually apologizes. And he's the same and at the same time so different. He kisses like a hurricane, Quinny. He sucks me up and consumes me, scattering little bits of me all over the place because I can't tell which direction is up. And now I'm so confused because it feels like maybe I have something to lose that I didn't have before," I ranted.

Quinn had let me go, and I started to pace in front of him, really getting on a roll as words poured out of my mouth faster than I could think about what I was saying.

"When I was a kid, I always imagined it'd be him and me riding off into the sunset, you know? I know it's cheesy, but it was what I wanted. I didn't even care what happened or where we were as long as we were together. He was my first best friend, my first protector outside of my dad, my first kiss, and my first love. When he left, it broke a part of me that I didn't think would ever heal. And then he came back, and those broken pieces started to sew themselves back together. When he apologized, I had no idea how much I needed that. And then he just shows up. Every day he's here, and he's putting in the effort to get to know me now. But not only me, you, too. He wants to know the people in my life, and I don't know what to do with all of this."

Quinn stepped in front of me and gripped my upper arms, a soft smile playing on his lips. "Take a deep breath, sweetie."

I did as he said and inhaled the thick afternoon air, blowing out slowly. "Look, from what I've seen, the guy can have anything and everything he wants. But the one thing he's never allowed himself to have is you. Now he's trying to make up for everything he fucked up in the first place. If I had to guess, I'd say he wants you to give him a chance," Quinn said.

"I don't know if I can. Giving him a chance means giving up on this place." I waved my hand around at the land that surrounded us.

"A place you don't even really want to be."

I hated when he was right, but that didn't change how I felt. "Doesn't matter, Quinny. Whether I want to be here or not, marrying Yates solves both problems. And if Maddox really wants me, he'll be willing to wait while I do this." My tone was final, and I was done talking about this. My stomach sank as I thought about whether Maddox would still be here in a year willing to give us a chance.

A lot of things could change in a year, and with a life like his where he'd no doubt be surrounded by adoring fans who'd give him whatever he wanted, I wasn't sure I stood a chance. Why would he ever want to stay here waiting for me?

Don't get me wrong - I knew I was a damn catch. But I was also realistic. I nudged Quinn's shoulder with mine. "C'mon, Quinny. Let's finish this pasture."

"Only if you promise to swim in the pond with me after," he countered, his eyes glinting with something I wasn't sure I liked the look of.

I sighed because he knew I needed his help today. "Fine."

"No backing out."

"I know," I snapped, completely over this conversation. "Now, get to work." I didn't know what he was up to, but I was pretty sure I wasn't going to like it.

𝄞

By the time we finished way too many hours later, I was drenched in sweat, covered in dirt, and bits of hay were in places I didn't want to think too hard about. My muscles ached, and I didn't know if I'd ever been more thirsty. I wouldn't admit it, but that swim with Quinn sounded like the perfect end to this day.

I followed his lead, riding over to the shady area near the pond that I liked to go when I needed a break or some time to myself. We stopped to let the horses drink from the pond before we tied them loosely to the trees. Quinn and I had gone swimming here probably hundreds of times, and even Maddox had swum here with me tons when we were kids. This was my favorite place on the entire property.

I watched as Quinn pulled his t-shirt over his head, admiring his toned body even if I wasn't actually attracted to him. I could still appreciate the view. He caught me staring and chuckled with a wink. "Glad at least one of us gets to enjoy the show," he teased.

I pulled my tank top over my head and tossed it at him playfully. "Just because you're gay doesn't mean I can't look."

"Oh, trust me, sweetie. I don't mind the attention," he assured before undoing the button on his jeans and sliding them and his boxer briefs down his legs. I did the same, and as we stood there, me in my underwear and Quinn completely naked, I grinned at my best friend before we both took off for the water at the same time, splashing into the warm pond.

I dove in, tucking my head so that the water would cover my body completely. I immediately relaxed as I felt the day wash away with every brush of the water surrounding me. When I surfaced, I sucked in a lungful of air and relished the water's feeling dripping down my skin. I slicked back my hair and turned at the sound of approaching hooves. Quinn surfaced next to me, and his gaze drifted to where I was watching Maddox ride up to the pond.

Any confusion I'd been feeling about him was quickly put to rest by the sudden racing of my pulse and the flutter in my stomach as he approached and hopped down off the black stallion he'd rode out here. The horse fit him like they'd been made to be together. He was no white knight riding in to save the day. He wore his darkness like armor he spent a lifetime earning, which made him that much more appealing.

"Damn," Quinn breathed next to me, and I just bit down on my lip to keep the stupid grin that wanted to escape in. I didn't want Maddox to know how much he affected me. That didn't mean I kept my eyes from wandering up and down every inch of his body, from his messy brown hair, down every peak and valley of his muscular torso. He was currently covered in black from head to toe, down to his heavy black boots with the laces untied.

He smirked as he caught me checking him out and I grinned right back. I didn't care to hide my interest, even if I didn't know what to do with it. I may be inexperienced, but that didn't mean I was shy. Maddox Everleigh had always been the sexiest guy I'd ever seen, and I didn't see that changing anytime soon.

"Mind if I join you guys?" he drawled, still wearing that hot as hell smirk on his face and reaching back to yank his shirt over his head, knowing neither Quinn nor I planned to say no. As his clothes hit the ground, I saw Quinn's jaw drop next to me, and I couldn't help the giggle that bubbled up and escaped my lips. I pulled my hand out of the water and used my index finger to push up on Quinn's jaw.

"I think you've got a little drool right there," I teased, wiping my hand across his chin. I looked back at Maddox, but his eyes were locked on mine and filled with heat. They were so dark they almost looked black, and as I watched him wade into the water, I was suddenly very aware of the fact I was wearing only a bra and panties.

When he dove under the water, swimming in our direction, Quinn finally tore his gaze off him, and his face broke into a boyish grin. "Like the view?" I asked.

"Fuck, yes. That man is sin personified, and I love every second I get to stare at him," Quinn said wistfully, splashing into the water to float on his back. I followed his lead, floating on the surface of the water, the sound around me muffled as I stared up at the cloudless blue sky before letting my eyes drift closed.

The waves around me gently lapped at my arms and legs as for a few minutes, I was weightless. I let my mind empty of everything before I felt arms wrap around my waist and pull me down into the water. I plugged my nose just before I was pulled under, submerged in the dark water, and held down with a pair of strong arms wrapped around me before he let me go, and I floated back to the surface.

When he popped up a second behind me and flung his wet hair out of his face, my breath caught at the dark beauty of this man. The way the sun glistened off of his wet, tan skin and the way his eyes were dark with intent. He didn't try to hide the desire in his gaze. Oh, no. Instead, his tongue played in the corner of his lips before a sinful smile crept across his face, telling me everything he wanted with just one look.

This was a man who wanted me just as much as I wanted him. Maybe more.

I tore my eyes away from his, shaking my head and trying to remind myself that I was engaged, even if it was bullshit. Maddox didn't know it wasn't real. To him, I was in love with Yates and tying my life to his. I had really and truly created a mess of epic proportions without even trying.

Moving to swim away and put a little distance between us, Maddox moved with me, grabbing my hand and pulling me back so he could wrap his hand around my waist. His thumb stroked the bare skin above my hip, and a shudder rolled through my body involuntarily at his touch. I wanted to wrap my legs around his waist, but that felt like an invitation to me, one I wasn't ready to extend.

It wasn't that I didn't want Maddox. It was the opposite. I spent my entire life wanting this man to be mine. To come home and claim me, tell me he wanted me as much as I wanted him. But the hurt was still there from what he did. I could tell he was trying to make up for it, and every day he came back and stuck around, showing me that he really had meant his apology, made me trust him a little bit more. But I needed time to figure out what to do with Yates and to be sure I wasn't just some fleeting challenge for Maddox.

"Hey, man. Glad you could make it," Quinn greeted him with a smug smile as he watched the two of us.

I rolled my eyes. "So, that was how he knew we'd be swimming."

Maddox chuckled darkly. "Quinn and I had a discussion after lunch. When he made the suggestion to your fiance, I thought it sounded like a fun walk down memory lane. Remember when we used to do this as kids?"

Nodding my head, I wrapped my arms around his neck so I could stop treading water with them, but I kept my legs firmly pointed toward the bottom, not giving into temptation. "Remember the rope swing?" I wondered.

Maddox lit up and moved his head from side to side, trying to find it. "Yeah, where'd it go?" he asked, adjusting his hold on my hips as he twisted his body back and forth.

Reluctantly pulling my hand off of him, I pointed at Quinn. "This guy thought it could take his very grown-up and muscular weight, and it snapped right off the branch mid-swing."

Quinn shrugged. "I had to test its limits. You never know unless you try, right?" He glanced at Maddox with an unreadable expression on his face.

Maddox smiled knowingly and nodded. "Right. Maybe we'll have to rebuild it."

My eyes lit up. "Can we?"

Maddox's turned his attention back to me, his eyes locking on mine as they searched deep into my soul like only he could. I wasn't sure what he was looking for, but I didn't want him to ever look away. "I'll build you anything you want, Freckles." He seemed totally serious, as if he meant more when he said it, and then he leaned in and placed a gentle kiss right on the tip of my nose.

I couldn't help the sigh that escaped my lips, but he didn't seem to mind. If anything, he held me closer to his body and his warm, smooth skin pressed against mine as he closed whatever distance was left between us.

"Okay, I'm starting to feel like a third wheel," Quinn complained. That broke the spell, and I put a little distance between Maddox and me. He seemed reluctant to let me move even a little but did it anyway.

"What do you want to do, Quinny?" I asked.

He grinned at me wickedly. I cringed because I knew whatever he was about to say would probably be something that would embarrass me. My awareness was brought to the fact that Maddox's hands were still holding me close to him but moving up before they stopped just underneath my bra. His thumbs stroked the skin just below my breasts, and electric tension flared between us.

Quinn's deep voice brought my attention back to him. "Truth or dare?"

I groaned, and Maddox let out a low chuckle. "Well played, Quinn," he grinned.

"I thought so."

Men.

Letting go of Maddox completely, I swam between the two of them, so we formed a triangle in the middle of the pond, all of us treading water. They'd roped me into this, and I honestly didn't know what to pick. If I chose truth, Quinn would undoubtedly ask me something embarrassing either about Maddox or about my pathetic love life up to this point. I wasn't sure I wanted Maddox to see how desperately I clung to the idea of my happily ever after being with him.

At the same time, if I picked dare, Quinn would find some way to embarrass me in front of the one guy I actually cared about what he thought of me. Ugh. "Dare," I decided, saying it out loud before I could chicken out.

Quinn was practically vibrating with excitement, and I knew I'd made a mistake. "I dare you to strip off whatever you still have left on and skinny dip."

I snuck a peek at Maddox, who was staring at me with what could only be described as pure lust. His eyes looked practically black in the shadows created with the sun at his back. Just that look made my thighs clench together as heat spiraled to my core.

In his gaze, I saw everything he wanted to do to me--every swirl of his tongue, every clench of my body, every spark of electricity and connection between us. I wanted it all, and we both knew it. But I couldn't go there. Not right now.

Damn Quinn and his dares. Taking off the last layers I wore would remove every last protection I had against Maddox. If I was naked and he pressed up against me, I wasn't sure I had the will to deny us both what we so clearly wanted.

But a dare's a dare. So, I tossed one last evil eye at Quinn before swimming toward shore. I stayed deep enough in the water that if I crouched down, I wouldn't expose myself to the guys, but I could still toss my clothes up on the shore so they wouldn't sink to the bottom of the pond. With my back facing them, I unhooked my bra before sliding the straps off my arms and tossing it to the shore. I looked back over my shoulder at Maddox, and I swore he'd moved closer.

Turning back toward the shore, I slid my thong down my legs and tossed the soaking fabric onto the sand beside my bra. I had a feeling it'd still be soaking even if we weren't swimming right now after being so close to Maddox.

The warm water caressed my newly exposed skin, and I turned back to face the guys. "Done. Now it's my turn." I swam out a little further until the water came up to just below my shoulders and faced Maddox, who was staring down into the water right at my breasts. I sucked in a breath, trying to act like I didn't care. In reality, his gaze felt like a warm caress, exactly where I wished his hands were.

"Maddox. Truth or dare?" I challenged.

I didn't think it was possible, but his eyes darkened even further. "Truth."

Swallowing hard, a million questions ran through my mind. There was so much I wanted to know, how could I possibly settle in on just one? But this was my chance to find out where we stood. More than anything in our past, this was what I needed to know most. "What do you want from me?" I asked, the words coming out louder than I'd intended because I was afraid if I didn't get them out, I wouldn't be able to.

A frown creased his brow as he watched me. "Isn't it obvious?" he answered my question with one of his own as he swam toward me. He stopped right in front of me, so he was looking down into my eyes, the intensity of his burning almost like fire. As he found his footing, he reached out and ran his fingertips down the side of my face, and I leaned into his touch but didn't break eye contact. "Everything," he whispered.

My heart clenched as my chest flooded with warmth. The way he was looking at me left no doubt as to his meaning. He wanted me. He wanted *more*. But could I believe he wouldn't walk away again when things got tough?

And even if I did, what would I do about the ranch? About Yates and the contract I signed?

My thoughts were obliterated when he lowered his mouth to mine. My hands moved on their own to glide up his chest and to the back of his neck, pulling him closer. I melted into him as he dotted my jaw with soft kisses. His lips covered mine again, and we devoured each other, both of us starved for the other. I didn't know what would happen in the future, but right now, I didn't care. Everything around us disappeared into nothingness as we got lost in each other.

A flood of heat rushed through my body as Maddox pressed himself against me, his hips pressing into mine. I felt the thick ridge of his growing erection press against me, and I moaned softly in the back of my throat, which just made him press closer.

Quinn clearing his throat behind us finally had me yanking my mouth away from Maddox, and I sucked in air. I didn't think I breathed for the entirety of that kiss, and my knees were weak and shaky.

"Goddamn," Maddox cursed under his breath, and I had to agree. Every time we kissed, it got better and better.

"As much fun as it is to watch you two suck face, we've got a game to finish," Quinn grumbled.

Maddox ran a hand up to his face and through his hair before focusing back on Quinn. "Truth or dare, Quinny?"

I didn't miss how he'd used my nickname for Quinn, and it gave me the warm fuzzies when Quinn didn't correct him. Instead, he flashed him a devilish smile. "Dare."

"You're feeling left out? I dare you to come kiss me," he said, and my eyebrows shot up in surprise. Maddox wore a smirk, and his eyes challenged Quinn. Maddox held up his finger. "One time only," he clarified.

Quinn practically dove for Maddox, and I giggled. "You just made his entire life," I told him, moving aside as Quinn stepped right in front of him. If Maddox thought Quinn was the type of guy who was shy and wouldn't take exactly what he wanted, he was in for quite the surprise.

Quinn gently placed his hands on both sides of Maddox's face and leaned in, kissing him once gently, and I was surprised when Maddox closed his eyes and leaned in, their lips connecting again. This time, Quinn deepened the kiss, and I watched basically the hottest thing I'd ever seen happen right in front of me. Both of their hands stayed above the shoulders, and the kiss was surprisingly gentle and over much too quickly. I could have watched them kiss all night long.

When Quinn pulled away, I watched his cheeks turn pink, and Maddox stepped back once and winked at me before he said, "Don't make it weird."

Quinn giggled, and I had to laugh with him. I'd only heard him giggle a couple of times, and it always made me laugh because he wasn't the giggling type. He was this big macho cowboy-type of guy, so when he lost it, I did, too. Finally, Maddox joined in, and all the tension that could have been there was just gone as we all cracked up.

I drifted backwards to float on my back again with a soft smile on my face, and I felt Maddox take my hand, weaving our fingers together. He tugged me upright and leaned in to whisper in my ear. "You know I did that for you, right? Did you enjoy the show?"

I bit my lip. "It was hot as hell."

He nodded once. "Burn it into your memory because it's not happening again. I may be comfortable with my sexuality, but I don't usually swing that way. Besides, I only want one person on this entire planet, and she's standing here in my arms." He snaked his arms around my waist and pulled me against his chest, but I didn't fight him.

Once Quinn had gathered himself, he came back over to us. "Last round. Maddox, truth or dare?"

Maddox sighed, resigned. "Last round." He moved his hand down until it rested on the curve right above my ass. If he inched it just a tiny bit lower, he'd be able to grab me, and I shimmied a little because I couldn't help myself, I wanted him to grab me and pull me against him. He chuckled darkly against my ear and lowered his hand, squeezing me once before moving it back up. "Dare."

"Strip off the rest of your clothes and go skinny dipping," Quinn dared.

"Not very original," Maddox said with a smirk before letting me go and wading toward the shore. Instead of staying in the water like I had, he waited until he was on the shoreline before stripping off his black boxer briefs. He turned back around before striking a pose and gave Quinn and me both an eyeful before he waded back into the water.

I didn't even try to hide the fact my eyes roamed every part of his body, and he did not disappoint. If anything, his muscular torso that led down to a delicious vee at his hips that pointed directly at his very big and semi-hard cock was better than I'd fantasized about. Real-life Maddox was temptation incarnate. I suddenly found myself fighting off a deep, intense craving to get up close and personal with every last part of the crazy hot man making his way toward me.

My cheeks heated up. I wasn't sure what to do with myself now that we were both naked. The look in his eye told me he had some ideas. As if on cue, Quinn cleared his throat. "Well, I think I'll head back and start dinner. You're staying the night, right, Mad?"

Maddox's smirk grew into a grin as he nodded. My head whipped around to Quinn, and I tried to catch his eye, but he was doing a great job of avoiding me. Instead, he swam toward the shore and climbed out completely naked. I'd seen Quinn naked so many times it didn't phase me at this point, but he was the only man I'd ever seen that way until today.

I was totally out of my depth, and now Quinn was leaving. I moved water with my arms while I balanced on the sandy lake bottom on my tiptoes with my eyes locked on Maddox. I was waiting to see what he was going to do.

A few seconds later, I got my answer when he stopped right in front of me and ran his fingertips down my arm before sliding his palm against my lower back and pulling me closer. "Looks like we're about to be all alone out here," he whispered against the shell of my ear, and I shivered under his touch.

"Looks like it," I managed to say, though I was surprised I got even that out. We were both breathing heavily, our chests pressing closer together with every breath. Just as I heard Quinn riding off on Daisy, Maddox lowered his mouth to my neck, sucking my skin gently. My head fell back as I closed my eyes, and he took advantage of it, nipping and kissing along my neck until he got up to my jaw.

He leaned back, his dark eyes looking back and forth between mine, the silent question in them. I closed my eyes slowly, letting him know I wanted this, and his warm lips covered mine. This kiss wasn't frantic, but it was consuming all the same. He was sweet, kissing me lazily, taking his time as if he had nowhere he'd rather be. His hand pressed harder into my lower back as his other hand slid up to my hair, where he gathered it into his fingers, tangling them in the wild mess of my curls.

I had no idea how much time had passed. All I knew was that my toes were curled into the lake's sandy bottom, and my body ached for him to be closer. No matter how close we pressed together, it wasn't close enough. His hard-on pressed into me, sliding against the slick skin of my hips and belly, and I moaned, letting my hand wander down his chest and lower until I'd explored every defined ridge of his abs.

I didn't let my hand drop below his abs, though. If I did, I knew I wouldn't be able to stop myself from taking this further, and there were no clothes between us to get in the way.

Maddox pulled back slightly, whispering against my lips, "Truth or dare?"

My lips curled into a smile against his as I kissed him again. "Truth."

He leaned even further back so that he could properly look into my eyes. He studied me for a long time before he sighed and asked me what he obviously had been wanting to know. "What's going on with you and this Yates guy?"

My whole body stiffened, and he tried to pull me closer, but I resisted. It wasn't that I didn't want to be in his arms. The opposite, actually. That was the *only* place I ever wanted to be. But not like this. Not when I was technically engaged to someone else, even if that person was a stranger. Not when I was lying to the man standing in front of me, doing his best to make up for all of his past mistakes.

God, I was a horrible person.

The worst part was I couldn't come clean and tell him the truth even if I wanted to. Maddox wasn't the kind of guy to take the deal Yates had cornered me into without doing something about it. He already hated my fake fiance. What would he do to him when he found out he'd taken advantage of the fact I was desperate and needed help?

And yeah, I was starting to see this whole deal for what it really was - Yates taking advantage of me. But I wasn't without blame, and I made my bed. Now it was time to lie in it. Besides, I still needed Yates's help to save this place, even if I had a feeling I didn't have even close to the whole picture as to why he wanted to marry me in the first place.

Did it really matter, though? I'd agreed, and now I was stuck.

"What do you mean? We're getting married." I thought I'd try to act like everything was fine.

Maddox let me go and growled in frustration as his eyes stayed locked on mine. I watched as he worked the muscles in his jaw, clenching them tightly while his eyes searched mine. "You know that's not what I meant. You're not stupid, so don't act like you are," he snapped. "I mean this. Right here." He waved his arm at me. "You're kissing me, and we're both naked. I can tell you want more from me, and you sure as fuck know I want more from you."

"We're naked because of truth or dare," I weakly pointed out.

He narrowed his eyes. "That's bullshit, and you know it. You could have said no. You could have left with Quinn. You could have slapped me across the face when I tried to kiss you. But you didn't. To any of it."

He moved closer to me again, his intense gaze bored into me. "Want to know what I think? I think you don't love him. You don't even like him. So, why are you doing this, Freckles? What does he have on you?" His fingers ran up and down my spine. I shivered as he left goosebumps in the wake of his touch.

Maddox leaned closer, close enough that I could kiss him if I just tilted my head up a tiny bit. "Look at how your body responds to my touch," he murmured, gently running his fingertips across my heated skin. "I know you don't want him. You've only ever wanted me, and we both know it. So, tell me why you're really marrying him and let me help you."

His voice was hypnotic to me, and I was putty in his hands again. I didn't think a time would come where I wouldn't be weak for this man. I'd spent my entire life wanting him, and he was serving himself up to me on a silver platter, and there was nothing I could do about it.

Maddox was the worst kind of torture.

"I can't," I whispered, and he shifted back to look at me again.

"Can't or won't?"

"Can't," I said, and he sighed, letting me go and putting some distance between us.

"Fuck. I don't know what to do here, Freckles. I can tell you don't want to do this. The expression on your face whenever he's around. The way your body responds to me and not him. It paints a picture I don't like, and I can't help feeling like there's a whole lot more going on here. I know I left, but I'm back now, and I'm sure as fuck not going anywhere. Maybe eventually you'll trust me enough to let me in," he said, his shoulders tense as he turned and made his way back to the shore.

"Where are you going?" I called after him as fear clawed up my throat, and my heart started to race. Was he going to leave? Would I ever see him again?

"Home. I need some time to think," he called out as he waded out of the water completely naked, bending to pick up his clothes and pulling them on before climbing up on his black stallion. He never even looked back at me.

As I watched him ride away, I couldn't help but wonder if I was making a huge mistake by not just coming clean and telling him the truth about what's going on. But if I broke the NDA and Yates found out, and I had to assume he would, there'd be no way I could handle the financial consequences of that, let alone save the farm.

Making my way to the shore, I watched Maddox on the horizon until he was only a tiny dot. I wanted to cling to every second I could and hoped that wasn't the last time I'd ever see him.

EIGHTEEN
MADDOX

Stepping out of the shower, I towel dried my hair. Droplets of water ran down my chest, and I drug the towel over my skin, catching them before they hit the floor. I slept like absolute shit last night, tossing and turning because I couldn't shut my goddamn brain off about Ryan and what she was hiding from me. Before I hopped in the shower this morning, I texted Connor and asked him to bring over coffee because I'd never make it through today if I didn't take in a fuck ton of caffeine.

I pulled on a black t-shirt and jeans, and I padded out to the kitchen where he already sat waiting. He nodded toward the styrofoam cup sitting on the table across from him, and I took the seat in front of it. "Thanks," I mumbled, lifting the cup to my mouth and enjoying the hot, bitter burn.

Connor watched me as he sipped his own coffee. The silence stretched out between us, but it wasn't uncomfortable. Finally, he spoke up. "You're up early," he noted.

I nodded. "I'm about to head next door for the day."

"You do realize you're not a rancher, right? You have three guys waiting for you to figure your shit out and get back so you can start working on your next album." He watched me over the top of his cup as he sipped again, his posture deceptively relaxed. I knew better.

"Of course I know I'm not a fucking rancher, Connor. And I don't want to be. But that girl over there?" I pointed in the direction of Ryan's house. "She needs help, and I need her. So until the guys need me back, I'm staying here until I can figure out what the fuck is going on between Ryan and that dickhead Yates."

Connor leaned forward and rested his arms on the tabletop, gripping his cup between his giant hands. It was almost funny how small the cup looked between them. He absently spun it around between his fingers. "I've started digging, but so far haven't turned up much on him. That's not all that surprising if he has something to hide. Someone with money like he has would hire the best to cover their tracks. I'll keep looking, but if I keep hitting walls and she doesn't give you anything, we need to decide if you want to dig deeper or just leave it alone and let her go."

My eyes narrowed as I glared at him across the table. "I will *never* let her go. Even if I have to wait forever. I spent so fucking long denying how I really felt, pushing it down and fucking around to forget. Now that I admitted that shit to myself, there's no going back. Ryan's what I want, and I'll do whatever I have to do to figure out what the fuck is going on. I know there's something not right about this whole situation. I can feel it in my fucking bones, Connor."

He sighed as if he'd already resigned himself, he knew that was what I was going to say. "I had a feeling. You know I'll call in my guys if I need to."

"I know. I really want her to tell me what's going on, though. I want to earn her trust, and so far, I've spent twelve years doing a terrible fucking job. I'm not surprised she won't talk to me. But I'm done running, so maybe I can get her to tell me, and we won't need your team." I glanced down at the digital screen on my wrist and realized I was going to be late for breakfast.

"Thanks for the coffee, but I gotta run. How much longer are you staying?" I asked, standing and tossing my empty cup in the trash. I made a mental note to hire a cleaning crew to come to deal with this place because I didn't have time to mess with that shit myself, and Russell hadn't exactly taken care of the house when he owned it.

"I'm heading back this afternoon, actually. True's got some promo stuff he's doing, and Zen wants to be with him. Kennedy called me this morning." He chuckled. "She's freaking the fuck out about me not being there. Hormones," he said with a grin as if that were the only reason she'd be freaking out. We both knew that wasn't it, though. She liked Julian, Sebastian, and Indy just fine, but the only one on Connor's team she really trusted with her husband's safety was the man himself, and he'd been gone long enough.

I smirked. "Don't let her hear you say that shit."

Connor laughed. "I won't. If you need me, call. Otherwise, I'll see you when you get back." He groaned. "Fuck. I just realized I'm gonna have to find a new wingman, aren't I?"

Walking around the table, I clapped him on the shoulder as he stood. "Sorry, man. Looks like it."

"You fucking rock stars. You're supposed to be debauched. Corrupt degenerates. Instead, I get stuck with the group who's *monogamous*." He said the last word like it tasted bad coming out of his mouth, and I laughed, not really able to believe that I was being included in that group. What the hell was happening to me?

"I'm starting to think with the right woman, monogamy isn't that bad." I shrugged. "It doesn't feel like a bad thing when she's the only one you want. Other girls just don't compare."

"Yeah, you go ahead and keep that shit to yourself. I don't want to catch it," he shuddered.

I stepped around him to the counter, grabbing my keys and my phone and shoving them in my pockets before sliding my sunglasses onto my face. "Can you lock up when you leave?"

He nodded. "I'll text you when my flight lands."

With one last glance around the house to make sure I had everything, I slid into my boots, quickly lacing them up and taking off for Ryan's. They'd be just starting breakfast, and I was already running late.

I started jogging and found myself climbing the steps to her front porch in only a few minutes.

I rapped my knuckles on the screen door and waited until Quinn swung the door open. He visibly relaxed when he saw it was me. "Morning, Quinny."

A smile tugged at his lips. "Fuck, am I glad to see you."

I chuckled. "That's exactly the reaction I want people to have when I grace them with my presence." I stepped inside, moving past him into the hall, noticing the warm, sweet smell in the air. "What's for breakfast?"

He closed the door and followed me down the hall toward the dining room. "Chocolate chip scones and avocado toast."

I raised my eyebrow. "You're not going all California on me, are you?"

"Just wanted you to feel at home with your snobby millennial breakfast foods."

I liked that Quinn didn't take my teasing lying down and instead volleyed that shit right back at me. "Dude, you're a millennial, too."

"Yeah, and I proudly fit the stereotype. I like avocado toast. Sue me," he laughed.

Pulling out one of the chairs, I plopped down in it, grabbing a scone and a piece of toast before Ryan walked in. She stopped mid-stride, stumbling as a little yelp escaped her throat when she saw me sitting here. My chest constricted at the sight of her. "You okay, Freckles?" I asked, knowing the pet name would probably make her squirm a little. My smirk turned into a grin when she started to stammer.

"Y-you... I..." She took a deep breath and stepped the rest of the way into the room, taking the seat next to Quinn. "I didn't expect to see you here this morning after you bailed on the movie last night," she admitted. I watched her, trying to figure out how she felt about last night, but all I saw in her eyes was fear and a little bit of relief. She thought I was going to leave again, and I couldn't blame anyone but myself for putting those doubts in her mind.

I got up from where I sat across from her and moved around the table, crouching down by her side. I pulled her hand into mine and looked up into her questioning gaze. "I know you might not believe me yet, but I'm not going anywhere unless you come with me. Even if you marry that absolute-"

Quinn interrupted with a well-placed throat clearing, and I swallowed back the words I wanted to say. My eyes darted over to him for a second, and I caught his wink and bit my cheek to stop from laughing.

Taking a deep breath, I continued. "Even if you marry Yates, I'll still be here."

"How can you promise that? You've got Shadow Phoenix. The guys depend on you, and you've got millions of fans around the world who look forward to your music. You can't stay here and wait around for me." She sounded so sure of herself, sure of what she thought I was capable of.

She had no fucking idea. "Oh, Freckles. I can and I will. Maybe you've forgotten since it's been a long time, but I get whatever the fuck I want, and I don't quit until it's mine. You… you've always been mine. We both just forgot for a while. But not anymore. You're what I want, and I don't care if it takes my whole goddamn life. I. Will. Wait."

She sucked in a breath and bit her lip. Reaching up, I brushed my thumb across and tugged her lip out from between her teeth. "If anyone's going to bite your lip, it's going to be me."

"Damn," I heard Quinn mutter from behind Ryan.

"I don't really know what to say," she confessed, playing with the hem of her white tank top. I noticed that it was a habit of hers. Her dark wavy hair fell over her shoulder, and I brushed it back, running my fingers through the silky strands so I could see her stunning face and those tiny light Freckles I loved so much that dotted almost every inch of it.

"Don't say anything. But you've got less than two weeks until the wedding, and I'm going to be here every single goddamn day proving to you that you belong with me, that I'm not going anywhere, and that no matter what you decide, I'll always be here. That's a motherfucking promise." I brought her hand to my mouth, kissing the back of it before letting go and sitting back down.

"What's the plan for the day?" Quinn asked, breaking the tension as he talked with his mouth full of scone. He spit a couple of crumbs out when he talked, and I shook my head.

"Christ, Quinny. At least swallow your mouth full of food first," I said, wrinkling my nose. Fucking gross.

He just laughed at me, though. I was starting to think he liked getting under my skin.

"We're clearing out ditches and checking the irrigation today," Ryan explained, and I bit back a groan. Fuck, I hated ranch chores. Digging ditches all day? It wasn't exactly a day in my regular life. From what she said, she and Quinn hated this shit just as much as I did, but they were stuck, and neither one of them was complaining, so I had to keep my mouth shut and try to keep up.

It didn't matter if we burned under the sun all goddamn day breaking our backs and sweating our asses off. As long as I was with Ryan, I'd never complain about a second of it. But fuck if I didn't want to hire her all the help she could use and set her free. Once I earned her trust, I'd bring it up but not a second sooner.

𝄞

The past few days went quickly and dragged at the same time. Every second I got to spend with Ryan that we weren't doing goddamn ranch chores went way too fast, and every minute we were breaking our bodies trying to keep up with the cattle and everything that needed to be done went way too fucking slow.

One thing was for sure - I was working muscles I never even knew I had, and when I got back to LA, my trainer would sure as fuck be impressed. I missed my normal daily workouts. They were easy compared to the shit I was doing this week. No wonder Quinn looked like a fucking fitness model.

After another grueling as fuck morning, I managed to plan ahead and pull off a surprise for my girl. Even if she wasn't ready to admit it yet, that's what she was to me. That's what she'd always be. So, I'd asked her to meet me by the pond for lunch today. I knew her favorite spot to chill was under the little grove of trees that grew right near the water's edge. There was a soft patch of grass underneath, and since I had a minute to set up, I pulled the blanket I'd tied to Hex's saddle down.

Once the blanket was spread out, I walked back to Hex, patting his side gently. Then, I unpacked the lunch I packed us and carried it over to the blanket. Sinking down, I stretched out my legs and closed my eyes, enjoying the shade while waiting for Ryan.

I didn't have to wait long. The sound of hooves approaching had me opening my eyes and taking her in. God, she was fucking perfect. Her long, dark wavy hair was down today flowing behind her as the breeze brushed past her face. Her hips swayed side to side with the motion of her horse, and her skin was sunkissed and glistened from the morning spent in the sun.

Watching her on top of the horse had me picturing her on top of me as her body writhed above, her head thrown back as I worshipped her. Swallowing hard, I sat up, trying to hide how hard my dick was right now. I didn't want to show how much I wanted to relieve the pressure by unzipping my jeans because the zipper was currently digging into the sensitive flesh of my cock.

I watched her pull back on the reins as she swung her leg over the saddle and stepped down. She had a playful tilt to her lips as she made her way over to me. "What's all this?" she asked, taking in the blanket and the lunch I'd packed for us.

"A picnic. Come sit," I answered, patting the blanket right next to me and hoping she'd take the invitation. She did, and my heart sped up at how close she was. Her orange and vanilla scent drifted past me, and I inhaled, taking her all in. This week I made it a point of stepping back, though. I made it clear where we stood, but until I'd earned her trust, I wasn't going to push her anymore. If she wanted me, I'd never turn her away. But she had to be the one to come to me.

She leaned against me, her back leaned up against my side while she kicked off her boots and grabbed a bottle of water and a sandwich. "You know, in all the years I've lived here, I don't think I've ever had a picnic out here," she mused.

"Glad I could be your first," I flirted, hoping she'd let me be more than one first by the time we'd figured everything out.

She just hummed against me as she ate her sandwich, the vibration carrying up my arm. I had an ulterior motive for this picnic. I wanted to know what her hopes and dreams were so I could help make them happen, and I planned to ask her all about them. I knew she didn't want to be stuck on this ranch for the rest of her life. "Hey, Freckles?"

She turned and looked up through her sinfully long eyelashes, her wide doe eyes captivating me and making me forget what I wanted to ask. "Yeah?"

"Uh…" I frantically searched my mind, trying to remember where I was going with this. "What do you want out of your life?" I finally asked, breathing a sigh of relief that I managed to come up with something and not make a total fool out of myself.

I watched as her eyebrows drew together, and an adorable little wrinkle formed between them on her forehead. "What do you mean?"

"I mean, where do you see yourself in the future? In a couple of years? Do you still want to be here doing this?" I wondered, scanning the miles of green grass spread out in front of us.

"I don't know," she mumbled around her sandwich, dropping her eyes down to the blanket.

I turned so that we were facing each other and she had to look at me. "That's not true, Freckles. I think you do know, but you're too afraid to admit it."

She huffed out a breath and finished swallowing her bite before lifting her eyes to meet mine. She stared back at me with determination and fire, which was one of the things I loved most about Ryan. She didn't cower or cry or pout. She owned her shit, and she worked hard to make it happen. I respected the fuck out of her.

"Fine. That dream I had? The one I told you about where I wanted to be a cop? I never let that go. I don't want to be stuck out here in the middle of fucking nowhere completely miserable and wasting away as my body slowly breaks down. And for what? So people can have their steaks and hamburgers? I fucking hate it, okay?"

She was breathing hard, and I was a little bit stunned at the way she just put it all out there. I didn't think I'd ever heard her talk like that before, but I liked it. I scooted closer to her and rubbed her arm with my hand. She was shaking underneath my palm, so I pulled her against me and wrapped her up in my arms. I couldn't keep my distance no matter how hard I tried.

I also hadn't missed that her dream of getting the fuck out of here and becoming a cop hadn't mentioned one thing about her future husband. I filed that away to analyze later. I figured if I brought it up now, she'd shut down, and that was the last thing I wanted.

"You can do anything you want, and I'll be right beside you to make sure it happens," I vowed, my words slightly muffled as I talked into her hair. But I didn't want to let her go.

She pulled out of my grasp but still held onto my hand. "I want to help people. I feel called to it in every cell of my being. Watching what you went through, Mad… It did something to me. I'll never forget how your face used to look when you'd show up at my window." My jaw clenched as the memories threatened to pop up, but I focused back on her, refusing to acknowledge my past right now.

The stormy determination shining in her eyes even inspired me. It made me want to be better, *do* better. "You were always my safe haven, Freckles. You'd make an excellent cop," I assured her. "But what's stopping you?"

She looked around and sighed, her shoulders slumping. "This place. It's like a chain around my neck. I can't let it go because it's my parent's dream. It's the only home my dad's ever known. But if I don't do something, I'll never get out."

"I can help with that, you know," I volunteered, but she shook her head.

"I can't let you do that. This is my mess, and I have to figure it out." She finished her sandwich and stood up, dusting off her hands. "Ready to get back to work?" I hadn't missed the change in subject when I offered to help, or how she said she needed to figure it out. I'd learned a lot at this lunch, even if she hadn't meant to give much away.

First, Ryan still held onto her dream of being a cop. Yates didn't seem like the kind of guy who was interested in anything other than a trophy wife, so I wondered how she figured she'd pull off convincing him to be okay with her plans.

Second, she hadn't mentioned anything about her soon-to-be husband in her future or any plans to start a family.

And third, and probably most important, she was actively looking for a way to get out of here. To free her of this place so she could follow her dream. And if she was so eager to leave, why wouldn't she take me up on my offer to help? Did she already have plans in motion? And was that what she was doing with the jackass she was marrying? Nothing added up.

My mind raced with so many thoughts, I hadn't heard Ryan talking to me. "What was that, Freckles?" I asked, my attention completely focused on her again as I silenced my thoughts. I'd figure all that shit out later. Right now, she was what was important.

"I asked you why you've been sort of distant this week. Did I do something wrong?"

"No. But you know where I stand, and I don't want to keep feeling like I'm pushing you somewhere you don't want to go. I'm here, I'm around every single day because I'm trying to show you that you can count on me. I'm not going anywhere. And I haven't made it a secret that I hope you'll call off the wedding and give me a chance." I reached out and grabbed her hand, pulling her closer to me so that we stood chest to chest. I smoothed her hair back out of her face and rested my palm against her neck, feeling her pulse racing under her skin.

"But make no mistake. If you come to me? It's game fucking *on*. I have no problems finishing whatever you want to start, Freckles," I promised with a dark chuckle.

"Oh, no?" she whispered, her lips brushing against mine before we crashed together. I wrapped my arms around her, tangling one of my hands in her hair as she pushed her tongue into my mouth. I walked us backward until I pinned her body up against a tree. I reached down and grabbed under her thighs, picking her up so her legs wrapped around my waist, and I groaned at the feeling of her perfection pressed against me.

I kissed her long and hard, neither of us wanting to be the first to let the other go. She gripped me between her thighs, so I moved one hand up her hip and under her shirt, caressing the silky skin of her stomach. My fingers danced up her body until I rubbed my thumb across the hardened nipple poking through the thin lace of her bra.

I swallowed her moan as she arched into my hand, silently begging for more. Moving my hand, I slid it underneath the thin material and pushed it up out of the way so my fingers could play with no barriers between us. I ran my thumb across her again, and she threw her head back and cried out. Lifting her shirt, I lowered my mouth, blowing my hot breath against her stiff peak before swirling my tongue around it.

When she pressed her pussy against me, I nearly lost it. It didn't matter that we both had multiple layers of fabric between us. I wanted to rip every fucking piece of cloth off our bodies and lay her down right here and claim her as mine.

But she deserved better.

She wasn't slowing down, but I needed to. I had to earn her trust, and to do that, I had to put her above myself. That wasn't something I'd ever tried to do before. I was a selfish motherfucker who got whatever he wanted. But if I wanted Ryan, I had to change starting right now.

I moved back, pulling her shirt back into place and slowing our kisses down until I placed one more on her lips and let her down. She looked incredible. Her hair was wild, and her lips were pink and swollen, and my chest swelled because *I* did that to her. I had as much of an effect on her as she did on me.

I rested my forehead against hers and closed my eyes while we both caught our breath. Her fingers moved lightly through the hair at the back of my neck as we stood in each other's arms, not saying anything. There wasn't anything else to say.

I had to figure out what her dickhead fiance had that I didn't and fast. With only a week until the wedding, I was starting to panic that I might actually lose her to another man. If that happened, I'd be broken.

As she shifted in my arms, I swore she was made for me, and I never wanted to let her go. No matter what it took, Ryan would always be mine, but the clock was ticking.

NINETEEN
RYAN

The past week had gone by so fast, my head was spinning. I guessed that was what happened when you were dreading what was coming next. I'd tried living in denial the entire week, pretending that I wasn't about to marry myself off to a perfect stranger, one I no longer had any interest in whatsoever.

Yates had been texting and calling all week, checking in with me and making sure I was still on board to do this. His tone hadn't been exactly threatening, but he was putting pressure on me. He'd also been trying to be sweet, telling me that his mother had hired a wedding planner, and I didn't need to worry about anything.

But here it was Friday morning, and I couldn't pretend this wasn't happening anymore. I had to drive to Dallas this morning with Quinn to meet up with my sisters at the Rutherford Estate. Yeah, I still couldn't believe I was about to marry into a family with an *estate*. Still, my disbelief didn't change the fact that this was happening.

The past two weeks almost felt like a dream. I'd gotten Maddox back, and he actually wanted me. I had no idea what I was doing or how any of this was going to work out. I just kept putting one foot in front of the other, living in a blissful state of denial where Yates only existed in this shiny little box I shoved him into in my mind, and he only popped out when he called or texted.

I wanted to tell Maddox everything so incredibly bad. There were multiple times since our picnic that the words almost spilled out of my mouth, confessing every sordid detail to him like he deserved. But, I held back. I didn't doubt that he meant everything he said. Over the past month, his actions proved to me that he really was still that protective and possessive boy he was all those years ago.

Yet I couldn't bring myself to ask for his help. I'd always been independent and strong, and for some reason asking him to dig me out of this situation felt wrong. I pulled out my phone to send him a text. We'd been texting nonstop all week when we weren't actually together. Whenever my phone buzzed or lit up this week, a smile would break out across my face.

Ryan: Getting ready to leave now. Taking Quinny with me. Wish you were coming too.

Maddox: Text me when you get there.

His message was a lot shorter than the ones he'd been sending all week, and I had to believe it was because I was still going through with all of this, and it weighed just as heavily on him as it was me. Maybe even more so because he didn't know the truth of the situation. I knew I was hurting him. I knew it, and I was doing it anyway. I was officially a terrible person.

With a heavy sigh, I pushed up off my bed and grabbed the bag I'd packed. I was leaving for Dallas as soon as Quinn was ready, and I wouldn't be coming home until after my honeymoon. I shuddered as I thought about a week away with Yates once we were married. Alone time with him was not what I wanted, but it was the price I had to pay.

Quinn popped his head into my room, looking as shitty as I felt. "Ready?" I knew he was a little bit mad at me for going through with this, too, especially since he was the only one who knew the truth. But he'd stand by my side no matter what, and I loved him for it.

"Not even a little bit," I answered, slinging my bag over my shoulders and taking one last glance back into my room. Every corner of this place held memories of time spent with the man I really loved and wanted but wasn't sure I'd ever get to have.

The car ride to Dallas with Quinn was mostly silent, outside of the country radio station he had playing quietly in the background. I knew everything he wanted to say to me, and he knew the reasons I'd tell him I had to go through with this. We'd talked ourselves out over the past month, and now there was nothing left to say.

I stared down at my phone, willing Maddox to send me something, *anything*, to show me he wasn't going to bail on me again. He was the main reason I got through these past two weeks without breaking down. I needed him even more now, even if I knew it wasn't fair.

"Jesus Christ," Quinn's murmured curse had me lifting my face off of the blank screen of my phone and looking out the windshield at the monstrous *Rutherford Estate*. "Are these people for real?" he asked, but I didn't think he expected me to answer.

"Unfortunately," I muttered.

Quinn turned to me, his jaw clenched. "Are you *seriously* going to go through with this bullshit, Ryan?"

Slumping down in the seat, I broke eye contact with him and stared back at the giant house looming in the distance. "I don't have a choice, Quinn."

He slammed his hand down on the steering wheel. "Yes, you fucking do, Ryan! Why are you so determined to fuck up your life by doing this? You don't have to. No one is making you but *you*. Stop being an idiot. Maddox would step in and help. You know he would."

I hesitated. "Quinn…"

"Don't give me whatever bullshit excuse you're about to. I don't want to hear it." His tone was final, and he turned back to stare out the windshield, shifting his truck back into gear and finishing the short drive to where all the other cars were parked. I hated that he was mad at me, but I knew it was between us. Once we left this car, he'd never show it to anyone else. And he'd come around. Quinn would always support me even if he didn't agree.

With one last sigh, I pried the door open, but I turned back to Quinn before I stepped out. "Quinny, please don't be mad at me. I'm trying to do the right thing here," I pleaded with him. I couldn't face this shitshow without my best friend. It already felt like Maddox was mad at me, and if Quinn was mad, I might just break down right here, and I couldn't afford to do that. My family couldn't afford my second thoughts and cold feet. It was time to pull on my big girl panties and lie in the bed I'd made for myself.

Quinn leaned forward and rested his forehead on the steering wheel, a long sigh escaping him. "I'm not mad at you, Ryan. I just think you're making an epically fucking huge mistake marrying this guy for the reasons you are. But you know I'll stand by your side no matter what," he vowed, turning his head and flashing me a small smile.

The tension that'd made its home deep in my chest unfurled at his words, and warmth took its place. I reached over and squeezed his hand. "Thank you," I whispered, fighting off the sting in my eyes. I couldn't show these people any weakness. Yates's mother would eat me alive. I let Quinn's hand go and blinked a few times before steeling myself and stepping out of the truck.

Out of the corner of my eye, I spotted wavy dark hair identical to my own, and I relaxed a little bit more. Justice and Charlie were waving at us from where they'd just pulled up and stepped out of Charlie's car. Quinn and I walked across the expansive circular driveway until I could pull my sisters in for a four-way hug. With arms wrapped around me from every angle, I finally felt strong enough to face this day.

"Just say the word, and we'll get you the hell out of here," Justice offered, squeezing me a little tighter into our makeshift circle.

Sighing, I step back and drop my arms. "No, I need to do this." Quinn shook his head, and Charlie narrowed her eyes, probably picking up on the fact I said *need* instead of *want*. I'd have to watch that more carefully. A bride should want to marry her future husband, not be dreading it or forcing herself to keep moving forward like I was.

"Should we go in? You can meet my future in-laws," I suggested, thumbing over my shoulder toward the monstrosity of a house behind me.

"Can't wait," Charlie muttered under her breath, but the other two stayed quiet and followed in my wake.

Before we could reach the front doors, they were flung open, and a bubbly woman in a skirt suit wearing a headset and carrying a clipboard stepped out. "Welcome! Come in, come in! You must be Ryan," she gushed, shoving her hand toward me. I slipped my hand lightly into hers, and she shook it vigorously before dropping it and gripping her clipboard, gesturing further into the house.

Before I could get a word in, she started talking again, her words moving so quickly they were almost hard to follow. "I'm Daphne. Mrs. Rutherford hired me to handle everything for your wedding tomorrow." She walked slightly in front of me, leading me through tons of halls and rooms until we stepped through a wide set of patio doors that were already open to the massive yard. Surprisingly, I hadn't seen any of Yates's family or the man himself. The house was eerily empty, but now I knew why.

Everyone was out back setting up. There were already a couple of huge white tents looming in the distance. Fabric-covered chairs were being placed strategically around round tables, and I was pretty sure I saw a dance floor being laid down in one of the tents. Rubbing my arm, I glanced around. This was all becoming too real very fast. My heart rate picked up, and my breaths were coming in shorter and shorter pants. If I couldn't calm myself down, I was in danger of freaking the hell out. And just as that realization hit me, Jacqueline strode up to us, her spine ramrod straight and her chin up in a haughty way, like although she was shorter than almost all of us, she thought she still looked down on us.

She definitely didn't look happy to see me if the downturn of her thin lips was any indication. "Ryan, nice to see you again," she said begrudgingly, and I plastered on my fakest smile.

"You, too, Jacqueline. You've done such a great job with everything. Yates and I can't thank you enough. I'm just sorry he couldn't join us this morning." I figured being diplomatic and gracious would be the best ways to get through this even though I had no clue what Yates felt about anything. I did know he'd go along with my speaking for him because he had just as much interest in selling the shit out of the fact we were in love as I did.

"Yes, well, it's not like I had much choice, is it?" she huffed. "Besides, his work is *very* important." She gave me a pointed look as if I should know better and also that I better not fuck up her son's future. Instead of rolling my eyes like I wanted to, I looked behind her and saw what I was assuming was a florist setting out red rose centerpieces, and I tried not to cringe as hard outwardly as I was inwardly. I *hated* red roses. They were so cliche, and in my mind, there was nothing original or romantic about them. If this were my forever wedding, the last thing I'd want was red roses, and her picking them for me showed just how little any of these people knew me.

"No, I suppose not, but I appreciate your help just the same," I acknowledged, gritting my teeth.

Quinn bumped his shoulder into mine, and the motion caught Jacqueline's attention. "Who's this?" she asked, tilting her head to the side as she studied Quinn and my sisters. She was looking at them as if they were a new species she'd never seen before.

"This is my best friend, Quinn, and my sisters Charlie and Justice," I introduced, pointing out who everyone was. Quinn gave her a little wave, and my sisters shot her twin nods of acknowledgment. No one in this group had the warm fuzzies toward one another, but we just had to get through today and tomorrow, and then my people could avoid Yates's people for the most part.

Unfortunately, things wouldn't be so easy for me. But that was the price I'd agreed to pay.

"Pleasure," Jacqueline finally choked out with a complete lack of sincerity before turning on her heel. She tossed over her shoulder, "If you'll excuse me, I've got too much to do to stand around entertaining you and your friends. Try and be on time to the rehearsal dinner, and for the love of god, wear something more respectable than that." She stopped to eye me up and down in a way that made my blood boil like she judged me and found me unworthy of breathing the same air she did.

I didn't bother with a response. Daphne, who reminded me of an excited puppy, didn't shoot me so much as one sympathetic glance before she trailed along at Jacqueline's heel she was hoping for scraps.

"Wow," Quinn marveled. "She's something alright." He pulled out his phone and started texting furiously.

"Who are you texting, Quinny?" I asked.

He snorted. "Maddox. He'd never believe this bitch." He held up his phone, snapping a not-so-discrete picture of Jacqueline's back and Daphne scurrying after her before tapping at his phone again.

I turned to my sisters. "You two want to get the hell out of here?"

They exchanged worried glances before Justice finally spoke up. "Thought you'd never ask."

"Burgers and beer?" Charlie was already pulling her keys out of her purse while Justice swiped at her phone.

Sighing, I tugged on the soft fabric of Quinn's t-shirt. "Let's go."

We all trudged back through the house and into the cars. Quinn's phone vibrated every couple of minutes, but once we finally started driving, he had to ignore it. I hadn't expected he and Maddox to become such good friends so soon, but it made warmth spread throughout my chest that they hit it off so well. Everything about being around Maddox just felt comfortable, the way a relationship should be.

But we didn't have a relationship. At least not more than a friendship with a mutual attraction. After this little excursion to see the progress on the wedding, I had to admit I was starting to freak the hell out. What the hell was I doing? This might be my only chance to be with the guy I'd loved since I was ten years old. Was I really so quick to throw that away?

I rested my forehead on the warm glass. I watched the scenery go by as my unfocused eyes stared out the window. My mind was swimming with scattered thoughts, and I had no idea what to do. Every minute that ticked by felt shorter, like time was speeding up. The panic starting to well up inside of me didn't bode well for me making it through this. Based on the identical *what the fuck is she doing* looks on Charlie and Justices' faces back at the estate, I knew I was in for one hell of an intervention over lunch.

I just hoped they waited until I had a couple of beers in me before they started in because I wasn't sure I had the strength to defend my decision right now. Because if my inhibitions were down, I didn't think I'd be able to lie to them or myself anymore. I might just blow the whole thing up. I was suddenly glad Maddox hadn't come with us because one look into his soulful brown eyes, and I had a feeling I'd make a run for it.

My stomach twisted into knots at the thought of hurting him. I was being unfair to him, asking him to stick around and stand by me through all of this, and I understood why he felt like he couldn't be here today. But that didn't change the fact that I missed him desperately.

We pulled into a low brick building with a black and white sign outside. Raising my eyebrows, I turned to Quinn. "Couldn't have picked a better place for you, could they?"

He chuckled and snatched his phone out of the cupholder, scrolling through the messages he'd missed. He tapped frantically on the glass before sliding it into his pocket and flinging his door open. I followed, hopping down out of his truck and feeling the shock of the impact of my heels on the parking lot's hard-packed dirt. We started walking toward the building as my sister's car pulled into the lot.

I turned to Quinn. "Is he okay?" I didn't have to clarify who I meant, Quinn knew.

He sighed. "Not really, Lancelot. He really thought you'd change your mind by now. To be honest, I thought you would, too. You know how fucked up this all is, right?" he asked gently.

My eyes stung, but I blinked and forced the tears back. If I let them out now, I wasn't sure I'd ever be able to stop. "I know," I whispered, keeping my eyes on my sisters approaching. "But I don't know what else to do."

"Give in to what you really want. Don't make him suffer, but more importantly, don't make *you* suffer. You deserve better than that asshole and his stuck up family, even if it's only temporary. Who knows what kind of shit he might try to pull once you sign on the dotted line?"

I bit my lip because I hadn't thought about that. Would Yates go back on our agreement if the marriage worked for what he needed? What if I couldn't get out once we were married? Shit.

I didn't have a chance to talk about it anymore because my sisters finally made it over to where we were standing by the front door.

"I don't know about you three, but I'm *so* ready for a beer," Charlie declared, pulling the door open. I let out a sigh of relief as the cold, air-conditioned air rushed out the open door and smacked me right in the face.

We found a booth and slid in, not wasting any time ordering a sample of every beer the brewery had on tap plus burgers, fries, and onion rings. Quinn looked like he'd died and gone to heaven. I was so nervous about this morning. I hadn't eaten anything for breakfast, so my stomach was growling loudly, and my mouth watered as the waitress set my burger down in front of me.

I raised one of my glasses of a light-colored beer with little bubbles rising up inside of it. "Thank you guys for being here with me. It means so much that I don't have to do this alone," I toasted, lifting my glass up and toward the middle of the table. The three of them lifted their glasses and clinked with mine before we all sipped.

"Now that we've all eaten and had a beer, I want to know what the hell is going on," Charlie demanded, leveling me with a probing stare.

"I second that," Justice echoed.

Quinn's eyes jumped to mine, but I wasn't sure what he was trying to communicate to me. "What do you mean?" I feigned innocence, blinking a couple of times and looking back at my sister with what I hoped would pass for a curious if not blank expression.

Justice scoffed and folded her arms across her chest. "This is how you're going to play this? Seriously?"

"Play what? I'm getting married tomorrow. It's not exactly a secret." I glanced down, picking at the chipped nail polish on my finger. I couldn't remember when I last painted my nails, and it suddenly dawned on me that I should probably do something about that before tomorrow.

Charlie leaned forward over the table and lowered her voice. "There's no goddamn way you love Yates, Ryan. We know you better than that. Remember how you always used to talk about Maddox? How whenever he came around when we were kids, you paraded him around because you were so smitten with him you couldn't stand to keep it to yourself? *That's* the real you. This?" She gestured at me. "There's something not right about this. I can see the dread in your eyes. There's something you're not telling us."

Justice's gaze softened, and she leaned forward, too. "We can get you out of this, Ryan. You don't even have to tell us what's going on, but please don't marry some guy you don't love. It's not fair to him, not fair to you, and not fair to the guy who actually loves you."

I shot a withering glare at Quinn because only he could have told my sisters about Maddox. He held up his hands. "Don't look at me."

Justice laughed. "Don't kill Quinn, mom told us."

I lowered my head into my hands and groaned. "This family is horrible at keeping secrets."

"Is that such a bad thing?" Charlie asked.

"Yes! This right here is why I can't tell you two what's going on. Just know that what I'm doing tomorrow I'm doing for all the best reasons," I promised, hoping they'd take that and let it go.

"You're really not going to tell us?" Justice questioned.

"Nope," I said, popping a fry into my mouth and washing it down with a sip of the dark beer I'd moved onto. It was much more my speed.

"Fine, keep your secrets, but the offer still stands. We'll drive the getaway car if you need it," Charlie finished, leaning back in her chair. My body relaxed as I realized the interrogation was over.

"Personally, I'm rooting for Maddox," Quinn chimed in with a sly grin.

Both of my sisters laughed. "I think we all are, Quinn," Justice agreed.

"Anyway," I cut in, not wanting to continue that line of conversation. Maddox was my weakness. He always had been. My resolve was weakening by the minute to go through with this sham. If I allowed my mind and heart to open up to the possibility that he could be mine, this whole thing would be over before it really began. "Who's up for mani-pedis?"

With a pretty decent buzz, a full stomach, and most of my favorite people at my side, I felt ready to face the rest of the day. Or at least the next hour.

The four of us had gone shopping after hitting up the nail salon because I needed an outfit to *impress* tonight. I didn't really give a shit what Yates's family and friends thought of me, but he'd been texting me all day about how important it was to him to keep up appearances. We weren't going through with this bogus wedding just for me. He needed something out of it, too, and I agreed to hold up my end of the bargain.

As I stared at myself in the mirror, studying the floor-length deep red jumpsuit I decided on for tonight, I couldn't help but smile as I took in my appearance. I never had any reason to wear anything like this before, but I had to admit it was kind of fun to dress up. The outfit looked like a cross between a dress and pants. It was strapless with a notch out at the front, making it almost look like it had a sweetheart neckline. The pants were wide-legged with a slit up each side, and there was a panel of fabric wrapped around the waist, contouring, and draping along the outside of each leg. The effect was gorgeous, and I didn't know if I'd ever felt this pretty in my life.

Too bad the one person I wanted to see me like this wouldn't be there tonight.

Quinn and I got ready in our hotel room, and my sisters were meeting us at the country club where Yates and his parents insisted we hold our rehearsal dinner. No part of this had been my decision, but I figured one day when I had my real wedding, I could make it into whatever I wanted. I wasn't paying for this one, so I didn't have a choice but to go along with whatever they wanted.

I hoped I'd get to have a real wedding someday to someone I actually loved. My mind flashed to Maddox, and I quickly shoved the unhelpful thought away as Quinn stepped out of the bathroom, looking incredible like he always did. "Damn, Quinny. Gonna try to find a groomsman tonight and work your magic?"

He ducked his head and blushed a little bit, clearing his throat. "Tonight's not about me, but thanks for the compliment, I think." He flashed me the crooked smile I loved so much. "You look stunning, Ryan. I don't think I can say this enough, but that fucktard doesn't deserve you." He lifted his phone at me and snapped a picture.

"What are you doing with that?" I asked, trying to look at his screen, but he held it away from me.

"Sending it to Maddox," he answered as if it were obvious.

"Why?" I screeched, still trying to grab his phone away, jumping to try to reach.

"Because that man is obsessed with you, and I still believe he's the only one who can talk some sense into you. I'm hoping if he sees what he's missing, he'll make a grand gesture."

I stop jumping to look at him suspiciously. "What kind of grand gesture? Because he *can't* embarrass me tonight, Quinn! As much as you don't like Yates, he doesn't deserve that. He's never done anything but be kind to me."

Quinn shook his head. "Maddox would never do that to you, Lancelot. You know better."

Groaning, I rested my head on his shoulder, and he wrapped his arm around me. "I've sure gotten myself into one hell of a mess, haven't I?"

I felt his nod against the top of my head. "But it's not too late to do something about it."

With those words, I retreated into my mind, lost in thought about what to do next.

TWENTY
MADDOX

Drumming my fingers impatiently on the steering wheel, I parked the truck I rented in front of the valet stand. I flung open the door, grabbing the ticket the attendant offered me as I stepped up on the sidewalk and watched Connor climb out of the passenger side.

He glanced into the back seat before shutting the door. "We won't be here long," I promised. "Sorry, there wasn't time to drop your bag at my house before we left."

Connor straightened his suit jacket, smoothing out the non-existent wrinkles. "It's fine," he waved me off. I called him this morning and asked him to fly out here on the band's jet and bring a suit. I was planning to come to this shit show even if he couldn't back me up, but I was sure as fuck glad he was here. If Ryan walked down that aisle tomorrow, I'd need him to save me from myself. Plus, having the jet here would help me make a quick escape if I needed to.

I figured I had one last night to convince her to change her mind, and I sure as fuck wasn't going to blow it. My eyes rose to take in the *Imperial Cedar Country Club*. What a fucking joke. I liked to surround myself with the nicest shit I could afford, but places like this where the environment was stuffy just because it could be always pissed me the fuck off. It was obvious this was the kind of place people came to make themselves feel better than people they considered *lesser*.

Brushing off my irritation, I turned back to Connor as he asked me a question. "What's the plan?"

Shrugging, I looked at the door. "I sort of figured I'd just wing it."

"That's the worst fucking idea I've ever heard," he berated.

"Well, what's your great idea then?"

He held up his hands. "Hey, I'm just here for backup."

Grunting, I rolled my eyes. "Thanks for all the help." I balled my fists and took a couple of deep breaths before relaxing my hands. "I think we should find Quinn and see if we convince him to give me an assist. I don't know what I'm going to do about getting her out, and I'm gonna need his help."

"Fine. So, we find Quinn. I'll run interference if I need to for the asshole," Connor agreed.

With the beginnings of a plan in place, we climbed the stairs to the club. We made our way inside, following the tasteful yet somehow still tacky signs that pointed us toward the event room at the back of the building.

I stopped right outside the door and held out my arm to stop Connor from stepping into the room. "Let me text Quinn so he can get us in," I said, pulling my phone out of my pocket. Quinn texted me all day, keeping me updated on what Ryan was doing, her state of mind, and throwing in plenty of hilarious jabs at Ryan's future in-laws and her husband-to-be.

My phone buzzed as Quinn returned my text, and before I had a chance to respond, he strode out of the doors like he owned the place. He grinned at me and winked at Connor. "Hey, man. I'm glad you came," he said, turning to me as his expression turned serious. "We need to save her from herself." I knew there was some shit going on with Ryan that she didn't want to tell me, or maybe she couldn't. It didn't really matter. At least Quinn was on my side, and I had a feeling that would make tonight a lot easier.

I had plans for my girl tonight, a big last-ditch grand gesture to show her that I wasn't going anywhere. And the truth was even if tomorrow she married the douchecanoe, I'd still do everything I could to be in her life. I didn't give a fuck what he thought or if he tried to keep her away from me. It'd never happen. I'd never allow it.

But I hoped it didn't come to that.

"Do you have any suggestions on how I get her out of here without making a scene?" I inquired.

Quinn shifted his weight from one foot to the other, looking past Connor and me into the expansive room behind us. His eyes locked on someone I assumed was Ryan. "Come in with me and try and lay low until you see an opportunity. Then grab her and make a run for it."

Connor raised his eyebrows but stayed silent.

"Not very sophisticated, is it?" I sighed.

"No, but it'll work. Maybe you can even dance with her and really piss the dickhead off," Quinn suggested, letting out a low chuckle.

My face broke into a devious smile. I fucking loved the idea of dancing with my girl and pissing her fiance off at the same time. Something about that asshole really rubbed me the wrong way, and I knew both Quinn and Connor felt the same way.

The phone I still held in my hand vibrated, and I lifted it to my face. As I read the message from Ryan, my chest flooded with warmth.

Ryan: I wish you were here.

Five simple words made my whole goddamn existence. She had no idea what was in store for her tonight, but I wasn't about to let her down. Somehow I'd known she'd need me here just like I needed her. If she married Yates, it'd be the biggest fucking mistake of her life. I knew it, Quinn knew it, and I hoped I could get her to see it too.

I was aware of Quinn and Connor both staring at me, waiting for me to fill them in. "Ryan texted that she wished I was here," I explained, fighting back my fucking huge-ass smile. But it was time for me to throw my best asshole face on because I was walking into enemy territory.

At least the dinner was over, and I didn't have to listen to a long line of pretentious assholes drone on about useless shit for hours and hours. I came late enough to miss all of that.

We finally stepped through the doors, and I took in the immense room where this spectacle was being held. Quinn scanned the room for Ryan. I took the opportunity to familiarize myself with the exits since I'd probably need to grab Ryan and get the fuck out of here as fast as I could.

This room was so ordinary it almost hurt to look at. It was what Ryan would call cringe-worthy. The room had beige walls, crystal chandeliers, and nothing about it showed any personality. It was fucking boring, and it proved to me that none of these people knew my girl. This place was beige and bougie, Ryan was cowboy boots and wildflowers. She was dancing in the rain and not caring about getting wet. She was warmth and fun and sass all rolled into one stunning package. And this wasn't her. Not even fucking close.

Someday maybe I'd get the chance to give her the wedding she deserved. But first, I had to plead my case and believe she'd hear me out.

When my eyes landed on her across the room, my breath caught in my throat. Everything around and between us faded into nothingness. I couldn't see anything else except the waves of her soft hair flowing down her bare back, her outfit low cut enough that it stopped just above the curve of her waist. The need to run my fingers along the soft skin slammed into me, and I flexed my fingers, trying to get my shit under control.

Taking a deep breath and steeling myself for whatever may happen next, I strode across the room as confidently as possible. I wanted to make sure it looked like I belonged here. In fact, as I saw it, I belonged here more than any of these assholes. Ryan was *mine*.

Finally, I stepped up behind her and danced my fingertips along the warm skin of her lower back. She stiffened until I leaned down and whispered in her ear, brushing my lips along the curve. "I'm all about making your wishes come true, Freckles."

As soon as she heard my voice, she melted against me, and I inhaled her citrus vanilla scent, her closeness calming my tightly wound nerves. Someone coughing softly nearby broke me out of my Ryan-induced spell, and suddenly it was like the volume in the room got turned up. My hand splayed across her lower back while my attention turned to the people standing in front of her.

Charlie and Justice both stared at me with matching incredulous expressions. Justice finally broke the stare-off when she turned to Ryan. "What's he doing here?" she whisper-yelled, and I chuckled, teasing the edge of Ryan's outfit with my fingertips. She shivered underneath my touch, and I didn't even try to hide the smile that broke out on my face.

I didn't wait for Ryan to answer her sister. "I'm here to dance with my girl,"

I proclaimed, even as I felt eyes burning into the back of my skull. My smile widened at the thought that Yates was watching how Ryan responded to my touch. I'd seen them together enough to know she didn't react the same way to him, and it fucking floored me.

Instead of paying attention to him, I reached my other hand down and wove our fingers together, leaning over to whisper in her ear again. "Dance with me." It wasn't a request, and we both knew it. I hadn't originally planned to spend much time here, only enough to grab Ryan and go. But I couldn't miss out on the opportunity to hold her in my arms and press her body to mine. It was made even sweeter by the fact that her fiance was too much of a coward to do anything about me staking my claim on her in public. He cared too much about what people thought.

Lucky for me, I didn't give a fuck.

A small smile lit up her face, and she nodded once, and that was all the permission I needed. I walked backward as I pulled her with me, not wanting to take my eyes off her for even a second. I tugged until her chest met mine, and I wrapped her arm around my neck.

Wrapping my arms around her small waist, she leaned into me, and I turned my head to the side, breathing her in. I closed my eyes for a second as we began to sway gently to the music. I'd never get sick of holding Ryan in my arms.

We made it about halfway through the song before I felt a hard tap on my shoulder. I glanced behind me, not letting go of Ryan even a little bit, to find Yates glaring at me with barely controlled fury. "Mind if I cut in to dance with my fiance?"

"Yeah, actually, I do. Wait for your fucking turn," I snapped before turning back and ignoring him. I could feel the anger radiating off him at my back, but I didn't give a shit. He cared more about how things looked than anything else, so I knew he wouldn't start shit with me right here in the middle of his rehearsal dinner. Finally, he huffed, and out of the corner of my eye, I watched him stalk off the dance floor.

Ryan shook with laughter against me, burying her face in my chest to mask her giggles, and she was so fucking cute. I felt myself smiling. "What's so funny, Freckles?"

She lifted her chin until she looked up at me, her deep brown eyes sparkling. "I don't think Yates is used to people talking to him like that. It was fun to watch," she admitted.

Tearing my gaze away from her, I scanned the room and saw him glowering from the back of the room, his angry glare locked onto Ryan and me. Fuck, I hadn't meant to cause problems at this thing for Ryan, but I knew Yates wasn't going to let my humiliating him go.

The song was wrapping up, so I focused my attention back on my girl. As the last notes played, I reluctantly loosened my grip on her waist and stepped back, feeling Connor step up beside me. One glance at him and I knew shit was about to go down, and I wanted Ryan far away from the drama.

Sliding my palm against her cheek, she leaned into my touch, and I pressed my lips to her forehead. I wanted so much more, but it was all I dared to do right now. "Do you trust me, Freckles?"

Her brow furrowed, and she bit her lip. "Yeah, I think I do."

It wasn't exactly a ringing endorsement, but it was a lot of progress in just a few short weeks. "Good. Meet me at the valet stand in fifteen minutes. I'm kidnapping you tonight."

"But-"

I pressed my finger against her lips, silencing her. "Nope. If I'm about to lose you to another guy, I deserve this one night with you to plead my case."

Her eyes darted between mine while she thought about it, and the moment she gave in, I saw it. Her shoulders relaxed, and her gaze dropped to my mouth, which made my dick twitch. I knew she wanted me just as bad as I wanted her, but she was resisting. Barely, but she was. Which meant I still had work to do and only one night to do it.

Nodding once, she squeezed my bicep before turning and walking off the dance floor and meeting up with her sisters. I didn't take my eyes off of her until she was safely engaged in conversation with the two of them. I refused to let her asshat fiance anywhere near her for the rest of the night.

"Where is he?" I demanded, walking off the dance floor with Connor at my side. Quinn caught my eye and started crossing the room to meet up with us.

"Over there," Connor grunted, pointing toward the back of the room by a set of doors that led outside.

We stopped our path toward Yates to wait for Quinn to catch up. "What's going on?" Quinn asked.

I jerked my head in Yates's direction, where he was surrounded by a couple of his douchebag Ivy League buddies. I bet none of them had ever been punched in the face before. I didn't mind rectifying that situation right now, and I flexed my fingers into a fist as my heart rate picked up. I'd been itching to smash my fist into that fucker's face since the moment I met him and based on the smirk on Connor's face, I knew he wouldn't mind hitting a couple of those guys, either.

And as for Quinn? Well, I had a feeling he hated Yates more than I did, and that was saying something.

Connor shifted his eyes toward where Yates and his cronies huddled near the exit. "The asshole fiance wants to start shit, and we're going to let him," he explained, cracking his knuckles. I swore he just grew a couple of inches and got even broader in the last thirty seconds. I was happy he was on my side.

"Fuck, finally. I get to punch him in the face if it comes to that," Quinn called dibs.

"Only the first punch. I want a shot at him, too," I countered.

"Fine, but that guy with the pink tie is mine," Connor added, narrowing his eyes even more in their direction.

I chuckled darkly. "What'd he do to you?"

He shrugged one massive shoulder. "I don't like how he's looking at me."

"That's enough reason for me. You two ready to do this? No one has ever deserved a punch in the face more than that group of assholes," I insisted, looking to both of the men at my sides.

"Fuck, yes. I've been waiting for this day forever," Quinn enthused with a glare of his own to the corner of the room. We now had their attention. There were four of them and three of us, but I had no doubt none of them would be able to connect so much as one punch. One of them even looked like he'd never spent a day in the gym in his entire life. I was pretty goddamn confident of the outcome of this little altercation Yates was leading us to.

His overconfidence would be his downfall.

We passed right by his group of friends on our way out the exit, one of them deciding to try and step in our path with his arms crossed. Connor's shoulder checked him so hard, he fell into a table and knocked a glass of wine to the floor, spilling sticky red liquid across the shiny marble. I smirked but held in my laugh. Time for that would come later.

Their glares were on my back as we made it out into the hall. Once the doors closed behind us, I spun around to face Yates and his soft as fuck friends. They were even more pathetic up close.

To his credit, Yates didn't immediately cower or try to make peace. He must have felt emboldened by his buddies at his back. Or maybe his ego refused to let him back down. Either way, I wouldn't throw the first punch. I'd wait for him to make his move.

He got within a couple of inches of me and stuck his finger in my face, his cheeks red and his eyes a little wild. "Stay the fuck away from Ryan. She's going to be my wife, and there isn't a goddamn thing you can do about it." He was breathing hard, and I laughed in his face before slapping his finger away.

"I'd love to see you make me, cocksucker," I taunted, my muscles tense and ready for a fight. I almost craved it, the feel of his bones crunching under my fists.

One of his friends stepped up beside him, and Connor tensed next to me but stayed where he was. He knew I could handle my own shit and didn't need him to step in. I flicked my eyes past a fuming Yates to his much smaller buddy beside him and then back again. "Looks like Digby over there wants to get his ass beat. Maybe you should tell him to step back in line," I goaded, chuckling again when the guy's cheeks flared red. I could practically see the steam pouring out of his ears.

One look at Yates's other friends, and I knew they had no intention of helping him out if this came to blows. The watch on my wrist vibrated as I got a text message, and I glanced down to look at it, seeing Ryan's name pop up.

Ryan: I'm at the valet stand. Where are you?

I smiled, and Yates stepped even closer until our chests were practically touching. We were almost the same height, but I was broader, all my time in the gym, and on the ranch paying off. He pressed his palms against my chest and shoved, but I held firm. I wouldn't let him move me even one goddamn inch. His eyes widened in surprise, and my smile grew until it turned menacing.

"Here's what's going to happen. You're going to back the fuck down like the little bitch you are, and then you're going to mind your own goddamn business. My relationship with Ryan? Not your business," I laid out, taking a step closer to him and chuckling when he stepped backward. "If you want to start shit with me, I promise you I have no fucking problem finishing it."

I waited a couple of seconds, but he didn't say anything, so I turned and walked toward the exit, not wanting to waste any more time getting to my girl. I stopped when he yelled out behind me. "Watch your fucking back, Everleigh. You have no idea who you're messing with."

"Bring it on, dickhead," I smirked. He could try, but he'd never actually be able to do shit to me. I'd been dealing with people trying to trap me and take me down for years. He wasn't even worth worrying about.

I refused to give him one more second of my time tonight. Stepping into the warm, humid air, I searched until I spotted Ryan. The way her eyes lit up when she saw me made my heart clench and then race out of control.

I turned back to Connor and Quinn. "Do you mind sharing your room with Connor tonight, Quinny? I'm going to kidnap Ryan."

Quinn looked Connor up and down before he cracked a little grin. "I think I can handle that."

Connor chuckled. "Sorry, bro. I don't swing that way."

They followed me to the valet stand, and I handed over my ticket before wrapping my arm around Ryan's shoulders and pulling her into my side. I dropped a kiss to the top of her head. It'd only been a few minutes since I'd seen her, but I missed her all the same. When we were apart, it felt like a piece of me was missing, and I fucking hated it. What would I do if she actually went through with this whole thing?

I couldn't let myself go there. Tonight, she was mine. That was what mattered right now.

When my black truck pulled up, I reached into the back and tossed Connor his bag. "See you guys in the morning," I told them before pulling open the passenger door and helping Ryan up into the seat.

I ran around and climbed in the driver's side, starting the engine and taking off. It was nearly dark, the last bits of sunlight making the sky pink and purple off toward the west, but the stars were already out above us, and the sky was beautiful.

I hadn't wanted distractions tonight. I wanted just Ryan and me surrounded by the night like a cocoon, fireflies and stars our only light. We drove in comfortable silence for about twenty minutes, our fingers twined together, and her body pressed against mine on the bench seat. Her head rested on my shoulder, and I steered with one hand gripping the top of the wheel. This was my version of heaven, and I could've just kept driving all night, taking us both away from the reality of tomorrow.

Instead, I pulled off the highway into a field filled with corn. It stood tall, and it didn't look like there were any roads through it, but I'd already made arrangements with the farmer earlier today and paid him for any damage my truck did to his crop. Once we were past the tallest stalks, I steered us toward a huge oak tree in the middle of a tall grass field that swayed gently in the light breeze. I parked us near the tree but not underneath it since I wanted to see the stars.

"Stay here," I said, jumping down into the thigh-high grass and walking around to lower the tailgate. I climbed into the truck's bed, unrolling the blankets I'd packed and creating a soft bed for us to stretch out in. I also brought my guitar and drinks and snacks. I'd never played guitar for a girl before. In the band, I played bass, so not many people knew I could play, but it felt too private and intimate for me to play for just anyone.

Satisfied with my setup, I walked back to the passenger side and opened the door, catching Ryan's hand and gently pulling her toward me. I let go of her to grip her hips and helped her out of the truck. I held her close and let her body slide down against mine before her feet touched the ground. Tilting my head down, our eyes locked, and the look of devotion in hers took my breath away until she blinked and it was gone.

"C'mon," I found myself whispering, not wanting to disturb the peacefulness of the night. Linking our hands together, we walked to the back of the truck, and I helped her up into the bed, enjoying the view of her toned ass as she practically shoved it in my face. My fingers twitched with the desire to reach out and slap it, leaving my red handprint behind as proof that she was mine. But I didn't. Now wasn't the time.

"I can't believe you did all this," she gasped, looking around in wonder. She deserved so much more. This was just a simple night out in the country, and I could give her so much. I could give her everything. But how she was looking at me right now like I'd made all her dreams come true? Yeah, I could get fucking used to that.

I shrugged and sat against the wheel well, pulling my guitar into my lap as she settled into the blanket, laying back on one of the pillows and staring up at the stars. "Want a beer?" I offered.

"Sure."

I reached into the cooler and wiped off the water droplets before popping the top, taking a swig, and handing it over to her. She sat up and watched me as I strummed a couple of chords, testing and tweaking the tuning on the guitar. "Are you going to play for me?" she asked, her eyes brightening.

Shrugging, I strummed a couple more chords, happy with how they sounded and started to play one of my favorite Shadow Phoenix songs from our last album. It was the one Zen wrote for Kennedy. I wasn't the best singer in the band, but I could hold my own, and as I quietly finished the last few notes, I heard Ryan sniffle. I looked up at her and saw her swipe at her eyes.

Setting my guitar down, I moved to her side, wrapping her in my arms and holding her against my chest as I rocked us slowly back and forth. "Are you okay?"

She shook her head against me but didn't say anything. We sat in silence for a few minutes before she pulled away and gave me a watery smile.

"What can I do to make you feel better?" I wanted to take away every ounce of hurt she was feeling and kill every motherfucker that caused her discomfort.

"Lay here with me," she pleaded, laying beside me and staring up at the stars. I stretched out on my side, watching her instead of the sky. "I only want to think about us tonight," she declared in a whisper so quiet it floated away on the breeze but not before I caught it.

To hear her talk about us? It was fucking addictive.

She shifted even closer, molding her body against mine so I could feel every soft curve. "Make me forget about tomorrow, Maddox," she begged, her breath ghosting along my skin and making me shiver. Being so close to her was tempting as fuck.

My heart felt like it might pound out of my chest. I was no saint. I'd been with so many women, I couldn't count. And yet it was like I was a virgin all over again. Ryan made me feel like I was brand new. Like no one else before her had ever mattered. Like they'd all been practice leading up to this moment.

Laying beside her with my weight balanced on my arm, I stared down at her reverently. The way she was looking up at me was magnetic, her wide, innocent eyes pulling me in closer and closer until I had no choice but to kiss her. To feel her lips under mine, hungry and needy and begging for more.

I fought with myself, the urge to rip her clothes off and claim her as mine so intense I had to squeeze my fingers into a tight fist, digging my nails into the soft flesh of my palm until I broke the skin to keep from acting on my animal impulses.

The way she kissed me, the little moans and whimpers escaping her lips and her fist bunched in my shirt, pulling me closer, lit my entire body on fire. My veins coursed with lava as every inch of me was consumed by Ryan.

I'd never needed anything as much as I needed to be inside of her right now.

But this wasn't about me and what I needed. I'd never hurt her again. So, I'd take my time and make sure she was ready. That she wanted me as much as I wanted her.

Releasing her lips, I trailed my tongue down her neck, nipping and kissing along the sweet skin until I reached the swell of her tits. Teasing the flesh until she arched her back to push closer to my mouth, I smiled against her skin, enjoying every goddamn second with her.

My fingers brushed along her side, down her ribs, looking for a zipper. They were so many fucking layers between us. I thought I might go insane. I needed to feel her skin against mine, searing this moment into my memory. I needed to believe it was real, that she was really here giving herself to me.

Ryan threaded her fingers through my hair, pulling until the tension on my scalp was almost painful, and she pulled me back up to her mouth, crushing her lips against mine. Her teeth scraped my bottom lip as we both took a second to catch our breath. I finally found the zipper on the side of her jumpsuit and slid it down, pushing the fabric down to her waist, I watched as her tits popped free.

Leaning back, I let my hungry gaze rake down newly exposed skin.

She was so goddamn beautiful. The hair on my arms raised as goosebumps broke out over my skin from just being this close to her, surrounded by her intoxicating scent. I leaned back to take a second to compose myself. My dick was so fucking hard it was trying to punch through the rough denim material caging it in.

I took a deep breath and exhaled slowly as Ryan stared up at me with glassy eyes, the fireflies fluttering around us reflecting in her eyes like stars. I'd never seen anything more enticing in my entire life.

"You're so fucking perfect," I breathed so quietly I wasn't sure if she heard me until she reached up and ran her hand down my face and across my stubble.

"And you're everything I've ever wanted," she confessed just as quietly as if the darkness surrounding us made us both brave enough to speak our truths out loud.

I leaned down and kissed her again, but something had shifted. Our kisses were deep but frenzied, and when I started to trail kisses down her chest and stomach, pulling the fabric of her outfit down further until I'd pulled it all the way off, she moaned, my name a whisper on her lips.

I'd never been more glad for the warm and humid air because now it wrapped her naked body like a blanket. I didn't have to worry about protecting her from the cold and could just sit back and appreciate the incredible view in front of me.

She sat up, her eyes hooded and filled with heat as she tugged at my shirt, trying to pull it off. I flashed her a wicked grin as I reached back and dragged my shirt over my head. I watched her closely as her eyes drifted down my body, and I didn't think it was possible, but my dick got even harder under her molten gaze.

I groaned as she pulled me down on top of her with clumsy hands. It was such a goddamn turn on that she didn't know what she was doing. Her fingers danced across my skin, creating little explosions of need that got stronger and stronger as they moved closer to my hard-on.

Shifting until our hips were locked together, I rocked against her once, and a needy whimper fell from her lips that made me want to say *fuck it* and bury myself in her right now. Instead, I kissed my way down her body, running my teeth gently along the soft skin between her hip bones before nipping the sensitive skin of her inner thigh.

Running my tongue over the spot I just bit, I let my hand drift up her stomach until my thumb rubbed softly across her nipple. I watched through heavy eyes as it puckered, and she arched into my hand again. Keeping my eyes on her tightened peaks, I lowered my mouth to her pussy. She froze at the first soft lick of my tongue, and I knew it was because she'd never done this with anyone before.

Again, the overwhelming weight of the gift she was giving me crashed over me, but I pushed those thoughts away to be dealt with later. Right now, I needed my focus on only showing Ryan exactly how good we were together and how much pleasure I could bring her.

I gently kissed her, moving back to her thighs, and relaxed bit by bit under my touch. Finally, I moved back to her clit and swirled my tongue before licking her in a steady rhythm with the flat of my tongue. She tasted so fucking good, and I groaned, sucking her clit into my mouth and running my finger along her slit.

She was fucking dripping, and my heart clenched because *I* had done that to her. Nothing else I'd accomplished in my life meant as much as this moment right here. I pushed my finger inside her, sliding in easily and curling it in a steady rhythm. The silence of the night was only broken by her whimpers and cries of pleasure as I brought her closer and closer to her release.

Reaching down, I unzipped my jeans while keeping my mouth and other hand on Ryan. My cock throbbed, and I couldn't take it anymore. I needed relief, or I was going to come in my jeans like some fucking amateur. But that was what Ryan did to me.

Watching her come undone under my tongue was almost too much, as her thighs squeezed against my head, trapping me between her legs. I licked and sucked until finally, her legs relaxed, shaking violently against my shoulders. I placed a couple last soft kisses against her clit before I moved up her body.

Heat spiraled to my groin as I pressed my lips to hers, her taste still on my tongue. She looked up, and our eyes met, locking together. I brushed a damp piece of hair off of her forehead. "Tell me now if you want me to stop, Freckles, because I'm barely hanging on, and in another ten seconds, there will be no going back," I growled out, my voice low and husky.

She locked her legs around my hips and lower back, settling my cock against her slick pussy. I rocked my hips, sliding my length along her slit, and her eyes rolled back as she moaned. She pushed herself against me, wiggling her hips and trying to push my cock inside her. I shifted until I was lined up with her entrance and waited until she looked at me. Her cheeks were flushed, her eyes a little wild and filled with heat, and she was breathing hard. I bent down and kissed her gently. "Tell me you want me," I demanded.

"I want you, Maddox. So bad. Please, I need you," she begged.

I pressed my hips forward, sliding slowly inside her heat inch by fucking inch. I inhaled sharply and held my breath at how tightly her walls were squeezing me, and I was only a couple of inches inside of her. I watched her face closely for any signs of pain or discomfort, and her eyes widened the further I slid inside. When I finally came up against the barrier, the one she'd saved just for me, I pressed a kiss to her lips. "This might hurt, baby, but I'll be as gentle as I can."

She nodded, and I thrust forward the rest of the way until I was buried balls deep inside her as she cried out, and it took everything in me not to immediately come. I breathed deeply, holding still and waiting for her to adjust to my size. I stroked her hair and tried to focus on her instead of how close I was to exploding.

She blinked a few times, and then a sexy little smile spread across her face. "I need you to move," she said, shifting her hips against mine. As we rocked together, her pussy clenched around me, and she cried out my name. My heart slammed against my ribcage as I tried to take in every single detail of this moment. Her hair fanned out on the pillow underneath her, her eyes closed and her head thrown back in pleasure. Her soft skin brushing against mine, and the way my name sounded like a prayer on her lips.

Pleasure pooled at the base of my spine, and I gritted my teeth. I fucking *would not* come before she did, especially for her first time. I picked up the pace, rolling my hips to hit just the right spot. She reacted immediately. Her walls tightened as I reached down and rubbed the rough pad of my thumb over her hardened nipple.

She was close, balanced right on the edge and wound so tight it would only be a few more seconds until she let go and came all over my dick. "Let go, baby.

Come for me," I coaxed her through clenched teeth, continuing my assault on her nipples.

The second she let go, I followed. I didn't stand a chance. Her inner walls milked me so hard she ripped the orgasm straight out of me. I swear my soul left my body, and I didn't even care if I got it back. If I died right now, I'd do it with so much peace and satisfaction, I wasn't sure anything could ever top it. When I finally came back down to earth, I looked down at the woman I loved with my entire being, and she stared up at me lazily, her eyes filled with wonder.

"Can we do that again?" she asked, her words almost slurred and a soft smile on her lips.

Chuckling, I pressed a gentle kiss to her lips. "Anytime you want, Freckles." I held myself over her body, not wanting to move. I didn't want to slip out of her and disconnect us. I never wanted to be apart from Ryan again.

Now that reality was seeping back in, I had to wonder. What would happen now?

TWENTY ONE
MADDOX

Waking up with my body wrapped around Ryan was an experience I wanted to have every fucking day until the day I died. I didn't want to open my eyes because that meant facing reality, and I didn't know what Ryan was going to do today or what last night meant for the two of us. All I knew was that if she went through with this wedding, I'd never recover.

It would wreck me.

I had no idea what time it was. All I knew was that the sun was shining brightly overhead, so when I finally cracked my eyes open, I had to immediately slam them closed. Ryan shifted in my arms, her hair tickling my face. She stretched, pressing her very naked body against mine and waking my dick right the fuck up.

My hand drifted down the curves of her body before I rested it on her hip, lightly digging my fingers in and pulling her ass back against me. "Fuck," I groaned, wanting nothing more than to bury myself inside of her and keep her here in my arms all day, forgetting about everything else.

Her sharp gasp had a grin breaking out across my face as she felt the effect she had on me. But the spell was broken when she abruptly sat up, the thin blanket we managed to pull over ourselves last night falling down and exposing her very naked tits. My eyes immediately dropped to them. I couldn't fucking help myself when it came to Ryan. Her body was worthy of worship, and I planned to throw myself at her alter again and again.

"What time is it?" she squeaked, frantically searching through all the bedding and discarded clothes for her phone.

I grabbed her hand and turned it over, placing a kiss on the inside of her wrist. "I think we both left our phones up front, Freckles."

"That's right." As much as I didn't want her to ever get dressed, I knew she'd never relax now. I handed her her clothes and watched as she quickly pulled them on, hopping down off the tailgate and throwing open the passenger door.

I laid back and stared at the clear blue sky while I waited, the events of last night replaying in my mind. Blood rushed to my cock when I thought about how, after the first time, Ryan climbed on top of me and rode me until she came so hard that we both passed out.

Finally, she came back around and climbed up into the back of the truck, a forlorn expression on her face. "It's already eleven. I was supposed to meet my sisters for hair and makeup an hour ago," she sighed.

Sitting up, I pulled her against me and ran my fingers through her tangled hair. "Please don't do this, Ryan. Don't marry Yates. I can tell you don't love him. I can tell you don't want to marry him. So why are you going through with it? Stay here with me. Whatever he's got on you, I can help. I'll never let anyone hurt you. I…" My mouth went dry. "I love you so fucking much. Please don't make me watch you marry another man. I don't know if I can survive it," I pleaded with her, my tone desperate.

She leaned back and looked at me, sliding her palm up my cheek and rubbing her thumb along the stubble of my jawline. Her dark eyes locked on mine, the depth of feeling I saw reflected my own back at me perfectly. "I love you, too. I always have, and I always will. But I gave my word. I have to go," she said gently, but the words might as well have been knives stabbed into my chest. Every single one hurt. How could she still go through with marrying that tool after what we'd shared last night?

My heart was shredding in my chest, ripping apart into a million tiny pieces that were then set on fire. But I didn't say anything, because after I left all those years ago, I deserved this. I hurt her, and she moved on. Swallowing down my anguish, I got dressed. I didn't say anything. I couldn't. If I opened my mouth, I didn't know what might come out.

I might yell or say things I didn't mean, lashing out at the fucking torture I was going through right now. Or I might beg, but she didn't need that from me right now.

Helping her down, I slammed the tailgate shut and walked around to the passenger door, pulling it open and waiting until she climbed in. She watched my face, but I refused to make eye contact. This was all my fucking fault, and I didn't want to lose my shit, even as she ripped my heart out. I loved her, more than I'd ever loved anyone, and even if it killed me if she was happy with Yates, I'd somehow learn to deal with it. Or I'd drink myself to death trying. Time would tell.

"Would you mind dropping me off at Charlie's?" she asked quietly as she played with a lock of her hair and stared out the window.

I tossed her my phone across the bench. She was sitting against the door so fucking far away it felt like a physical blow, a loss of something I'd barely had just yesterday. "Put her address in the GPS," I grunted, barely keeping control over my emotions. I needed to hit something, scream, drink, *something* before I completely fell apart. But I was trapped in this truck with Ryan, and I couldn't do any of it. Instead, I gripped the wheel even tighter, my knuckles already white and aching, and gritted my teeth.

Thank fuck we were only about ten minutes away from Charlie's, and as I pulled up, Ryan finally turned to me. "Are you still coming to the ceremony?" she whispered, and I wanted to be so goddamn angry at her for having the balls to ask that of me, but I couldn't. Lifting my gaze, I searched her eyes, and I saw the desperation and fear in them. She was afraid and needed me. No matter how I felt, I'd never abandon her again.

I slumped against the seat, the anger in me momentarily fading as Ryan's despair filled me up instead. "Yeah, I'll be there," I confirmed.

She slid across the bench toward me and leaned forward slowly as if she were afraid I'd snap at her for touching me. In reality, her touch was the only thing I wanted. Leaning up, she pressed her lips to my cheek, and I closed my eyes, breathing her in one last time. I had no idea what would happen to us after today. I had a life in LA. I'd make sure I was always available to her, but I wouldn't physically be here. And she was about to start a new life with someone else.

"Thank you," she murmured before turning and quickly hopping out of the car. She didn't look back as she hurried into the building where her sister lived. I squeezed my eyes shut and took a deep breath before fumbling for my phone.

Maddox: What hotel are you at?

Connor: Quinn drove me to your house this morning.

Maddox: Meet you there in 45.

Tossing my phone onto the seat, I shifted into drive and started the long drive home, blasting angry music and hoping that if I got it loud enough, it'd block out my thoughts. It didn't work.

Turning onto the short, dusty drive that led to Everleigh Ranch, the anger I'd been trying to contain for the past hour or so bubbled to the surface with a vengeance. I stopped in front of the house and slammed my door, my heart banging against my ribs and my chest heaving as I tried to breathe. How the fuck could she marry someone else? Someone I *knew* she didn't love?

Connor stepped onto the porch, his eyes narrowing as he looked me over. He turned and went back inside, the screen door slamming behind his retreating form. Letting some of the rage I was feeling out, I roared like a goddamn animal, but it wasn't even close to enough. I watched as Connor opened the came back outside, jogging down the steps and tossing me a set of boxing gloves. He shoved his own hands into some padded gloves and held them out in front of me.

"Put on the goddamn gloves and hit me," he demanded.

I crammed my shaking hands into the gloves, tightening and securing the velcro before curling my fingers into fists. I unleashed jab after jab into Connor's gloved hands, letting out all the rage, frustration, hurt, regret, and self-loathing bottled up until reality started to seep in. I was breathing hard, and sweat dripped down my forehead and stung my eyes. The fight in me subsided as agony took its place.

Fuck, my heart hurt.

Ripping the gloves off my hands, I stalked into the house and straight for the shower, not bothering to say anything to Connor. Deep down, I appreciated that he knew what I needed, and right now, he'd leave me alone to work through my shit.

After I took the shortest possible shower, not wanting to spend time with my thoughts, I got out and dried off, throwing on some joggers and stomping out to the kitchen. I tore through the cabinets looking for the bottle of whiskey I bought last week. There was still plenty left. I hadn't been drinking much since I was spending more time with Ryan.

Reaching for a glass, I poured a couple of fingers and tossed them back, relishing in the burn. I heard Connor step into the room behind me. I lifted the glass in his direction and raised my eyebrow, and he nodded, so I pulled him down a glass and refilled my glass and his. Handing his drink over, we both sipped our liquor in silence.

"Are we going to the wedding?" he finally asked.

"Fuck. I would give literally anything to not have to go to this today, but yeah, we are."

"Why?" He lifted his glass and took another sip, eyeing me over the rim.

"Because she asked me to," I answered simply, the words tearing their way up my throat.

"Okay," he agreed. "I'll bring an extra flask and have the plane ready as soon as it's over."

I nodded, finishing my drink and walking back to my room to get dressed. The wedding was in a couple of hours, and we had a long drive into Dallas.

The suit I asked Connor to bring me was hanging in my closet, and it was so fucking fitting for this day. I wanted to be prepared in case Ryan decided to go through with this clusterfuck. Getting dressed to watch the woman who possessed me on a level I wasn't even prepared to examine, marry another man felt like a funeral. So, I decided to dress like it. Head to toe black.

A slim-cut black Italian wool suit with a black button-down and a skinny black tie underneath was what I had him bring, and staring at my reflection in the mirror, I hardly recognized myself. My eyes were clouded with grief, and I'd let my stubble grow out a little longer than normal, but I didn't give a shit. I wanted to look good for Ryan today, show her what she could have if she'd just change her mind, but I didn't have it in me to try.

I already asked, and she turned me down. I wasn't holding any hope as the wedding got closer that she'd have a change of heart.

With one final deep breath, I stepped out of the room and into the kitchen, pocketing all my essentials. I didn't plan on coming back here after the wedding. I needed to put some distance between Ryan and me for a little while so I could try and deal with the misery of what today meant for me, for us, for the future we could've had.

Connor stood in the kitchen, his suit more neutral in navy blue. He passed me a flask and tucked another into his inner jacket pocket. "Your spare," he explained.

"Thanks," I mumbled, knowing the alcohol wouldn't really help, but what the fuck else could I do to numb the torment?

Connor watched me closely as if he weren't sure if I was going to explode and tear the house apart or break down, but I could hold my shit in until we got on the plane at least. He grabbed the keys off the counter. "We don't have to do this," he reminded me.

"I promised her, Connor. I let her down once, and this is the goddamn price I have to pay for my fuck up. I won't disappoint her again." Clenching my jaw, I walked to the car and slid in, slamming the door closed.

A few minutes later, Connor joined me, and we started the long drive into Dallas. Neither one of us said much, I lost in my misery and Connor giving me space. I didn't know if more space was a good thing right now, but I couldn't think of anything to say.

He pulled up to the gates of the Rutherford Estate and gave our names, waiting for them to swing open. Driving onto these grounds, my stomach rolled, and I pulled the flask out of my pocket. I never thought this was a possibility, that Ryan would actually go through with the wedding. Over the past two weeks, we'd gotten so close it was like no time at all had gone by. I saw the way she looked at me. It was the same way I looked at her. With adoration and devotion and a fuck ton of love and desire mixed in, too.

The way she looked at Yates? It was thinly masked annoyance on her best day, straight up contempt on her worst. So why the fuck was she marrying him? I didn't understand it, and maybe I never would. Maybe the way I abandoned her all those years ago was too much for her to forgive and overcome.

I ran a hand through my messy hair as I climbed out of the car. There were guests parking and walking to the back of the grounds, following a path lined with red roses. I rolled my eyes, knowing Ryan had no part in picking those. They were too cliche for her, and if she saw them, I had a feeling she'd hate them. The thought brought a small smile to my lips that disappeared as quickly as it came.

Connor walked around the car and stood next to me, our shoulders almost touching. With the looks he'd given me all day, I knew he'd have my back no matter what went down. He'd be there to clean up whatever mess I made of myself. It struck me how good a friend he became over the past year and how much I depended on him.

He glanced down at the watch on his wrist. "Wedding starts in half an hour," he pointed out. My stomach rolled again as I forced my feet forward, following that fucking path of red roses across the soft grass. As we rounded the house, a couple of huge white tents came into view. Off to the side was an aisle with two giant pedestals at the front overflowing with arrangements of red roses. I'd gone to a couple of weddings in the past year or so, and even I knew this style was severely outdated.

Connor and I finished trudging across the grass, and I found us two seats at the very back. I sunk into mine, but they were filling up fast. The only two open together were toward the middle of the row, so I had no choice but to be sandwiched between a stranger and Connor.

I kept my sunglasses on and tried to avoid making eye contact with anyone. I saw Yates out of the corner of my eye at the front of the room, and when he spotted me in the back row, a smug smile stretched across his shitbag face. Clenching my jaw, I reached for the flask in my pocket, taking a healthy swig while watching him walk out of the room. It'd be fun to follow him and break both of his legs so he couldn't stand up there and marry my girl today, but I wouldn't do that to Ryan.

Sliding even further down in my seat, the effects of all the whiskey I had today started to numb the sharp edges of my pain. It probably wouldn't do shit when I had to watch Ryan walk down the aisle, but for now, I was floating along with a mostly pleasant buzz.

My hand shook slightly as I looked at the digital display on my wrist. *Fuck.* Five minutes. A cold sweat broke out across my forehead, and despite the Texas heat, a chill ran down my spine. Connor looked relaxed next to me with his ankle crossed over his knee, but I knew better. He kept checking on me out of the corner of his eye, probably making sure I wasn't going to do anything too stupid.

His patience for my antics would only go so far in public. Like mine, his instinct was to protect, so I didn't mind losing my shit in front of him.

Four minutes.

My phone buzzed in my pocket, and I was so fucking glad to have the distraction. I pulled up the message and shot up out of my chair, almost knocking it over as I read the screen.

Ryan: I need you.

Ryan: Please.

I didn't give a fuck about the strangers around me who were now staring at me distastefully for causing a scene. Fuck them all. "I've gotta find her," I blurted, kicking the chair out of my way so I could get out of this aisle without passing twenty-five people along the way. My girl needed me. Hope bloomed in my chest. Had something happened? Had she changed her mind?

Sprinting out of the tent, I was suddenly completely sober, but I realized I had no idea where to find her. I pulled out my phone and shot off a quick message.

Maddox: I'm coming. Where are you?

It took the longest fucking ten seconds of my life for her to respond.

Ryan: Just inside the back door of the estate. Go left, first door on the left. Hurry.

I sprinted across the grass with Connor right behind me. Bursting through the back door, I frantically scanned the huge room I found myself in. There were so many goddamn doors, but I would spend all day opening every single one if it meant getting to my girl when she needed me. Nothing would stop me.

There was a hallway off to the left, so I decided to start there, flinging the first door open. The anger melted out of me when I saw Ryan standing near the window with tears streaking down her face. She was alone in the room, and Connor discretely stepped out behind me, closing the door behind him. I knew he'd stand guard and not let anyone in here to figure out whatever the fuck was happening right now.

My breath caught when my gaze raked down her body and took in how the white lace dress she wore hugged every curve, falling and pooling around her feet. "You look beautiful," I breathed, moving up beside her. I let my fingers trace down her arm, the feel of her skin igniting electric sparks under my fingertips.

"Thank you," she sniffled, wiping at her eyes before throwing herself into my arms, sobbing against my chest. I held her tight against me, breathing her in and never wanting to let go. I wasn't sure what was going on, but I didn't care if we stood here like this forever. At this moment, she didn't belong to anyone but me. There was no one else in the world, but Ryan and I.

Her body trembled against mine while she quietly cried, and I hated that she was sad and hurting. If I could take her pain on myself, I'd do it in a goddamn second.

"Shh," I cooed. "Everything's going to be okay, Freckles. I promise." And I meant it. I'd do anything to make Ryan happy.

She leaned back a little, but still clung to me as if she were afraid I'd disappear and leave her alone to face reality, her fist bunched at the back of my jacket. Her red-rimmed eyes and mascara-streaked cheeks made me want to kill someone for making her cry. She looked as miserable as I felt.

"What's going on?" I finally asked after staring into her eyes for an eternity trying to figure out what was going through her head but being no closer to an answer.

She took a deep breath, exhaling shakily and gripping me even tighter. "I have something to tell you."

TWENTY TWO
RYAN

My body shook so hard my teeth clacked together. Maddox tightened his grip on me, his eyes filled with concern. I sniffled because my nose was starting to run, but I couldn't really find it in me to care. The guilt I felt for going this far with the agreement I made with Yates was weighing down on me so heavily, if Maddox loosened his grip, I thought I might collapse.

Tears streamed down my face, and I was sure I looked like a complete disaster.

He brushed the stray hair that had fallen across my face away. "What did you need to tell me?" he asked softly. My stomach twisted at the thought of confessing my secret to Maddox. If he left me here by myself right now, I didn't know if I could handle it.

Now that I was getting ready to spill all the sordid details of my arrangement with Yates, nondisclosure agreement be damned, I was picking a side. I was choosing Maddox. I hoped once he heard what I did, he'd still want me.

"Before I tell you, please believe me when I say I thought I was out of options. I thought it didn't matter. It was before you came back, and I finally started to give up on my last bits of hope that you'd ever return home."

He flinched lightly but quickly recovered, his thumb brushing back and forth across my upper back in a comforting motion. He still had his arms wrapped around me, holding me up. "It's okay, Freckles. Just tell me."

The nerves made his voice tremble. He was on edge, waiting for me to explain, and I couldn't blame him. Taking one last deep breath, I began. "A little over a month ago, I intercepted a notice from the bank that our ranch was being foreclosed. It had progressed far enough that they set a date for the auction. My parents never told me."

He sucked in a sharp breath, his grip around me tightening a little, but he didn't say anything. So I kept going. "Quinn and I talked it over, and I decided I needed to do something. The hopelessness and resignation in my dad's eyes killed me."

Maddox nodded. "That land is his entire life. I know." I loved that I didn't have to explain it to him. He just knew how important this was to my parents.

Instead of keeping the distance between us so that I could look into his eyes, I rested my cheek against his chest and listened to his steady heartbeat instead, letting it calm me. "The next day, I went to the bank and applied for a loan. That was where I met Yates. He was the one I talked to about everything, and he denied my application. But then he asked me to dinner."

Maddox's muscles tensed, and his heartbeat quickened, but he stayed silent. "That was the day you were a jerk and refused the cookies I'd baked you. Do you remember?"

He sagged a little against me. "I remember," he muttered.

"Well, when he asked, I was so mad and so hurt about everything I agreed to go. You have to understand I never dated. Ever. You've really been it for me since I was ten years old, even before I really knew what a crush was. No one else ever caught my attention." I gripped the handful of his jacket I was clutching in my fist a little tighter, wanting him even closer for this next part even if it was impossible. In this position, I was pretty sure we were already as close as we could get.

"I thought maybe he was interested in dating me, and he seemed like a nice guy and was decently good looking, so I took a chance. Except at that dinner, he made me a proposal I wasn't expecting. Marry him so he could get access to his trust fund, and he'd buy the ranch and sign the deed over to me so we'd never owe anyone for it again. He made me decide that night, so I didn't really have a chance to think it over, but I made him put into the contract that it'd only be for a year." The air wooshed out of me now that I got the worst parts out. The weight still hadn't lifted off me yet because I didn't know how Maddox was going to react.

He stepped back, loosening his hold on me and leaving me feeling cold and terrified he was going to walk away again. Maybe all of this was too much for him. But his words surprised me. "I could've helped you," he whispered, his eyes so full of compassion and love, tears started to stream down my face again at the massive relief washing over me.

Shaking my head, I pulled him closer again. "No. I couldn't ask that of you. And even if I could have, you weren't exactly happy to see me. How would that have gone over? 'Hey, Maddox. Haven't seen you in twelve years but do you mind lending me hundreds of thousands of dollars?'"

He chuckled. "Yeah, I guess I see your point. But why didn't you tell me these past few weeks what the deal was? Or even last night?"

Hanging my head, I stared at the lacy fabric pooling around my bare feet. "Yates made me sign a nondisclosure agreement. If I told anyone, not only would he not save the ranch, but he could sue me for more than a million dollars. I was too afraid he'd somehow find out."

Lifting my eyes, I watched as Maddox's jaw clenched, and his eyes blazed with barely-contained fury. I hoped it wasn't because of me. He blinked and looked down at me, the rage still in his eyes, but now it swirled with something else I couldn't quite place. "Why did you finally decide to tell me now?"

Shrugging, I bit my lip before answering. "I guess now I trust you. I trust that you're not going to leave again, that you mean it when you say you're here for me."

He ran his palm along the side of my neck and gripped me with his fingers, this thumb rubbing soothingly along my jaw. "Good," he whispered just before he lowered his head and covered my lips with his.

A noise outside broke the spell, and I startled away from him, but he pushed me behind his body protectively as the door swung open, and Quinn rushed in, followed by an irritated-looking Connor. Quinn took in Maddox standing in front of me as I peeked around his broad shoulders, finally looking over my hot mess of a face. "You told him," he stated.

"You knew?" Maddox asked Quinn accusingly. "And you didn't bother telling me?"

Quinn crossed his arms defiantly. "Dude, I like you, but my loyalty will always be to Ryan first. I did everything I could to encourage you without actually breaking her trust."

"Thanks, Quinny," I murmured from where I still stood behind Maddox.

"Hate to break whatever this is up, but we need to get the fuck out of here. Now," Connor insisted from where he stood looking out of the window towards the ceremony.

"I've got your bag and your phone," Quinn announced, slinging the duffle bag I'd grabbed from my sister's this morning over his shoulder.

Looking down at my bare feet, I spun around frantically searching for the wedges I planned to wear today. "Where are my shoes?"

"No time to find them. Go! Now!" Connor boomed, and we all reacted instantly, Maddox grabbing my hand and pulling me with him. My bare feet slapped against the polished marble floor as we followed Connor toward the front of the estate. He flung the door open, and we all piled out onto the front steps. There was a valet attendant, but we didn't have time to wait for them to find the car.

Connor strode confidently but quickly up to him, demanded the keys, and asked him to point us in the direction where Maddox's truck was parked.

Connor and Quinn took off, but I wasn't wearing shoes, and the idea of running through whatever kind of terrain was on the ground out here barefoot sucked. Maddox felt my hesitation and didn't miss a beat, bending down and lifting me bridal-style into his arms, the irony of which wasn't lost on me as the small train of my lacy, white wedding dress trailed behind us.

"Hold on, Freckles. We're getting the hell out of here and never coming back," he promised, tightening his grip on me as he hurried to catch up to Quinn and Connor. By the time we got to them, they'd found the truck and unlocked it. Maddox slid me into the backseat and climbed up after to me. Quinn hopped in the passenger side, and Connor started the engine, backing out of the spot before he'd even buckled up.

As he turned toward the heavy iron gates that stood open at the front of the grounds, I looked back through the small rear window just as Yates and his cronies spilled out the front door, his glare visible even from this far away. Maddox reached up and turned my face with gentle fingers until our eyes locked. "No looking back. Now that I know the truth, everything's going to change. I won't let him do shit to you," he vowed. "He'll have to go through me first, and I promise you he doesn't stand a chance in hell."

Connor chuckled darkly from the front seat but didn't say anything as we cruised down the two-lane highway. We moved in the opposite direction of home, though. "Where are we going?" I asked, watching another field fly by.

"Private airstrip," Connor grunted. I was starting to figure out he didn't talk much, but that was fine with me.

Maddox gripped my hand in his. "I'm not taking you back to either of our places right now. Yates is going to be on the warpath after you just embarrassed him. We need to get out of town for a couple of days, but I'll bring you back once things settle down, okay?"

Letting out a shuddering breath, I nodded once. I was glad he was thinking more clearly than me. "Yeah. Yeah, okay. Where are we going? And don't we have to buy tickets or something? What if there aren't four seats together?" I started to ramble, the emotions of everything that happened today too much for me to process.

Maddox laughed softly before pressing a warm kiss to the inside of my wrist. "I thought we'd go to LA if that's okay with you. And don't worry about the seats or the tickets. I've got it covered." The smug smirk on his face like he knew something I didn't made me want to smack him, but I didn't have the energy, so I let it go. I'd wait and see where we ended up. I trusted he knew what he was doing, and honestly, it was such a relief to let someone else handle things for a little while.

I rested my head against Maddox's strong shoulder and closed my eyes, relishing the feel of his sturdy body underneath my head. I must've dozed off because I startled awake when the truck suddenly came to a stop. Blinking, I winced as I sat up and rotated my neck, the stiff muscles aching. Maddox smiled softly down at me and gripped the back of my neck in his large palm, squeezing gently, the rough calluses on his fingertips somehow soothing against my skin.

"I'll give you a massage when we're in the air," he promised before letting me go and opening the door. He climbed out, and I squealed when he grabbed my ankle and pulled, yanking me toward him with a mischievous grin.

"You're barefoot, remember?" he justified, lifting me into his arms like I weighed nothing and stalking toward a big building with huge doors that were wide open. I raised my hand to shield my eyes from the sun and squinted, trying to see where we were going.

I gasped when I saw the jet parked inside. "Is that what we're taking to LA?"

Maddox smirked again. "Told you I had it covered," he laughed.

"Yes, yes, you did." I gripped his neck a little tighter as he carried me up the steps and set me down at the top so I could walk through the small open door.

The woman just inside wore a friendly, welcoming smile, and my eyes dropped to the tag pinned to her chest before returning her grin. "Hey, Hilda. I'm Ryan. Nice to meet you," I greeted, sticking my hand out for her to shake.

She took it, shaking briefly before grabbing my bag from Quinn, who'd followed us up the steps and into the cabin. Quinn whistled. "Damn, buddy. I could get used to this," he praised before flopping backward across a couple of seats.

Maddox laughed as Connor brushed past us, grabbing a seat across from Quinn. I followed him down the aisle with Maddox behind me, so close I could feel his warmth against my back. Instead of focusing on that, I sank into the soft leather seat and buckled up. Maddox leaned down and pressed a kiss to my forehead. "I'm going to go find out how long until we take off." He looked up and nodded at someone behind us. "Hilda's going to get you guys whatever you want to drink. I'll be right back."

I watched as he retreated up the aisle toward the cockpit, his muscles bunching and flexing underneath his black suit as he walked. The fact he was in all black just now registered in my brain. My heart hurt for what I put him through, but the fact that he showed up anyway meant everything.

Quinn looked across the table that separated us and raised his eyebrow before lifting the glass Hilda had just placed in his hand in a mock toast. I couldn't help but laugh. I'd have to face reality at some point, the consequences of what I agreed to a month ago, and, more importantly, what I did today, were hanging out there. But they could wait. Right now, I needed to block it out for a couple of days and just process everything.

My family would understand. Everybody else? I really didn't give a crap.

"Quinny, can you pass me my phone, please?" I asked, leaning forward to look for my bag.

"No can do, Lancelot. But don't worry. I texted Justice while we were in the car and let her know the wedding was off, and you wouldn't be reachable for a couple of days," he spelled out, sipping his drink.

I leaned back against the seat, reveling in the cool leather on my heated skin. "Thanks. Was she freaking out?"

He shrugged. "No clue. I turned your phone off right after I made sure the message went through. I love you, but I'm not dealing with that drama right now."

I laughed softly, and before I knew what was happening, it turned into a full belly laugh complete with tears streaming down my face. Quinn joined me, and we were both gasping for air. Connor silently watched with an amused tilt to his lips.

I was still trying to catch my breath when Maddox took the seat next to me, fastening his seat belt. "Less than ten minutes," he announced to all of us. He reached for my hand, entwining our fingers and kissing the back before settling in.

I'd only flown a couple of times in my life, but I loved it. The feeling of the engines revving up and shooting us into the sky was like nothing else I'd experienced, and I couldn't wait. My stomach fluttered as I lifted the window covering and stared out at the wing, watching the flaps tilt up and down, no doubt part of the pre-flight check.

Hilda slamming the door closed and locking it brought my attention back to the cabin, and across from me, Connor watched, his eyes filled with amusement. "I take it you're not a nervous flyer," he remarked, crossing his ankles and settling into his seat. He didn't look at all impressed by his surroundings, so

I guessed this wasn't his first time flying on this jet.

"Not at all. I haven't done it much, but I love it. It's such a rush. Well, taking off and landing. The rest I could take or leave," I clarified.

Maddox leaned over, his warm breath tickling my ear as he whispered, "I could think of a few ways we could make the time pass faster."

A shiver ran down my spine at his words. My whole body clenched, the idea of passing the time locked in some tiny bathroom with Maddox not as unappealing as I might've thought a couple of days ago. I knew what it felt like having him inside of me, and that was a feeling I wanted to repeat over and over again.

But Quinn's hard stare was like a bucket of cold water over my heated body, and Maddox must have sensed the shift because he sat back in his seat, shooting Quinn a death glare that made me giggle. As we taxied down the runway, I watched out the window, but none of us really spoke.

Once we were in the air, I wanted to take my mind off the unproductive thoughts threatening to overrun my brain. "Let's do some shots," I suggested, unbuckling my seatbelt and sliding past Maddox. He smacked my ass, and I yelped, a devious smile spread across his face. If that was how he wanted to play, I could keep up.

I decided right then and there I'd spend the entire flight to LA teasing Maddox but not giving in. I wondered how turned on I could get him. Well, I was about to find out. I caught Hilda's attention and asked for a bottle of whiskey and four glasses, thanking her and moving back to my seat. But instead of sitting in mine, I lowered myself onto Maddox's lap, shifting around more than necessary before finally settling in.

His hands gripped my hips, fingers digging deliciously into my skin, and I smiled inwardly knowing I was getting to him. I could already feel him thickening underneath me, and my heartbeat quickened at the dangerous game I was playing. Pouring the first shots, I passed them around. "Wait," I ordered as they all lifted their glasses to their lips.

Holding out my own, I made sure to arch my back just enough to make Maddox groan and shift underneath me. I gnawed on my cheek to keep from laughing. "To broken engagements and new beginnings," I toasted, and the guys all clinked glasses with me before swallowing their liquor.

I coughed as the whiskey burned down my throat and warmed my stomach from the inside. "Okay," Connor said, slamming his glass back on the table so hard I was surprised it didn't shatter under his giant, meaty hand. "What's your deal?" he asked me, folding his arms over his chest.

"My deal?" I asked, lifting my eyebrow while I refilled his glass.

"Yeah, what the hell was that back there? Not that I'm not all for taking guys like that down a few notches, but Jesus Christ." I let his words hang in the air for a couple seconds while I decided what to say. I mean, I'd broken the NDA already, right? Might as well go all in.

Sucking in a deep breath, I let the words pour out of me. "Long story short, I was desperate and went to the bank Yates's family owns for help. He turned me down but asked me to dinner and gave me a proposal, a fake marriage that would benefit both of us. I didn't have any other options, so I accepted."

"Which I, for the record, thought was the worst fucking idea I'd ever heard, and I hadn't even met the fucker yet," Quinn chimed in.

"You haven't exactly kept that a secret, Quinny," I grumbled, leaning back against Maddox's chest and writhing a little on top of him just to make him squirm. He bent forward and kissed the spot where my shoulder and neck met, and I bit back a moan. He pulled my hips back, so my ass pressed even harder into his erection, but then I sat up and turned my attention back to Connor, ignoring the low growl from behind me.

"Now my turn to ask a question," I started, downing the refill I'd just poured myself. "How do you and Maddox know each other? I know you're not in the band."

Connor chuckled. "No, I couldn't play an instrument or sing if my life depended on it."

"Fuck, no. You do *not* want to hear this guy sing. It'll make your ears bleed," Maddox teased.

Ignoring Maddox's jab, he continued. "Zen hired me as his bodyguard a few years ago. I'd just gotten out of the Marines and was trying to figure out how the fuck I was going to adjust to civilian life. A buddy of mine knew someone who heard Zen was looking after he dealt with a couple of stalker situations. So,

I reached out. He hired me, and the rest is history."

"So, if you're Zen's bodyguard, why are you with Maddox so much?" I questioned, leaning back against Maddox's chest and reaching my hand up to play with his hair, running my fingers through the silky strands.

"Because he likes to stir shit up and cause trouble. Someone's got to make sure his ass stays out of trouble." Connor slid his suit jacket off and tossed it over the arm of his chair, unfastening his cufflinks and rolling his sleeves up to his elbows.

"*Liked* to stir shit up," Maddox corrected, wrapping an arm around my waist and stroking my hip with his fingers. My nipples hardened under his touch as we drove each other crazy. I hoped the flight wasn't much longer. I didn't know how long I could hold out. There was a tingle that started in my core and spread throughout my body, a neediness that I hadn't experienced before.

"And I'm going to need details," Quinn insisted, reclining his seat back and settling in for the story he assumed he'd be getting.

Maddox shot Connor a warning glare that I didn't see but felt in the way he tensed around me. Rolling my eyes, I reached back and patted his cheek a little bit condescendingly. "Don't worry, Romeo. I'm well aware of your whorish ways. I've got eyes and access to the internet, remember?"

He grabbed my hand and kissed it before putting my fingers back into his hair. "No one wants to hear about my antics. And that's all in the past now anyway," Maddox assured me.

"Fuck, of course you decide to reconnect and then get boring. I'm gonna need a wingman when we get to LA since Ryan's obviously out," Quinn declared, eyeing Connor, who held out his glass for Quinn to tap with his own.

"I've got you, Q. Tonight, we'll hit my favorite club." Connor yawned, reclining his seat next to Quinn, and suddenly I felt tired, too.

Closing my eyes as the conversation died down, I let myself be lulled by the rise and fall of Maddox's chest and the gentle rocking of the airplane. Before I knew it, I was completely out.

TWENTY THREE
RYAN

It'd only been twenty-four hours since I gave myself to Maddox, but it almost felt like a lifetime ago. Our mouths crashed together after that torturous plane ride. We were like magnets, drawn to each other without the ability to resist. And last night we'd given in for the first time. Now there would be no stopping the force that pulled us together.

The reality of Maddox inside of me was better than any fantasy I'd ever had. And I wanted him again. Badly.

We barely made it through the front door before his hands were all over me, ripping at the layers of lace still wrapping around my body. We were both panting as I watched his muscles ripple and bulge under his black suit jacket while he grabbed my dress and pulled. The tearing sound that filled the room further fueled my desire.

The ruined dress pooled around my feet. Maddox growled as he closed the few inches of distance between us, wrapping his arms around me, one hand gripping my ass and pulling me against the hard ridge in his slacks. The other hand skated up and tangled in my hair, grabbing a handful and pulling my head to the side. I didn't fight. I wanted this. I wanted *him*. I wanted him to make me forget everything and everyone except us.

He sucked and bit at my neck, his day-old scruff scratching the sensitive skin and making me shiver. I couldn't get close enough, and I lifted my leg and wrapped it around his waist. He stood taller and slammed his mouth down on mine, and I instantly opened for him, wanting him deeper, harder, just *more*. I wanted more of everything he had to give.

Pleasure clawed through me as he lowered his hand and tweaked my nipple until it tightened almost painfully. The rough pads of his fingers brushed across the sensitive peaks again and again until I writhed against him, burning up from the inside out. I needed him closer.

He reached down and lifted me like I weighed nothing, and I wrapped my legs around his waist. He never stopped the way he ravished my mouth, and I met him stroke for stroke, wrapping my arms around his neck and digging my nails into his scalp lightly. He growled into my mouth and started walking fast and with purpose somewhere deeper into the house.

I'd never been here before, so I wasn't sure where he was going, but I didn't care. At some point, he pushed me up against the wall and yanked my white lace thong right off of my body, shredding it and tossing it to the side before sinking a finger inside my center. "Fuck," I whimpered and tried to grind against him, but he had me pinned down. The wicked smile that crossed his face told me he knew exactly what he was doing when his thumb found my clit and started tracing slow, deliberate circles.

He was still fully dressed, and I needed to feel his skin against mine, so even as my body shook and pulsed, I ripped at his tie, yanking it off. He pulled his finger out of me long enough to drop his jacket off of his body before sliding not only one but two fingers back inside me. "You're fucking dripping, Freckles." The words sounded almost pained as he grit them out, and even though I wasn't experienced, I could tell he was on the verge of losing it.

"For you," I purred, wanting to see how far I could push him before he lost it completely. He watched his hand moving in and out of me and then glanced up at me with eyes that were almost entirely black. I shivered from that one look, feeling both burning heat and icy cold.

With shaky hands, I undid as many buttons as I could on his shirt before ripping the rest apart, almost moaning as the clink of buttons hitting the floor meant that his smooth, tanned, and incredibly sculpted chest was finally revealed. My mouth watered, and I leaned forward and bit the silver barbell through his right nipple, tugging it gently. He cursed and moaned, pulling his fingers from me and sucking them into his mouth while his dark eyes were locked with mine.

"So fucking good, Freckles. You have no idea," he grunted, pulling my body closer against his and finally pushing us through the door to his bedroom. He crossed it quickly, dropping me on the bed and standing back. His eyes raked over every naked inch of my body, and I reveled in his perusal. I wasn't ashamed of my body at all, and I watched as he reached down and flicked the button on his slacks open, pulling the zipper down achingly slow.

Dropping his pants, he stepped out of them and stood in front of me in just his black boxer briefs, the evidence of how turned on he was obvious. I longed to touch him, to run my hands over every inch of his perfect body. Maddox was every girl's fantasy come to life. Last night, it'd been dark, and he made everything about me. Tonight, I could study every bit of him and damn if he wasn't incredible. He was built and toned in all the right places, and his cock was so big I'd been a little sore this morning.

One look at the smug smirk on his face told me he knew exactly what he was doing to me. I slid off the bed onto my knees in front of him. I'd never done anything like this, but I wasn't stupid. I knew the mechanics of how blow jobs worked, and I wanted to see how far I could push his control. I never felt this need to get someone to lose control like Maddox brought out in me. He was always in charge and demanding. Could I get him to lose control? To act on every impulse without thinking it all through first? Without worrying about the consequences?

His eyes darkened even more as I reached up and ran my palm along the length of his hardness. "Freckles…" he warned, but I ignored him. I wanted what I wanted, and I was going to take it.

I leaned forward and pressed my lips to the head of his cock, and he groaned, shoving his hand into my hair. I opened my mouth, testing the feel of him in my mouth. He tasted a little salty, but I liked it. I ran my tongue along the head and closed my mouth around him, sliding my lips up and down until he hit the back of my throat. He gripped my hair tighter, pushing his hips against me almost involuntarily. I fought off a smile, trying to focus on what I was doing. I suctioned him deeper into my throat, gagging a little, but the way he cursed and moaned distracted me.

"Fuck, I'm going to come if you don't stop." I wanted him to. I wanted to taste him and swallow him down and get him to unravel in my mouth, but he had other plans. He pulled himself out of my mouth with a loud *pop* and lifted me up by my upper arms, tossing me back on the bed and crawling over my body, ravaging my mouth with his.

I bet he could taste himself on my lips, but he didn't seem to care. He settled himself between my legs, pressing the head of his cock against my opening. Desire flooded me, and we both moaned as he slammed deep inside. This wasn't like last night, though. This was hot and needy and more possessive than sweet. I loved every damn second.

As he relentlessly rocked into me again and again, he hit every spot until I was wound so tight I knew I'd explode any second. He drove me higher and higher toward ecstasy.

"Who's pussy is this?" he demanded, his voice gruff.

"Yours," I whimpered.

"Who has it always belonged to?"

"You. Always you."

"That's right. *Mine,*" he growled.

His words pushed me over the edge, and I dug my fingernails into his back as I lost myself to the waves of pleasure crashing through me. I cried out his name, and his guttural moan joined mine as he emptied himself inside of me.

Our harsh breathing filled the room until he finally pressed a kiss to my forehead and looked deep into my eyes. His gaze was so open and vulnerable, I'd never seen him like this. "I mean it, Freckles. I love you so fucking much it hurts, and I always have. And now you're mine and only mine. And I'm yours. There's no going back."

I could only nod, trying to fight off the sting of tears as my eyes welled. A lone tear managed to escape, and I cursed it. I was *not* the type of girl who cried. But there were so many emotions warring inside me right now I couldn't process them. Here, lying in the afterglow of the best orgasm I'd ever had, I finally found the one thing I'd always wanted. Maddox Everleigh loved me like I loved him. As he wiped the tear from my cheek, I whispered the words I'd longed to say aloud for as long as I could remember. "I love you, too."

After the best nap of my life, I untangled myself from Maddox, and we got ready to go out for what he called *family dinner*. I knew he didn't have any family out here, so I figured he meant his group of friends. They'd be like his family now.

After a quick shower and change of clothes, we climbed into a car, but I couldn't have told you what it was. He leaned over and kissed me quickly before starting the engine on the ridiculously expensive sports car. I hadn't had a lot of time earlier to check out his house, but what I saw was luxurious and bright and beautiful.

Music played softly from the speakers as we cruised along the streets of LA, the blue sky and palm trees, and brief glimpses of the ocean as we approached Malibu, filling me up with a feeling like coming home. I hadn't been back here since I left the academy, and I hadn't realized just how much I missed it. I rolled down the window and let the wind tear through my hair, not giving a second thought to the fact that the strands of my hair were about to become a giant tangled mess. This was me, and if his friends didn't like it, I didn't care.

We pulled up to a gorgeous house right on the beach, and I gawked up at it. This was what Maddox's world was like, the type of place his friends lived. I would never be able to afford to live in a place like this. Maddox seemed to thrive in this environment. A little insecurity wiggled its way inside of me, wondering if I was good enough for him. I looked over at this stunningly complex man, the carefree smile on his face one I hadn't seen since we were kids, and even then, he hadn't been this light.

His smile dropped as he walked around the car and took in the look on my face. "What's wrong?"

I bit my lip, not wanting to ruin the good mood from earlier. I was looking forward to meeting his friends, and he seemed excited about it, too. And I knew Quinn would be here with Connor since they had the good sense to leave Maddox and me alone for a few hours.

Sighing, I gave in. "Look at this place," I offered, waving my hand at the house in front of us. "I'm not sure if I fit in here."

He stepped in front of me, his body pressing against mine so I could feel every inch of him from his chest down while he snaked his arms around my waist. "I know you're not being serious right now, Freckles, because the girl I know and love doesn't doubt how incredible she is. She doesn't question whether she belongs. She walks in and commands the goddamn room."

His words washed over me, and I realized he was right. This self-doubt bullshit wasn't who I was. I lifted my chin and stood a little taller, and his face lit up with his smile again. "There she is," he noted, bending to press a kiss to the tip of my nose. "Now, let's go inside. You're going to love them."

I noticed he didn't say whether they'd love me. Maybe that wasn't important to him. Maybe that's where my nervousness came from, and the bitch manifested herself as self-doubt. Well, I was done with that.

He didn't bother knocking, opening the heavy wooden door and walking right inside. Laughter echoed from deeper in the house, the sounds of food sizzling and pans clanging filling the entire space with a very lived-in vibe. While the house was beautiful, this place was no museum. It was a home, and I immediately felt more relaxed with that realization.

We rounded the corner into the kitchen, and as soon as one person noticed us, everyone surrounded Maddox and me. I wasn't sure who was who except for Zen, True, Connor, and of course, Quinn. Zen had a beautiful blonde woman who was obviously pregnant glued to his side. They almost looked like they were one person. It made me think of the saying *attached at the hip*, and I almost giggled out loud at the thought. Her eyes were bright blue and sparkling as she looked me over. "You must be Ryan. I'd say we've heard a lot about you, but this douchecanoe kept you a secret from us." She pointed at Maddox.

Laughing, she stepped briefly away from her husband and pulled me into a tight hug. "I'm Kennedy, and you already met my husband, Zen. Let me introduce you to everyone." She threaded her arm through mine and dragged me away from Maddox, who just grinned at me before turning back to his friends. I didn't mind. I'd never had girlfriends before, except for my sisters. There weren't exactly a lot of options when you lived in the middle of nowhere.

Pulling me into the living room where the biggest TV I'd ever seen in my life was mounted to the wall, and a huge sectional sofa that looked perfect for naps sat, a couple of women were having what looked to be a spirited conversation, but I couldn't tell what about. "Okay, you two. Knock your shit off and meet Mad's girl. This is Ryan," she introduced, shifting me closer to the two women who stood up off the couch and were looking at me with matching wide grins.

"Well, fuck me, I never thought I'd see the day Maddox brought a girl around the fam," the redhead with an adorable baby perched on her hip remarked.

"You guys are going to scare her off," the exotic brunette chided. "I'm Amara. This is Montana, and this little parasite is my daughter, Phoenix," she added, before leaning down and tickling her daughter's chubby little tummy. Phoenix's giggle was infectious, and I felt myself smiling down at her as her bright blue eyes locked on her mom.

"Who haven't you met yet?" Kennedy wondered aloud, scanning the room. "Oh! Jericho and Grayson. Harrison's not here yet," she explained as if I had any idea who those people were.

"It was nice meeting you!" I called out over my shoulder as Kennedy dragged me away, but based on the looks the girls gave me, I had a feeling this wasn't the last I'd be seeing of them.

She pulled me into the kitchen where Maddox was nowhere to be found, but a tall blonde guy with bright blue eyes was chopping an onion so fast, I cringed, sure he was about to cut his finger off. "Gray, this is Ryan, Maddox's girl," Kennedy introduced me again, emphasizing Maddox's name like this whole thing was so unbelievable. Maybe it was. Maybe my brain had gone into safe mode, and this was all a hallucination I created to forget the tragic reality of marrying Yates.

But my stinging, watering eyes told me otherwise—stupid onions. "Hi," I said with a small wave. Wiping away a stray tear.

"Hey, I'm Grayson, this one's older brother," he said, ruffling Kennedy's hair as she rolled her eyes.

"He's a couple minutes older and thinks that gives him the right to tell me what to do. Pshh," she scoffed. Then she cracked up and leaned closer to me, almost conspiratorial. "Did you know one time Zen thought Grayson and I were dating? Can you imagine?"

I found myself laughing with her. She was so warm and made me feel like we'd known each other forever. It was a comfort I hadn't experienced before.

"Okay," she straightened, resting her hand on her stomach. "This little guy kicks the crap out of my insides when I laugh. I can't tell if he thinks he's funny or not," she mused, lovingly rubbing her stomach. Over her shoulder, I noticed Zen hovering nearby but trying to act like he was giving her some space. It was sweet and amusing at the same time.

"Okay, Jericho. I think he's in the pool room with the rest of the guys," she explained, walking faster than I thought she'd be able to with her stomach as big as it was. We stepped into the room at the front of the house. A pool table sat in the middle, and another huge TV was spread across the wall. Maddox set down his pool stick and crossed the room, wrapping me in his arms. "You okay?" he whispered so only I could hear, and I nodded, relishing his closeness. Even though everyone was great, fantastic even, it was still a lot to take in meeting them all at once like this.

He leaned down to kiss me before letting me go. Kennedy watched him with a look on his face like he'd grown a second head. Then a sly smile spread across her face. "Okay then. Last but not least is my favorite. Jericho," she said, stepping up behind the Asian guy on the couch who had a game controller in his hand. "I heard that," Zen called out from the other side of the room, and Kennedy winked at me.

"Sorry. *Second* favorite," she corrected, and he grumbled, but her smile just got wider.

"Who are you?" he asked as he looked me over, and I had no idea what he was thinking.

"Ryan, Maddox's..." I paused to think it over. "Childhood best friend slash sometimes safe person slash girl who's been pining over him for *way* too long," I gushed before clamping my mouth shut. "Yeah, so, it's complicated," I said with a laugh, and he grinned.

"Right. Well, welcome to the fam. If you ever want to throw down on some Xbox, I'm your guy. And for the love of Christ, don't let Montana mix you a drink," he warned before turning back to his game. I wasn't sure what to make of him, but I liked him all the same.

"Okay, I think that's everyone," Kennedy hesitated, looking around the room. "Pregnancy brain makes me forget all sorts of shit."

"I have literally no idea what pregnancy brain is but sure if you say so," I said, glancing at where Maddox stood with his eyes locked on me, his gaze turning darker and more heated by the second. I squirmed under his scrutiny.

"Hey, Ryan," True called out from where he stepped up next to Maddox, and sometime in the last ten minutes, he managed to snag his daughter from Montana and carried her in a wrap across his chest. I waved. Watching these rock legends become giant piles of tattooed and muscled mush around their wives and kids would have been hilarious if it wasn't so endearing.

"Good, now we can eat. Did you know Gray's a world-class chef? You're about to have a foodgasm. Prepare yourself," Kennedy cautioned. I followed her back to the kitchen, wondering what the hell a foodgasm was and whether or not I wanted one.

TWENTY FOUR
MADDOX

She chose me, and I still couldn't believe it. The past two days were a goddamn fantasy come to life. Ryan fit seamlessly into my life in LA, better than I could have ever even hoped. And even Quinn felt like he was meant to be here with us. He and Grayson had hit it off at dinner Saturday night, and he even hung out at the restaurant with Gray on Sunday.

That was perfect because it meant Ryan and I didn't even get out of bed yesterday. I looked over at where she sat beside me on the plane, and I squeezed the hand I held. She glanced up from the magazine she was reading, and her eyes crinkled at the corners as she gave me a soft smile that fucking melted me.

The amount of love I felt for this woman was overwhelming in the best way.

She settled back in, leaning her head against my shoulder for a few minutes before she sat back up and gnawed on her lower lip. I reached over and gently tugged it out from between her teeth. "What's wrong, Freckles?"

Quinn chuckled from where he sat across from us, and my eyes flicked to him before settling back on my girl. He had dark sunglasses still perched on his face even though we were inside the body of the plane with all the window covers pulled down. It looked like he had even more fun with Connor that I thought.

An adorable crease formed between her eyebrows. "I'm so nervous about facing my parents and my family when we get back. What can I even say to explain everything that happened? And then just running away like I did and leaving them all to deal with the fallout. I'm terrified they're all going to hate me."

I moved my hands up to her face, gently turning her, so I stared directly into her eyes. "Remember what I promised you? I'm not going anywhere. I'll be right next to you for every second, and I won't let anything happen. Your parents are some of the most understanding people I've ever met. And when they find out why you agreed to that whole sham in the first place? I have a feeling any anger they might have will go up in smoke."

"He's right," Quinn agreed, his usual snark missing while he suffered from what looked like one hell of a hangover.

She closed her eyes and took a deep breath, and I watched as some of the tension melted out of her body as she leaned into my touch. "You don't think they'll hate me?"

Shaking my head, I let her go and pulled her against me instead. "Shannon and Alex love you. They'll forgive you. I'd bet my Maclaren on it."

She giggled lightly. "You love that car too much."

"Not as much as you," I countered, wanting to pull her into my lap, but we were flying through a shit ton of turbulence right now, and I'd always put Ryan's well being above my wants and needs. I always had, even when we were kids. It was why I left and stayed away without contacting her. I think deep down, I always knew I was fucking lost when it came to her. That there wouldn't ever be anyone else for me, but I didn't want to admit it because she deserved so much more than me.

I knew she'd never walk away, so I had to be the strong one and keep her safe from me. But the older I got, the more I faced my own demons, the more I realized they didn't control me. *I* controlled *them*. Which meant I could have her and be confident I wasn't going to turn into my dad. I'd rather die than hurt Ryan in any way.

"You two would make me sick if I wasn't so fucking jealous," Quinn complained, lifting the soda water he was nursing up to his lips and taking the smallest possible sip.

"Don't worry, Quinny. When you move to LA, it won't take long for you to find someone," I promised, and he sat up a little straighter, his eyebrows lifting.

"What do you mean *when I move to LA?*" he asked, leaning forward.

I glanced down at Ryan, whose breathing had evened out as she slept against my shoulder. "Well, I can't stay in the band and live in fucking *Texas*. Not that I'd want to live here anyway," I whispered, wrinkling my nose.

"Sure," Quinn agreed, waving me on.

"I know Ryan doesn't want to stay and work the ranch. She has dreams, and I plan to make every single one come true. But I know she'd never leave you behind. And truthfully, I don't want to leave you here, either. You're a good guy, and I like having you around. You want to protect Ryan as much as I do, not that she needs it."

He chuckled softly again then winced, rubbing his temples. "Fuck, no. She's no scared little girl. She's badass. That's part of why I love her so much," he confessed in a whisper as his eyes flicked down to take her in, and I could've sworn I caught something in his gaze that shouldn't be there, but I shook it off. Quinn had never been anything but a good friend to Ryan.

Dismissing that thought, I closed my eyes and thought about what we were going to be facing. As much as I wanted to put on a brave face for Ryan, I really had no idea how her parents were going to react. And I knew there was no fucking way Yates was going to just let this go.

He had plans for my girl, and when she walked away from that, it was a blow to his considerable ego. I didn't know what he had the reach to make happen, but he had money. He might not have access to a lot of it, but he was a clever and sneaky son of a bitch, and I couldn't underestimate him.

Not knowing what I'd be dealing with when it came to his retribution had me stressed the fuck out, but I'd never tell Ryan. She was already worried enough. I could handle that asshole myself. I had to admit it was unsettling as fuck that Connor hadn't been able to dig up even a speeding ticket on Yates. There was no way he was that clean.

The question was, what was he hiding? I intended to find out.

The plane shook again, and I tightened my grip on Ryan, but she didn't wake up. The rest of the plane ride, I tried to clear my mind and stay as calm as possible so that Ryan could rest. I didn't let shit rattle me. I was smarter than that. I needed more information, and until I had it, there was no point worrying about it.

I tried to relax the rest of the flight, planning what steps to take next in my mind and then letting them go. Ryan slept, resting her body against mine, and she fit like she was made to be there. I hated to wake her up, considering neither of us got a lot of sleep over the past couple of days. A grin broke out on my face as I relieved my favorite memories of Ryan's body wrapped around mine all weekend long.

Just before we touched down, I gently woke her by kissing her entire face, everywhere but her lips. Her eyelids fluttered open, and she looked up at me with tired eyes. "Time to wake up, Freckles. Wouldn't want you to miss out on your favorite part."

Glancing over at Quinn, he was slumped in the seat, his glasses askew on his face. He looked like a fucking wreck after the weekend, but it made me happy that he fit in just as well as Ryan with my friends.

Ryan sat up straighter and leaned over to look out the window. Her passion for every new thing was like a breath of fresh air in my lungs. It was infectious. I'd flown around the entire world. I'd flown so many miles that I barely paid attention to it anymore, let alone appreciated the parts that used to be exciting. But watching the world through Ryan's eyes was like rediscovering it.

I was quickly getting addicted to life with her by my side. I never imagined I could actually have her, and now that she'd walked away from everything for me, I planned to do everything to show her she'd made the right choice.

The wheels touched down with a jolt, and the engines roared as we barrelled down the runway before slowing. "Well, Freckles, you ready to do this?" I asked, capturing her hand in mine and pulling her attention away from the window, back to me and reality.

She sighed heavily, looking back at me through unsure eyes. "No, but I'm never going to be more ready to face it than I am right now."

"That's my girl," I praised before Quinn sleepily interjected, "Our girl."

Laughing, I stood and led us to the front of the plane where Hilda had our bags ready. After a quick thanks, we climbed down the steps and got into the truck I'd bought and had delivered to the hanger. If we were going to be spending more time out here, I didn't want to have to keep renting cars. It was a pain in the ass.

The ranch was about half an hour away, and the entire way, Ryan alternated between nervously chatting about nothing at all and complete silence as I watched her chew her lip until it looked like she drew blood. Quinn dozed off and on and kept to himself most of the ride. "Do you think your sisters will be there?" I asked, trying to get her talking so she'd quit hurting herself. My motivation was partly selfish. If her lip was injured, I wouldn't be able to kiss it without causing her pain, and I couldn't have that.

Not kissing her wasn't an option either. So talking it was, even if it made her think about what she didn't want to. We were going to have to face it in just a few minutes anyway.

"I hadn't really thought about it. I hope not. They don't forgive as easily as my parents, and they don't let things go. Charlie's like a bloodhound with a scent. She'll never give up until she's unearthed every single detail more than once just to be sure," she explained, sighing. "I *really* hope it's just mom and dad."

I rubbed her upper thigh in circles gently, hoping I could calm her down a little bit with my touch the way she did to me whenever I was just in her presence. It seemed to work as she leaned against me. She was lost in thought, but luckily she gave up the assault on her lower lip.

"Fuck, Lancelot. You better hope the girls aren't there, or they're going to make it so much more difficult on you," Quinn unhelpfully added from the back seat, and I shot him a glare in the rearview mirror.

He shifted his eyes away from me before rubbing Ryan's shoulder. "But I'm sure they won't be there. They're way too busy with their own lives," he added, trying to be reassuring, but the damage was already done as Ryan stiffened next to me.

"Quinn and I will run interference if we have to, Freckles. Don't worry about your sisters. This isn't about them. Really, this is between you and your parents," I gently reminded her.

"You're right. And once we talk to them, we can figure out what to do about the ranch. Right?" she asked, her big, doe eyes pleading with me to have all the answers.

"Right," I agreed, squeezing her thigh and feeling a zing shoot straight to my dick. We stayed in bed until the last possible second before we flew back, and still, my body reacted as if I hadn't spent the weekend fucking her in every room of my house.

And I had a big goddamn house.

I had some ideas about what I wanted to do with both of our ranches, but we needed to first deal with the wedding fallout. There were so many issues flying around with this situation I wanted to take them one at a time.

Turning down the long dirt drive, Ryan sucked in a breath. Even Quinn's quiet reassurances and my touch weren't enough to keep her from breathing hard and tensing every muscle in her body. Finally, I parked the truck and turned toward her. "Everything's going to be fine, Freckles. I promise. Okay?"

She nodded, but her eyes were still wild, and her body was still stiff as fuck. The front door opened, and her mom stepped out onto the porch, shielding her eyes with her hand against the sun and watching us. She didn't move closer, and despite us not having called and my truck being unfamiliar, I had no doubt she knew exactly who just drove up.

"Go be the confident fighter I know you are and stand up for what you know is right. They'll understand," I nudged, grabbing the door handle and swinging my door open. Quinn followed my lead, and I rounded the front of the truck and pulled open her door. She straightened her spine and flashed me a small smile, the confidence seeping back into her eyes.

Quinn and I hung back and let Ryan take the lead. She marched up the stairs like she had a spine made of steel, not an ounce of the nerves I knew she was feeling showing on the outside. I didn't know if she was fooling anyone, but I appreciated the effort. My girl was fierce and brave, and I was the lucky bastard that got to stand at her side.

"Hey, mom," she greeted Shannon with a hug which her mom returned, and I let out the breath I'd been holding. My experience with parents wasn't typical or positive in any way, so I had no idea how this was going to go down. If I based what was coming on my own experiences, there'd be a lot of yelling, a lot of insults, and probably some violence on the horizon.

But Ryan's parents weren't like that, and her mom welcomed us into the house with a watery smile. When I stepped through the door, followed by Quinn at my back, I sniffed at the air and smelled cinnamon. I wondered if Shannon had expected us to come by.

We stepped into the living room where Alexander sat in his wheelchair, staring out the window at the green rolling fields behind the house with an unreadable expression on his face. Ryan sank down onto the sofa while her mom left the room, probably to grab snacks. I sat down beside her, and Quinn took the other side. We flanked her like sentries, both of us ready to go to battle on her behalf.

Shannon came back into the room, carrying a tray of cinnamon rolls and set the tray down on the coffee table in front of us, but nobody reached for them. The air was thick with tension, and I could see Quinn squirming out of the corner of my eye. I was used to being put in all sorts of uncomfortable as fuck situations. I'd been training for that shit my entire life. But he clearly wanted to do something to break the tension.

I hoped he wouldn't step in and would let Ryan handle this. She needed to.

Shannon sat in the armchair across from me. "Alex? Come join us," she softly insisted.

He sighed and wheeled himself over to take his place next to her.

"Dad-" Ryan started, and he held up his hand, stopping her.

"No. I'm sorry," he apologized.

I glanced down at Ryan, and she looked like she'd been slapped. "You're sorry? For what?" she asked incredulously.

"For not telling you about the foreclosure sooner. For making you come back home in the first place. For not being able to handle this myself. And most of all, for making you think you had to marry an asshole like Yates to solve my problems," he clarified. "For so many things."

He looked tired, like he'd aged ten years overnight. All of this shit was looked like it weighed heavily on him.

Ryan stood up and crossed the room, kneeling down in front of her dad and pulling his hand into hers. "Please don't apologize. I was happy to come home and help if it meant you could recover and keep the ranch. And yeah, I wish you would've told me about the foreclosure sooner, but what's done is done.

I never should have agreed to marry Yates. The price was too heavy. Quinn tried to tell me, but I didn't want to listen."

Alex's eyes shot over to Quinn and narrowed for a second, but Quinn didn't even flinch. He was fucking loyal, I'd give him that. Ryan drew her dad's attention back to her. "But now that I didn't go through with the wedding, Yates isn't going to help save this place. We only have a few days left, and I'm not sure what we're going to do."

Shannon's eyebrows furrowed. "He emailed a couple of weeks ago and asked for the bank paperwork, so I sent it over. We've gone back and forth a bit, signing forms and granting access and everything, so I don't know what's happening with the foreclosure. You know paperwork has never been something I'm very good at," she mumbled.

Something about her explanation didn't sit well with me. If she didn't remember what she'd signed or given Yates access to, I had no idea what we'd be dealing with when it came to him. I had a sinking feeling he'd done more damage than I'd thought when we came here today. I made a mental note to text Connor and ask him to look into it when we were done.

"Honey, we aren't upset. We're *proud*. Proud as hell, actually," Shannon said with a grin that lit up her whole face, and Alexander nodded in agreement. "Your mother's right. You were willing to go so far to help us, and then then you realized how wrong it was and walked away."

A shadow passed over Shannon's face as her smile fell. "I'm so relieved we're not going to be related to those people. That woman is a monster, and her son is just as bad. Maybe worse. We want so much better for you."

Turning toward me, she smiled, and I got her message loud and clear. They approved of our relationship, but I better treat their daughter like the goddamn gift she was. Ryan stood halfway and hugged her dad before moving to her mom and wrapping her arms around her.

"Thank you," she told them before moving across the room to where Quinn and I sat on the couch. "Now, I think we have some chores to get done."

I stood up and pulled her against me, the relief in the room palpable. The energy felt good, hopeful even despite all the unknowns surrounding all of us. And yes, I included myself in that. I had no idea what would be coming, but I hoped we'd have enough time to gather information and make a plan.

Ryan pulled out of my arms, and I tried to tug her back, but she just chuckled and turned around instead, letting me pull her back against my chest and wrap my arms around her while she addressed her parents.

"What about Charlie and Justice? Are they mad?" she wondered.

"At first they were. When they found out you left, Yates and his friends tried to surround them and get them to tell them where you were. But Charlie threatened to call the cops, and Justice kicked one in the balls. Dropped him like a sack of potatoes," Alex recounted, pride shining in his eyes as he chuckled. "But now they're just relieved we're not going to have any connection to that horrible family."

Ryan relaxed against my body as stress flowed out of her. "We'll be moving the herd from the east pasture to the west," I informed them before glancing down to Ryan, who nodded at me. It was easy to slip right into the old habits I formed when I was a kid working way too hard as a ranch hand for my dad.

"I need a shower and a bottle of Tylenol," Quinn stated, lifting himself shakily off the couch. By the look of him, his hangover was still kicking his ass.

"That's fine, Quinny. We'll meet back here for lunch, and you can help after," Ryan decided, and we both turned and walked hand-in-hand outside. Once the door was firmly closed behind us and we were on our way to the barn, I wanted to check in with my girl.

"How are you feeling, Freckles?" I asked, swinging our joined hands between us as we trudged through the soft grass to the old barn.

"Relieved," she breathed as a slow smile spread across her face. "I didn't think it'd be that easy with them. I thought they'd hate me for what I did."

"I told you they wouldn't. Your parents are the best I know, outside of True's mom and dad. I knew they wouldn't be too mad."

"Yeah, but they didn't even seem mad at all. I wasn't expecting that, but I'm really thankful they're being so understanding." She stopped walking and dropped my hand, instead launching herself at me. I caught her, barely stumbling, as she wrapped her legs around my waist and peppered my face with kisses.

"I love you," she repeated over and over, her carefree laughter was a sound of pure joy that had reduced my heart to a puddle of mush and sent electric jolts of need through my body. My dick was quickly hardening between us as she ground her body against mine. We were in a grassy field with nothing around. I couldn't push her against a wall and press into her like I wanted, and the living room looked right out onto us. I couldn't lay her down on the ground here and finish what she started, either.

Sighing, I pulled back, and she slid down my body, and I hated every fucking second of it because my body was screaming for her. Her eyes dropped to my hard-as-fuck cock before she lifted them up to my face, inch by agonizing fucking inch. "Thanks for having my back in there, and, well, with everything. I don't think I've thanked you yet."

"You never have to thank me, Freckles. I'll always have your back. You don't have to go through anything you don't want to alone again," I vowed as we started our walk back to the barn.

She stayed silent the rest of the way, and I got the feeling she was processing what my words meant. But fuck if I was going to let her go through this life alone when I could have her by my side.

We saddled up the horses and rode out to the east pasture, circling the cattle and starting the slow process of herding them toward the west. It was boring as fuck, and I'd have probably fallen asleep on the back of my horse if I hadn't been entranced by watching Ryan work. The way her hips moved on the back of her horse, her absolute control and command of the animal beneath her, her quiet confidence in every fluid movement of her body.

By the time the sun crawled its way to the highest point in the sky, I didn't know which part of my body needed more attention: my growling stomach or my throbbing dick. I watched Ryan bounce on the back of Storm as she rode toward me, my eyes obviously dropping to her tits. Fuck, she had great tits.

I snapped my gaze back up to her face and instantly sobered at the look on her face.

"Quinn just texted me," she seethed, and I wondered what the hell he'd done to piss her off so bad.

"What'd he do?" I asked, tightening my grip on Hex's reins.

"It's not him. Yates is here," she grit out. "We've gotta go."

I followed her out, stopping only to lock the pasture gate before we took off at a solid gallop across the rolling fields. As we approached the house, Ryan nudged Storm into a trot before stopping in front of the house. She threw her leg over the saddle, jumping down. So was so goddamn graceful even when she was fiery and pissed off. She entranced me, and I could watch her all day.

Instead, we were here dealing with this fucker. Again.

He held paperwork in his hands and wore a smug-as-fuck smile on his face I didn't like the look of. Quinn stood off to the side with a death glare on his face pointed right at Yates. The screen door slammed as Alexander rolled out onto the porch behind us. His shotgun laid in his lap with his hand resting on top of it, making his point without ever having to say a word. I made a mental note to buy a shotgun and keep it around for situations just like this because it just hit me where Ryan learned to be a badass. I looked at Alexander with newfound respect, his jaw clenched, and his eyes focused on Yates.

"What the fuck do you want?" I finally asked since it seemed like everyone else was content to just glare at each other.

"This doesn't concern you," he fumed before turning to Ryan with an evil smile that showed more teeth than necessary. I automatically got down off of Hex and stepped up behind her.

"I own this whole goddamn place, and you've got a week to get the fuck off my property," he demanded with a sneer on his face. "You're lucky I'm giving you that long."

Fuck, I underestimated how bad he'd want to hurt Ryan after she humiliated him. The rage that was starting to course through my veins had adrenaline flooding my system. My fists clenched and I saw red, wanting to destroy him. I didn't just want to make him hurt. I wanted to fucking *demolish* him. I wanted to dismantle every goddamn piece of his life until there was nothing left.

Maybe in my early twenties, I would have said fuck it and knocked his evil ass out. But I'd learned and grown, and now I played the long game. We had a week to figure shit out and make a plan to take this fucker out. As I watched him retreat back to his stupid vintage car, I glanced at Quinn, who looked at least as pissed off as I felt. Maybe even more.

I knew what my next move was, though. I had Connor in my corner, and that motherfucker could take anyone down. I'd seen him do it with minimal effort. If this was how Yates wanted to play, he'd get the game of his fucking life.

TWENTY FIVE
MADDOX

Watching that fucker disappear in a cloud of dust and taillights down the driveway, we collectively stood in silence. No one wanted to admit that we were fucked. Ryan must be devastated after everything, but she wasn't the kind of girl to collapse under the weight of her emotions. At least not in front of people.

I ran my hand up her back and clasped her shoulder, squeezing gently, and she spun, wrapping her arms around me and burying her face in my chest. "I hate him," she mumbled, and I chuckled darkly.

"Freckles, I think it's safe to say you're in good company." I rubbed her back and looked at Quinn, who stood next to me, his jaw working as he continued to glare at the dissipating dust.

"We'll deal with him, Quinny," I promised, and he shifted his gaze to me.

"How? Do you have a plan?"

I looked past him to the porch, where Alexander shook his head before retreating back into the house. Once he was inside, I answered. "We need information, and Connor will know how to get it. Once we know what exactly we're up against, we'll figure out what we're going to do. But there's not one goddamn chance I'm letting him take this ranch."

Ryan lifted her head, her stormy eyes meeting mine. "This is all my fault."

"Did you bring Yates into this situation? Yes. But did you make him act like an asshole? No, that's all him. What he's doing? That's on him, not you."

I pressed a kiss to the top of her head before letting her go. "You two go finish the chores," I said, climbing back up onto Hex and grabbing his reins. "I'm going home to call in the cavalry."

Turning away from the two of them, I rode back to my barn, handing Hex over to Joel before striding inside the house, my brain churning the entire time. We were going to have a more formidable foe than I anticipated in Yates, and I was going to have to be smart and patient with how I dealt with him.

He thought he had Ryan where he wanted her, and he wasn't about to give that up easily. Pulling my cell out of my pocket, I shot a text to Connor.

Maddox: I need you back in TX.

Connor: Can it wait?

Maddox: No. Bring the whole team.

Connor: K.

I didn't need to do much else now but wait. Connor and his team would hop on the jet and be here this afternoon. And after I was done strategizing with them, I had plans for Ryan and I. Grabbing my keys, I hopped in my truck and took off into town. The hardware store would help me pass the time nicely.

🎼

The low hum of the air conditioner rumbled through the room as we all sat around my living room, staring at each other. I wasn't quite sure where to begin explaining the shitshow that Yates brought to my doorstep, but I was sure as fuck glad that I had the men in this room surrounding me.

I purposefully left Ryan out of this meeting, not wanting her to derail any plans that might come up for ethical reasons. I had morals, but I had a feeling mine were a fuck of a lot more flexible than hers were.

As for Quinn? Well, I preferred to deal with professionals, and while I had no doubt the dude could hold his own, I also knew the team sitting around my living room would get this shit handled without any fuckups. It was what they did. Connor only brought the fucking best onto his team.

Connor didn't even need to clear his throat to get everyone's attention. He sat up taller in his seat, the ink on his arms and shoulders poking out of the sleeves and collar of his t-shirt. His dirty blonde hair was messy like he'd been running his hands through it for hours, but his eyes were focused. Everyone's attention snapped to him while we waited to see what he was going to say.

"This is the target," he announced, slapping a picture of Yates's smug face down onto the ottoman we sat around. Indy, Connor's main muscle and ex-MMA fighter, reached over and picked up the picture, studying it carefully.

"Looks like an egotistical asshole," he observed before passing the picture to his hacker, Sebastian.

He adjusted his glasses, pushing them further up his nose as he squinted at the picture. "He has a punchable face," Sebastian noted, setting the picture back onto the ottoman. We all looked back at Connor.

"His name is Yates Rutherford. His family's in the banking business. He's had a hard-on for Maddox's girl for a couple of months, and they were getting married. Turns out the wedding was all a setup," he explained, laying a folder down on the ottoman again. "Inside is the contract and NDA he had her sign."

Indy grabbed for the file and flipped through it while Connor continued. "The way he had all of it drawn up and pulled Ryan into his plan is really fucking suspicious. Add to that that he now claims to own her family's ranch and is kicking them off and, well, this shit just got personal."

"What do you need from us, boss?" Sebastian asked, his gaze flicking between Connor and me. In Connor's crew, if you fucked with anyone they considered friend or family, they were all in, very few questions asked.

"He's given the Knight's a week until he has them removed from their ranch. I want constant surveillance on Yates for the next forty-eight hours. Audio, video, night vision. Use it all. Collect everything. I want to know who he's with, where he goes, what his routines are." Connor turned to face Indy and Julian, his second in command, who'd been silent until now. "You two will take eight-hour rotating shifts. If he so much as sneezes, I want to know about it."

He turned to Sebastian. "I've done a little digging into him myself and couldn't find shit. One personal bank account with hardly anything in it, which is suspicious as fuck, because he's supposed to be rich. Nothing else. Not even a library card or parking ticket. He's too clean. Do what you do and see how far it takes you. I also need to know if he bought the Knight ranch and how much he paid."

Sebastian pulled out his tablet, flipped open the cover, and started tapping. He tuned the rest of us out now that he had his assignment. Finally, Connor turned to me. "I'm going to alternate with Julian and Indy on surveillance. You stick by your girl. Tell her not to worry. We'll take this fucker down."

Indy locked his intense brown eyes on me. "He's right. We've never had a problem making shit go away before, and this asshole is no exception."

Nodding, I asked, "When will the surveillance start?"

Connor dropped his gaze to the watch on his wrist. "As soon as Indy and Julian load up the equipment they'll need, and Bas gets us an address to start."

Sebastian didn't even look up from where he was tapping quickly on his tablet. "Already sent, check your phones. He's at the bank until four o'clock."

Indy and Julian stood, and on their way out, Julian stopped and squeezed my shoulder briefly, flashing me a sympathetic look before his eyes hardened as he focused back on the mission and followed Indy outside. We'd been through some shit, Julian and me, and I knew he wouldn't let me down. I trusted him as much as I did Connor.

Lifting myself off the couch, Sebastian didn't even look up as the cushions next to him shifted. I needed to do something. Anything. I felt completely useless right now. "Want to help me with a side project?" I asked Connor, who nodded.

I led the way out to my truck and pulled the supplies I purchased earlier out, tossing some rope at Connor. "We're taking horses," I announced before turning and making my way toward the barn, a smile stretching across my face as I thought about what we were about to do.

𝄞

Connor took his horse back to the barn to check in with his team once we finished my secret project. The sun hung low in the sky, and by the time I got back home, everyone would be gone, scattered to their own hotel rooms and assignments.

I pulled out my phone and shot Quinn a text.

Maddox: Send Freckles to the pond

Quinn: Say please

Maddox: …now

Quinn: So bossy

Maddox: Make sure she has a swimsuit

Quinn: Yes, sir

A smirk played across my lips as I imagined the level of snark in that last text. Quinn was quickly becoming one of my favorite people. I made sure Hex was tied up before pulling my shirt off and slipping out of my jeans. My swim trunks molded to my body in a flattering as fuck way, and I couldn't wait to watch Ryan's eyes rake over my body.

The way her eyes both lit up and darkened at the same time whenever she looked at me set my body ablaze. My heart was thrumming steadily faster in my chest as I watched the horizon with sunglass-covered eyes, waiting for any sign of my girl.

Finally, a fucking eternity later, she and Quinn both on the back of Daisy came into view. What the fuck was he doing here? Had my instructions been anything but clear? I gritted my teeth, not wanting to let Quinn's tagging along ruin my good mood.

Finally, they came to a stop a few steps away, Ryan moving to dismount the horse but Quinn didn't move to get down. He smirked knowingly at me, tiling the rim of his cowboy hat down briefly. "Thought I'd drop our girl off." He let his eyes wander all over my body. I didn't give a shit if Quinn wanted to look at me. Better me than my girl.

Ryan stepped up close so that the soft curves of her body were pressed against me. She rested both palms on my bare chest, her hands running up to clasp together behind my neck, stopping only briefly to flick against the ring I wore in my right nipple.

I ran my hands down her back, which was still covered by a thin cotton t-shirt, my fingers itching to touch her bare skin. I couldn't resist the urge anymore and snuck my thumb underneath the hem of her shirt, stroking the silky skin underneath.

The sound of fading hooves was the only signal Quinn left us as Ryan and I stared into each other's eyes. I lowered my head while she pushed up on her toes, and our mouths met in the middle, wildly clashing together, tongues colliding in a frantic kiss that completely consumed me.

A reminder of why we were out here popped up in my mind, and I debated whether I should ignore that shit, but I couldn't wait to see the look on Ryan's face when she saw what I did. Pulling back from the kiss by placing some soft, gentle kisses first on her lips, then on either side of her mouth, and finally on both cheeks before kissing the tip of her nose, I looked down at her darkened eyes and swollen lips as pride swelled up inside me.

But I beat it back and instead gripped her hand in mine. "Miss me, Freckles?" I breathed as I ran my nose along the curve of her neck and inhaled. She smelled like fresh air and creamsicles. Summer personified. I couldn't stay away from her, I was fucking addicted.

"Isn't it obvious?" she hummed, leaning into me. She was like fucking gasoline, and I was a match. With every touch, she reacted, and the chemistry between us blazed to life.

"If we don't stop, we both know where this is going to lead, and I didn't bring you out here to fuck you."

She stepped back, a naughty grin on her face. "Why *did* you bring me out here?"

"Close your eyes," I demanded instead of answering.

Her eyelids fluttered closed without hesitation, and I fucking preened at how far we'd come in the trust department over the last month. Stepping over the soft grass and patches of dusty dirt, I slowly led her up a small hill with a tree on the top of it that had somehow grown out over the deep part of the pond. I stopped her right underneath the tree, close to the trunk. Moving behind her and pressing my chest up against her back, I lowered my hands to grip her hips. I leaned forward and whispered in her ear, "Open your eyes."

I watched as she shivered at my breath drifting over her skin. I chuckled softly, watching her blink her eyes open before they widened. "Oh, my god. Did you…" She turned to me, her eyes sparkling. "I can't believe you did this!" she squealed, throwing herself against me again and squeezing me hard.

"Better strip out of those clothes, Freckles, so you can try it out," I suggested, leaning against the tree and folding my arms over my chest, settling in for the show. Her eyes met mine as she pulled the shirt over her head and tossed it aside. She wore a tiny black bikini that barely covered her fucking nipples, and I found myself moving toward her.

"You don't wear this for anyone but me," I growled out the demand, and her eyes flashed with a fiery challenge.

"Oh? And what if I wear it to the beach?" she asked innocently, knowing exactly what she was fucking doing to me.

"I'd have to take you home, strip you out of it," I promised, dropping kisses to her shoulder. "And remind you exactly who you belong to."

"Mmm," she murmured in agreement, and fuck if it didn't make me so goddamn hard how she reveled in my possessiveness.

"Okay, Freckles. Time to give it a try." I moved away from her and toward the tree, gripping the rope swing Connor, and I put up and reinforced in the thickest branch earlier today. The lust cleared from her eyes as she took the rope into her hands, stepping backward slowly.

With every step, the smile on her face grew bigger. Finally, she ran forward, jumping at the last second and landing on the step at the end of the rope, swinging out over the water. Her joyful screaming echoed around us and made me laugh. Her elation was infectious as she let go of the rope at the perfect moment and splashed into the water, disappearing under the inky surface.

The rope swung back toward me, and I caught it easily, pulling it back and following her into the water. As I crashed into the cool liquid, I let myself sink for a couple of seconds before breaching the surface with a huge fucking smile on my face. Nobody could make me smile like Ryan could.

She swam up to me, looking like fucking joy and warmth and wonder in the most gorgeous package I'd ever seen. She wrapped herself around me as I swam in place, and her eyes were practically glowing with happiness. "Thank you," she whispered, pressing her lips to mine before pushing away and splashing water at my face.

I laughed as she swam away, calling out over her shoulder, "Race you back to the swing!"

And I couldn't help but follow.

We spent a couple of hours playing and swimming at the pond, and by some goddamn miracle, I kept my dick out of my girlfriend. But it wasn't easy. And now that the sun had set, the stars were twinkling in the sky, I'd reached my limit. With my arms wrapped around Ryan, she leaned against my chest, contented sighs escaping her lips every few minutes as we rode home on Hex.

Fireflies danced around us as my stallion strolled across the open fields, the wide-open sky sparkling with stars. Before we started the ride home, I ordered a pizza. I'd never had a relaxing night at home with a girl except for Ryan, but they were quickly becoming my favorite way to spend an evening.

Stopping at the barn to take care of Hex, I put everything away, gave him a quick brush, and grabbed Ryan's hand. We walked to the house together, and just as we stepped inside, the doorbell rang.

"Who's that?" she asked curiously, her eyebrows furrowing.

"Pizza." I moved toward the door. "Why don't you find a movie or something, and I'll grab dinner?"

She nodded, flopping down onto the giant-ass sectional that took up most of the space in this room. It was perfect for lounging around. My place in LA was professionally decorated, but this place was comfortable. Relaxing. Something I never thought I'd say about the fucking hellhole I grew up in. But I'd officially taken it back.

And Ryan made this house feel like a home. Having her here was everything I always denied I wanted. But I did want it. So fucking bad.

Tearing my eyes off of her, I turned toward the door, swinging it open. Before I could take in who was standing there, a bright light flashed in my face. I threw up my hand instinctively to block it and tried to blink away the spots now dancing in my eyes. "What the fuck?" I snapped.

"Pizza delivery," the guy's bored tone announced, and I only knew it was a fucking guy because of his voice. I still couldn't see a goddamn thing.

I reached out, groping for the cardboard box and snatching it from his hands as he came into focus. He was most definitely *not* a pizza delivery guy. He didn't wear any sort of uniform, and he had more than one camera slung around his neck. Fucking press.

A thought tickled at the back of my brain, but I couldn't grasp it and deal with the questions the "delivery guy" was now hurling my way at the same time.

"Get the fuck off of my property, and if you come back, I'll have the police deal with you," I threatened before slamming the door closed right in his face. I was breathing hard, and the pizza box in my hand was shaking with my rage.

"Hey, Romeo. You okay over there?" Ryan's soft voice carried across the room, concern laced with curiosity.

Taking a deep breath, I shook off the unsettling feeling creeping up my spine. A photographer showing up on my doorstep hadn't been an accident. It was fucking Yates. It had to be. Reporters were like goddamn cockroaches. Where there was one, there were a shit ton more hiding in dark crevices waiting to pop out. It was only a matter of time before they had this place swarmed, and my carefree escape became nothing more than another fucking prison.

My desire to shatter Yates's life just increased tenfold. He was fucking with my girl, my career, and it was only a matter of time before he really came after me.

This shit needed to end. Now.

TWENTY SIX
MADDOX

Despite holding Ryan in my arms all night, I barely got any sleep. That fucking reporter had me on edge. In LA, I had security set up for that sort of shit. But here? Here we were basically sitting ducks. There was nothing to keep the hordes at bay, and it was only a matter of time before they swarmed us.

And I had no doubt who made the call letting them know where I was. Of all the guys in the band, I had to be the most careful with the media. I was a wreck for a lot of my career, which to them, meant a great story. So, they followed me around the most relentlessly trying to get any hint of a potential fuck up.

But I wasn't ready to share this part of my life with the world. Them finding my childhood home meant digging into my past, and there was plenty of shit buried deep, deep down that I didn't want anyone finding out about.

Staring down at the beautiful woman still asleep in my bed, her head resting on my chest and her dark, wild curls scattered across the sheets, I watched her sleep. Soft breaths left her lips in a steady rhythm, every worry erased momentarily off of her face, so she looked peaceful and relaxed.

As much as I wanted to lay here all day, I couldn't. I was restless as fuck, and I wouldn't wait around for whatever was going to happen next. Fuck that. I needed to take control of this situation, and then I needed to get Ryan, Quinn, and I the fuck out of Texas.

Gently moving my body out from under Ryan, I slid slowly across the sheets to be sure I wasn't going to wake her up. She hadn't been sleeping well, and I didn't want to interrupt what must've been a completely exhausted rest.

Finally, I froze, standing perfectly still beside the bed, watching to see if she was going to wake. When she didn't, I turned and grabbed some black joggers, pulling them up before stepping out of the room in search of coffee and my phone. It was still early, but Ryan was, for sure, going to be late to help Quinn this morning.

I left my phone on the ottoman last night, but before I bent to grab it, a flash of light caught my eye. I moved toward the big window in the living room, brushing the curtains back to look out through a tiny slit.

Fuck.

At least a dozen photographers were crowding around my short driveway, and I cursed Russell for building this place so goddamn close to the road. I could keep them off of my property with one call to the local Sheriff, but I couldn't do shit about them camping on the public highway that ran right in front of my house.

Letting the curtains flutter closed, I reached for my phone, intending to call Connor. Instead, it vibrated in my hand with an incoming call from Harrison. I fucking hated talking on the phone, and because of that, I only got calls when shit was really fucking bad.

Bracing myself, I answered the call. "What's wrong, Harry?"

A long sigh greeted me on the other end. "I've fucking told you lot a *thousand. Fucking. Times,*" he gritted out. "My name is Harrison. And to think I was calling to do you a bloody favor," he grumbled.

I bit back a laugh. It was too easy to get under my publicist's skin, and all the guys in Shadow Phoenix did it. "Fine. *Harrison.* What nightmare awaits me on the other end of this call?"

"I got a disturbing email this morning from my contact over at CNT. Let me start by saying you must have some luck on your side that he was the one that got it, and I convinced him to kill it," Harrison shared.

"What email? Who sent it?" I asked, lowering myself to the couch and not liking the churning starting to happen in my gut.

"Hold on," he muttered, clicking sounds crawling their way through the phone. "I just sent it to you."

Lowering my phone away from my ear, I put him on speaker. "Let me pull it up."

Tapping into the new message notification, I quickly scanned the body of the email, my muscles bunching, and tensing the further I read. "What the fuck is this?" I snarled into the phone, unable to keep my anger in check.

"Don't shoot the messenger, mate. I'm here to help you, remember?" Harrison reminded me firmly, his voice full of a whole lot of *don't fuck with me* that helped me calm down a little. Breathing in deeply, I filled my lungs with so much air they ached before exhaling loudly.

"Someone was trying to sell this to the media?" I asked in a somewhat calmer voice.

"Unfortunately, yes. Is any of it true?" he asked me casually, as if it didn't matter to him either way. But I knew better.

"Did I sexually assault anyone? Are you serious right now?" I fumed. By now, he should fucking know me better than that.

"Look. I know you had a few years where things might be a bit hazy. I just need to know if there could possibly be any validity to this rubbish so I can figure out how to deal with it," he clarified.

"No, it's not fucking true. Not even one sentence of this goddamn thing is true. But I bet I know where it came from. I'm going to fucking kill him," I vowed, feeling like my heart was trying to launch itself out of my chest with how hard it was pounding.

"Good," Harrison agreed. "CNT is the biggest outlet, and they're not running with it. Even if they did, you could sue them for slander since there's no evidence to back up their claims. Still, whoever did this isn't trying to do you any favors."

"Just let me know if you come across anything else. I'll handle this," I decided, ending the call without waiting to hear his response. Was it a dick move? Maybe. I had bigger shit to worry about right now.

Yates was trying to fuck me over in a big way. Lifting my phone back up, I tapped out a message to Sebastian, forwarding him the email Harrison had sent. Tossing my phone down and trying to ignore the growing crowd at the end of my driveway, I stalked down the hall to the shower. I wasn't used to playing from behind, and Yates was about to learn what kind of man I was deep down. It was time I took the fight to him.

Stepping out of the shower, I walked into my room to find Ryan securing the last couple of buttons on her shirt. Her eyes drank me in hungrily as they raked over my bare chest, water droplets still dripping down my skin. "Going somewhere?" I asked, moving across the room and watching as her mouth dropped open a little, her tongue teasing her bottom lip.

"I..." she started before swallowing hard and forcing her eyes back up to my face. I chuckled darkly, thinking of everything I wanted to do to her. I'd start by laying her out on my bed and peeling every piece of fabric off of her. Then I'd-

"I have to get back. Quinn texted, and he needs help," her words broke through my dirty fantasies. Fucking Quinn.

Running a frustrated hand through my hair, I went into the closet and quickly pulled on some jeans and a black t-shirt. "You're going to have to sneak back home, Freckles," I called out so she'd hear me outside of the closet.

She poked her head in as I was sliding my watch onto my wrist. "Why?"

"Because there's a fuck ton of reporters at the end of my driveway thanks to your ex-fiance. If they see you leaving, you're going to be all over the internet within the hour," I warned, pulling her into my arms and brushing her hair off her face, letting my fingers linger on the soft skin of her cheek. "Trust me on this, please. Go back to the barn, take Hex, and ride home. I'll come to get him later this afternoon."

"Can I at least get some coffee before you kick me out?" she teased, flashing me a fake glare.

I pointed toward the bedside table where I left her a travel mug before I got into the shower. "I'd have cooked you breakfast, but we both know Quinn will have something better waiting for you at home."

"Facts," she said, laughing. I leaned down, peppering her face with as many kisses as I could while she wrinkled her nose and giggled, trying to squirm out of my arms. Finally, I released her, and she grabbed the mug, taking a healthy sip before I followed her out to the barn. I watched as she stroked Hex's nose lovingly, cooing at him and he turned into a puddle of mush at her feet. Ryan just had that way about her. Men of all species worshipped at her feet, and she didn't even have to try.

Once she climbed up on the black stallion, I looked up at her, in awe of how she looked like a fiery goddess, the sun blazing behind her creating a glow that surrounded her body. "Text me when you get home," I demanded, leaving no room for her to question or argue in my tone.

"You sure know how to make a girl feel special, Romeo," she teased with a grin.

"Blow Quinn off, and I'll show you *exactly* how special you are to me, Freckles," I called her bluff.

"Can't, but raincheck." With a sexy as fuck wink, she turned and sauntered off on the back of my horse, taking my whole heart with her as I stood there like an idiot watching her go.

𝄞

Stepping out of the car, the sun beat down on the black fabric of my t-shirt like a goddamn magnet. I slammed the door closed, already feeling the rush of adrenaline tearing through my veins. I didn't want to tip my hand just yet, but I couldn't let this motherfucker get away with the shit he was trying to pull.

If I didn't have a rock-solid and loyal team surrounding me, I'd be dealing with a whole shitstorm that would distract me from what Yates is really doing. But I was focused as fuck, and nothing would divert me from my goal.

Dismantling Yates's entire goddamn life.

I hadn't planned to confront him so soon, but I couldn't let what he did slide. Accusing me of hurting women? I wasn't that kind of guy. In fact, I'd let the darker side of me come out and taken care of more than one guy who'd done that type of shit to women I knew in the past. I wasn't just against it, I took fucking action.

I met Ryan because I couldn't stand the little shits bullying her. I was a protector at heart, always had been. To think I'd hurt anyone who didn't deserve it was fucking gross and that Yates tried to make me into something so far from what I actually was made me want to remove his head from his body. With my bare hands.

Yanking open the door to the bank, I strode inside straight to the first desk I saw. "Where's Yates Rutherford's office?" I asked through clenched teeth.

The teller looked up with wide eyes, pointing to a set of heavy wooden doors in the middle of the building. Turning, I stalked off toward them as she called out after me, but I didn't give a shit about whatever she had to say. She wouldn't be able to stop me.

Grabbing the handle of the door, I threw it open. Yates jerked upright from where he was leaned back in his chair, some chick kneeling between his knees. He jumped up from his chair, shoving his dick back into his pants. I rolled my eyes, holding the door open for the girl who was wiping her mouth while she scurried out of the room. She'd barely crossed the threshold when I slammed the door shut behind her.

"What the fuck do you think you're doing?" he raged, his skin flushing as his hands bunched into fists.

Stepping closer to him, I got within punching distance before shoving the file I carried in with me into his chest with more force than necessary. He stumbled as he grabbed for the papers starting to fall out of it. "I know what you're trying to do, and I'm warning you not to push me. Keep this shit up, and not only will I destroy you in court for slander, but I'll start digging. And I won't stop until I fucking destroy everything in your pathetic little life. This is your one and only warning. I suggest you heed it." Barely-controlled fury laced my voice.

Not waiting on his response, I turned and stalked from the room and out of the bank feeling an odd sort of satisfaction wash over me. Thank fuck Ryan hadn't married that douche. And soon, he was going to be out of our lives for good, even if I had to end him myself.

"Freckles?" I called out, my voice carrying throughout the Knight barn. I had to come back for Hex, and I needed to talk to my girl.

"Over here," her answering voice sounded from the other side of the barn where my horse blocked my view of her. When I stepped into the stable, I watched as she used a curry comb to brush over his body in long strokes. Was it possible to be jealous of a horse?

"Hi," I whispered, leaning into her body and wrapping my arm around her waist, splaying my hand across her stomach. I pressed a kiss to her neck, letting my lips linger, and tasted salt on her skin.

"Mmm, I missed you today," she murmured, her body sinking into mine and her hand dropping from Hex's side. He snorted impatiently, and we both laughed.

"Hex doesn't appreciate being cheated out of his brushing," I noted, stepping back and grabbing the brush off the ground before lifting it to the smooth black fur and running it through. I finished brushing my horse while Ryan's gaze burned into my back, the heavy heat of it sending sparks of electricity shooting through my body.

Setting the tools down, I turned around and faced Ryan. As much as I wanted to pin her up against the stable wall and fuck her into next week, we needed to have a conversation about what went down today. There was some shit from the past I hoped would stay buried but now had a very real chance of coming out.

And I wouldn't let her hear it from anyone but me.

"Can we go home? We need to talk about what happened today," I stated, stepping outside the stall and waiting for her to follow.

Her eyebrows raised as she stepped past me. "What happened today?"

I captured her hand, giving it a gentle squeeze. "I went to Dallas. To the bank."

She inhaled sharply. "Why would you go see Yates?" she asked hesitantly.

"C'mon. We'll sneak in the back way. The walk isn't that long, and I could use the exercise."

When we finally walked through the back door of my house, I could tell she'd spent the entire walk coming up with every worst-case scenario to the point where she was wound so tightly, she was on the verge of snapping. Her body was tense as I coaxed her down into the couch. I followed and sat facing her.

"This morning, I got a call from my publicist, Harrison. One of his contacts at CNT let him know someone sent in an anonymous tip about me," I began, trying to keep my voice even.

"What kind of tip?" she asked, leaning against me.

"The kind that accused me of some fucked up shit I'd never do."

"Okay, well, why'd you go to Dallas?"

"Because Sebastian traced the email and that asshole Yates sent it," I explained, getting angry all over again at the motherfucker's audacity.

"Why would he do that? He's already taken the ranch," she mused, absently stroking my arm.

"He lost, Freckles. That's why. You hurt his pride, and then I came along and shoved it in his face. Now he wants to make us pay. The problem with that is he has no idea what I'm capable of."

"And what exactly are you capable of?" she wondered.

"I'm the guy that handles shit. The guy who doesn't let anyone hurt the people I care about. And I'm also the guy willing to do whatever it takes to keep those people safe."

"I know all of this. It's one of the things I love about you the most." She looked up at me with wonder in her eyes that I wasn't sure I deserved.

"Well, you don't know everything that I've done. And I don't know how far Yates will go to try and break me or break us apart."

"It doesn't matter what you've done or what he does. He'll never break us apart because I know the kind of man you are in here," she proclaimed, laying her palm flat against my chest over my heart.

"Not everything I've done has been good. Or legal," I added, covering her palm with my hand.

"Did the people you take care of deserve it?" she asked, her expressive coffee-colored eyes staring into mine.

I nodded slowly. "Every single one."

"Then I don't need to know. I trust you, and I know you'd never hurt anyone unless you had to."

Tugging on the hand she had resting on my chest, I pulled until she fell against me, leaning back until she lay sprawled out on top of me. Wrapping her in my arms, I stroked the skin just underneath the hem of her shirt. "How the fuck did I get so lucky to get to call you mine?"

"You're the only one who proved himself worthy of me," she whispered, her lips moving against my chest, which warmed at her words.

And I'd never stop doing everything I could to continue proving to her how deserving of her I was.

TWENTY SEVEN
MADDOX

Almost like a bad case of deja vu, Connor and his team, me, Quinny, and Ryan all crowded around the sectional in my living room. The last forty-eight hours had gone by both fast and slow at the same time, and my head felt like it was starting to spin Exorcist-style.

If it weren't for Ryan's calming hand stroking my arm up and down in a steady rhythm, I'd be completely on edge. Shit didn't get to me. I was always in control, always planned ahead and knew what was coming. But Yates was an unknown. He was purposefully trying to fuck with Ryan, and now he'd set his sights on me.

I didn't want to drag shit out. I wanted to take him down before he could do any more damage. And right now, we were about to find out what tools we'd have at our disposal to do it. What kind of ammunition was he hiding from the world?

And how could I exploit that shit for maximum pain and entertainment?

Connor leaned forward, grabbing the iPad off of the ottoman in front of him. "It's been an interesting forty-eight hours," he started, flipping the cover open. "Buckle up for the circus because shit's about to get wild."

I exhaled, sinking back into the cushions and draping my arm across Ryan's shoulders, pulling her into my side. Bit by bit, I started to relax. I hadn't even admitted it to myself, but there was a part of me that'd been afraid despite all the digging, Yates was as clean as he appeared to be. It looked like my gut feeling about him had been right.

Julian and Indy glanced at each other, and it looked like they were having a silent conversation between themselves. Finally, Julian spoke up. "We watched him in rotating shifts for the past two days. There was really only one thing of interest, and that was that he likes hookers."

"A *lot*," Indy added. "Like a disgusting amount. I'm surprised his dick hasn't fallen off yet." He turned to me. "And I'm billing you for a gallon of fucking brain bleach to wash out some of the shit I've seen."

"Worth it if we get to take him down," I chuckled.

"Oh, he's fucking done. There's no doubt about that anymore," Connor confirmed, swiping across the screen of the tablet he held. "Thank fuck you didn't marry this pervert, Ryan."

Her eyebrows shot up, and she paled. "Oh, Jesus. What kind of sick shit is he into?"

"Prostitutes aren't bad enough for you?" Quinn joked from her other side, and I bit back a smile.

Sebastian pulled a file out of the messenger bag that sat on the floor next to his feet, setting it down on the ottoman and flipping it open. "Where do you want to start? The women suing him for paternity tests and back child support for his alleged kids? The sex tape one of his many prostitutes is blackmailing him over? The transsexual fetish porn he watches every day? Or how about the fact he's stealing from his family's bank?" He finished pulling out page after page, setting each one down as he explained what they were.

And my smile got a little wider with every item Sebastian tossed out like a fucked up checklist of depravity. I was ecstatic that Ryan chose me and not walked down the aisle to that prick, but hearing how fucked up he really was deep down? Now I was beside myself happy that I convinced her I deserved a shot.

I glanced over at my girl, her freckled nose wrinkled like she'd smelled something bad. She looked horrified, disgusted, but, most of all, really fucking pissed off. My heart fucking sang, watching her strength shine through, like a goddamn avenging angel as fury took over her beautiful features.

She smoothed down her hair, taking a deep breath as she reigned in her anger. Her shoulders relaxed a fraction, and her flushed skin started to fade back to its normal tan-with-freckles that I loved so much. "I don't even know where to start," she admitted finally.

"How about we start with the easiest thing first?" I suggested, taking the opportunity to rub soothing circles across her back.

She laughed, but I wasn't sure if she actually found any of this funny or not. My guess was not. "Easiest? What on that disgusting list would you refer to as *easy?*"

Shrugging, I answered, "The porn, probably."

Sebastian nodded along with me. "Mad's right. What you see is mostly what you get with that one. He looks at porn a *lot*. Enough that I started to wonder how the hell he has time to do anything else with his day. But when he looks, it's always the same kind. The kind where the woman has both boobs and a cock."

I bit my lip to keep from laughing, and Ryan must have heard the really fucking unsexy snort that popped out of my mouth before I could stop it. I tried to cover it up with a cough, but judging by the glare she shot me, I'd say it hadn't worked. "Sorry, baby. It sounds like you weren't exactly his type." I leaned close enough that I whispered the next part into her ear. "But you're definitely mine, and when we're done here, I'll take my time showing you exactly what you do to me." It was a dirty promise I intended to keep.

But first, we had plans to make.

"Next up is the sex tape," Connor decided, turning his tablet so it faced Ryan, Quinn, and me. I assumed the rest of them had already seen it, so he was showing it for our benefit. Turning to Ryan, I waited for her to meet my eyes. "I don't think you have to watch this, Freckles."

Her gaze hardened as she turned back to the screen, her spine straightening. "I need to know everything we're up against. That asshole is messing with everyone I love, and I don't want to miss anything that we can use against him." Her tone left no room for argument, so I moved my body closer until our legs were molded together and tucked her into my side. She melted into me, and I breathed another sigh of relief. I hated it when she was mad at me.

"Anyone care if I take a quick break to make some popcorn first?" Quinn asked, jumping up without waiting for an answer and striding into the kitchen. Cabinet doors opened and closed before the telltale sounds of the microwave starting carried across the room. Connor looked at me with a shake of his head and a twitch of his lips.

The scent of butter wafted through the house as Quinn came out of the kitchen with a giant bowl filled to almost overflowing with popcorn. He settled in next to Ryan, grabbing a huge handful and shoving it straight in his mouth, crunching loudly. Ryan giggled softly beside me and reached her hand into the bowl, taking some for herself.

"Fuck it," I gave in, grabbing a handful, too. We all settled back into the couch, making ourselves as comfortable as possible for the horror we were about to endure.

"Anyone need a drink? Any other refreshments?" Connor mocked before glaring at each of us individually.

"Nope," I snarked, popping the *P* just because I knew it'd piss him off.

He held the iPad balanced on his lap, pointed in our direction, and pushed play. All of us stilled and watched in silent disgust and revulsion as frame after frame flew by, a variety of positions, more of Yates than I ever cared to see, and enough offensive dialogue to make even me uncomfortable painted a disturbing as fuck picture of the guy Ryan almost tied herself to.

I held her a lot tighter as the video finally came to an end, and she shuddered against me. It wasn't the same way she usually did, either. Instead of her shuddering in reaction to my touch, this was distaste and nausea.

"Well, that was informative," Quinn piped up, continuing to munch away on popcorn as if we hadn't all just watched Yates going to town on some prostitute he picked up and did unspeakable shit to. How the fuck he could still eat after that was beyond me.

I didn't know if I'd ever be able to eat again.

"I think the damage that could do is pretty self-explanatory," Connor said, flipping the cover shut on the tablet and setting it down. "Now's where we get into the really juicy stuff."

Sliding a couple of the papers out of the folder Sebastian laid out, he handed them over to Ryan. I read over her shoulder, and I noticed Quinn doing the same thing. "How many women are suing him?" I finally asked.

"Three, from what I can tell," Sebastian answered, pushing his glasses up the bridge of his nose. "If I had more than two days to dig into it, I could tell you if there'd been others he's settled with in the past. Apparently, your boy doesn't know how to use a goddamn condom."

"Don't call him my boy," Ryan snapped with a look of pure disgust on her face. I pressed a kiss to her temple, and she leaned into me, closing her eyes for a second. I breathed her in, closing my own eyes and pretending that it was just her and me in this room, and we weren't dealing with any of this bullshit.

Forcing my eyes open, I sighed. "So, he's got three women who claim he fathered their kids?" I asked Sebastian.

He nodded. "He's been trying to fight them, but they're asking for DNA tests. He can only put that off so long unless he comes to a settlement."

"This is good, Freckles. We can use all of this against him," I reminded her, and I saw Quinn nodding in agreement on her other side. He held her hand in his and shot me a concerned look. We both knew Ryan was strong. I wasn't worried about her breaking down or not being able to handle this. But she carried a fuck ton of guilt when it came to not being able to protect the people she loved just like I did. She'd be worried this wouldn't be enough or it wouldn't work. But I'd make absolutely sure that motherfucker went down.

There wasn't another option.

"Yeah, and we will. I'm not going to let him get away with coming after my family, coming after you," she said vehemently, cupping my rough cheek with her warm palm. "I'll kill him before I let him get away with the shit he's pulled."

"I don't think you're going to have to kill anybody, Lancelot," Quinn chimed in. "What was the last thing?"

Connor straightened up, digging through the papers in the file and swapping them out for the ones about the paternity suits. "Embezzlement. From what Bas was able to dig up, Yates has been stealing from his family for over a year." He pointed to a couple of highlighted transactions on the bank statement Ryan was staring intently at.

"When I first started digging into Yates's financials, his main bank account was nearly empty. I figured it was just a cover or something, and he was hiding his wealth somewhere else, maybe somewhere offshore. Instead, we found that this is his main account, but he shuffles money from Rutherford Financial into an offshore account and then transfers it here," Connor explained.

"His accountant probably told him it wouldn't be traceable. It took me two hours," Sebastian announced, a hint of pride in his voice.

"Where'd all his money go?" I asked. Reputation was everything to his family, and I doubted his parents would've sent him off to college empty-handed. Especially after I'd gotten a look at the Ivy League douche squad he called friends.

Sebastian shrugged. "I can only trace parts of it since he took cash out for a lot of his spending. If I had more time, I might know more. But legal fees, failed business ventures, and insane spending habits mostly. Prostitutes, leasing cars, houses, boats. You name it, he's bought it at some point."

"What kind of failed business ventures?" Ryan wondered, still scanning the pages of transactions lying across her lap.

A smile stretched across Sebastian's face. "He tried to start his own cologne company. Oh, and then there was the pocket square business. And then the porn production company. Too bad everyone watches that shit on the internet for free."

Ryan stacked all the papers together and set them back in the folder, closing the blue file and pushing it back toward Sebastian. "Okay, we have all of this information, but what are we going to do with it?"

"We're going to sit on it for a couple of days while we decide on the best course of action," I decided. "We have something more important to deal with first."

"What?" she asked.

"The fact that Sebastian dug in and that fucker really does own the ranch. But I'm going to get it back, Freckles," I promised. "He's stealing because he needs money, right?"

She nodded.

"He's going to wait until he gets the satisfaction of kicking your family out, and then he's going to try to offload it as fast as he can for as much as he can. But I'm going to make him an offer he can't refuse, so you don't have to worry about it."

"How the fuck do you plan to do that? He knows who you are," Connor pointed out.

"No, shit. I'm going to need Sebastian's help."

At the mention of his name, he perked up, lifting his eyes off the tablet he'd snatched from Connor and buried his face in it. "What's up?"

"I need you to create some sort of mask or shell company or something to make the offer through. And then I need you to contact Yates's lawyer and make an offer above market. Well above. I don't want him to counter or get suspicious. Make it seem like I'm a big-time ag company wanting to buy up farms in the area or something. I don't give a fuck as long as it works."

Ryan had pulled my hand into her lap, threading our fingers together and squeezing. I knew she hated letting me do this, but she was out of options. So, she stayed silent with a look of appreciation sparking in her eyes.

"You got it. When do you want it done?" He was already tapping aggressively on the tablet's screen.

"As soon as possible. Today if you can."

"Done," he assured, lost in whatever he was doing.

"Anything else?" I questioned.

"Now we talk about the best way to decimate one perverted asshole," Connor announced with a menacing grin that stretched almost unnaturally across his face making him look goddamn terrifying.

"I'm listening."

𝄞

An uneasy feeling crept through me as the rest of the day was quiet. After everything Yates pulled, I didn't think for one goddamn second he would quit after I threatened him at the bank. At best, I thought I might buy myself a day or two while he figured out a new strategy. He didn't seem like the kind of guy to let shit go.

When my phone buzzed on the nightstand, I jolted out of bed still fully naked. Ryan shifted, sitting up as the sheet fell away from her enticing body, blinking the post-orgasm haze from her eyes as she watched me.

"Fuck," I cursed as I answered the call. "Please tell me you've got good news."

""Fraid not, mate," Harrison's soft voice confirmed. "Have you had the TV on at all tonight?"

"No, I was busy doing something more fun," I answered, eyeing Ryan as she laughed softly and winked at me. She was so goddamn sexy, even though I knew I was about to get a gut punch in the form of some retaliation by Yates, my cock hadn't gotten the memo. It sprung to life and, like a goddamn divining rod, pointed right at Ryan.

She crawled across the bed, letting the sheet completely drop away. I groaned as she wrapped her fingers around me, pressing light kisses to the head of my dick before running her tongue along my entire shaft. Harrison's voice slammed me back to reality, though. "Turn it on CNT."

Ryan made a protesting sound as I pulled away from her. I sure as fuck didn't like it any more than she did. Stalking out to the living room completely fucking naked, hard on bobbing between my legs, I gripped the remote and turned the TV on, flipping through the channels until I found the right one.

And when I did? It was like dipping my cock in ice water, it went down so fast. Sinking down into the soft cushion, I clenched my jaw. "What the fuck is this?"

On the screen in front of me was Russell, my *dad*, talking about shit he had no goddamn business discussing with anyone, let alone publicly. All I could see was fucking vengeance because I knew, I fucking *knew*, Yates was behind this. I'd been a public figure for years, and Russell had never once tried to profit from it. It was the only decent thing he'd ever done.

And now here he was, laying all of my personal shit out for the public to judge. I didn't want to listen to any more of his bullshit. As Ryan slid down next to me, her eyes narrowed at the TV, I turned it off. "How bad is it?" I asked Harrison.

"Not bad per se. He was clearly not sober, so there's the embarrassment factor. And he ranted a lot about what a horrible son you are and how you kicked him out of his own house and threw him out on the street," he finished.

I scoffed. "Right, the street. I guess that's what you call it when you give someone fair market value for a ranch worth half."

"The way I see it, you have two options. You can make a statement or do an interview telling your side of the story. Or you can ignore his ranting and let it blow over. I don't think you can lose either way."

I looked over at Ryan, the worry in her eyes softening my anger momentarily. I rubbed my hand along her bare thigh, and her involuntary shiver at my touch made my lips twitch in an almost-smile. "How long do I have to decide?"

"Not long. Maybe a couple of hours. Let me know," he finished, ending the call.

"What was that?" Ryan leaned closer to me, running her fingers through my hair, and I closed my eyes as she scraped her nails along my scalp. I shouldn't be surprised anymore by anything Russell did to me, but I was. I hadn't expected him to do something like this. He'd never been a father, leaving scars that went far deeper than skin-level, and I was stupid to think buying him out would rid my life of him permanently.

"I think Yates somehow got Russell to do an interview about me on TV," I explained, the anger and hurt reigniting as I told her about what happened and what my options were. "What do you think I should do?"

"I think you should ignore it. Don't fuel the fire. That's what Yates wants. He wants to see that he got under your skin. Don't give him the satisfaction. Soon enough, he'll pay for what he's done to us, to our families."

She was right. As much as I wanted to explain my side and lash out at Yates, I had to be smart about it. I had to play to win, and I wouldn't be derailed by cheap shots. That motherfucker knew my family was a weak spot for me, and he exploited it. The gloves were fucking off. I had the ammunition, and it was time to load the goddamn gun, point it at his fucking head, and pull the trigger.

TWENTY EIGHT
RYAN

Leaving a naked, wet Maddox in the shower by himself was a lesson in restraint I never wanted to learn. But I could tell everything that'd happened weighed on him. He liked to pretend that his dad doing that interview last night was no big deal, but I knew better.

I also knew he needed space to deal with everything he was going through. But I wouldn't go far. In fact, the kitchen was about as far as I wanted to be away from him right now. I may not be as good of a cook as Quinn or even my mom, but I could handle bacon, eggs, and toast just fine.

Rummaging through the fridge, I pulled out everything I'd need and got to work. Just as I was pushing the button to start the coffee maker, a loud banging on the front door made me jump. Gripping my chest with my hand, trying to get the sudden frantic beating of my heart under control, I strode to the front door, lifting up onto my toes to look out the peephole.

A man stood on the porch, but he was turned away from me, and I couldn't see his face. From the back, he didn't look like anyone I recognized. Warily, I pulled the door open, just enough to catch his attention and speak through.

He whirled around, a mostly blank expression on his face as if he couldn't be bothered to care who I was. "Ms. Everleigh?" he asked.

"No, but you've got the right house," I confirmed.

He looked off into the distance for a second before shrugging and handing me a sealed manilla envelope. Goddamn yellow envelopes from hell, always popping up to screw up my life. I took it gingerly as if it were a bomb about to explode. For all I knew, it might be.

"Have a nice day," he said mildly before walking off back toward his car.

I closed the door behind me, wondering if I should open the envelope or leave it for Maddox. I know it's meant for him, and yet he was already going through so much. I didn't want to hand this over to him, whatever it was. At least not without solutions.

With my mind made up, I tore into the seal, pulling out glossy photo paper and flipping it over. My eyes fell to the picture of a woman standing next to a guy who looked to be in his early twenties. He didn't look familiar to me, but one look at her and I knew what this was.

"Monica," I whispered, my gaze dropping to the yellow sticky note attached to the front.

For $5 million, they'll stay your little secret.

All that followed was a series of nine digits, an account number I assumed. After last night, it wasn't hard to figure out who sent this picture. It was clear that Yates had figured out Maddox's weakness and had no issue exploiting it.

I had no intention of hiding this from Maddox, but I didn't want to tell him about it until I dealt with it myself. And I had no qualms handling it. I'd taken self-defense and martial arts training since I was a teenager. I regularly kicked ass in my jiu-jitsu classes, and Yates was soft. A lot softer than me.

Sure, he spent time in the gym. But that was different. My knuckles had been hardened over the years from boxing, from smashing my fists into a heavy bag over and over and over again. I'd broken more noses than I could count. The thought of making Yates feel the kind of pain he was inflicting on the man I loved made me almost gleeful.

He was going to pay, and it was going to be at my hands.

I shoved the picture back into the envelope as I heard Maddox's coming down the hallway, his footfalls soft as his bare feet hit the wood floor. Plastering a smile on my face and forcing the plans I was making in my brain to the side,

I sidled up to him and wrapped my arms around his waist, burying my face in his chest. "Ready for breakfast?" I mumbled against his taut muscles, the ones he hadn't bothered to cover up with a shirt.

I was pretty sure I could stare at his mouth-watering body all day, all year even, and never get sick of the view. I reluctantly stepped out of his arms and went to dish him up a plateful of food. Carrying it out to the couch, he followed as I sank down into one of the super soft and cushy seats, passing him the plate I carried over for him as soon as he sat down beside me.

After he took a couple of bites, I asked, "What are you up to today?"

"I have a call with Harrison in about twenty minutes. My morning after that is open for whatever he needs me to do after last night. And this afternoon I've got a video meeting with the guys to go over where we're at with the new album. How about you?"

I sipped my coffee carefully, lingering longer than normal to be sure I thought out my answer. I didn't want to lie to him, but I wasn't ready to tell him everything either. Not yet. Not until it was fixed. "I'll check in with Quinn and see if he needs any help, then I thought I'd get in a workout. Maybe boxing," I mused, picturing all the possibilities and ways my fists and feet, knees and elbows could connect with the soft, fleshy places on Yates's body.

Maddox side-eyed me a little suspiciously. "You box?"

Letting out a small breath of relief, I nod. "I do. Among other things."

"Since when?" he asked around a mouthful of food.

"Since college. I started self-defense before that, but I wanted to be a cop, remember? I needed to be at least as strong as the guys I was going up against for a spot. So I started learning how to most effectively defend myself. Around here, there aren't any places to take classes anymore, but I still spar with Quinn all the time."

"That's hot," he noted, letting his eyes wander down my body with newfound appreciation. "You'll have to show me sometime, naked, of course."

"Of course," I agreed, rolling my eyes but laughing to let him know I'd be down to give that a try, even if I seriously doubted he'd ever relinquish enough control in the bedroom to let it happen.

Finishing my breakfast quickly, I left him on the couch and slipped back to the bedroom, taking his phone and scrolling to find the contact I was looking for. Entering the number in my phone, I set his back on the nightstand and slid into my shoes.

I hurried out to the living room, dropped a quick but heated kiss on Maddox's enticing lips, and practically ran out the back door, envelope hidden inside my purse. I couldn't risk him seeing it before I talked to Connor.

I waited until I'd safely snuck past the lingering crowd of photographers at the front of the house before I pulled out my phone and dialed the one person I needed to talk to before I took any action against Yates.

"What?" his barking voice was impatient, but I didn't intend to mess around.

"I need your help," I divulged, slightly breathless from my run across the space between Maddox's house and my own.

"Ryan?" Something ruffled in the background on Connor's end of the line, muffling his voice slightly.

"Yep, that's me. Do you think we could meet somewhere? Maybe *On Tap* in half an hour?"

"Sure, see you there," he agreed easily, ending the call. Maybe I should've asked him not to tell Maddox, but I just had to hope he wouldn't for now. I didn't want to ask him to hide anything. It wasn't fair to Maddox, and I didn't want to risk his trust in me that way. If he found out, it wasn't the end of the world.

I crept into the house, avoiding every floorboard that squeaked along the way. Living in the house I grew up in had its advantages. I finally made it into my room, glad I hadn't run into Quinn. If he had any idea what I was about to do, he'd have been all up in my business, trying to stop me or convince me to take him along. But I couldn't risk him, either.

Changing my clothes quickly into some black yoga pants and a black tank top, I tied my shoes and swiped my keys off the dresser. I cracked open my bedroom door, listening for any sign of anyone in the house, but all was quiet. I crept back out the way I came, softly closing the screen door behind me. I felt terrible that Quinn was stuck doing the ranch work on his own again today, but with any luck, he wouldn't be doing any of that much longer.

I never dared to hope that he'd get the chance to pursue his passions, but now it almost felt within reach, as if my fingertips were just brushing along the future we were meant to have. And it was all thanks to Maddox.

That was why I was doing what I was right now. I wanted to carry my own weight, to show him that he didn't have to be my savior, that I could shoulder the burden at his side. Opening my car door, I tossed my purse on the seat, checking and then double-checking that the envelope was still nestled safely inside.

The short drive to *On Tap* went quickly, and I found myself in the nearly-empty bar at almost lunchtime with only the bartender and a lone patron at the far end of the counter. I was early, so I nodded once at the bartender and took the booth furthest in the back to wait for Connor.

I scrolled through my phone while I waited, but thankfully he was early, too. The bell above the door chimed as he pulled it open forcefully, striding inside and pulling off his sunglasses as he scanned the empty room. When our eyes met, he offered me a little wave before making his way over and sinking down into the booth across from where I sat.

"I've gotta say I was surprised to get your call," he started, lifting his hand to signal the bartender.

"Yeah, well, I was surprised to get this," I countered, sliding the envelope across the table. He picked it up, his eyebrows shooting up before narrowing as he studied the picture first, then the note attached.

"What the actual fuck does he think he's going to accomplish with this?" Connor questioned, shoving the picture back into the envelope.

"I don't know. But I plan to do something about it." I picked up the menu the bartender dropped off. I wasn't hungry, but I was fidgety and wanted something to do with my hands.

"And what's that?" Connor studied me from across the table, his expression unreadable. I got the feeling my answer was about to determine whether or not he brought Maddox into this.

"I intercepted that delivery this morning meant for Maddox. I assume you heard what his dad did last night?"

Connor nodded, so I continued. "When I saw this, I couldn't let him see it. Not yet. I want to know for sure that Yates sent it. And then I want to pay him a visit where I kick him in the balls so hard, he'll never have to worry about another hooker suing him for his worthless DNA."

He chuckled, an appraising glint in his eye before finally pulling out his phone and making a short call to Sebastian, asking him to find out what he could. There had to be a record of him hiring a PI or photographer or someone to snap that photo.

"Do you know who the guy in the picture is?" I asked Connor, pulling the picture back out and pointing at his face, noting the tattoos running up his neck and down both arms.

He shifted his gaze away from me, dropping it down to the picture. "I do."

"And are you going to tell me?"

He sighed heavily. "That's Griffin, Maddox's half brother. That's all I'm going to say. If you want to know the rest, ask your boyfriend."

"I'll do that."

I ordered an ice tea as we sat and waited for Sebastian to get back to us. "So, what's your plan here? Go rushing in there by yourself, and what exactly?" Connor asked, his tone conversational, but the look in his eyes anything but. His look dared me to admit I planned on facing down my sort of ex on my own. The same guy who apparently had the balls to think he could go toe-to-toe with and blackmail one of the biggest celebrities on the planet.

I figured his overconfidence would be his downfall. I just had to be patient. Patient but not silent. I wasn't about to sit here and let him cause as much chaos as he wanted before we took action. I figured I could at least make him hurt a little.

Connor's phone vibrated across the table, and he picked it up, pressing it to his ear. His eyes shot over to me, and we stared at each other as he listened. When he hung up after a hurried *thanks*, I waited with bated breath for the verdict.

"It was him, alright. Hired a PI, used his damn credit card like a moron," he confirmed. "So, what do you want to do?"

My whole body stiffened as I fumed, a storm tearing through my veins, the need to make him pay clawing at my insides, demanding to be unleashed. "I want to pay the jackass a visit," I declared, rising out of my seat and pulling out my wallet to throw some money onto the table. "Coming?"

𝄞

After stopping by Connor's hotel room and making another quick stop to have Sebastian figure out where Yates was right now, we packed a small bag with a few necessities like first aid supplies, water bottles, and ice packs. We drove to the dive bar my ex apparently liked to frequent.

When we pulled into the half-empty gravel parking lot, I understood why. This was more than likely the place he went to pick up the *working girls* he couldn't keep his diseased dick out of. My stomach rolled at the thought I'd actually considered for the briefest of seconds, giving him a real chance.

Gross.

Connor parked the black SUV we'd driven, and he turned to me as I reached for the door handle. "Wait." The commanding tone in his voice made me pause. "How do you want to do this?"

"I'm going to walk right up to that jerk and convince him to follow me outside. Then I'm going to kick the shit out of him for everything he's doing," I rattled off, adrenaline flooding my system.

"And what do you want to accomplish by doing this? Maddox already threatened him, and it didn't make him stop. In fact, that fucker only started coming after him harder," Connor pointed out, grabbing the bag we brought out of the back seat and rifling through it.

"Accomplish? I want to make myself feel better, and I want to make Yates feel pain. I don't think anyone has ever actually kicked his ass before, and I want to be the first." I lowered the visor, flipping open the mirror and checking my reflection. If I was going to convince him to follow me outside, I might have to use my looks to do it, and if I looked like shit, it wouldn't work.

Connor chuckled, setting the bag in the back seat after he pulled out the dreaded manilla envelope. The sun had just sunk below the horizon, and the first stars were starting to wink into existence. I unceremoniously flung my door open, stepping into the warm evening air.

I lifted my chin, straightened my spine, and walked confidently through the parking lot, the gravel crunching under the heels of my shoes. Connor followed right behind me, but he didn't try to take over. I got the feeling he wanted to see how I handled myself, what I was going to do next. We didn't know each other very well yet, but I liked the guy, and I respected that he was willing to let me take the lead.

A lot of guys like him, ex-military, muscle-bound tough guys, looked at women as lesser beings with smaller brains or too many emotions to be taken seriously. Connor didn't seem to be like that, and my opinion of him went up a couple more notches at how he handled today.

We stepped into the bar, the hot and stuffy air immediately making my hair stick to the back of my neck. It must've been a hundred and twenty degrees in here, the air conditioner long out of commission. The smell of sweat and alcohol hung heavy in the air, and I had the sudden urge to get the hell out of here just so I could fill my lungs with fresh, clean oxygen.

"He's over there," Connor's gruff voice sounded near my ear, his hand casually pointing to the middle of the bar where Yates sat with his back to us. He had a glass in his hand, his suit jacket wrinkled and askew as if he'd been there for hours.

Connor stepped back, slipping into the crowd near the door, and I stepped forward, deeper into this craptastic place. Finally, I slid onto the stool beside Yates, and he didn't even bother looking up before he started hitting on me. "Hey, sexy-"

"Save it for someone who cares," I snapped, waiting until his eyes finally made their way up to my face. When it registered who I was, his gaze narrowed slightly. Surprisingly, he was fully sober despite looking like he'd made himself a permanent home on the barstool he occupied.

"You," he spluttered, hate shining out of his eyes. "What are you doing here?"

I placed the envelope on the table but snatched it away when he tried to grab it. "I think we need to talk. Outside," I ordered, slipping off the stool and making my way toward the door. When he didn't immediately follow, I turned back. "Now."

Rolling his eyes, he downed the last of his drink and stood, slamming into my shoulder as he tried to bypass me on the way to the door. He also knocked into almost every table on the way to the door, sloshing people's drinks and being the general asshole that he was. It was like that's what he was made to do. He didn't even have to try.

Stepping outside the door, the air felt crisp and fresh as it brushed across my skin, and I inhaled deeply. I stepped around the side of the building, noting that Yates was following me, mumbling about how much I'd wronged him. I noticed Connor had slipped behind Yates when he stepped out of the bar.

When we turned the corner to the side of the building, I took a quick look around before spinning back to face Yates. There was a field behind the bar, and it looked like no one had ventured to this side of the building in years. The gravel was overgrown by green weeds, and as I discreetly scanned the building itself, I didn't spot any security cameras.

Perfect.

"I see you got my note," Yates taunted, a cocky grin crossing his face as he stood, leaning against the brick wall of the bar. "Come to pay up?"

"You could say that," I began, prowling closer to him step by step.

"We could have a little fun first." His eyes filled with lust, and my stomach lurched.

"I wouldn't touch your disease-riddled dick if my life depended on it." I moved until our chests were almost touching but not quite. The smell of liquor wafted off of him, permeating the air all around me and making my eyes water.

"You fucking bitch," he seethed, and I held up my hand right in his face.

"I'm tired of you thinking you can hurt anyone you want without consequences. And there *will* be consequences," I threatened.

"Oh yeah?" he smirked. "What the fuck is a weak little cunt like you going to do about it?"

That was all it took, and I snapped. My fingers curled into a fist, and I jabbed, striking him right in the throat. His eyes bulged, and his hands flew up to his neck. Spittle gathered at the corners of his lips as he gasped and wheezed.

He managed to catch his breath quickly, though, reaching out and fisting his hand in my hair. He yanked until my eyes watered. The burning pain on my scalp was intense but not as harsh as the pain that exploded behind my eye as his fist connected with my face.

If he thought that'd be enough to get me to back down, he had a surprise coming his way because I wasn't done yet.

Oh, no.

I heard a whispered, "Holy shit," out of Connor, but I couldn't pay attention to what he was doing right now. I was laser-focused on Yates and unloading on him for all the pain he caused. I reached up and gripped his shoulders, digging my nails in through his stupid suit jacket and bringing my knee up until it connected with his balls. He dropped to the ground, and when he did, I jumped on him, smashing my fist into his face a couple of times, hearing the crack of his nose, watching blood splatter the broken concrete sidewalk underneath him.

He finally got his arms up in front of his bloody face, so I took the opportunity to stand and deliver a couple of swift kicks to the ribs before I straightened to my full height, towering over him. I looked down at the pathetic excuse for a man that lay crumpled and ruined at my feet, and a surge of pride and peace washed over me. I didn't think anyone could call me weak again.

He groaned, spitting a mouthful of blood out before cracking open his eyes, the left one already starting to swell. "I'm going to call the fucking cops."

"Do it," I dared. "And I'll show them how you blackmailed Maddox."

"Fuck," he moaned, curling up even tighter on the ground.

"That's what I thought." I finally glanced up at Connor, who was putting his phone away with an approving grin on his face. "Last warning, Yates. Stay the hell away from my family and my boyfriend."

I stepped over his body, moving back toward the parking lot with Connor at my side. My knuckles ached, and I glanced down at them. They were already swelling, bruises forming, and little cuts dotting the skin. But I couldn't feel anything except the adrenaline and elation at what I'd done. I was strong enough to protect myself and those I loved most, and that was a feeling I never wanted to forget.

𝄞

"You're going to have to tell him," Connor brought up as we were pulling up to Maddox's house. He glanced down at where I held an ice pack over my swollen knuckles. I winced, pulling it off and looking down at the damage. Even in the cover of darkness, I could tell they were pretty banged up.

Worth it.

"I planned on telling him anyway, as soon as it was done. I never wanted to hide it from him." I grabbed my bag off the floor, checking to be sure the envelope was inside. After the talk I was about to have, I hoped I'd never see another damn manilla envelope as long as I lived.

"Hey. Thanks for going with me today. And thanks for letting me tell Maddox myself," I added.

"Anytime." Connor's lips lifted in a small smile, and I let myself out of his SUV. I'd need to get my car back from the hotel later, but I'd have Maddox drive me if he wasn't too mad, and Quinn take me if he was. Time would tell which of them would be more pissed off.

Stepping up onto the porch, I knocked lightly, hoping that with the light off out here, the few paparazzi who were left camped out at the end of the drive wouldn't be able to see me well enough to get a picture. Maddox swung the door open and pulled me inside, shutting it behind me and pressing me up against it. "And where the fuck have you been? Quinn and I have been going out of our minds looking for you," he exploded, breathing heavy.

His eyes were studying me, running over every inch, no doubt checking for injuries. When he was satisfied, he crashed his lips down on mine, pouring every bit of fear, anger, and frustration he'd been feeling into the kiss. He pulled away, resting his forehead on mine until he pulled back, grabbing my hand and bringing it up to his face.

He inspected my bruised knuckles, a crease forming on his forehead between his eyebrows. "What the fuck is this?"

"This is what happens when someone screws with the people I love," I answered vaguely, pushing off from the door. "Come sit down with me, and I'll explain."

He followed me to the couch, not letting go of my hand, but he did stop to pick up the bag I dropped at my feet when he'd pulled me inside. It was like he didn't want to let me out of his sight, and I felt bad that I'd scared him.

Unfortunately, things with Yates had taken longer than I expected.

He sat first, pulling me down onto his lap and wrapping his arms around my waist. "Talk," he demanded.

"Let me have my bag." I reached out for it, and he slid the handle into my hand. I pulled out the envelope and handed it to him. "Open it."

He eyed me warily before he pulled out the picture, his gaze instantly growing murderous like I knew it would. "What the everloving fuck is this?"

"Um. Your mom?" I answered as if it should be obvious.

He scowled at me. "You know what I meant."

"I know." I ran my hand through his hair.

"So?"

"When you were in the shower this morning, that came. A guy rang the doorbell and delivered it to me."

"And you opened it?" he asked, his voice on edge.

I nodded. "And I'm not sorry I did. You feel like you have to handle all of this on your own, but you don't. I'm strong enough to stand by your side and help. I'm not some helpless girl anymore, Maddox."

He deflated a little. "I know you're not. I love your strength. I love how you challenge me, how you're my equal. But you shouldn't have to deal with this alone, either."

"I wasn't alone. I took Connor. We verified Yates sent that before I decided to get a little payback. I know it wasn't much, but I needed to do it," I explained.

"Do what exactly?" He watched me carefully, but his grip tightened around my waist, and I leaned against him, suddenly exhausted from this entire day and wanting nothing more than for him to carry me to bed.

"Beat the hell out of Yates," I blurted like it was no big deal.

His eyebrows shot up, and a slow smile stretched across his face. "You beat him up?"

I nodded. "Kneed him in the balls, too."

"That's my girl," Maddox laughed. "I think you deserve a reward." He stood, carrying me with him, the picture of his mother and brother fluttering to the floor, already forgotten.

"You're not mad?"

"I'm only mad I didn't get to witness you being such a badass. I bet it was sexy as hell." He kicked the bedroom door open and threw me down onto the bed. I squealed as I bounced in the air before he crawled over me. "And now I'm going to show you *exactly* how much I worship the ground you walk on."

TWENTY NINE
MADDOX

I lifted the steaming mug of coffee to my mouth, slurping the bitter liquid so it wouldn't burn my tongue. Ryan left a few minutes ago, and now I was sitting in the quiet of my kitchen, figuring out what to do about Yates fucking with my family.

I had to hand it to the douchebag. He'd taken shit further than I ever thought he would. He seemed like the kind of guy who backed down when threatened, who ran home to daddy sniveling about life being *unfair*. But he surprised me when he found Russell, and when Ryan handed over the picture of my mom and brother last night? I was fucking floored.

So many emotions spiraled through me. I was fucking pissed, worried, and I didn't know what to do about my mom and brother. Russell could fuck off as far as I was concerned. There was absolutely nothing I wanted from him. But did I want something from them?

My front door opened and closed, whoever it was not bothering to knock. I glanced away from the wall I was staring at to catch Connor striding across my house. "I heard you and my girl got into some shit last night," I prodded without so much as a fucking hello. I was still pissed at him for not, at the very least, giving me a heads up.

"Your girl is a complete badass," he said as he pulled out the chair across from me and sat down. "See for yourself." He pulled his phone out of his pocket and tapped a few times before sliding it across the table to me.

Picking it up, I hit play and watched as Ryan beat the absolute fuck out of Yates. My chest swelled with pride every time her knuckles connected with his face. But when he pulled her hair and punched her in the face, I clenched my jaw so hard I thought I heard a tooth crack. "He hit her?" I asked, my voice deadly calm, but the murderous rage was simmering inside of me. He fucking put his hands on her, and I wanted him dead.

"Yeah, but keep watching." Connor nodded back at the phone gripped tightly in my hand.

Ryan proved time and time again she could defend herself. "Wow." I slid his phone back and shifted in my seat, trying to hide the sudden hard-on I was sporting because Ryan pummelling Yates was hot as fuck once the anger subsided a little.

I still wanted the motherfucker to disappear in a shallow grave somewhere in the fucking expanse of north Texas. My mind wandered to all the ways I could make it happen.

"Yeah, that's what I thought, too. She's got a bigger set of balls on her than a lot of men I've met. And that was all her idea. She was mad as hell when she saw how exactly Yates was coming after you. She had this fire lit in her eyes, and I'm sure you're not exactly thrilled that I didn't stop her from going after him alone, but she'd made up her mind. No one was going to stop her from doing this. The best I could do was go along and make sure she didn't get hurt."

My shoulders deflated a little. "Thanks for that," I mumbled, taking another sip of my now lukewarm coffee.

"I've got good news." Connor stood from the chair and grabbed a mug from the cupboard, pouring himself some coffee.

"Better good news than Yates getting his ass beat by my sexy as fuck girlfriend?" I wondered with a smirk.

He nodded before sitting back down across from me. "Sebastian made the offer yesterday, and this morning he got the notice that Yates accepted it. Since you just went straight up cash, as soon as it clears escrow, the place is all yours."

"So, he won't be able to kick them out?" I wanted to be sure.

"No. He must've signed everything before Ryan confronted him because if she'd done that before, I bet he would've hung onto it a few extra days just to give her one extra *fuck you*."

"Well, that's a fucking relief," I sighed before a smile crept up on my face. "I can't wait to tell her and see the look on her face."

"Dude, I can't believe you're so gone for a girl. I never thought I'd see the day," Connor noted, leaning back in the chair, his bulky frame making it creak ominously.

"Believe it. I buried that shit deep, *deep* down when I was a kid, but now all the feelings are out, and I don't want to put them back. She's incredible, and I'm never letting her go again. I was such a fucking idiot."

"Hell, you better hold onto her tight because women like her are one in a billion." He sounded almost wistful. I narrowed my eyes, wondering if I needed to worry about him hitting on my girlfriend.

He held up his hand in surrender, a smirk on his face. "I'd never lay a finger on your girl. Unless you asked." My glare melted into a low chuckle. It'd been a while, but it wasn't like we hadn't shared before. Unfortunately for him, I'd never share Ryan with anyone.

My phone buzzed on the table, and I groaned when I saw who was calling.

I pressed the phone to my ear. "No offense, but I'm getting real fucking sick of talking to you this week," I answered, not bothering with any pleasantries. Whenever my publicist called, it meant some bad shit was happening, and I'd had enough of that lately to last me a few decades at least.

"Yeah, well, right back at you," Harrison snapped, his British accent making him sound extra pissy. "What's up with all of your family drama coming out of the woodwork this week?"

A cold sweat broke out immediately across my forehead at his words. What other family bullshit could there be? "What do you mean?"

"Your father the other night with his lovely interview, and now your long-lost mum and brother hitting the headlines? I've been working with you for years, and I never knew you had anyone but the guys in the band," he noted, a question in his voice.

"Fuck. How bad is it?" I pinched the bridge of my nose, closing my eyes and taking a deep breath. An unfamiliar emotion gripped me as my hands turned clammy, and my stomach churned. Ryan tried to deal with Yates, and it worked about as well as my going to his office and threatening him had. At least he wasn't five million dollars richer.

"Not bad. At least not yet. But you may want to warn them because right now only one outlet is covering it, but it's about to be picked up by them all. You know what that bloody well means for them, right?"

"A fuck ton of reporters all over them. Yeah, I'm familiar." Especially considering that was how I pretty much lived my life every goddamn day.

"Good. So, I'm thinking we spin the reunion as you making peace with your estranged family, and maybe we do an interview or two? I think it'd actually help smooth the edges of your bad boy image," he suggested.

"Is that something I need to do? Smooth the edges?" I tossed his words back at him. "I like my reputation just how it is. I've worked hard to build it so that people don't fuck with me, and their expectations aren't too high."

"No, you don't need to do anything. Like with your father-"

"Russell," I spit out, hating the taste of his name in my mouth.

"Right. With *Russell*, you ignored it, and it's mostly old news. There's no reason you can't do the same here. I don't know what the person doing this is trying to accomplish."

Sighing, I leaned forward, resting my elbow on the table to prop my phone up to my ear as Connor watched me with only mild interest. "He's trying to hurt me the only way he thinks he can, by using my family against me."

"Is it working?" I could hear the smile in Harrison's voice. He worked in the right field, considering how much he lived for people's drama.

"I'll admit putting Russell on TV pissed me the fuck off. But I'm not sure how to feel about my mom and my brother. I don't even know them."

"Well, maybe now's the time. I've gotta go. Hopefully, I won't need to talk to you until you're back in town with a new album to promote."

"With any luck," I agreed before ending the call.

"Yates?" Connor asked as if he already knew the answer.

"Is there anyone else who doesn't realize how dangerous it is to fuck with me?" I countered, practically growling. I hoped this was the last card he had to play, and if it was, it wasn't a very good one. What did I care if my mom got thrown to the wolves? She'd abandoned me and never looked back.

I didn't like to admit that it still fucking stung.

Connor's laugh was interrupted by my goddamn phone ringing again, a number I didn't recognize. I usually just let that shit go to voicemail, but with everything happening, I decided to pick it up. "What?" I snapped into the phone, not really caring who was on the other end.

"Maddox?" A woman's voice filtered through the line, and my mouth went slack as I inhaled sharply. I hadn't heard it in years, but I'd recognize that voice anywhere.

"Mom?" I whispered before clearing my throat and straightening my spine. I wasn't a helpless little boy anymore.

I heard her sniffle on the other end, followed by a soft sob. "I'm… I'm so sorry." Her words rushed out, carried on her gentle voice laced with tears and regret.

"You're sorry?" I didn't know how to feel or what to say. My words were tinged with disbelief. I never understood why she left all those years ago and didn't take me with her or even come back for me. I had a thousand questions all on the tip of my tongue.

"Can… Would you be willing to meet me? I'll come to you. I just want the chance to explain, even if I don't deserve it," she begged, and my curiosity got the better of me.

"When?" I knew I was being short, but she'd fucking abandoned me. I wasn't going into this with any illusions that we'd be one big happy fucking family. But still, the prospect of getting answers to questions I'd had most of my life piqued my interest enough to agree to a meeting.

"This afternoon? I can be there in two hours."

"Fine. Come to the old house."

Her sharp intake of breath told me she hated this place probably more than I did. "Russell's gone so you don't have to worry about that, and I remodeled, so it doesn't look the same." I didn't know why I felt the need to comfort her.

"Fine. I'll be there," she agreed before hanging up.

I scrubbed my hands over my face. "What a weird fucking day."

"I'll text Ryan." Connor's fingers were already flying over his phone. My mind was spinning in so many different directions, I couldn't focus. I needed her, and he was smart enough to see it.

I sat staring blankly at the wall for what felt like hours but must have only been a few minutes. When the back door opened and closed with a soft click, it broke me out of my trance, and my gaze settled on Ryan walking across the room toward me.

She kneeled in front of me, a soft smile on her lips. "Hey, Romeo. You look a little lost."

I pulled her to me, breathing her in as my body instantly relaxed. She was better than a fucking Xanax. "I love you so fucking much, Freckles," I murmured against her hair.

"I love you, too," she chuckled, rubbing my back. "Come on, why don't we sit and you can tell me what happened?" she offered, pulling me up by my arm and lacing her fingers with mine as we walked to the couch. She guided me to sit and then sat beside me, pulling off her boots and draping her legs across my lap. I rested my hand on the rough denim material covering her smooth skin.

"Tell me what happened."

"Yates leaked the picture of my mom and Griffin," I sighed.

Her eyes narrowed into slits. "That *mother*fucker. I swear to god if I get my hands on him-"

"Whoa, Freckles. I saw the video, I think he got the worse end of the deal. That's not the part that has me spun out."

Her eyes softened as she reached up to play with the short hair at the back of my neck. "Then what does?"

"My mom called me."

The silence stretched on as she stilled. "*Monica* called you?"

I nodded.

"Whoa."

"I told you," I chuckled softly, running my palm up and down her thigh. "Know what's even crazier?"

"Crazier than your mom calling you after pretending you don't exist for twenty-two years? Sure." Her lips were pursed, and she was so fucking cute. I almost forgot to be weirded out about the situation. All I wanted to do was kiss her and not think about any of the other shit going on.

"She's coming here. Today."

"What?!" Ryan asked, bolting upright. "Today? When?"

"In about an hour and a half," I answered, checking the time on my phone.

"Wow. How do you feel about that?" Her eyes were now filled with concern as she watched me for any signs of distress. After what she'd done to Yates yesterday, if I hadn't known it before I knew it now, Ryan was protective as fuck of me just like I was of her. We were equally matched in our defense and possessiveness of each other.

Shrugging, I moved my hands down to pick up one of her feet so I could massage it. She groaned as my thumbs pressed into the arch. "I don't know how to feel. I guess I'm looking forward to hearing why the fuck she abandoned me. And I'm a little bit curious about my brother," I added.

"Is he coming with her?"

"I don't know, I didn't think to ask."

She sat up, pulling her foot from my grasp and running her fingers up the side of my face. "Do you want me to be here with you when she comes?"

Warmth bloomed in my body, starting in my chest and pushing its way out to my limbs, filling me up with comfort and love. For the first time in my life, I didn't have to go through something alone. Ryan would be here with me. I could lean on her strength if I needed to and fuck if that wasn't a weight off my shoulders. I nodded, and she grinned before tucking herself up against me, resting her head on my shoulder as we both sat in the quiet, lost in our own thoughts.

My heart hammered furiously in my chest as I listened to the knocking sound on the front door. I knew it was coming. I watched almost every minute tick down on the clock. I'd also seen the car pull up the short driveway and park.

And I'd seen the two figures stepping out and moving toward my porch.

Not only had my mom come, but she brought my brother.

Ryan squeezed my hand, trying to reassure me. "I've got this," she volunteered, moving to the front door and, with one last soft smile aimed in my direction, she swung it open. Ryan had been too young to really remember my mom when she left, but she was the only person in the world who knew everything about how I felt about it.

Once, when we were kids, I broke down one night after a particularly bad beating from my dad and told her everything. Every bit of sadness, anguish, and despair I'd felt when she'd left. The hope I held onto for years that she'd come back for me, and how every day it didn't happen hardened my heart more and more.

Now, she was coming face-to-face with the source of my pain, and I didn't know if I hoped she'd be welcoming or lash out. I had my answer a few seconds later. "Welcome, come in," Ryan greeted my mom and brother, whose gaze lingered on my girlfriend a few seconds too long. "I'm Griffin," he introduced, holding his palm out for Ryan. A cocky smirk not unlike my own crossed his face, and I stepped closer to her, pulling her into my side as they passed by.

"Ryan and this is Maddox." She shook his hand quickly as I nodded my head at my brother. Fuck, this was like an alternate reality. I couldn't believe I was standing face-to-face with my *brother*.

Once Ryan shut the door, we all stood staring awkwardly at each other; no one really sure where to start. My mom looked the same but different. She looked older, of course, but better. Healthier. Her light brown hair was pulled back in a bun, and she was dressed casually. She looked like she'd been crying, though. Her eyes were rimmed with red, and her face was pale.

Finally, my mom hurried forward and wrapped her arms around me. She was a lot shorter than I was, so her head only came up to my chest, but I hugged her back hesitantly as she cried softly. "I'm sorry, Maddox. So, so sorry."

I was lost. How the hell was I supposed to react right now? She stepped back, and Ryan suggested we move to the living room, so we all followed her, taking spots around the sectional. "What are you sorry for exactly?" I asked, holding back the tsunami of questions wanting to pour out of my mouth.

"I'm not sorry for leaving. I'll never apologize for that. Your father would have killed me if I stayed," she began.

"What did you think he would do to me?" I countered, anger simmering underneath my words.

"I never planned to leave you here with him. I planned to leave, to get my life settled, and then to come back for you. It took me a lot longer than I thought. I didn't have anywhere for you to stay because I lived on friend's couches or in my car. At least here you had a roof over your head. You had food. You could go to school."

"I didn't have food, and I missed school all the time because I couldn't hide the bruises.".

A scowl crossed Griffin's face, and he gripped our mother's hand tightly. "I should have come back for you, but honestly, I was scared. I was scared of your father, and I was scared that you hated me."

I softened a little toward the soul-deep sadness I saw in her eyes. It was finally sinking in that she didn't hate me or regret having me. Russell had always told me that my mom never wanted me and that she wished I'd never been born. But looking into her morose gaze, I saw the truth, and something inside of me was set free.

"I never hated you," I whispered softly, staring down at my hand held tightly in Ryan's. "I only wanted you to want me." The admission surprised me as it left my lips, but it felt right.

Her sniffles caught my attention, and I lifted my head to watch her as tears rolled down her cheeks. "Not one single second has gone by since I left that I didn't think about you, that I didn't feel an ache in my chest at the thought you could be out in the world needing me or hating me for what I did. I can never make up for the time we lost, and for that, I'll never forgive myself. I know I don't deserve it, but I'd like the chance to get to know you."

I glanced at Ryan, who was studying my mom intently. "If he lets you back in, you can't just walk out again. Either of you." She stared my mom down first and then turned her narrowed eyes on my brother.

"I just found out I have a brother. And not only a brother but also a fucking rock star, the bassist for my favorite band of all time. I feel like I'm in a damn dream," Griffin gushed, and my lips twitched in an almost smile. "So yeah, if you want to let me hang out and get to know you, you might never get rid of me."

"I... think I'd like that," I admitted. "And you, too, mom."

She smiled at me brighter than I think I'd ever seen, and something inside me clicked into place. I never thought I'd get this chance, and I didn't want to let it go. And it was made all the better with Ryan by my side. With her, anything was possible.

THIRTY
MADDOX

My mind was actively being blown. I could only imagine how Maddox felt right now. Seeing him tentatively make amends with his mom was better than I even dared to hope when he told me she was coming over.

I looked up at where he sat beside me, a boyish smile on his face as he caught up with the family he never thought he'd have. He looked younger and lighter than I'd ever seen him. He had a carefree energy around him that seriously made my heart sing. His mom looked lighter, too. They both needed this, and I couldn't believe it took Yates trying to hurt him to bring him the kind of freedom he always wished for.

And Griffin? He could almost be Maddox's twin, except he was covered in tattoos. While Maddox had a rebellious reputation, I had a feeling his little brother could give him a run for his money. He was *bad boy* personified with his dark eyes, tattoos, and cocky smirk. He even walked with a swagger meant to make all the panties in a three-block radius spontaneously combust.

He kept shooting me flirty glances that I hoped his brother didn't pick up on because Maddox was possessive as hell, and I wanted them to have a good relationship. So, I glared at him in return, not wanting to give him any signals at all that could be interpreted as anything other than *not interested*.

"So, Ryan," Monica turned to me with a bright smile on her face, the tears that streaked down her face just an hour ago long since dried and scrubbed away. "How long have you and my son been together?"

I tried to choke back a giggle, but it burst out, and before I knew it, I was full-on laughing. The head thrown back kind that wasn't cute. But, what a loaded question, one I really didn't know how to answer. Maddox's grip on me tightened as he chuckled and pressed a kiss to my temple.

"Sorry," I apologized, wiping my eyes. "That's a really complicated question to answer. I know it shouldn't be, but you're not the only one who left and took way too long to come back. I think it must be genetics," I teased, and Maddox's eyes narrowed slightly, almost like he was wondering if I was taking a shot at him or just teasing.

I smiled lovingly up at him, and he dropped a kiss on the tip of my nose. I melted a little because I loved it when he did that. "I was head over heels in love with this guy before I even really knew what love was," I started, poking him in the ribs as I turned to face his mom and Griffin, who made himself more comfortable on the couch. It seemed like he'd gotten the message and toned it down.

"I was ten, and he saved me from a couple of bullies. We'd been neighbors our whole lives, but I'd only seen him from a distance until that day," I recalled.

"She was so small, and it was heartbreaking watching the boys pick on her. Especially over something so stupid," he added, jumping in to tell a little bit of his side of that day.

"What were they picking on you about?" Griffin asked, leaning forward. He actually looked curious, which surprised me since he also looked like the kind of guy who only got to know you well enough to get in your pants but forgot your name as soon as he got off.

"My name." I shrugged. "Little boys are mostly all dicks, no offense."

Maddox and Griffin both laughed, and the sounds were eerily similar. "None taken, Freckles." Maddox's thumb rubbed gently along my shoulder, making me shiver like he always did. Every little way he touched me today was slowly building, making it harder to concentrate on anything but his touch. I wanted more, but I'd have to wait until later when we were alone. He flashed me a quick grin that said he knew exactly what he was doing to me.

"What's wrong with your name?" Griffin asked, genuine curiosity on his face as he picked up the bottle of water I'd brought out for him, twisting open the top and taking a sip."

I rolled my eyes. "Nothing except it's usually a boy's name. So they'd tease me about having boy 'parts'." I made air quotes. "Or being a boy or whatever. Now it seems kind of ridiculous, but at the time, it was relentless until Maddox stepped in."

"Aww, I'm proud of you," Monica said, pressing her palm to her chest with a warm smile on her face.

"Thanks." Maddox almost looked like he was blushing, and I *really* wanted to tease him, but I'd let him have a freebie. It was a big deal for him to have his mom tell him she was proud of him. It had probably never happened before in his life. He deserved to enjoy it.

"I'd seen it happen a few times, but the bus came, and I didn't want to get in more trouble. But that day, the bus was nowhere to be found, and they had her pinned. They were going to pull down her pants and try and prove she was really a boy. You should've seen the look on her face. She was this terrified, angry little girl who was trying desperately to save herself. But she couldn't. It was two against one, and she tried to fight them off, but it wasn't a battle she could win."

"What'd you do?" Griffin questioned, and he looked like he was genuinely invested in this story. It made me wonder if he was actually the kind of guy his outward appearance and attitude suggested or if there was more to him. Maybe he didn't even know yet since he was only twenty-two.

Maddox smirked. "All I had to do was tell them to let her go. They took one look at me towering over them and twice as broad and got the hell away from her."

I pulled his hand into mine. "And he didn't let me wait for the bus alone for the rest of the year. He walked me home every day. And those two little jerks never messed with me again."

"Damn, my big bro's a knight in shining armor," Griffin snickered.

"More like a wolf in sheep's clothing," I corrected as Maddox's hand moved from my shoulder to my thigh, squeezing and making desire pool inside of me. He was driving me insane with need. Was it possible to die from sexual frustration?

"What's wrong, Freckles?" he whispered darkly into my ear, his warm breath making goosebumps break out over my entire body. Damn him.

"Is it hot in here?" Griffin asked loudly, making my cheeks heat up.

"That's enough," Monica chastised her younger son gently, a soft smile on her face. She looked happy to have both of her boys in the same room. I couldn't imagine the weight of guilt and longing she'd been carrying all these years. "I think we're going to go, but I thought we'd stick around a few days if you don't mind. We'll get a hotel room, of course."

Maddox smiled and stood when his mom and brother did, smoothing out his shirt. He almost looked… nervous? "Are you sure? You guys can stay here, we have room."

My heart soared at the fact he'd included me as someone who lived here with him even if I wasn't.

"No, I… I can't stay here," Monica shook her head, shadows crossing her face before she blinked, and her smile was back. "The hotel will be fine. Griffin might want to stay, though."

"Would you mind?" he asked, his dark eyes locking with Maddox's.

"Not at all. Let's go grab your bag," Maddox offered, walking out the front door with his family. Before he stepped over the threshold, he looked back and gave me a smile of pure joy. He was radiating such happiness tears sprang to my eyes. Seeing him so happy made my heart full.

By the time Monica left for the hotel and Maddox got Griffin settled in his room, the three of us were sitting back around in the living room, and Connor walked in the front door with Sebastian. I didn't know where the other guys were, but then again, I hadn't known we were supposed to meet up with Connor today, either.

Everything but dealing with Maddox's family had fallen away today. I even forgot about Yates and what a mess we were dealing with. It was hard to be mad about his latest attempt to sabotage my boyfriend when it ended up bringing him so much happiness. The only times I'd seen him happier was when we had sex for the first time and when I chose him over Yates.

Connor plopped down across from where Maddox and I were tangled with each other on one side of the sectional. It was huge and in a U-shape, so there was plenty of room for everyone as Sebastian sat next to Connor. Griffin sat in the middle as he and Connor studied each other wordlessly.

"You're the little brother?" Connor finally asked, his eyes still unreadable. I looked at Maddox, who was watching his friend get a read on his brother. Truthfully, we didn't know anything about the guy. But I'd be willing to bet Connor had a file thicker than a dictionary on Griffin. If he gave his approval for him to be here and a part of everything going on, we could relax. If not, well… We'd figure it out.

"Apparently so," Griffin drawled, relaxing back against the cushions and crossing his ankle over his knee.

"There's a lot of shit going on that you know nothing about. If you stay, you can't breathe a fucking word to anyone outside of this room. Do you understand?" Connor demanded. It was as good as an approval from him that he was giving Griffin the choice. I relaxed back against Maddox and felt the tension melt from his body at the same time. That would go a long way towards Maddox accepting and trusting his brother.

Griffin nodded, suddenly more serious. The indifferent and somewhat asshole-ish expression he'd had on his face when the guys walked in dropped away, and now he just looked concerned. It looked like the protective instinct wasn't only strong in Maddox but his brother, too.

Sebastian dropped the messenger bag he always kept with him onto the ottoman and started pulling out thick files. "These are everything we've gathered on Yates. This one's every transactional record I could find between Rutherford Bank and his offshore account." He passed the folder to Maddox.

"And this one's all the transactions from the offshore account to his private account." He set another folder onto the ottoman.

"And lastly, but definitely most disgusting, pictures from the past couple of days along with transaction records of his interactions with a couple of different prostitutes," Sebastian finished, plopping the disturbingly thick file down and then squirting a huge amount of hand sanitizer in his hand and rubbing it in. "Too bad this doesn't work on my eyes." He looked at the bottle wistfully.

Griffin grabbed for the folder with the pictures in it and flipped it open. His eyes widened, and his lip curled. "Jesus," he muttered, slamming the folder closed and setting it back down. "Mind if I get some of that?" he asked Sebastian, pointing to the bottle of hand sanitizer.

"Sure," Sebastian agreed, tossing it to him.

As he rubbed his hands together, Griffin glanced down at the folders. "What is all of this?"

Connor looked to Maddox, his head cocked to the side, and his eyebrow raised. Maddox turned to his brother. "Yeah, so didn't you wonder how your picture suddenly ended up all over the media?"

He shrugged. "Once mom told me who you were, it made sense. I'm surprised it didn't happen sooner."

"Well, I've always kept my past private. I preferred to make as many distractions in the present as I could so everyone focused on that shit instead." I never realized Maddox had calculated and planned so much of his image. I always sort of figured it was just the way he was.

Griffin nodded along as Maddox continued. "Until someone tried to take Freckles from me. When I fought back, he played dirty. Now it's time I play dirtier. That motherfucker's going to regret not just letting her go."

"I think I missed a lot," Griffin noted, his eyes darting between Maddox and me.

"You did, but the most important thing to know is that despite your brother threatening him and me rearranging his balls back up into his body, he keeps coming at us. And at this point, we're convinced he's not going to stop. Plus, he deserves to pay for everything he's done," I explained, leaning my head against Maddox's shoulder. He brushed the hair off of my forehead gently.

"Wait, is this why I saw Russell on TV the other night?" Griffin asked, anger suddenly replacing his concern.

Connor nodded. "That was all Yates, Sebastian confirmed it by hacking his email."

"I'm not even going to touch his ridiculous name," Griffin started. "But mom told me on the way here about Russell and everything he did to her. She kept it to herself all these years. I never knew I had a brother, and I never knew she was married before my dad. But if I ever meet him, I'll fucking kill him," he vowed, his voice dark with his threat. The mood had gotten a lot more serious.

"You're going to have to get in line," Connor agreed.

"Getting back on track," I cut in because we could talk about how much of a dick Russell was and how much we all wanted a turn ripping into him all night. We had a mission and needed to stay focused.

"First, we hand this all over to the cops. Then, we crash a party," Connor outlined, gathering the files up and stuffing them back into Sebastian's bag.

"How is crashing a party going to help us?" I asked.

"It's not just any party," Sebastian grinned deviously. "It's Yates's parents' quarterly charity ball. They throw it at the country club for some ridiculous, undeserving charity that doesn't actually help anyone. This quarter's is happening tomorrow night, coincidentally. It's the perfect place to expose Yates as the thief he is. Among other things."

"We're going to embarrass him in front of everyone." The more of this plan I heard, the more I liked it.

"Right. Sebastian's done here, so he's going back to the hotel. The three of us have got a date with Sergeant Ferraro in," Connor glanced down at his watch. "A little more than an hour, so let's go."

"What about me?" Griffin asked, sitting up.

"Just hang out. It's a long drive, and it's going to be boring. We'll be back in a couple of hours, and then we'll get some dinner." Maddox stood up and pulled me with him. "Feel free to drink all my beer."

He glanced around. "Do you have a music room?" It would've been a weird question if he was talking to someone not in a world-famous band. But Maddox always had his bass or a guitar nearby.

"You play?" Maddox asked his brother, who nodded.

"Drums."

"It's the last door on the left. There are a couple of guitars, a couple of basses, and a drum set in case Jericho visits."

"I still can't believe you not only know those guys but are part of the band," Griffin marveled, looking a little star-struck for a minute before he snapped out of it. I giggled but tried to hide it behind my hand.

"Have fun, little brother." Maddox tested the words like a new food he wasn't sure he liked the taste of, but Griffin didn't seem to mind.

"We'll pick up dinner on the way home," I added, pulling out my phone. "Put your number in my phone, and I'll text so we can decide what we want." I handed my phone over to Griffin, and he tapped the screen before handing it back. I sent a quick text back. "I texted you Maddox's number, so you have it, too."

He nodded, pulling out his own phone and getting lost in it as I grabbed my purse and slid my boots back on. We stepped out of the house, ducking quickly into Connor's waiting SUV. The crowd of reporters outside had thinned considerably since we'd been avoiding them and not giving them anything usable picture-wise.

The drive to the police station passed quickly since I rested my head on Maddox's shoulder and dozed the entire trip. He was lost in thought, and I wanted to give him some space.

We pulled up to the station, following Connor inside. It was one of his old Marine buddies we were seeing, a guy he served with, who was a sergeant here with the DPD. The building was taller than I expected, this precinct one of the larger ones if I had to guess. It looked like it'd been recently remodeled, and it had a modern feel to it.

Judging by the fact Yates's parents lived in this area, I wasn't surprised.

Connor checked in with the front desk while Maddox and I hung back. Before we could even sit down, a surprisingly young man walked into the room, greeting Connor like old friends. "This must be the guy," Maddox murmured near my ear before kissing my cheek and weaving his fingers between mine.

Connor turned toward us, waving us over. "Maddox, Ryan, this is Sergeant Ferraro."

He held out his hand for me to shake first, then Maddox. His smile was open and friendly, and I couldn't help but smile back. "Call me Lucas. Please."

Maddox's hand dropped to my lower back as we followed Lucas and Connor back to his office. Once the door was safely closed, Connor pulled out the three files and handed them over. "These are yours to keep, I've got copies."

"And what am I looking at?" Lucas asked, thumbing through the pages.

"Are you familiar with the Rutherfords?" Connor asked instead of answering his question.

"Sure, everyone around here is. Old money, they own the bank downtown."

"As I'm sure you're aware, they have a son. Yates," Connor continued.

Lucas's happy demeanor shifted to something a little less friendly and a little bit more annoyed. I could relate. "I'm familiar with him. I wish I wasn't."

"A sentiment we all share," I offered with a soft laugh.

"He's been skimming from the company. And, as you'll see, he really enjoys prostitutes. Tread carefully when flipping through that file," Connor suggested, pointing out the folder with the prostitute pictures in it as if it were radioactive, keeping a fair distance.

Sergeant Ferraro looked at it like it might bite him, and I fought off a laugh. "I'll keep that in mind. What do you need from me?"

"We were hoping you'd arrest him tomorrow night at the charity ball his parents are throwing."

Lucas sighed. "At the Imperial Cedar Country Club, right?"

Maddox nodded.

"This is either going to go really, really well, or fuck up my whole day," Lucas noted, resigned.

"We're going to make a speech, and once it's done, we want you and your men to move in and take him. We plan to show his parents and all his parent's snobby friends the kind of man he truly is. But we need your help," Connor laid out, explaining the details of what we planned to do tomorrow night.

"I'll get everything set up and in place. I'll need to get a warrant," Lucas confirmed after he'd flipped through the evidence we brought him.

"We don't want anyone to know this is going down until it happens. If we don't surprise him, he'll run," Connor added, lifting himself out of the chair. Maddox and I did the same, and Lucas followed.

"I'll only bring in my most trusted guys. We'll get him," he promised, holding out his hand for Connor to shake. If Connor trusted him, Maddox and I did, too. I couldn't wait for tomorrow night and the end of the nightmare that I'd started for all of us a couple of months ago.

I couldn't wait to watch Yates get everything he deserved.

THIRTY ONE
MADDOX

I was no stranger to tuxes. Black tie was my bitch. But this was the first time that I wasn't focused at all on myself. Griffin had insisted on coming with us, and I tore my gaze off the hallway where I was waiting for Ryan to step out in her dress as he stepped into my line of sight. My little brother borrowed one of my tuxes, and I swear to god he wore it better than me.

Fucker.

And it was weird as fuck that I had a brother, but not a bad weird. I was getting used to it, and it was actually kind of… nice. He moved to stand next to me, turning his head toward the empty hall as he adjusted his sleeves and toyed with gold cufflinks. "What are you staring at?"

I rolled my shoulders back, standing taller. I still had an inch or so on him, and I planned to use it. "I'm waiting for Ryan."

"Bro, you're going to be waiting until you're old. This thing will probably be over before she's ready," he commented, patting me on the shoulder and walking off.

"She's not like that," I tossed back just as the door to my room opened, and she stepped out. I sucked in a breath as I took her in, starting from her feet strapped into gold heels that looked uncomfortable as fuck, up the slit in her dress that showed her bare leg all the way up to her hip. The desire to run my tongue over the exposed skin slammed into me as I stalked forward, my legs moving on their own.

Stepping in front of her, my hands skimmed along her waist over the soft fabric that hugged every curve. I dropped my lips to her exposed collarbone, inhaling her sweet scent. "There aren't words for how good you look, Freckles," I complimented. "I don't think we can leave the house. I'm not going to be able to kill everyone who looks at you in this dress and still be able to deal with Yates."

Anticipation crackled between us as she giggled, a soft, charming sound that made me smile against her warm skin.

"Unless you plan to share, we need to go or we're going to be late," Griffin's gruff voice came from somewhere behind me and made me want to take back all the somewhat warm and fuzzies I'd been feeling toward him just a few minutes ago.

Ryan's hands slid up my chest, pressing me gently back as she looked up at me with enchanting eyes I wanted to fall into and never find my way back out of. "Just think about how good it'll be later when we've been building anticipation all night," she murmured as she stepped away from me, letting her hand drag across my chest. I groaned, holding myself back with a lot of fucking effort from throwing her over my shoulder and carrying her back to my room.

Instead, I slapped her on the ass as she passed by me, enjoying the yelp she let out and the sting in my hand. It'd have to do for now. We filed out of the house in a single file line, Griffin stepping into the waiting limo first, followed by Ryan and then me. We had to keep up appearances, so I rented this thing for the night.

Griffin immediately reached for the bottle of champagne chilling, popping the top. "Take it fucking easy with that shit. We're not going there to party. We have a job to do," I reminded him. I'd been really hesitant to take him with us, but he insisted, and I didn't want to fight him on it. I had too much other shit to worry about. He was a big boy. He could take care of himself. But if he fucked this up for us, I was going to be pissed.

We stopped by the hotel in town and picked up Connor, Julian, and Indy. From what I could tell, Sebastian didn't typically get himself mixed up in the physical part of protecting people. He preferred to stay behind a computer monitor.

With six of us in the limo, it was a bit more crowded, and I hadn't missed how everyone had quickly roamed their gaze over my girl as they climbed in before respectfully keeping their goddamn eyes to themselves. My arm rested across her lap with my hand possessively gripping her bare thigh. My fingers itched to slide higher, and I sure a fuck wasn't shy, but there were four other guys in here, and even I had my limits. Letting them watch my girlfriend come was a hard line.

Griffin actually helped keep the atmosphere light, pouring champagne and handing it out and joking around with Connor and his guys. He seemed like the type of guy who could get along with anyone without really having to try that hard. The alcohol helped take the edge off, but we all stopped before it went any further. We needed to stay sharp, and we all knew it.

I may not have been a member of Connor's team, but I'd taken care of shit both by myself and with him enough times to know how things needed to go to be successful.

And we *would* be successful.

The limo pulled up to the ostentatious club, and the driver opened the door. Connor, Julian, and Indy stepped out first, followed by Griffin, and Ryan and I were left alone in the cab. "Are you ready, Freckles?" I asked, stroking my thumb against her soft cheek. She leaned into my touch and briefly closed her eyes, exhaling.

"I'm beyond ready. I can't wait to make him pay for messing with my family and the man I love," she assured me.

"Don't do anything reckless, Ryan. I mean it. He's more dangerous than we've given him credit for. I know you can kick his ass if you need to, but we have no idea what he's capable of when he's trapped," I warned.

"I'll be careful," she promised, kissing me once, twice, and three times before her soft lips lifted in a smirk, and she stepped out of the limo. I took in the incredible view of her body draped in that fucking red dress that would haunt my dreams for weeks. With one final exhale, I pushed myself off the seat and followed her out. The door closed behind us, and the limo pulled away.

We were gathered in a loose circle, going over our plans one final time. Ryan wrapped her fingers around my arm. I escorted her inside, still hating the idea of anyone but me seeing her in her dress. Connor had gotten a text message from Sergeant Ferraro letting us know he was inside and ready. He got the warrant, and his men were getting in place right now.

All we had to do was get in, and Ryan was going to steal the microphone and make a speech. And then Yates would be arrested, and everything could go back to normal. No, better than normal because I'd have Ryan. We hadn't talked about it, but she'd fit in perfectly with my friends in LA. Her and Quinn. And I had no intention of going back without either of them.

Connor went ahead of us, talking to the man guarding the door. I didn't know what he said, but the man let us all pass. He didn't look happy about it and scowled at me as I passed. I gave him a little salute because I was an asshole, and sticking it to these kinds of people made me happy.

Right outside the ballroom, I had a flashback to a few weeks ago when I crashed Ryan's engagement party in this very same room. It looked exactly the same as if they couldn't have been bothered to decorate it the way she wanted for such a special day.

Someday when we get married, it will be different.

Shoving those thoughts aside, I caught Ryan's attention. I was worried she had a flash of the same memories I did only worse, and I wanted to make sure she was okay. She gave me a small smile, and her eyes sparkled as if she were excited. She continued to impress me time and time again. I wondered when I'd stop doubting how amazing she was.

I kept underestimating her, and I needed to knock that shit off.

Outside, we decided we would step into the ballroom in pairs. Connor and Julian would go first and blend into the crowd. Two minutes later, Indy and Griffin would make their appearance, and we'd give them a couple of minutes to mix and mingle. And then Ryan and I would go in last because we were the most likely to be recognized.

Right after Connor and Julian stepped through the doors, I spotted Lucas down the hall with a couple of his guys. His blue uniform stood out in the ridiculous setting of this place, and I welcomed the stark contrast. I was practically giddy at the thought of seeing Yates in handcuffs being dragged out of the room in front of me in a matter of minutes.

He nodded at us as he approached. "We're ready. I've got officers stationed at every exit. He won't be able to get past us."

I appreciated his confidence and how quickly he pulled everything together. We wouldn't get another chance like this for a while. "Perfect," Ryan approved, tightening her grip on my arm. She hadn't let me go since the huddle outside.

Griffin and Indy had gone inside a minute ago, and so we waited, the last minute going on forever. "Our turn," Ryan grinned, lifting onto her toes to press a kiss to my cheek. I briefly wondered if she'd left her lipstick there, and I hoped she had. The idea of her marking me as hers turned me the fuck on, even if now wasn't the best time.

We slipped through the double doors, and the room was incredibly crowded. No one even glanced our way. We moved together toward the front of the room, not getting too close just yet. The plan was to wait until Jacqueline got up to make her speech. So for now, we'd blend in. I had no interest in talking to any of these people, but I pulled my girl into my arms on the edge of the dance floor, and we started to sway.

My hands wrapped around Ryan, one resting on her hip and the other moving around her back and pulling her closer. Her body pressed against mine was distracting, but I couldn't find it in me to care. I hadn't bothered looking for Yates yet. Where he was didn't matter. He wasn't getting out of this room a free man, and really, that was all that mattered.

I spun and twirled and swayed with my girl for so long, I almost forgot why we were here. If I hadn't been on edge, waiting for the right moment, I could've gotten lost in Ryan's magnetic eyes.

The feedback from a microphone caught our attention, and I spun Ryan out of my arms, still holding onto her while we looked toward the stage. Jacqueline stepped up to the microphone, her chin tilted up haughtily as she stared down at her subjects.

"Showtime," Ryan murmured, winking at me with a wicked grin before letting me go and starting to weave her way through the crowd. The other guys were supposed to be on Yates duty, making sure they kept an eye on him, and he didn't leave the room before this moment.

I'd been glued to Ryan's side all night because I refused to let her go through this alone. Shit was unpredictable, and no matter how much we planned, things didn't always go the way we thought they should. Just look at what had happened when we tried to get evidence on Chloe, Zen's stalker. She walked in with a gun, and almost fucking shot me.

You could plan for a goddamn year, but it wouldn't matter in the moment if shit went off the rails. I turned my attention back to the stage where Ryan was climbing the stairs, her eyes focused on the podium. She stepped up beside Jacqueline, and reached across the podium, snatching the microphone out of its holder.

She looked like vengeance in her fiery red dress, a wild mess of curls on her head, and the fierce look in her eyes. My chest actually ached from the amount of love trying to burst out of me right now. It felt like a struggle to contain it all inside.

Jacqueline made a weak attempt to pull the microphone back, but to save face, she plastered a thin smile on her face and stepped back and to the side, giving Ryan the floor.

"Ladies and gentlemen, excuse the interruption. I couldn't miss out on the opportunity to address you all here this evening. You see, I don't know if you're aware, but I almost became a Rutherford myself earlier this month," she started. Murmurs broke out across the crowd as people shifted around, their rapt attention on her as they anticipated what she might say. These people lived for gossip and drama, and they were eating this shit up.

"The problem was I was in love with someone else, and shouldn't real, honest, and intense love always win out in the end?" Ryan mused, not really paying attention to the crowd's reaction as her eyes found mine, and she smiled.

Movement to my right caught my attention as Yates slithered through the crowd, trying to get to the stage. "My ex-fiance, well, he didn't appreciate me walking away. So he thought he'd try and get me back. Isn't that right, Yates?"

Her warm gaze hardened and shifted away from me and instead focused on Yates as he got closer to where she stood. "Except he really didn't know me that well. He didn't know that when someone messes with the people I love, I don't just take it lying down. I fight back. I'm a fighter, and he's about to learn the lengths I'll go to to defend myself and the people I love."

Every exit door opened, and the officers plus Sergeant Ferraro stepped into the door frames, blocking them all. Yates spun around, his eyes starting to get frantic, and he tried to figure out what was happening. "What are you doing?" he demanded through clenched teeth. His fury was barely under control, but he was obviously still trying to save face in front of his parents.

"I'm showing everyone what kind of man you really are," she said sweetly, raising her head to address the crowd again. "Now, Yates here. He's a Rutherford. Old money. Prestigious as they come. And yet... there's more here than meets the eye, isn't there, *darling*?" Her tone dripped with condescension.

"I don't know what you're talking about," he scoffed.

"You don't? Well, normally, when you're going to marry someone, you should tell them about your kids, don't you think?" she asked, turning to Jacqueline. "Congratulations, you're a grandma... at least a few times over."

Jacqueline paled and swayed where she stood. "What's the meaning of this? Yates, what is she talking about?" she sputtered, her eyes darting around the room where the whispers were getting louder. This looked like her nightmare come to life.

"I don't know, mother," he answered robotically as his eyes narrowed at Ryan. His fists were balled at his sides, and I glanced around. All Lucas's guys were at the exits, but none were near the stage close enough to stop him from hurting the woman I loved. I edged closer.

"Maybe you'll remember last night then? At the *Cloud Inn*? You were there most of the night with Candy?" Ryan pulled a folded picture out of the tiny clutch she'd been carrying around all night, and now I wondered what else she had in there. She held the picture up, smoothing it out before passing it to Jacqueline.

Yates dove for the stage, climbing up and trying to snatch the picture out from Ryan's grasp, but his mother was quicker. She paled even further when her eyes scanned the image, her skin going a sickly shade between gray and green. "We'll discuss this later," she hissed at Yates before setting her sights on Ryan. "I think you've done enough-"

Ryan held up her finger. "Oh, no. I haven't done *nearly* enough yet. Sergeant Ferraro? Would you come into the ballroom, please?"

Lucas walked in, his navy blue uniform crisp and perfectly out of place. He walked up to the stage, climbing the steps, and standing next to Ryan. I relaxed a little knowing he was up there with her, and he had a gun strapped to his waist. "This is Sergeant Lucas Ferraro with the Dallas Police Department. We'll get to why he's here in just a second."

Yates's mother was glaring at him. The crowd watched with complete silent fascination except for a few people who had their phones out, furiously tapping on the screens. I hoped they were live Tweeting this shit show. The thought made me almost giddy.

"So, on top of the multiple random kids Yates has fathered-"

"Allegedly," he fumed, and his mom elbowed him in the ribs.

"Right. *Allegedly*. On top of that, Yates here has a couple pretty nasty habits. Remember the picture of him with Candy last night? The hooker who charges fifty dollars an hour? Well, he also has a fascinating porn viewing addiction." Ryan reached into that magical bag of tricks she was carrying around and pulled out several folded pieces of paper, tossing them out into the crowd.

"What the fuck are you doing?" Yates bellowed, jumping off the stage and attempting to grab as many pages as he could. The sheets might as well have been money for how people were diving after them.

"Just showing people who you really are," Ryan said with a shrug. "Now, as for Sergeant Ferraro," she announced, looking at Lucas with a small smile. "He's here for something a lot more important than all of this." Ryan waved her hand at the sheets of paper currently being ripped apart as people fought to get a look at his internet history.

"He's here because Yates has been stealing from Rutherford Bank for almost a year," she concluded as the crowd gasped.

"He what?!" Jacqueline exploded at her son as Yates stepped menacingly toward Ryan.

Lucas stepped forward, unfolding a piece of paper. "I have a warrant here for the arrest of Yates Rutherford."

The collective gasp in the room was so loud and satisfying, I closed my eyes for a second and reveled in it. Everything had come together perfectly so far. I should've known that it wouldn't be that easy.

Yates ran straight at Ryan, punching her in the stomach and grabbing her so fast she didn't have time to react other than to hunch over, gasping for air. His mother was shrieking, and I only felt a thrum coursing through my body, demanding pain. I needed to fucking hurt him for what he'd just done. He fucking hit her.

But then he wrapped his arm around her neck in the front in a sleeper hold, his other hand behind her head. He started dragging her toward one of the entrances as his eyes darted around, looking for anything to help him. I began to move toward where he was pulling her down the stairs, my explosion of rage morphing into fear.

Ryan's eyes met mine, but she looked calm. I wasn't calm, though. I was on the verge of screaming. What if he hurt her? What if he did worse? He was capable of anything because he was so desperate I scanned the room and watched as Connor, Julian, Indy, and Griffin all moved toward us in what looked like slow motion. Yates was almost to the exit, facing inward as he backed away, a cruel smile on his face. He thought he was going to get away with this.

He wasn't.

I would follow him to the ends of the fucking earth if it meant saving Ryan. Lucas had one hand on his gun, but it was still in the holster. He was following Yates as he backed toward the exit, his eyes never leaving them. He watched every single movement with the trained eyes of a professional. Where I was a fucking mess right now, he was completely composed as if he did this shit every day.

Hell, he probably did.

Yates took another step back, dragging Ryan along with him. She stumbled, undoubtedly trying to make it harder for him to pull her along because that was just the kind of badass my girl was. He was getting frustrated with her, I could tell. But she was also his ticket out of here, and he wasn't about to let her go.

I was watching Lucas when his eyes flicked for a fraction of a second over Yates's shoulder, but it was so quick, I doubted Yates had noticed with his gaze still frantically scanning the room. "Stay the fuck back, or I'll hurt her," he threatened.

He took one more step back. Just one more and one of Lucas's officers moved within striking distance, pulling out his taser and pulling the trigger. The electrodes cracked ominously as they flew through the air, sinking into Yates's back. As soon as they made contact, he dropped to the ground in a heap, taking Ryan with him. His muscles tensed and spasmed as his full weight landed on top of her.

"Get the hell off of me," she gritted out, pain flashing in her eyes as she shoved Yates off and crawled out from underneath him. Sergeant Ferraro rushed forward and snapped Yates's wrists into his cuffs, reading him his rights.

All I wanted to do was pull Ryan into my arms and rush her out of here. Fuck, he could have seriously hurt her. He could have found a weapon and killed her. There was a panic bubbling underneath the surface of my emotions right now because Yates could've taken Ryan from me permanently tonight.

I ran to her side, diving onto the floor on my knees and pulling her into my arms. I ran my hands over every inch of her that I could reach, but she seemed okay. "Shit, that taser hurt. Quinn's going to kill me for not inviting him to come to this," she noted, and I laughed. I couldn't believe how okay with all of this she was. Then again, she'd always wanted to be a cop, so maybe she was good with all of this stuff.

Lucas looked perfectly calm when I glanced up at him. "EMS is en route. They'll be here to check you over soon." He looked over at Yates. "And deal with him."

She shook her head. "Yates got the worst of it. I'm maybe a little tense and achy, but I'll be fine. I don't need paramedics."

Lucas crouched down next to us as the rest of the guys formed a loose half-circle behind us, shielding us from the pandemonium that'd broken out all over the ballroom. I had a feeling these people would be talking about this for years to come. "You okay?" he asked Ryan, his eyes filled with concern.

"I'm fine. I wish everyone would stop asking me," she huffed, and I chuckled. So fucking stubborn.

"In that case, I'm going to need you to give a statement," he stated, standing up and holding out his hand to help her stand.

"I'll go grab the limo," Julian offered, turning and walking quickly out of the room.

"I'm going to grab a drink." Griffin turned and moved toward the open bar.

"Just one!" I called after him. He still had to make a statement. He waved me off.

Connor and Indy watched everything. "Even I have to admit that shit was fucking satisfying," Connor said.

"Right? I wish we could do this every day," Indy agreed.

Connor pulled out his phone. "Julian's got the limo ready. You guys ready to head out?"

I nodded. Ryan took a step, winced, and I reached down, scooping her into my arms. She was still in pain from the taser, and I wasn't going to let her just tough her way through this. Once we were settled in the limo, I didn't want to take my hands off her. Things could have been so much worse tonight than they were, and I'd never stop being grateful for every second I had to spend with her.

A simple statement at the police station had taken fucking hours. We both nodded off on the drive home, but once we got there, I had big plans for Ryan. This need inside me had grown over the past several hours, minute by minute building into something completely primal. As if sensing how on edge I was, she looked up at me with darkened eyes, my own desire reflected back at me.

I tossed my keys to Griffin and told him to go ahead of us. I wanted him locked in his room because Ryan and I? We weren't going to be quiet tonight. Things were going to be intense.

As soon as the door closed behind us, I pulled her tightly against my body. I was shaking, and emotion clogged my throat, so I didn't talk. I still couldn't believe Ryan was here with me, my arms wrapped tightly around her. Yates could've taken her from me tonight. Fuck, the thought of that made me want to burn down the world. What kind of life would I be able to live without her in it?

But right now, it didn't matter. I needed to show her how much she meant to me. I wanted to run my hands over every curve of her body, but I also didn't want to let her go. I didn't want to loosen my grip because I was almost afraid if I let her go, she'd disappear, and right now, I was shaken to my core.

Breathing her in one last time, I finally let her go, trailing my fingers down her arm and taking her hand in mine. Fuck, I never want to stop touching her.

Right now, though, I needed to bury myself inside my girl and forget about everything that happened tonight. I wanted to release all the fear, anger, and uncertainty and replace it with love, passion, and devotion.

I wanted to worship at the temple of Ryan.

Turning to face her, I placed my hands on both sides of her face until she looked me in the eye. Stroking the soft skin of her cheeks gently with my thumbs, I leaned forward and kissed her lips before resting my forehead against hers. "Baby, right now, I need to be inside you." The words came out both demanding and as a plea.

She nodded once, and I led us down the hall to the master suite that had been transformed into mine. Leading her through the doorway, soft lights clicked on automatically overhead, dim enough to not be harsh but with enough light to cast Ryan in a soft glow. She tugged my hand, and I followed her across the room until she stopped in front of the bed.

She sat down on the edge and looked up at me with so much wonder in her eyes, for a second, I couldn't catch my goddamn breath. I sifted my fingers through her hair while we clung to each other, her hands stroking up and down my back as I stood between her thighs.

Wanting Ryan was a given, something that was a constant in my life these past few weeks. If I was honest with myself, even before that. But this moment right here was different. Of course, I wanted her, but it was more than that. I *needed* her. I needed the closeness, the connection to chase away the darkness and fear.

My thumb brushed against her bottom lip before I leaned down and captured her mouth with mine. The kiss started out sweet but turned heated fast. "I love you," she whispered against my lips, and I was lost to the sensations flooding my body. Her fingers against my back, pulling me closer, her hardened nipples brushing against my chest even through the layers we both still wore. The small sounds she made as I devoured her mouth lit me on fire.

Finally, fucking *finally*, she ripped at my shirt, needing it off as much as I did. I stopped kissing her just long enough to yank it over my head and toss it away before I watched her slip out of her dress quickly. We reached for each other at the same time, drawn together and unable to fight off the pull as I kissed her, claiming her again and again as mine with every stroke of my tongue against hers.

My dick was already straining against my jeans, demanding to be let out, but my focus was entirely on Ryan. She leaned back, and I crawled on top of her, wanting to feel her skin pressed against mine. Her legs opened for me, and I settled between them, pressing the hard ridge of my erection against her and groaning at the friction.

Her fingers danced down my body, tracing every ridge and muscle until she found the button on my jeans and flicked it open. She plunged her hand into my jeans and down my boxer briefs, shoving them off and palming my erection before wrapping her fingers around it. While her hand slid up and down my shaft, I reached around her back and unclasped her bra, watching as it fell off and the most incredible pair of tits I'd ever laid eyes on popped out.

Leaning down, my open mouth drifted across her nipple, and I watched as it puckered before pulling it into my mouth and sucking. Hard.

She gasped and released my hard as fuck dick from her hand to instead tangle her fingers in my hair. Suddenly kissing her wasn't enough. I wanted to feel her come undone on my tongue. I didn't think it was possible, but even more blood rushed to my groin as I started kissing a path down toward the juncture of her thighs.

I inhaled sharply when I realized she wasn't wearing underwear. "Fuck. You were a naughty girl tonight, weren't you?" I growled, barely recognizing my own voice.

She bit her lip and nodded as she stared up at me through hooded eyes. "Just for you."

I bit down on her hip, making her squeal and thrash underneath me. "You're goddamn right just for me." I cupped her bare pussy with my hand. "This. Is. Mine."

Ryan threw her head back and moaned, arching her back and pushing her perfect tits into the air, where I had a fantastic view of her tightened buds.

I let go of her and instead lowered my face down to her bare slit, which was already glistening. She was so damn intoxicating, I was greedy for her. A fucking ravenous wild animal that couldn't wait to show her who she belonged to.

Her sweet-tangy flavor exploded on my tongue as I dove in, licking circles around her clit in a steady rhythm as I slid my finger along her slick pussy. She bucked against me, and I splayed my other hand across her hips, holding her down against the bed so she'd hold still while I pushed my finger inside her body.

Her walls clenched around my finger as my dick jumped in response. I was painfully hard and on the verge of coming all over myself, but I couldn't let that happen. Instead, I refocused on her, sucking and licking at her clit with long strokes as I added a second finger.

I opened my mouth and sighed against her, my hot breath ghosting along her clit and making her squirm. I knew she was close. Her muscles tightened up, and she clawed at my hair, tugging on the ends almost painfully. With one final lick, she plunged over the edge, tightening around my fingers and trapping my face between her thighs as she screamed out my name.

Placing barely-there kisses on each of her quivering thighs, I crawled my way up, taking my time and letting my eyes rake over every inch of her irresistible body. When I finally covered her body with mine, I propped myself up on my forearms, bracing myself above her and settling my cock between her thighs. I rocked my hips a little, the head of my erection sliding against her slick entrance.

"Oh, god," she moaned, using her heels wrapped around my hips to push me forward.

I chuckled darkly, teasing her by letting just the tip slide inside her before pulling myself back out. Every part of my body screamed at me to push inside her until I couldn't go any further, but I wanted to tease her a little bit first.

"You want to feel me inside of you, Freckles?" I murmured against her lips, and she whimpered, shifting herself again.

"You shouldn't have teased me today by not wearing underwear. Good girls don't tease, Freckles." I pushed the head of my cock inside of her again before gritting my teeth and pulling it back out. It was hard as fuck to fight against the way her body tried to suck me inside of her slippery heat, and I wanted to give in so fucking bad, but playing with my girl a little was too much fun to resist.

"I'm s-sorry," she stuttered over her words as her body continued to writhe and shake underneath me. Finally, I reached my breaking point, and without another word, I plunged into her warmth as far as I could go. I let out a pleasure-filled groan at the feel of her wrapped around my dick, squeezing and pulling me in further than I thought I could go.

My balls tightened as I thrust inside her again and again. My heart raced, and I clenched my teeth to keep from blowing my load. Reaching down, I pinched her nipple between my thumb and finger, tugging gently as her eyes met mine. Her pupils were nearly black, and her eyes were wild and filled with lust as they rolled back in her head, my name a prayer on her lips.

I tilted my hips so I hit the spot that I'd quickly learned drove her almost instantly into an orgasm and her pussy clenched around me so goddamn hard when she came that I shattered right behind her, erupting inside of her with a roar, unlike any sound that had ever come out of me before.

Rolling onto my back with my semi-hard dick still inside Ryan, I pulled her on top of me and wrapped my arms around her back while she laid completely sprawled out and relaxed on top of my body. "Never leave me," I pleaded in a husky whisper.

"Never," she promised before her eyes fluttered closed and, completely exhausted from everything that'd happened, she drifted off to sleep.

THIRTY TWO
RYAN

When I woke up, I was wrapped up in warmth. I was so comfortable, I didn't want to open my eyes. Snuggling in deeper, I nestled my head against Maddox's hard chest. My forehead fit perfectly between his pecs, and I let out a contented sigh.

His skin was warm and contrasted against the cold air blowing gently through the room from the vent on the ceiling. I burrowed deeper into the blankets and Maddox, and a rumbling laugh vibrated through his chest, making my forehead tickle. The sun had moved pretty far across the wall, and I had a strong feeling it wasn't morning anymore, and we'd moved into early afternoon.

I whined a little as he pulled away from me and sat up. He chuckled and ran his hand down my bare back, and his touch woke up every part of my body. I stretched languidly as I watched him slide out of bed, the sheet dropping away. My gaze raked over every inch of his rock-hard body as he strode across the room to the bathroom.

Sighing, I rolled over onto my back and stared at the ceiling waiting impatiently for him to come back to bed. Now that all the drama was over, Yates was in jail, and the ranch was safe, I wanted to spend the entire day in bed. I stretched, and my muscles were deliciously sore from yesterday, more from what happened in this bed last night than anything that happened at the ball.

Just as Maddox stepped out of the bathroom, a wicked grin flashing across his face, yelling from down the hall stopped him in his tracks. Maddox quickly grabbed a pair of joggers out of the closet and threw them on just as the door burst open.

"What the actual fuck is wrong with you?" Quinn yelled with an angry-looking Griffin on his heels.

Griffin shot Maddox an apologetic look. "I tried to stop him, but the dude's faster than he looks."

"I figured you were a lot of things, Quinny, but a cockblocker wasn't one of them," Maddox joked, looking only slightly irritated at his interruption. He probably expected this. We hadn't taken Quinn with us last night, and both of us knew he'd be pissed off about it.

"Shut the fuck up, Maddox. I can't believe you blindsided Yates without me. I was a part of this even before you were. What if something had gone wrong? Fuck, Ryan," he ranted, turning to me. "Why the fuck wouldn't you let me be there?"

I pulled the sheet around myself because Griffin still stood outside, and I didn't need the drama of him checking out my naked body. Confirming I'd made the right move, a taunting smile lifted the corner of his lips, and I looked away, instead focusing my attention on Quinn. Rising from the bed, I crossed the room until I stood in front of my best friend.

"My dad called me yesterday afternoon and told me a couple of the cattle were sick, and the vet was coming out. He wanted me to be there, but I couldn't. The only other person that could was you. I'm sorry I didn't tell you, but if I had, you'd have forced me to take you, and we could've lost the cattle. I hate that you couldn't be there, Quinny. I wanted you to be there. But you can always watch the video."

His eyes softened as he sighed and ruffled the top of my hair. "You're forgiven. But I swear to Christ if you ever leave me out of anything again, I'll dunk your hand in warm water when you sleep and make you pee the bed every night for a month."

I giggled, and Maddox chuckled as he moved behind me, wrapping his arms around my waist. "Sorry, buddy. Won't happen again," Maddox promised.

"Want me to put the video on the big screen?" Griffin offered from over

Quinn's shoulder, holding up his phone and giving it a shake.

"Fuck, yes." Quinn turned and followed Griffin down the hall. "And who exactly are you?" I heard him ask, and I giggled.

I dropped the sheet, and Maddox's heated gaze dropped right along with it. I pushed lightly on his chest. "I'm going to get dressed. We can continue this later."

He groaned, but let me go, lounging on the bed and watching every bend and shimmy I made as I pulled a pair of cutoffs and a tank top on. When I was done, he sat up. "I thought we could go over and talk to your parents this afternoon," Maddox suggested.

"Not that I don't want to spend time with my parents, but why?"

He ducked his head, looking uncharacteristically shy. "I thought maybe they could meet my mom and Griff. What do you think?"

I sat down on the bed next to him, the mattress dipping and moving him closer to me. I pulled his hand into mine and gave him a soft smile. "I think that sounds perfect."

He brightened. "Yeah?"

I nodded, and he continued. "I want to talk to everyone at once about the future of the ranch and what I want to happen."

"Aren't you going to at least give me a hint?" I questioned, batting my eyelashes up at him.

He chuckled darkly. "No, Freckles. But if you keep looking at me like that, I'm going to give you something else."

I let go of his hand and jumped up off the bed as it was on fire, jogging out of the room with him hot on my heels. I almost made it to the living room before he caught me, his arms snagging me around the waist and pulling me back against his hard chest. He pressed his lips to my neck, sending shivers down my spine. "Caught you," he pointed out smugly.

"So you did." I spun in his arms and lifted up to kiss his lips before moving away. I stepped into the living room where Quinn and Griffin were both intently staring at the giant TV mounted to the wall watching last night's events unfold in all their glory.

I pulled on my cowboy boots while I waited for them to finish their video.

It was too fresh for me. I didn't care to watch it yet. Maybe someday I would, but my memories were vivid enough, and I was ready to move forward from the nightmare.

"Quinny, did you make breakfast this morning?" I asked, my stomach growling so loudly I wondered if everyone could hear it. I hadn't eaten anything since lunch yesterday.

He nodded. "Biscuits and gravy. There's plenty of leftovers."

"Griff, can you text mom and ask her to meet us next door?" Maddox asked his brother, and I was struck by how relaxed and comfortable he sounded. He accepted his family back into his life a lot more quickly than I expected.

"Yup," his brother agreed, pulling out his phone.

"I'm out the door. You guys can take your time, but I need food," I declared, moving quickly through the house and flinging open the door. The hot sun beat down on me, but it didn't matter. I had one singular focus: food.

Quinn jogged to catch up with me, slowing down so we could walk at the same pace. "I need to talk to you about something, Ry."

I stopped, glancing over my shoulder at the guys still a long way behind us before locking eyes with my best friend. "What's up?"

He sighed, running his fingers through his tousled hair. "I'm not really sure where to start."

"That's easy. Start at the beginning," I teased, flashing him a smile.

When he didn't laugh, my heart sped up a little. I could count the times I saw Quinn be nervous about anything on one hand and have fingers left over. "You remember when I came out in high school?"

Nodding, I turned and started slowly walking again. The guys behind us were starting to gain ground, and I could tell Quinn wanted to talk just the two of us.

"I didn't know back then that things aren't always so black and white," he said cryptically.

"I'm not really sure what that means, Quinny."

"It means that I don't just love you, Ryan. I'm *in* love with you," he rushed out, the words stumbling over each other as my breath caught.

I stopped in my tracks, turning to face him. "Quinn-"

His eyes were soft and full of regret. "I should have told you sooner, but I wanted to be sure it wasn't just some phase. You're my best friend, and you're beautiful and incredible. We'll never lose what we have, Lancelot. That's a fucking promise. But you're with Maddox, and really, even when it was just the two of us, he was there in the middle in spirit. I know that, and I'm not telling you this because I'm asking for anything. I don't want you to change your mind or be with me. I'm telling you because I needed to admit it out loud to myself. I needed my best friend, even if you are the one I love. I want to broaden my horizons, and this is how I begin."

I pulled him into my arms, tears stinging my eyes at how incredibly brave Quinn was to confide this in me. "I love you so much, Quinny. And truth?"

He pulled away, grinning down at me. "Always."

"If you'd told me this a year ago, I'd have totally had my way with you."

He laughed, the tension dissipating. "Seriously?"

"You have no idea how many times I wished you weren't gay," I confirmed, and he groaned.

"Well, shit."

"Sorry," I shrugged, patting him on the back as he slung his arm across my shoulders. "Thank you for telling me. I'm really proud of you."

"I'm just relieved you don't hate me," he admitted, twisting one of my curls around his finger as we walked.

"I could never hate you, Quinn. You're my other half. Where you go, I go. That's for life right there."

The boys trudged along slowly behind us, laughing and joking around about the video and last night with Yates. We hurried ahead, though. I had needs, and Quinn's biscuits and gravy were nothing short of heavenly.

Jogging up the front steps, I pulled open the screen and then the front door, the familiar creak of the hinges welcoming. I let it slam after Quinn stepped inside. My mom would kill me if I let all the cool air out. That shit was expensive, and I'd been trained well.

I didn't stop to look for my mom or dad, just beelined for the kitchen, pulling open the fridge as the front door opened again, and the three men moved inside. My dad rolled into the kitchen as I stuck my breakfast in the microwave. "Hey, kiddo," he greeted with a warm smile.

"Hi, dad. Maddox, Quinn, and Maddox's brother Griffin are here, too," I announced just as they walked into the room.

My dad's gaze lifted to the three men, flickering between them before landing on Griffin. "You're Griffin?"

"That's me," he confirmed, a little of his cockiness shining through.

"And he's your brother?" my dad asked again, turning to Maddox.

"He is. Pretty freaky, right?" Maddox grinned at my dad, whose eyes were currently darting between the brothers, no doubt looking for similarities.

The microwave beeped, and I turned to pull my scalding bowl out, grabbing a fork and moving to the kitchen table. I blew on the steaming bite sitting on my fork before eating it, moaning at how the biscuit melted on my tongue.

"Slow down, Freckles, or you'll choke," Maddox warned as he moved the chair next to me closer and sat down, draping his arm across the back of my chair seat and watching me intently as I shoveled food in my mouth.

"It's your fault I'm so hungry," I complained, and he laughed, reaching over to wipe a little bit of gravy off of my lip with his thumb and sticking it in his own mouth to lick off. It was hot, and my eyes locked on his mouth before my dad rolled up across from me and broke me out of the trance he'd caught me in.

Quinn and Griffin joined us a few minutes later, and Quinn slid a plate in front of Maddox. "Thanks, Quinny. Looks great." Maddox looked across the table to his brother, who was attacking his food hungrily. "When's mom going to be here?"

"Any minute," Griffin answered around a mouthful of food.

My dad's eyebrows lifted. "Your mom's coming here? Monica Everleigh?"

"It's Spencer now," Griffin corrected after swallowing his bite.

"Who's coming here?" my mom asked as she breezed into the room. "Hi, boys. Hi, sweetheart," she said, bending to kiss me on the top of my head like I was five years old. I didn't mind, though. It made me feel safe in a cozy sort of way.

"My mom," Maddox answered, taking a sip of the coffee my mom slid in front of him. She stepped further into the kitchen and returned with mugs for Quinn and Griffin, too, pouring them their own steaming cups. That was just who my mom was, always the caretaker. She wasn't much for ranch work, but she'd always been a helluva mom. She didn't even know who Griffin was other than a strange tattooed man sitting at her table. But it didn't matter to her. He was with Maddox, so he was family.

"Monica's back?" my mom asked with a gasp, a look of disbelief on her face. "When did that happen?"

"A couple of days ago. There's a lot to explain, but Maddox wanted you guys to meet his family. It's all really new," I explained, scraping my almost clean plate to get every last crumb.

There was a soft knock on the door, and we all looked at each other. Griffin ultimately jumped up and walked to the door, pulling it open for Monica. She stepped inside and looked around nervously, twisting the strap of her purse between her fingers.

As Maddox's mom stepped into the kitchen, all eyes turned to her. A soft smile crossed her face but didn't quite mask the nervousness in her eyes. I slid my chair back and crossed the room, pulling her into a hug. "I'm glad you came," I whispered before stepping back, and the relief in her eyes told me my instinct to welcome her was the right one.

"I can't believe you're here," my mom gushed before she enveloped Monica in a hug. Once upon a time, they were either friends, or my mom wished they had been. I doubted Russell let Monica have many friends back in those days, but my mom was persistent.

Both of the women's eyes shined with unshed tears. "It's so good to see you again, Shannon. Thank you for treating my son like one of your own. I can never repay the kindness you've shown him."

With one last squeeze of Monica's hand, my mom let her go, waving her off. "He's the son I never had. He and Quinn both."

Maddox sat up straighter at my mom's admission, gratitude swirling in his eyes. It just felt right having him here, and it was made even sweeter with Monica and Griffin joining us.

"And you remember Alexander?" my mom gestured to my dad, who held his hand up for Monica to squeeze.

"I do. It's really nice to see you again," Monica beamed. She looked genuinely happy, and I could see the shackles of her past falling off of her with every bridge she rebuilt from what was probably the worst time in her life. I couldn't imagine what she'd suffered at the hands of her husband.

Women like her were the reason I wanted to be a cop. Not everyone was strong enough to stand up to their bullies. And when they weren't? I'd be there to step in.

"Can we go sit in the living room?" Maddox asked, grabbing his plate and mine and standing up, putting them in the sink and then coming back for me. He wrapped his arm around my shoulders, and I leaned against him as we made our way to the couch. Griffin sat next to his brother, and Quinn sat on my other side. Mom and Monica took the chairs, and my dad wheeled himself between them.

Maddox clasped out hands together before he looked around the room. "I wanted everyone to meet and catch up because there's a lot we need to talk about. I don't know what information everyone has at this point. But I managed to buy this place back from Yates at the last second. I have my attorney drawing up the paperwork to transfer it to you, and as soon as I get it, we'll sign, and you'll own the land free and clear."

My mom gasped, and my dad looked tearful before gruffly clearing his throat. "I… Thank you. I won't ever be able to repay what you've done for my family."

Maddox kissed my forehead. Before staring down at me reverently. "You've done more for me than I could ever do for you. You gave me this amazing woman. You took me in when I didn't have a safe place to escape to. You stepped in, and for a few important years, you became the parents I didn't have."

Monica flinched a little, but Maddox gave her a soft smile. I never thought I'd see the day he forgave his mom. "This family is as much mine as it is Ryan's. I'm just sorry I stayed away so long. But that's never happening again," he promised.

"We're glad to hear it, son." My dad gave Maddox a warm smile, one that my boyfriend returned.

"So, that brings me to my next point. Neither Ryan nor Quinn want to be working this ranch," he began, and both Quinn and I started to protest, but Maddox squeezed my hand. "I talked to Joel, and he's willing to oversee both ranches. I think the smart move would be to combine our operations into one, and Joel agrees. If you allow it, Joel will hire all the staff we'll need. And I'll upgrade whatever we need equipment-wise so everything's running like it should."

My dad looked like he was at a loss for words. It was unsettling. My shoulders were tense as I watched him, my breath caught in my throat, waiting for him to decide. I hadn't known Maddox was going to do this, but if my dad agreed, I'd be free. Free to chase my dream, free to follow Maddox to LA. And even better? Quinn would be able to live the life he deserved, too. I quickly turned my head, meeting Quinn's wide, stunned eyes for a second before looking back at my dad.

"I can't ask you to do that. You've already done so much," my dad tried to refuse.

"It's a smart business decision, Alex. If we want to be profitable, and I don't invest to lose money, this is the smartest move. I've gone over all the numbers myself and had my accountant take a look, too," Maddox argued.

My dad blew out a breath. "Sounds like I can't refuse then, can I?"

"Plus, with the new study, you're going to need all your time for healing," my mom pointed out.

"You got in?" I squeaked, moving to the edge of the couch. This study had the potential to help my dad regain some use of his legs, and I was beyond excited.

"I did," he confirmed, his eyes filled with a hope I hadn't seen in years. It seemed like happiness was free-flowing this morning.

The smile that lit up Maddox's face was nearly blinding. "Congrats, Alex." He loved my dad like his own, and I'd never seen him look happier. He turned to me. "As for you," he said, running his palm along the side of my neck and rubbing his thumb along my jaw. "Come to LA with me."

I was nodding before he finished the sentence. "I'd love to. When do we leave?" My body was humming with excitement. I couldn't wait to go back. I missed LA from college, and the little taste I got a couple of weeks ago wasn't nearly enough.

He chuckled. "I have a couple of other people to ask first, Freckles." He turned to Quinn. "I want you to come with us. Grayson texted me about you, and he wants to get you into his kitchen. There's a spot waiting for you if you want it."

"Fuck, seriously?" Quinn breathed, his elbows resting on his knees. His head fell into his hands as he took deep breaths.

I turned and rubbed his back. "Come on, Quinny. I don't want to go to LA without you."

"I don't know what to say." He lifted his head and grinned at Maddox. "Except, fuck, yes. I'm *so* in."

"To answer your question, Freckles, now that Quinn's in, we're flying home tomorrow," Maddox answered. *Home.* I couldn't wait.

He finally turned to his brother. "What about you? What are your plans?"

Griffin shrugged. "I've been lifeguarding for the summer, but that's almost done."

"Feel like coming with us?" Maddox offered, eyeing his brother.

"I'm with Quinn. Fuck, yes. Not to sound like a fangirl, but will I get to meet the band?" he enthused. At that moment, despite all the piercings and the tattoos and his overflowing confidence, he looked like a little boy.

"Considering we're recording a new album, and we're fucking glued at the hip whenever we're in the studio, I'm going to say that's a yes."

Griffin tried to play it cool, but I could see the excitement in his eyes. I think there was some part of him deep down that really, truly worshipped his big brother. He hadn't been anything but open, happy, and enthusiastic since he'd stepped into Maddox's life.

"So we're all agreed?" Maddox asked finally, looking around the room. "Joel's going to handle day-to-day ranch operations for both properties, and Quinn, Ryan, and Griffin are coming back with me to LA?"

We all nodded our agreement. "What about you, mom?" he asked Monica.

"I'm going to head home tomorrow morning. I've got a life there, Griffin's dad and I have been wanting to take a cruise, so maybe we'll do that," she mused. "And hopefully it won't be too long before we get the chance to visit you all. I'd love to see what your life in California's like."

"Sure, mom. Just say the word, and I'll have you on the next flight," he assured her.

"Well, I don't know about you all, but I need a nap before I start packing for tomorrow. It was good to see you again," I said, turning to Monica before pulling Maddox up with me and stalking off for my room. I'd had one overarching fantasy in all the years I'd known him: Maddox Everleigh naked in my bed. And this afternoon was the last chance I'd get for a long time to make my wish come true. Quinn's knowing laugh followed us down the hall, but I didn't care.

Maddox had swooped in again, the beautiful man before me delivering every daydream I'd ever had on a silver platter. I couldn't wait to start my new life, but right now, I wanted to live in the past just a little longer.

THIRTY THREE
MADDOX

I watched Ryan's lithe form as she moved around her bedroom, folding and shoving clothes into her suitcase. Her long hair brushed across her bare shoulders. My eyes dropped, following the curve of her waist and traveling down her toned ass before lazily taking in the smooth skin that covered her long legs.

My phone buzzed with a text, and I reluctantly tore my eyes away from the most enticing show I'd ever seen.

Connor: Meet me at your place. We need to talk

Sighing heavily, I pushed off the bed, shoving my phone in my pocket. I crossed the room to Ryan, leaning down and capturing her lips in a quick but heated kiss. As much as my dick was perpetually hard around her and I could spend every fucking second buried inside her, sometimes real life called. "I'm running next door to talk to Connor. Bring Quinn and come over when you're done, and we'll head to the airstrip."

She nodded, smiling against my lips. I was having a real fucking hard time making my body move away from her. "We won't be long," she promised, her voice somewhere between a purr and a whisper that shot straight to my cock. No one had ever affected me the way Ryan did.

Pulling back, I let my eyes drift over her one more time before turning and leaving the room. I wasn't sure when it happened, but I didn't like to be away from her even for short periods of time. When she wasn't with me, life was colder, less expressive, more empty. I hated it.

I'd never been dependent on anybody, but Ryan made me reliant on her happiness and warmth. She was sexy and confident and fun in a combination unique to her, one I wanted to get completely fucking lost in. But for now, I had shit to do, so I had to rip myself away.

It didn't take me long to walk through the front door of my house, Connor was already comfortable on my couch sitting across from Sebastian and Griffin. I lifted my chin in greeting before flopping down onto an empty spot on the plush sofa.

"What's up?" I asked, leaning back into the cushion and resting my arm across the back of the couch.

"We have an update on Yates," Connor announced, nodding at Sebastian, who leaned forward and clasped his hands together, resting his elbows on his knees like he had a secret he wanted to confide.

"He had his bail hearing this morning, and the judge granted him home detention, but his parents refused to let him come home after what he did. So, essentially he's stuck in jail until the trial," Sebastian explained, and a slow smile stretched across my face.

"Serves the asshole right. He tried to use Ryan as a goddamn hostage. He deserves to rot in jail for fucking ever for what he did," I fumed, the firey licks of anger kicking up in my veins.

"I've gotta admit, watching her kick his ass was the highlight of my year so far," Connor noted, a huge grin taking over his face.

"Same," agreed Griffin, leaning over to pat me on the back. "Yous girlfriend is hot as fuck, bro."

"Stay the fuck away," I growled, and he laughed, holding up his hands in surrender.

"I'd never touch her. Bro code and all that. Just saying," Griffin backtracked, and I glared at him, daring him to even try. The thought of Ryan kneeing him in the balls loosened the intensity of my anger, and I almost laughed. Because if he tried to make a move on her, there was no doubt that's what she would do.

"If you two are done, I want to talk to you about something else." Connor shifted, so he was directly facing me, his observant eyes boring into mine. I'd known him long enough to know he was watching for my reaction to whatever he was about to say, which put me on guard.

My shoulders tensed, and I sat up straighter. "What?"

"I know Ryan wanted to become a cop, but I want her on my team," Connor started, studying my face as he let the words fall slowly from his lips as if he was afraid I'd lose my shit on him for suggesting my girlfriend go work for him.

"Huh." I turned his words over in my mind, but the more I thought about it, the more it made sense. I didn't know if it was what Ryan wanted, but I thought she could fit in well with the guys. "Are you sure?"

Connor's eyebrows shot up. "Am I sure that I want someone on my team who has the balls to take down a grown-ass man? Who isn't afraid to work hard? Who's completely loyal to the people she loves and trusts to the point she's willing to do whatever it takes to keep them safe?" he scoffed. "Yeah, I'm pretty fucking sure."

I sighed, rubbing my rough stubbled cheek with my palm. My eyes flicked over to Sebastian. "And, your guys are fine with a girl joining the team?"

"Don't look at me, man. She could kick my ass, and she's not stepping on my toes. I'm happy to have her join up if it's what she wants. If Connor trusts her, I trust her. I know the other guys feel the same." Sebastian's eyes shone back at me with his truth, and I knew he meant what he said.

Turning my attention back to Connor, I was struck by how much everyone around him trusted his instincts. He was so careful who he gave his trust to that when he deemed someone trustworthy, we all followed. He was a powerful and formidable ally to have, and I'd never been more glad to call him my friend.

"The question isn't are the guys okay, which they are. The question is, are *you* okay with her doing this? Because she's going to be in danger. If she's on my team, I'll protect her as much as I can, but she'll be the one sticking her neck out and protecting the people we work for. I need you to understand that," Connor pointed out.

"Look, I know she'll be in danger. But I trust that she can handle it. She wanted to be a cop. At least this way, I know you'll do everything you can to make situations as safe for her as possible. And I know you won't send her into anything until she's trained and up to your standards. I'm not the type of guy who's going to hold her back from doing what she loves. She doesn't need my permission. But if something happens to her, I reserve the right to kill you." I leveled him with my hardened, unblinking stare making sure he got my fucking point.

"Noted," he agreed, an almost smile tilting his lips up.

The front door swung open, and Ryan and Quinn shoved through the entryway. The bags and suitcases draped all over them and hanging from their arms making it hard for them to move through the narrow opening. Quinn cursed and dropped all his bags at once with a loud thud. Ryan looked at him appreciatively before doing the same thing with a loud sigh. "Good thinking, Quinny."

She glanced around the room at all of us as Quinn moved into the kitchen and pulled a beer out of my refrigerator. "What's going on in here?" she asked.

"We were actually just talking about you, Freckles," I told her, pulling her down into my lap. She shifted as I wrapped my arms around her waist, resting one on her hip. Her ass pushed right against my dick, and I groaned at the feel of her.

She flashed me a knowing smile. "Oh? What about?"

"Connor thinks you're a badass and wants you for his team," Griffin stole Connor's thunder, and the big guy shot him a harsh glare. Griffin just grinned, looking smug as fuck, and I chuckled.

Connor turned to her. "The little asshole's right. I think you'd fit in with my team, and you've already got skills and haven't even had much training."

She bit her lip, looking a little lost in thought. I rubbed my fingers along her hip, watching as she shivered beneath my touch. I fucking loved that she did that. "What would I be doing?" she finally asked.

"We'd evaluate your skills, but if I had to say right now, probably guarding like I do." Connor leaned back, crossing his ankle over his knee and watching Ryan intently.

"And how's that different than being a cop?" She was absently running her fingers through the short hairs at the back of my neck and driving me fucking insane. Shivers wracked my body under her light touch.

"The training would be similar but in more areas and more one-on-one so it'll be really fucking intense. Then you'll get assigned someone to guard. It'll probably be someone from the band because we all feel more comfortable with people we trust on both sides. But if something comes up like this Yates situation, you might get pulled off of your detail and be asked to apply your skills to whatever problem or case we're working on," he told her as she nodded along.

"I like that." She looked down at me. "And you're okay with me doing this?"

"If it's what you want to do, Freckles, I'm more than okay. I think you should do it," I confirmed, loving how her eyes lit up and sparkled as she considered her new future.

"I want to do it. Yes, I'm in! I'm in." She was practically bouncing in my lap, and I was cursing the audience we had right now, so I couldn't take advantage of the hard-on I was sporting.

She jumped off of me and strode across the room, hauling her bag up onto her shoulder while four sets of eyes watched her with curiosity, and I tried to figure out how long it would take me to rip her clothes off. "What are you doing, Freckles?"

"Aren't we going? What's the holdup?" She lifted one of Quinn's bags and dragged it across the room, flinging it at him. He caught it with a wince as it narrowly missed his junk.

Chuckling, I stood up. "You heard the lady. Let's get the fuck out of here."

It didn't take us long to gather everything, lock up, and go. I said my goodbyes to Joel, who promised to keep me up to date on finding staff and combining the ranch operations. I was sure that with my someday in-laws living next door, we'd be back to see how things were going for ourselves pretty often.

The drive to the airstrip went quickly with Ryan pushed up against me in the back seat. I could get lost in her anytime and anywhere. She was everything to me, and despite what we went through with Yates, we came out the other side better than I ever could have imagined.

"What are you thinking?" she whispered, her body relaxed against mine with her head resting on my shoulder.

I pressed a kiss to her temple, brushing back the soft strands of her hair. Running my fingers through the dark waves had become one of my favorite things to do. "About how much I love you, how glad I am that I came back and everything turned out the way it did."

"Who knew you had this sweet, sentimental side to you?" she teased with a soft laugh.

"What can I say? You make me fucking weak, Freckles. In the best possible way." Turned out, I did have a heart buried under all of my cynicism and anger. I just needed the right girl to make it beat again.

She turned her head, facing me, so our eyes connected. "I've never loved anyone the way I've always loved you. Thank you for coming back for me, even if it took you a lot longer than I ever expected."

I captured her lips with mine but didn't get carried away. "I hope you like having me around because I'm not leaving again."

"If you do, I'll kill you," she said sweetly, her eyes drifting closed as she settled in for the rest of the drive. I believed her. If anyone could plot my death and carry it out, it'd be Ryan. As fucked up as it sounded, that was one of many reasons I loved her.

"I know."

I stared out the window as the ground shrunk below the powerful engines hurtling us into the air. When I first came back to Texas, I carried a heavy weight on my shoulders of guilt, anger, anguish, and regret. But I was free of that now.

The gorgeous woman sitting next to me helped release me. She smiled and squeezed my hand as I lifted it to my lips, pressing a kiss to her wrist before pulling our joined hands into my lap. I knew we'd be back here, to the place we met and grew up. The place our families still lived. But it wouldn't be home.

As the plane lifted into the clouds, the past fell away. It would always be a part of me, a part of us. But now we could look to the future, a future that held so much promise. Ryan and I had our whole lives ahead of us. And I was so fucking proud of her. When she joined Connor's team, she'd be fulfilling a long-held desire to make a difference in people's lives. I didn't think anything could make me happier than bringing her joy and experiencing life through her eyes.

Glancing around at the plane full of the people closest to us, complete contentment settled inside me, and for the first time in my life, my soul was peaceful. In only a matter of hours, our new life together would begin, and I couldn't fucking wait.

EPILOGUE
MADDOX

Two months later...

Getting used to being back with the band and away from Ryan was hard as fuck. A few times over the past few weeks, I'd wanted to say *fuck it* and throw her over my shoulder and run back to Texas. Even though I knew we were both working, and we both loved our careers, that didn't make shit any easier.

I'd been gone in the studio for forty-eight goddamn hours, and every one felt like an eternity. Ryan texted me earlier that she'd be with True and Amara until the morning when Julian relieved her, so needless to say, I was fucking cranky at the prospect of coming home to an empty house and having to wait another twelve miserable hours to see her.

Saying I was fine with her working with Connor's team and actually *feeling* fine with it were two different things. I loved seeing her happy, but I missed her when she wasn't around.

Walking through my front door, I slammed it harder than necessary, taking out my irritation on the innocent piece of wood but not giving a single fuck. I threw my keys onto the table, but with so much force, they slid off the top and fell onto the floor. Not bothering to pick them up, I stalked into the kitchen, planning to pour myself a shit ton of whiskey.

Instead, my goddamn jaw almost hit the floor when I crossed the threshold into the room. Ryan stood behind the island dressed like a fucking

Playboy bunny, complete with ears. My gaze raked hungrily down her body, taking in the bright blue satin bunny ears on her head, the black bowtie at her neck, and the curve-hugging blue satin bustier her tits were spilling out of.

Her long legs were wrapped in black fishnet stockings, and my cock had never been harder. She was my fantasy come to life. "What are you doing, Freckles?" I managed to choke out despite the fact my brain was exploding into ten thousand tiny pieces because of how goddamn incredible this was.

Instead of answering, she sauntered across the kitchen and handed me a glass of whiskey just how I liked it. I gripped the glass and lifted it to my lips, letting the drink burn its way down my throat, but my eyes never left hers.

"What? Aren't you happy to see me?" she purred, running her index finger down my chest and abs before grabbing my dick through my jeans.

"Fuck," I groaned as she suddenly spun and pressed her ass into me, fluffy bunny tail and all. I reached over and set my glass on the island, grabbing her hips with both of my hands and pulling her closer as she ground herself against me.

"Don't you remember?" she murmured. "Miss August 2003?"

If I wasn't so goddamn turned on right now, I might ask her how the hell she remembered my favorite Playboy Playmate of all time. The one that I jerked off to so many times when I was twelve, I'm surprised my dick didn't fall off. But at this moment? The how didn't matter. The fact that she was standing in front of me as my living fantasy in more ways than one had my pulse skyrocketing as my heart tried to pump all my blood to my cock.

"As if I could forget," I ground out, my hands finding their way around to the front of her body and gliding up and down every silky inch of her costume as she pressed herself harder back against me.

Slowly, she lowered herself, dragging her body down mine until she was on her hands and knees, her ass in the air as she wiggled her hips, that goddamn bunny tail taunting me like a red cape to a bull. Ryan glanced back at me over her shoulder with a wicked grin on her face and one last wiggle of that tail before turning around and kneeling in front of me.

I was surprised my dick hadn't punched a hole in my jeans to free itself at this point, but when she reached up and unzipped my fly, I practically moaned at how good it felt when I popped free of the confining denim. Her nails scratched down my thighs, making me shiver.

She yanked my jeans down, and I stepped out of them, and then she practically tore my boxers off of me. I almost fell over trying to step out of them as fast as she wanted me to, and she giggled and flashed me that wicked smile of hers again.

"Careful, Freckles," I warned, not minding the idea of taking this whole situation over and showing her who's really in control.

"Or what?" she challenged, a mischievous glint in her eye.

I reached down and tugged at her bowtie, running my finger around the inside of it before wrapping my fingers around the band and pulling her slightly forward. "Or I'll show you exactly what happens to bunnies who misbehave."

She stood up and kissed me, her tongue swirling with mine before she pulled back and slid that goddamn satin outfit down along my body until my cock was wedged between her tits. She moved up and down a few times, letting my shaft glide along the silky material. I'd never felt anything like it, and I never wanted her to stop.

My head fell back on my shoulders, and I closed my eyes, letting the feel of her perky tits sliding along my dick wash over me and mentally saying the alphabet backward to keep from coming. I had big plans for that bunny outfit, and coming in the first five minutes was not part of them.

Cool air rushed across the heated skin of my erection catching my attention, and I looked down just as Ryan stuck her tongue out and ran it along the entire length of my shaft before pulling me into her mouth. She sucked, bobbing her head up and down as she gripped the base of my cock in her fist. As much as I'd already learned her body, she'd paid attention and discovered mine, too. I was already close to coming, so I pulled her off of me.

"On your hands and knees," I ordered. My cock swelled even more as I watched her follow my command. I walked around her slowly, taking my time as she watched my every move with lust-filled eyes.

Stopping behind her, I got on my knees, pressing my dick up against her satin-covered ass. I reached down, running my hand along the curve of her ass before grabbing a handful of her fishnet and tearing it apart. No part of me wanted her out of this bunny outfit when I fucked her.

No, I was going to fuck her while she was wrapped in bright blue satin, fluffy tail and all. Sliding the satin material to the side, I slipped a finger inside her soaking pussy. "Already so wet for me," I murmured as she rocked back against me. Pulling my finger out, I slapped her ass, and she yelped before moaning.

"Hold still, Freckles, or you'll get another one," I demanded, and she stilled under my palm. Pushing my finger back inside of her, I worked it in and out a few times before adding a second. She squirmed again, and I bit my lip while I slapped her ass again, rubbing away the sting as she cried out.

"Had enough?" I asked.

"Have you?" she countered and fuck if I didn't love how this girl always challenged me.

Rather than answer, I moved the satin fabric further over and replaced my fingers with my cock, pushing inside Ryan until I was buried balls deep. She let out an excited gasp before rocking back against me again.

"Haven't you learned who's in charge yet?" I questioned as I pulled out and slammed back inside of her again and again. Leaning forward, I grabbed the back of the bow tie collar she wore and wrapped my fingers around it, holding on while I set a punishing pace, our hips slamming together relentlessly

Letting go of the collar, I reached around and rubbed her clit in the same rhythm I fucked her, and she bucked against me, clawing at the floor and cursing like I'd never heard out of her before. As I picked up my pace, she tensed around me, and I knew she was about to come. "Come for me, Freckles," I urged as she squeezed my dick and shook around me. Her inner walls contracted, and I was fucking done. My eyes rolled back in my head as I slammed into her one last time before I surrendered and rode wave after wave of pleasure until I couldn't hold myself up anymore.

Pulling out of Ryan with a wince, I flopped down on the floor beside where she'd fallen. Both of us breathed heavy, and she crawled over to me, resting her head on my stomach and looking up at me with a satisfied smile, bunny ears askew. "We're definitely doing that again," she panted.

"Fuck, yes, we are," I agreed, running my fingers through the tangles of her hair and humming contentedly. My earlier irritation was completely forgotten.

𝄞

"What is this?" Ryan asked as she dropped her bag on the floor of the entryway. Our house's open floor plan meant she looked right into the kitchen where I was covered head to toe in flour and other powdery baking shit, but fuck it. I tried.

I held up a plate of darker-than-they-should-be chocolate chip oatmeal cookies for her. "I made you our favorite."

Her lips twitched as her gaze roamed over the plate. "Your favorite, you mean." She picked up one of the cookies and took a tentative bite. I didn't miss the flinch she made when she crunched off a small piece.

"They're my favorite now," she confirmed, lifting her eyes until I was lost in her gaze. "You made them for me."

I laughed as she shoved the rest of the cookie in her mouth, chomping down loudly and obnoxiously. She slid closer to me, wrapping her arms around my neck as she laughed and dropped crumbs out of her mouth. They added to the mess I already was as they fell against my black shirt.

"Sooooo gooooood," she moaned, rolling her eyes back as she swallowed. Once she got the bite down, I reached over the counter and passed her a cup of milk.

My cookies sucked, and it was no secret; they were dry as fuck.

Still, she ate them with a somewhat inappropriate reaction, and I loved her all the more for it.

"Thank you for doing this for me, Romeo. I love them," she murmured, pressing herself against me as I leaned down to kiss her. "And you're forgiven for being an epic asshole to me and my cookies," she added.

I laughed, bending to pick her up and carry her off to our bed, ignoring the mess I made in the kitchen.

Life with Ryan would never be boring and fuck if I wasn't looking forward to seeing how she kept me on my toes for the rest of my life.

𝄞

"Show me what you've got," I prompted Griffin, where he sat behind the drum set in the studio we were recording in. Our new album was underway, but we were messing with some new shit and hadn't gotten the sounds we wanted. Nothing had been coming out right, and all of us were frustrated as fuck. So, we were taking a well-deserved break.

Griffin had been my shadow since we got to LA, and I had to admit he was impressive as hell. Apparently, musical talent was in our blood, so that was something we bonded over right away when he came to LA with me.

He spun the wooden stick in his hand before slamming it onto the snare drum's surface, his arms flying so fast they were almost a blur as he pounded out a beat. I glanced at the other guys who were behind the glass panel watching. Jericho was our drummer, that wasn't in question. But there was no doubt in my mind that Griffin needed to be making music.

I wanted to help him however I could, and I had connections. For now, he was happy to hang with the four of us watching and learning. But he was a fast learner, and I doubted that'd be enough for him for long. He was also fucking wild, and if he brought one more hookup home from some random club, I was going to make him get his own place.

Ryan didn't need to be around that shit, and neither did I. I was done with all that and didn't have room for it in my life anymore. I understood him, though. I was the same when I was his age, trying to lose myself in anything I could that might make me *feel* but not feel too much. Anything that might make me forget.

It was fun until it wasn't.

A small part of me worried for him, my stint in rehab coming to mind. So, I tried to give him direction. To give him something productive to focus on. He had all the talent, and I wanted to see him use it. I hated to admit it, but he might be a better drummer than Jericho, and Jericho was the fucking *best*.

Griffin finished his piece, grinning up at me while he panted lightly from the exertion of flinging his body around behind the drums. "Well?"

"It was good." I shrugged, holding back my praise. He didn't need to go and develop a fucking ego.

Jericho walked into the room and stepped up to the drums. He held out his hand, and Griffin passed him the sticks before sliding off of the stool. Jericho eyed me and tilted his head in a way that said *I've got this* and went to fucking town, playing the drum line from one of our most popular songs. When he finished, Griffin gaped at him as he absently grabbed the sticks back from where our drummer offered them out to him.

Jer stood and came to stand next to me, leaning against the wall and looking completely disinterested as Griffin played back from memory the exact pattern Jericho had just played. I was impressed as fuck, but I schooled my features, not wanting to give that shit away. When he finished, Jericho pushed off the wall. "You finished two bars ahead," was his only comment before turning and leaving the room.

Even I thought that shit was cold.

Griffin's smile dropped a little. "Is he always that much of an asshole?"

I grinned. "Yeah, pretty much. Ready to go home? Quinn's making dinner."

Griffin perked up. "Is Ryan going to be there?"

I pulled my phone out and checked my messages, smiling like an idiot. "Yeah, she's home tonight."

"Fuck, I'm going out. I can't listen to you two fucking all night again. I don't know how Quinn does it. I'm done with that shit," he complained, grabbing his bottle of water as we walked out of the studio.

"Don't bring any goddamn randos you find tonight home with you," I warned.

He rolled his eyes and sighed. "Fine."

Zen laughed. "Fuck, I'm glad to be done with that shit," he said.

"Same," I agreed.

"Thirded," True chimed in.

"What, nothing to add?" Griffin taunted Jericho, who rolled his eyes but said nothing. "Ugh," he complained. "You guys are fucking rock *legends*. Why the fuck are you all so boring?"

We all looked at each other before bursting out laughing. "Someday, you'll get it," I promised before grabbing my stuff and following my best friends out the door.

I finally understood what they'd been going through the past couple of years, how everything was worth it to find that piece of you that made you whole. Ryan was my missing piece, the person who patched my soul up and made it complete, and I wouldn't give her up for anything.

Our future was wide open, and for the first time in my life, I was looking forward to seeing where it took me.

SIGN UP FOR A HEATHER ASHLEY

NEWSLETTER

And get exclusive sneak peeks, previews, and behind the scenes info from author Heather Ashley that you won't find anywhere else! You'll even get a free bonus as a thank you!

heatherashleywrites.com/newsletter

JOIN MY READER GROUP AND
BECOME A MEMBER OF THE

WILD RIDE CREW

Want to talk about what you just read? Join us backstage in my reader group!

facebook.com/groups/thewildridecrew

NEXT IN THE SERIES:

VICIOUS ICON

If anyone finds out his scret, it will destroy him.

Jericho Cole has always been a mystery. The world knows him as Shadow Phoenix's moody drummer, but what lies underneath the dark, tattooed exterior would scacre away even the most die-hard fans.

IF THEY KNEW THE TRUTH. THAT IS.

Pounding his drums into oblivion helps keep the demons at bay, but every day they creep clcoser. Soon, music may not be enough at all.

When Moon Mahem storms into Jericho's life all color and chaos, he can't help but take notice. She drags him into a whirlwind of sultry days and steamy nights that tempts him to give up everything but her.

But when her past catches up to her, Moon has to decide whether the drummer with the shadows lurking behind his eyes can protect her...

OR IF HE'LL BE THE ONE TO BRING HER TO RUIN.

www.amazon.com/dp/B08CD42NYV

Printed in Great Britain
by Amazon